To Eileen & Danny

the ghosts that come between us

Nargis's Journey, a Novel

Best wishes
Dr. Bahuguna

BULBUL BAHUGUNA, M.D.

DRONA PRODUCTIONS
Chicago, IL

Copyright © Bulbul Bahuguna, 2011
All rights reserved

LIABRARY OF CONGRESS CONTROL NUMBER   2012938628

Hardcover ISBN: 978-0-9854222-1-9
Paperback ISBN: 978-0-9854222-0-2
Ebook   ISBN: 978-0-9854222-2-6

Publisher: Drona Productions, Chicago, IL
Printed in the United States of America
First Edition, 2012

This is a work of fiction. Names, characters, places and incidents are either the product of the author's imagination or are used fictitiously. Any resemblance to actual person living or dead,   business establishments, events or locales is entirely coincidental.

This book is available for special promotions at a discount. For details write to
Drona Productions, 2232 N. Clybourn Avenue, Chicago, IL 60614
or visit www.dronaproductions.com

To all those who understand ...
and to those who need understanding

ACKNOWLEDGEMENTS

I do believe that I am usually able to articulate my feelings through written expression. However, I find myself at a loss for words that would adequately convey my thankfulness, not only for Anita Sinha's commitment to this writing project, but, also, for the thoughtfulness and love I felt every time we met. Thank you.

My deepest gratitude to Mita Kapur, Jay Winuk, Brian Feinblum, Lisa Mora and Yashpal Singh, and all those who have been a huge part of taking this manuscript forward.

Thanks to my family for their honest feedback and ongoing support, and for holding my hand throughout the writing of this novel.

PROLOGUE

I pray that one day, I will have an opportunity to ask God why this happened. If at all possible, I would prefer the answer in person.

My name is Nargis, and I have a lot of questions for God.

Is it true, that man must go through the wringer at least once in his life so he can grow from the experience? And that if pain does not kill, it will only make him stronger?

How does wrong become right? Can man mute his soul? Does his spirit die? Is it humanly possible in this one life to live, to un-skew, detangle, and re-fix the mangled mess between people?

Do some things happen without reason, even though they bear sweeping and devastating consequences? Does a Supreme Justice get to decide how culpability and punishment is honorably matched with wrong and hurt? How on earth does a criminal manage to dodge any blame or penalty? Can one calibrate a dent made on the soul?

Will there ever come a time in a man's life when he can graciously accept, without batting an eyelid or stifling a nervous twitch, the wrongs that have happened to him that he does not yet fully understand? Or does life's struggle end only with death?

If age cannot cure everything, death certainly will. Is this the nemesis of life?

There are many questions I must ask God, if He indeed exists, some of which I have still not clearly formulated in my mind. But most of all, I want to ask God why this happened to me.

My life journey can be told in a few sentences, or it can run into several pages. I have chosen the longer version. Once I get started, I learned a long time ago not to take any pit stops.

I have been thinking about writing my story for some time now, not fully understanding why I feel compelled to do so. Will I finally hear from my reader what I have wanted to hear from my family every waking moment of my life, and *how* I have wanted to hear it? Does the story change with who gets to tell it first and how it is told, or who gets to hear it last and how it is heard?

When you write about truth the way you know it, do some people still hear it a tad muffled like the noise of drums-in-retreat fading into oblivion? How many truths have been eternally lost to mankind since the beginning of time? How many truths have been carried by the careless wind over the edge of the globe, and unceremoniously tossed over into the nothingness of the Universe?

Can reality be botched and bungled? Buried and forgotten? Does it lapse with time from having a short shelf-life, and even a shorter half-life? Does it die? What is real, and what is distortion? Is it humanly possible for both reality and distortion to honestly represent complete and absolute truth in the same breath? But then, is there even such a thing as complete and absolute truth?

I am a prisoner of my own thoughts that ping-pong back and forth in disquiet harmony inside the concavity of my skull. I live in a mind filled with mindless clutter that brutally grates at my insides as it seeps into my soul to find a permanent home, while I desperately search for answers to a volley of questions that continue to befuddle me. When I think I have finally nailed down a few, many more crop up sticking out like obstinate and forgotten weeds in the late autumn grass.

I feel as if I have been trying to pull at obstinate and forgotten weeds most of my life.

Sometimes, when I would drive in the snow on a cold blustery day in the Windy City of Chicago, something from a song would remind me of my story. Just a simple line from Holly Dunn's country song, *Daddy's Hands*, could easily evoke a body memory and pull me into a whirlpool of strong, sometimes opposing emotions. Sometimes, they were so pervasive that I could not tell them apart. It reminds me of the shade a child creates when he randomly chooses all the watercolors in his box, but does not bother to wash the brush between the colors. A sure way to make the canvas muddy and murky.

And mud and murk is what I am talking about.

I try to shut out the feeling by turning up the car radio to the max until I cannot hear even my own thoughts, let alone an ambulance blinking wildly and blaring dangerously behind me, ready to run me over. If it does not, I know the emotions surely will. Sometimes, I do not have names for these feelings. Feelings that I continue to sweep under the rug until I stumble on the very mound they create. In a frenzy of this all-out in-house anguish, I try to snuff out the inflamed and smoldering hurt attached to certain memories. Smoke is still rising from them. Like it does from shit dropped on cold ground.

When I am not successful at blunting out these jagged edges of pain, the feelings start to have a life of their own, swirling around me and building into a crescendo akin to a whirlpool made from an entire ocean. A bit like that vortex in the original version of the movie, *Journey to the Center of the Earth*, it jack-knifes into a bottomless black hole and swallows everything that comes in its path --- and ends up swallowing me. I want to run away from it, run away from everything, run away from myself. But there is no place to escape, no place to hide. I cannot even feel the ground under my now inordinately heavy and weary feet. The ones that are still complaining, but have forgotten how to run.

This is when I feel alone, betrayed, and helpless. I am angry that I cannot express anger, except in tears that build on themselves into shameful outbursts that even shock me when they get out of control. Especially in public. Getting control back is hard, arduous and exhausting, and leaves me feeling empty and drained.

Sometimes it is not a song, but silence that brings back the past. Being with silence can also be quite painful. I need to surround myself with sounds that prevent me from hearing the jumbled tapes in my head. At other times, when I cannot stand the stillness, I resort to obsessively engaging in senseless mundane chores of cleaning and organizing. Or simply picking at my skin to numb my very being.

I feel a lot of shame about picking at my skin, so I do it when I think no one is watching. But that is not the worst shame I have ever felt. My fingers are often bleeding, ugly, and sore with pain. But that is not the worst pain I have ever felt. Actually, by now my hands no longer seem to hurt. My thoughts get muddled, the feelings get dulled, and the tsunami of thought-feeling-angst mounting inside me ebbs for maybe just a second. Or two.

But it can never change what happened. Nothing can ever change what happened to me.

How my life journey is told and retold, fudged and forgotten, cannot change what happened. Running the risk of being perceived as repetitive and thankless --- or repetitively thankless, overly-sensitive and attention-seeking, or just plain hysterical, cannot change what happened. What happened, though, did change me. It made me overtly strong-willed but quietly codependent, seemingly clear-headed but privately confused, wanting to please but not fully trusting. And always wanting to forget.

As you can understand, I have been hesitant about telling my story, at the risk of remorse over self-disclosure and the agony of feeling the pain again. But nothing can stop me now. Because finally now, I know that this is the right thing to do. *For me.*

Right and wrong was never clear growing up. Almost as fuzzy as the many blurred memories I try so hard to separate. Nor was good or evil. A person was good only as long as he was good enough for our family. And especially, only if he was good enough for my father. Daddy could juggle right and wrong, good and bad, like a magician. He did it so fast, I could never make out what he was holding in his hands --- the ones with the long tapering artistic fingers, and what he was hiding up his sleeve: the docile fluffy white dove, or the frightened scrawny brown rabbit. But for sure, I was bad if I did not agree with Daddy, believe in him, or follow his every command. A chance glance, or a hint of a grimace, could easily give me away. And I knew he was always watching. I had no choice but to become who Daddy was, and dared not spill out of the mould he had painstakingly preset at my birth. *Just for me.* And just for that reason alone, I could never be myself. Reflexively, he assumed control over those around him and was systematically contemptuous and rejecting of those he could not.

If I ever risked my very existence to act differently — and God help me if I even made an invisible attempt to think or feel differently, it was perceived as a deliberate betrayal of him. This was punishable by protracted volatile anger or endless brooding silence.

I am not sure which sentence was worse. All I knew was that something awful had happened, and it was only up to me to correct it. *Immediately.*

Or else my whole life would fall apart. Or else —

"NARGIS, YOU CAN BEAT ANYTHING."

It was now my last year at medical school in Moscow. Arjun had already graduated and gone back home to oh-so-far-away India, and was an attending physician at a hospital in New Delhi. I missed him terribly, and do not remember ever feeling so alone in my life. I wrote to him several times a week, but it was never enough. I had a nagging feeling that this would be one long year. What kept me going was the singular thought that in just under three hundred and sixty five days I would be done with school for good, and we would be reunited together forever. I liked the notions of 'for good' and 'forever.' If you can hang on to a few words, a whole year can go by faster. I dismissed any lurking fears that we may never meet again, in spite of being hopelessly certain that our families would never bless this union. Our families did not matter anymore. Nobody else mattered anymore.

My Russian roommate at the dorm, Vera, was a couple of years older than me. Soon she and I had become close. Her husband was serving in the Soviet army and was posted abroad in Egypt. We became two despondent women who would share our lonely time together, pining for the missing men in our lives. A little bit like forlorn *Russki* chicken, with our heads cut off! On some long and never-ending nights, I would lay the shirt Arjun had left behind, gently spread it out on my pillow, bury my head in it, take in the smell of him, and cry myself to sleep. To the rhythm of pangs of longing. This is what love is.

My ever watchful and caring roommate reminded me to eat regularly, since I had started to lose weight. I was now less than a size zero, which could make even Twiggy jealous. Somehow, I had not anticipated any new problems. In my mind, without Arjun by my side, I felt that I had been doled out more than my share of grief. So what happened next came as a complete shock!

Since my clothes had now started to hang over me like on a solitary doornail, it was becoming easier to look cool and spiffy in the miniskirts that I had recently acquired from Sweden. It was not so easy, though, to ignore the hacking cough that had crept up on me, resistant to routine expectorants and grandmother cures, and was threatening to become chronic. Like a bad habit.

When final exams came around, all I cared about was to be on the Honor Roll as usual. Simply so that I could write home about it. I studied hard, biting my nails even harder. When there were no more cuticles left to get my teeth into, I resorted to picking at the skin around my fingertips until I drew blood thus putting my platelets to test. Needless to say, they tested well. I would wake up in the middle of the night in my PJs, swamped with homework, with my incandescent marker-underscored thick medicine and surgery textbooks strewn around me, and find myself bathed in my own sweat. I dismissed this as examination fatigue. Gradually, I began to develop an unrelenting low-grade fever. Then I started to tire easily.

One day, I was stunned when I coughed up frank blood. This is when Vera insisted that I go to the university clinic right away.

A balding specialist, in a starched white coat that perfectly matched his stiff demeanor, emerged from behind the curtain waving an x-ray film in one hand and clutching a fat folder in the crook of the other armpit.

If by any reason that hefty medical record is mine, fat chance of getting a clear verdict! I thought.

He was briskly flipping through the pages, and nodding to himself as he went along, happy that the content so robustly agreed with him. Then, he nonchalantly proceeded to throw a battery of questions in my general direction barely taking his eyes off the written word as he continued to doodle in my chart. Nor did he pause to hear my complete answers. As if my answers did not matter. I am not entirely sure that they did. Clearly, he had already made up his mind by just sizing me up the moment I had walked in through the door of his office, as, I believe, all top specialists are trained to do.

How much weight had I lost? Did I feel tired all the time? Did my ribcage hurt when I coughed? Was my sputum streaked with occult blood? Had I noticed night sweats?

When he asked me that last question, as if on cue, I started to sweat profusely: on my brow, over my upper lip, under my armpits, and along the insides of my legs all the way down to my toes.

I remember feeling paralyzed in the bright fluorescent lights of the x-ray screen. My denial was rapidly ebbing. As was any hope of escaping through that exit door without a diagnosis. In that moment, I could almost predict what he was about to say.

"You have advanced tuberculosis," the pulmonologist declared in a calm and matter-of-fact voice, as if he was announcing the next train station on a PA system. He explained the shadows and shades on the black and white x-ray film in his general aseptic clinical manner.

"Nargis, you have a cavity in your left lung, the size of a walnut, and you *will* die if you don't get help," he continued with detached concern.

Why are doctors so fond of employing images of fruits and nuts to describe serious lesions: cherry, orange, grapefruit, watermelon? Or the size of balls from popular sports: golf, tennis, baseball, football? Or better still, coin sizes of the legal currency on hand: penny, nickel, dime, quarter?

When you are that sick, money is usually the last thing on your mind.

And, why do specialists convey the prognosis only in absolute terms: "Will. Or will not? Black. Or white? Life. Or death?"

All I heard was the dreaded abbreviation TB, as the syllable reverberated through my entire being. I think it is probably similar to how people must feel when the verdict of Cancer or Death Row is pronounced.

That nervous truth: "Guilty! Guilty! Guilty of TB!"

Suddenly I was feeling sicker and weaker, as a TB patient should feel. My entire anatomy started to revolt: the innocuous otoliths in the vestibular cochlea of my ears instantly tried to summersault like ping-pong lottery balls, enough to make the room spin in the opposite direction; the unfortunate duodenum in my abdomen immediately began to gurgle audibly and attempted a reverse U-turn to protest on my behalf; and the yielding gluteus muscle punctually drained all its potassium to coax my legs to buckle down from under me. As if the protoplasm in every cell of my body was crying out, both objecting and resigned at the same time, "Live! No, die! Yes, live!" I was sure that the ground under my very feet would cave in, and I would be swallowed into the confines of a stony cold vault.

This is what happens when you die.

My first thought was that only poor people get TB. This *could* not be happening to me. This *should* not be happening to me. At that moment, I could picture those blasted bacilli, footloose and fancy free, carousing and scuba-diving in my vena cava with the cheerful abandon of squatters in newly occupied no-man's-land; their smooth bodies squeezing into the recesses of my capillaries, guided by their bulging eyeballs, and ogling for victuals to suck into their gluttonous mouths. Food made of *my* body. A body reeling from shellshock and combat fatigue.

I felt as if I was within an inch of my life. Where all roads lead to death. Where the cliff ends abruptly before the final freefall into an abyss that lies beyond the unknown. Where carbon atoms join other carbon atoms.

I'm a strong *Jaat* girl, I told myself. I'm sure that my body will never fail me. I'm too young to die.

Since the spot diagnosis met with no resistance, the Communist Medical System went into autopilot. I was whisked off to a sanatorium sixty miles away on the fringe of Moscow, far away from school and the people I knew. I had no hope of graduating with my class next summer, or ever being reunited with Arjun again. It was like being dead already.

When I entered through those gates in the high walls of the sanatorium, and was ushered into a foyer with the vaulted cathedral ceiling, I felt like the walking dead. A lower-division Czar must have lived there before he was, in all probability, guillotined in the name of the common people after the Great Revolution. The efficient staff in cult-like uniforms greeted me politely, handed me a brand new toothbrush and a clean comb, and escorted me to a room occupied by three Russian girls. On a plain firm mattress by the barred window lay crisp white sheets, folded up nicely by comrades. For comrades.

This would now become *my* bed, and *my* window. So different from my window in the pink bedroom back home at the Red Fort in Dehradun, from where I would watch lighthearted bees fussing over vines loaded with sticky purple grapes; or my window in Lilliputian house, where I would wonder what it would be like to dance up-close and personal with the teenage boy who I had the latest crush on; or my window in Bombay, from where I could hear the waves crashing gently against the rocks.

Windows tell the story of my life.

Very soon, I discovered that I was the only foreign-born patient at the sanatorium. In the weeks ahead, I would have no option but to get accustomed to unshaven legs, matted hair, and wardrobe malfunction from mismatched strings of hospital gowns. I would learn to stifle the inaudible wince every time the needle would first prick my skin, and mute the angst on my face every time the doctor would begin to clear his throat before pronouncing a sentence on my recovery.

"Six more months, my dear Nargis ---" or, "Prepare for ---," or, "I'm so sorry to inform you that ---"

Sitting on the edge of my bed, wringing my now continuously sweaty palms, I realized this would be my home for the next several months. When I buried my head in my pillow that first night and lulled myself to sleep, languishing in pain as I rocked my body, curled up like a fetus, I felt alone in this world. The last person left on Earth.

I woke up the next day dreading the morning light. Sitting on my bed cupping my face in my hands, I knew that I would witness a change of seasons through that lonely barricaded window.

Is this how incarcerated criminals feel in solitary confinement?

I would miss a whole winter and spring. The nights were eternal. The outside world appeared cold, gray, and forbidding. When dark looks even darker. And low feels even lower. When every day is Groundhog Day. When the tired fir trees on the hospital grounds seem to groan under the load of snow. And the birches are utterly denuded, save for that one lonesome leaf left over from last fall fluttering hopelessly in the cold blast from the Arctic Circle. The last leaf left on Earth.

The favorite part of my day was when I went to sleep. Deep, deep, sleep. Like death. When you hang on the pendulum to stop the needle, and time stands still to intersect with eternity.

Until one day, a solitary sparrow stopped by to chirp ever so timidly on the window sill, its feathers puffed out to conceal continuous shivering. Overhead, the icicles had started to hesitantly drip-drip, then constantly pitter-patter, signaling the end of another long Russian winter.

If that lonesome leaf signifies yesterday, I consoled myself, this chirpy sparrow must represent tomorrow.

Slowly my Russian roommates drew me out of my depression. They helped put back the scaffolding to repair my spirits, and gave me a reason to smile again. They taught me how to laugh. At nothing. These were simple common people, who shared simple stories with me from their ordinary lives. The redhead was a hairdresser, a nonstop chatterbox, who could not get over her boyfriend cheating on her. She vowed that she would be sure to kill him with cyanide concentrate the moment she was released from the sanatorium. She said that after suffering TB, jail would be a cinch! The brunette was a shop assistant, who talked about her father having rage attacks whenever he was under the influence, which happened to be every single day of her entire life. She said that suffering his anger was worse than having TB. The third, a strawberry-blonde mill worker and single mother, encouraged me to get a new boyfriend.

"That's the only way to get over Arjun," she advised. "I've done it. Ask me how."

She said it was so easy. And she had enough spare time to do so, because her son was being raised by his grandmother. Most Russian children are.

Specialists love to practice a war strategy for disease: it has to be killed in situ. So, in order to end this slow dance with Death and prevent the bacillus from rearing its ugly head ever again, my doctors pulled out all the stops. I went into intensive treatment, alternately subjecting my now pincushion behind to daily injections of streptomycin. The nurse seemed to leap from several feet away straight at my naked rear-end, needle in hand. As I lay on the gurney staring at the ceiling, receiving my protracted intravenous cocktail of anti-tuberculosis concoctions that caused unrelenting nausea, I felt as if I was on a medical leash. A bit like how a convict must feel when he is dragged out of his cell every morning at sunrise, escorted by two burly men to face the firing squad, wondering when the captain will say, "Fire!" I thought how far away India was from where my body lay, slowly   burning with fever, and wondered whether I would ever step on her soil again.

Steadily gaining back both weight and spirits on chunky

borshch and heavy-duty prednisone, I learned to be content with very little, except a wish to survive and see Arjun that one last time. I was so petrified that I would never be able to complete the coursework required to graduate with my class, having missed two semesters at school. So, I studied with new vigor, poring over every conceivable treatment approach to scoliosis, septicemia, and schizophrenia, even as I breathed in thick sickly-yellow and wild-orange fumes of every potent poison known to mankind that would certainly kill the recalcitrant bacillus that had invaded my body. I wrote to Arjun every night, reassuring him that I would be released soon, and would go to bed memorizing his letters of love and longing to be reunited.

Daddy's distressed letters also punctually arrived at the sanatorium, albeit well over a month late. Most likely intercepted by a top-shelf, overzealous, underpaid, and largely obsessive recent recruit at the KGB. Father wrote that both Mummy and he were shocked to hear about my illness. They hugged each other and cried together when they read about my struggle for life.

"It's so terrible that we can't be with you at such a difficult time," Daddy wrote. "Unfortunately, obtaining a visa from India could take several months. Nargis, you are a strong girl, I'm cent percent sure that you can beat this disease. You'll kill it before it can kill you. Remember, no one knows this better than I do. Nargis, you can beat anything."

Does he really mean *anything*? I wondered.

One

THE BURDEN OF LOVE

NARCISSUSES AND NIGHTINGALES

I was born in a charming little English cottage nestled in the Himalayan mountains on a cold frosty day, when winter was getting ready to say goodbye. My father was posted at Dalhousie by the Indian army, and my parents had been married for six years or so. Most of the stories about my birth and every other aspect of my life, as well as the lives of everyone else around me, have been told by my father. He was *the* storyteller in the family. And he always told the best stories.

Daddy would narrate the events around my birth while sipping an evening cocktail, savoring Mummy's crisp spinach *pakoras* flavored with homemade mint chutney; or while negotiating a desolate treacherous mountain road; or halting and honking at bullock carts, rickshaws, and horse-drawn carriages as we passed through crowded nondescript towns in Northern India. He would embellish the story with surreal detail, interspersed with natural wit and fun exclamations thrown in for effect. On every such occasion, I wanted to believe that I was hearing the chronicle about my debut on this planet for the very first time. Over the years the legend would attain the distinction of a fable.

I never understood why my siblings did not have birth stories, but, nevertheless, they seemed to listen just as attentively. Mostly, I believe, out of sheer courtesy to the legacy. As for myself, I did not care to ponder for more than the duration of a neuron's momentary synaptic kindling on why I was flying solo. It was *my* story, and it was about *my* birth.

Mummy did not know she was pregnant again, only a few months after my brother Sanjay was born. As a youngster I remember hearing that a woman may not be aware she is carrying a child, while still nursing a newborn. Who else would educate me about this fundamental fact concerning normal female physiology other than Daddy?

When Mummy first heard she was going to have me, she burst into tears. She did not feel ready to have another child so soon. Her hands were plenty full caring for a toddler, my sister Anjali, who innocently ran around the house and garden touching every object within and outside her reach, and for an infant, my brother Sanjay, who suckled poorly at her breast. She felt overwhelmed. The notion of carrying and caring for a baby a third time over in such quick succession, was, understandably, reason enough to cause distress and tumult.

It was Daddy who insisted they keep the baby.

"Mani, believe me, this'll be our wonder child," he told her, again and again, so she would conquer her ambivalence.

And his decision prevailed like it always had in the past, and always would in the future.

During the fall months, Mummy carried me with her everywhere she went cozy and snug inside her expanding girth. The garden was ready with plums, pears, and peaches. Mummy had a renewed craving for fruit and ate them all, especially the ripe-red cherries that hung low on the branches in the orchard around our cottage. Today, when I think fondly of my mother, I still like to believe that I especially favor that fruit group because Mummy ate it so ravenously to feed the hungry miniature me in her growing tummy.

Around the time when I was getting ready to emerge from the darkness, warmth, and safety of my mother's womb, "When you were still a twinkle in my eye," as Daddy would often narrate, the snow had started to melt on the Himalayan peaks, and there was a promise of spring in the air. The birds had returned after a long winter away to warm up their abandoned nests, perch precariously on tree branches, chirp in an unremitting high-pitch monologue, and hop around on the veranda with carefree abandon --- the chatterbox sparrows, the industrious woodpeckers, and the melodious nightingales. Meanwhile, the garden was coming alive once again with bright-eyed daffodils, innocent daisies, and beautiful *nargises*, the Indo-Persian name for narcissuses.

That is why Daddy decided to name me Nargis.

I was a bouncy, rounded eight-pounder, and even shocked my mother when I announced myself with a full-throttle all-cylinders-firing cry that resounded past the mountain tops and into the valleys.

"I'm here! Look at me. Look at me. I've landed!"

The final proof that I was alive.

"That's how Nargis learned to cry about everything right from day one," Daddy would tease.

I arrived unannounced before Dr. Ezkiah, a Jewish gynecologist previously hired explicitly for the birthing event, could appear on the scene. And the scene was happening in my parents' bedroom, and I was out there, bloody and slimy, wriggling and squirming, on my mother's bed.

Mummy, meanwhile, was bleeding to death. Somewhere a large artery had burst and there was blood spewing in every direction, flying all the way down to the wall by her bedside.

"That's how, my dear," Daddy concluded with a loving smile, "you were born in my hands." Then he continued, "But I must tell you, around you there was complete mayhem! Yes, sir! Hell had broken loose! There was blood all over! And you, little baby Nargis, were crying nonstop on sheets soaked in red. As you were getting louder and more pink, Mummy was becoming quieter and more pale! I didn't know what to do with you, because Mummy was sinking! 'Mani,' I pleaded with your mother, 'you *have* to stay alive for all of us.'"

And Mummy mustered up all her strength to stay alive, just like Daddy had instructed her to do.

Finally, after what seemed like an eternity, Dr. Ezkiah came rushing through the front door almost half an hour late, in time only to cut the cord. Sometimes I question today, whether she was really able to completely accomplish that.

Who really feels more pain when the cord is cut? I'd wonder. Mother or child?

Then Dr. Ezkiah turned to Daddy, "Major Shiv Yadav, you deserve a Gold Medal of Honor for the courage you've shown today."

And I remember thinking, of course, Daddy deserves the highest Medal of Honor. Had he not been there to take charge, I would've never been born!

I am told that very quickly I ousted Sanjay from his nursing position. He was a weak baby and a finicky eater. My parents were quite concerned about his failure to gain weight, which made him more prone to a myriad of illnesses. Especially diarrhea. Meanwhile, I had quickly found my place at my mother's breast and would not let go. Boys from the UP farmland are expected to be able-bodied and tough like stallions and it bothered Daddy that Sanjay was not what he had always wanted in a son. Sometimes, I used to think that Mummy favored my brother when she would load his plate with extras at meal times.

From what I have been told, Anjali would point excitedly to where I lay gurgling and cooing on the cot. She would call me "baby" and poke me with her pointer finger to verify whether I was just another blinking doll, the one who coyly shuts her eyes when you lay her down, or an alive and wide-eyed girl child: Exhibit E, Youngest Member, Second Daughter, Number Five.

I believe most children have an alternative story of their birth. This one was also told by Daddy. My parents were quite happy and content with having two children. A 'complete' family with a boy and a girl, as most families are supposed to be. One day, when Daddy was driving this rather complete family on a completely lonely mountain road, he chanced upon a black leather bag by the roadside in a ditch with something moving and whimpering inside.

"Surprise! Surprise! It was you in that bag, baby Nargis, abandoned there by some hill people, pleading to be adopted by us."

Daddy said I looked so lonely and cute. As if I had been laying there forever, all geared up and waiting to be chosen, held, and owned. By *our* family.

Daddy would be quick to add, "So we took pity on you, my dear, and brought you home with us."

I am not sure whether there was ever a moment in my life, when I truly fully believed this black-leather-bag story. But it never ceased to intrigue me. The idea of having another set of parents elsewhere, who would one day come looking for me was appealing enough. The notion of being found and then claimed back later was past fascinating. I remember rationalizing that I did look different from my siblings, especially my sister. How I hated it when people would point out similarities between us! It felt so good to be different and special --- a feeling I would carry, neatly folded and stacked-up in my back-satchel, all the way into my adult years.

So, it's just remotely possible that the black-leather-bag story's actually true, I'd think. But then, what about that other story, the one with blood spraying all over the wall through a hosepipe, and Mummy sinking? That sounds just as real.

In my mind, I would play along with the fantasy that one sunny day, another family would come knocking on our front door asking for me by a different name. Like Lorraine. Or Larissa. These phantom faceless parents were always more affluent --- and on occasion, from foreign lands located mostly in the Western Hemisphere.

But then, why did these mysterious parents throw me to the winds? Was there something wrong with me? I'd wonder. And why is Daddy smiling when he tells the story? It's just a tease, isn't it?

I was always such an easy tease.

On some occasions, after Daddy was done telling this story, I would feel left out from being an integral part of the rest of the family. At other times, it would feel strangely special to be singled out in this manner. In my heart, though, I knew that there was no such thing as a black leather bag.

For reasons still not very clear to me, my paternal grandfather, Dada, along with the rest of the extended family in the village, did not know that my parents had just recently had a third child. It seems that in the early fifties, lorries carrying mail straggled for days on the long and winding journey from the mountains down to the plains.

Were there no telegrams in those days, I wondered? Or, did Daddy have yet another dispute with his father, an adjunct to the endless list of conflicts --- how Dada was raising his younger children, and having so many of them? Or, did my parents want to skip the announcement altogether and go straight to the show-and-tell?

Or, did they want to excuse themselves from the predictably insufferable muted response toward the birth of another girl child, instead of a male heir?

The first winter after I was born, our family traveled back to Daddy's village, Raipur, on his annual furlough from the military. From the train station in Mawana, we took the only horse-drawn carriage in that one-street town to the ancestral home. When we arrived, I lay fast asleep in my mother's arms, bundled up in the folds of an intricately embroidered Kashmiri shawl. Aunty Tara, the youngest of my father's three sisters, received us at the tired wooden swing door of Dada's home. She was a plump, talkative, and somatically focused woman, who attributed all her ailments to abdominal gas that, curiously, defied normal human anatomy and could travel to remote parts of her body until it reached the recesses of her mind. Most likely, this was the reason for her hearty laugh and clever wit.

As she ambled up to greet us at the swing door, aunty asked my mother, "And who is this you are hiding in this beautiful shawl?"

"That's your new niece," Mummy replied, as she swaddled me even closer.

Frumpily dressed roly-poly Aunt Tara remarked, "I thought that is a doll you're carrying."

She would tell me I looked so tiny, pink, and cute. Just like a toy. I picture myself looking innocent, unhurt, and trusting. Eyes and mouth wide open. Not knowing anyone from anything. Quite lost then, I would feel quite lost again. For a long time in my life. I would eagerly go to anyone who cared to pick me up. Never mind that I was a girl. Daddy made sure I got extra attention and was thoroughly pampered for the simple reason that not only was I his daughter, but I was also his youngest child.

In those days of unisex one-size-fits-all garments, there is an early photograph of Sanjay in a frock. He is suspended on the driver's seat of Grandfather's tractor in the farm, smiling weakly into the camera, looking rather slight and undernourished, with loopy ears that had the curious habit of sticking out like flags at half-mast, especially after haircuts. I still tease him about those appendages.

On that same page in the family album, where black-and-white photos were stuck between triangular gold-colored corner-brackets and protected from wandering greasy fingers by flimsy translucent gray paper, there is a faded-out photo of Anjali from before I was born. She looks the picture of happiness, backed into a stonewall with a daisy in her hair, with that endearing I-got-your-attention-didn't-I look, which most three-year-olds are allowed to have. Did my arrival change that?

And then, there is a photograph of the four of them. I like to insist that I am also somewhere in there, because Mummy must have been pregnant with me at the time. Strangely enough though, and I hate to admit, it *does* seem like a complete family. Daddy appears in control, complete with a perfectly horizontal bowtie running absolutely parallel to thin lips. Lips that are sandwiched between a stiffly leveled moustache and an impeccably manicured beard. He is looking sternly with those soft honey-brown eyes capped with muddy-blue crescents into the camera and at the rest of the world.

"Make sure that your hair is always in place, and your shoes never forget to shine," he would instruct. "Children, you must pay attention to those two ends of your body. Namely: your head and your feet. Remember, you can be shabbily dressed, but with your hair flawlessly combed and your shoes perfectly brushed, everything else in between will definitely look elegant and proper. Now, there is actually a method to this. The best way to shine your shoes is to spit on them, brush hard, then spit again. It's as simple as that. Spit and shine --- shine and spit --- brush and shine --- like this --- A British officer taught me how to do that. And children, don't stop shining your shoes until you can see your own confident face gleaming in them, telling you what a good job you've done!" Daddy would declare, looking up briefly from his own reflection in his shoe to size up his audience, as he continued to demonstrate the spit-'n'-shine paradigm.

Daddy knows *something* about *everything*, I'd agree.

In the same photo, I see my sister leaning on Mummy. Nowadays, they still lean on each other. I see my brother, thumb in mouth, looking somewhat weak. Sometimes, he looks just as weak today. Mummy is wearing her hair twisted in place on either side of the parting with hairpins. That was the fashion of the day, before she learned to use curlers. She looks hesitant and unsure. Some things never change. Mummy has kept that chiffon sari till today. Mummy always kept everything.

In those days Mummy used to match her sari with her bindi until, one day, Daddy reprimanded her, "Only illiterate and ignorant Hindu women allow themselves to be tagged in this rustic manner!"

And Mummy abruptly stopped this primordial practice of dotting her forehead. Daddy never had to say it a second time.

Another episode that I remember was told by Aunty Sundri, one of Mummy's three sisters, and perhaps the least good looking one of them all. It goes without saying that Mummy was the prettiest in her family. Simply because she was my mother. I remember being out-and-out awash with embarrassment by Aunty Sundri's looks, or lack thereof, so much so that I would pretend we did not know each other when we went to the movies together. In my general avoidance mode, I would take the lead and make sure that I walked several steps ahead of her at any given time.

According to aunty, one time Daddy had fought long and bitterly with his father during annual leave. Most fights generally happened during annual vacation. And generally, they were between Daddy and Dada. And, also generally, they were rather long and never-ending. Daddy had moved us for the remainder of that month to Mummy's village home in Dharampur, for yet another round of self-imposed exile. I had just learned to crawl, and would follow Sanjay everywhere he went. My brother, who was usually prone to the runs, had had another bout of explosive summer diarrhea.

I would pucker my nose in disgust every time Daddy expounded on any embarrassing sibling GI routine. But privately, this was also something that tickled me pink. After all, Sanjay was my buddy, my partner in crime, my kindred spirit, and *kumbaya* soul-mate all in one. I loved the idea of trailing behind him, even if it was for the wrong reason. We were after all, almost like twins not separated at birth, albeit of unequal yolk. Or yoke? Under his generous tutelage, I would learn how to wink, snap my fingers, and whistle. Except, I could never really learn how to whistle.

Sanjay was older, but more importantly, he was a boy. I remember wishing I was a boy just like him. Boys were definitely more

at school, with the usual my-name-is routine leading to casual acquaintances that entailed matching name to face. I spoke of my family only in glowing terms. My father was Superman in army fatigue. In order to save our country, he had killed hundreds of Japanese soldiers in the line of duty during the Second World War. My mother was a college graduate from the "good ole days," when most women were less than matric-pass and could not even accurately count up to the number of the last standard they had failed at school.

While relationships with new and hitherto anonymous friends remained superficial, they remained even more distant with the remotely located extended family that lived mostly in a village in the largest state, UP. We would visit with them every couple of years or so. They spoke little or no English, yet strived hard to make our family feel welcome when we arrived. Even though a better part of the vacation was spent being a passive spectator to spontaneous and animated discussions between Dada's male progeny over the property he had once owned and developed with pride. Who would be bequeathed which lot of land: the fertile one where the brown sugarcane grew the tallest and fattest in the district; or the mango grove, where, in the height of the season, the trees bent double saluting the yellow juicy fruit. Or the cracked earth on the distant sloped acres where even a single drop of water dare not linger; or the sandpit, which had become home to a family of sleepy cobras with split tongues that protruded ominously without warning especially when rattled. And, whatever happened to the houses? The car? The tube well? The tractor? And everything else? Everything had value, after all. These discussions would easily graduate to full-blown arguments that would get loud and thunderous as they continued late into the night, trying to keep up with the rumbling in the monsoon clouds overhead. Generally, the debate would not end without speculating, within which wall of the ancestral home were stashed the manifold earthenware pitchers laden with gold and silver coins.

"Why the hell does nobody have the courage to own up to the loot? Or, has the booty already been secretly plundered away?" Daddy would enquire repeatedly, trying to size up the guilty party.

The still of the night would be broken by heated words, name-calling, finger pointing and someone (usually Daddy) making a dash for the front door and unceremoniously storming out of the house in the middle of a treacherous rainstorm raging outside.

It always felt as if Daddy started and ended these negotiations. It also usually felt as if he was doing the family a favor. As a testament to his largess, he had volunteered to accept the worst fourth of Dada's estate leaving the rest for the other three brothers.

"That's what happens when you don't care to leave a will," Daddy would say. "Dada was too afraid of death to prepare a will. Most people are." Then, he would go on to complain about his brothers, blatantly labeling them as, "capricious and selfish, forgetful and thankless," all at once.

After all, Daddy had bankrolled the education of his siblings, dutifully sending funds home to Dada from his officer's salary. He had bought trunk-full and car-loads of gifts and whatnot from the military commissary every time he came home on annual leave. I even remember seeing some gray army blankets being discarded as throwaway rugs that eventually lay gathering dirt off the kitchen floor at the ancestral home.

"The family never took care of those gifts, which I selected so thoughtfully and had given to them with so much love. That's what happens when you get freebies. And what short memories they have! By the way, most of our relatives even had the audacity to return those presents with recycled items, and tally them in their own favor. Children, now always remember this. Never trust anyone. No one is as sincere and honest as your parents."

How lucky we are to be born into our family! I'd conclude. How privileged we are to have Daddy and Mummy for parents. I have not known anyone to be as decent and honest as Daddy.

We were but a few relatives removed from simple country folk who were amply content with feeding the flickering fires with cow dung patties. Or packing ground spinach and chopped mustard saag alongside thick yogurt lassi for the farmhands. Usually seen with a kid on each hip, their noses running like a faucet, and at least a dozen or so trailing behind kicking up dust. Just to announce themselves.

Phew! I'd think. What a narrow miss! We must stay together, and be strong together.

It was hard to be polite to our uncles after hearing Daddy's testimony on their whimsical behavior, even though they were usually unusually kind to us. It made the family get-togethers so much more relaxed and fun when Daddy would sometimes laugh and joke around with them.

"They are all self-centered, dull, and uncouth. And, mark my words, without an education they'll never amount to anything," Daddy would often predict privately with us.

And I'd obligingly think, Daddy's always right. Because Daddy *knows*.

Later in life, I would hear other conflicting stories of the property distribution, adapted but not-so-abridged versions from various disgruntled relatives. I know that sometimes Daddy appeared different to different people. What I do know for sure, though, was that he was always different to me.

I never understood whether we grew up rich or poor. Sometimes we lived in epically palatial homes, and attended some of the most exclusive schools in the country. Yet, at other times, we slept on makeshift beds prepared with trunks stacked against each other and cushioned with mattresses. I do not ever remember our family not owning a car.

But then, I'd ask myself, why do we scrimp for pennies?

Well, rich or poor, the village trips were always a lot of fun --- and a lot of heat and dust.

Just preparing for the trip was more than half the fun. There was a buildup of anticipated thrill in the air, since we usually packed for days. Everything went into the car, with mattresses piled into the legroom at the back. The dickey of the meticulously airbrushed and hand-buffed white Ambassador was burgeoning with the oddities of generic baggage. Even a kerosene stove traveled with us for those sporadic roadside picnics, as did a flashlight loaded with fresh batteries in case we got stranded on a moonless night on a lonely country road. Needless to say, we could never leave home without Daddy's pistol --- always ready and loaded to gun down random dacoits, tucked safely away between the folds of yesterday's newspaper in the glove compartment, and at least a couple of thermoses for tea.

"You know, your mother cannot function without tea," Daddy would tease.

And Mummy would smile quietly to herself.

Daddy would praise us for never stopping for water. So we never stopped for water. We made jolly well sure that our respective bladders behaved and stayed in compliance as well.

We would leave at the crack of dawn, splashing water into our eyes glued with fragmented sleep. Then we would simply crash on the backseat like sacks of tired potatoes, until the sun would wake us up with those first fine rays emerging from the horizon.

"It's simple. The sun rises in the East, so where does it set?"

And I would be super impatient, just to be the first one to pipe in and get it right.

Or, "When you are facing the South, what comes to your left?"

And Daddy would call on me to answer, the moment he would notice my eager and ever-ready hand shooting up in the rearview mirror.

In those days there were very few cars on the road, so it was rather quiet. Even the dust raised by the previously shiny Ambassador car as we passed through those abandoned country roads would take a long time to settle. After dusk, the haystacks on the bullock carts going home would protrude dangerously up-close against my window as we drove past. Daddy would caution us to keep our body parts close to us, and not crane our necks out of the window, or else we would end up getting our heads chopped off like those that had rolled off and flown asunder at a guillotine during the French Revolution. In the darkness, the eyes of wandering animals would light up orange-red like menacing twin wolverines. Even harmless indentations on the road looked like ominous craters. Daddy was the best (and only) driver we knew, so we felt safe enough to fall into deep slumber on the mattresses in the back, dreaming of sweet sugarcane, rollicking hayrides, and juicy *chusne-wale* mangoes that would surely welcome us at the end of our long journey. The ones that would turn from raw-green to ripe-yellow just by looking at each other while they waited for us. Then we would sing, joke around, throw banana peels out of the windows, and scoop out the pulp from custard-apples.

"Now, let me tell you something, Nargis," Sanjay would start in real earnest. "If by some silly mistake you swallow the seeds of a custard-apple, the little black beans will germinate in your stomach.

And believe it or not, in a few days the branches of a whole tree will sprout straight through your mouth! Don't blame me then, that I didn't warn you first."

That's downright scary! I'd think. How can a tree actually grow right in the pit of my stomach? Like a baby does in a pregnant woman? Will the branches then stick out wildly straight through my mouth?! What if by accident, I ingest the seeds of the fruits hanging from those branches too? Will the cycle keep repeating itself? Will new leaves then start budding and growing out of my nose? Or my ears? Or through my eyes? I could easily become blind! But, it can't be true! It's impossible! Sanju's just bullying me. He's gone completely bonkers! I bet he's been reading too much of *Ripley's Believe it or Not*!

Nevertheless, I would swiftly savor the soft jelly-like pulp using my tongue against my palate as a sieve. To protect all visible body orifices and receptacles, I would focus my entire anatomy on shooting out the seeds as far away from my body as was humanly possible, making sure I could still see where they landed so that they could later germinate there if they must. That is, *outside* my body.

After a fruit-break, the three of us children would sing and fight, and sing again.

There were lots of songs to choose from. An old favorite was the *Gunner's Song* passed down from the army clubs.

"She wore, she wore, she wore a yellow ribbon
She wore a yellow ribbon in the
Merry month of May
Hey, hey
If you ask, why the hell she wore it
She wore it for a gunner who lives
Far, faraway
Far, faraway, far, faraway
She wore it for a gunner who lives far, far away

She bounced, she bounced
She bounced a bonnie baby
She bounced a bonnie baby in the
Merry month of May ---"

(And then, the best part.)
"Her father, her father, her father bought a shotgun
Her father bought a shotgun in the
Merry month of May
Hey, hey
If, you ask, why the hell he bought it
He bought it for a doctor who is six feet down
Far, faraway, far, faraway
He bought it for a doctor who is six feet down"

And we would all roar with laughter thinking of the poor pathetic doctor, laying six feet under. Then we would start over again, with Daddy leading us into chorus.

"Come on Mani, if you can't sing, at least you can smile for us," he would coax. "My dear, why must you always look so serious?"

Daddy would then turn around to us in the backseat with only one hand on the steering wheel, while we would hold a cumulative breath to gauge whether he was playful and good-humoredly cajoling, or serious and truly upset with Mummy.

"You know children, your mother must always have something to worry about. And when there's nothing to fret about, she worries about being worried! By the way, have you noticed the permanent crease on her forehead?!"

And Mummy would slowly shake her head and allow herself a hint of a smile to ease her frown. *She* knew when he was cajoling, and when he was upset. Even then, the frown never went away completely.

Mummy's momentary relaxed silhouette would allow us to heave a sigh of collective relief in the backseat. I was quite sure that Daddy could drive equally well with just one hand on the steering. That was the least of my worries.

Then we would sing, *Take Me Home, Country Roads*, followed by *Que Sera Sera, What Ever Will Be, Will Be*, and finish up with *Five Hundred Miles Away from Home*.

Daddy would point out how expertly he drove, "One must learn to take a calculated risk and drive defensively, keeping in mind time and distance. It's all about time and distance," he would say knowledgeably. "And, about taking *calculated* risks in life. Children, you'll understand this better only when you become older."

And I'd worry, why is getting older taking such a heck of a long time?

We would fight about getting the window seats and would trick each other after every stop. Somehow, all three of us managed to take turns to mist up the windowpane with our breath. Sometimes, I would stick a towel against the glass frame to keep the sun out, to save the freckles on my cheeks from growing into the rest of my face. Surely that would make me as dark as the wind-chapped brown faces of those urchins, the ones who would jubilantly greet us with prolonged snorts of glee the moment our car hit the dirt road.

Even on a detour, the Grand Trunk Road would certainly take us to our final destination. I used to think that we absolutely *had* to take it to travel to any place in the country. That famous GT Road, lined with rows of grand eucalyptus with their erect ivory trunks and the sporadic not-so-grand kikar trees with their fledgling random branches, interspersed with dusty dhabas alongside country-inn flophouses. The thatched huts were contentedly surrounded by a configuration of dodder, comfortably settled on unsuspecting shrubs, looking like witches' hair.

"It's an obstinate parasite that thrives off its host plant," Daddy would take his eyes off the road for a few moments to explain."That's called symbiosis, children. When *both* sides benefit from each other."

Then we would zoom through lonely ring-roads, chasing mirages of heat vapors rising above the blacktop that would magically evaporate as we approached. I knew the journey was almost over, when we would turn onto the one-lane narrow dirt road cut between the tall sugarcane lined with thorny cactus loaded with pale-yellow flowers. The trick was to swerve the oncoming vehicle into the mud or slush --- depending on the season, and on Daddy's mood, as we passed it. He would use choice words if, for some reason beyond his control, he was not able to accomplish this. And of course, we would all root for Daddy.

Suddenly, we would come upon Daddy's brother, Uncle Shankar, riding his bike home into the sunset. Daddy had this on-again, off-again (but mostly off-again) relationship with brother Shankar. It never ceased to fascinate me that we could be halfway across the country, and come upon our own uncle biking with complete abandon so randomly in, what appeared to be, the middle of nowhere.

And it was the middle of nowhere where all our immediate and distant cousins lived in quiet disharmony, with other nth-degree cousins-removed in attendance. They would come out in large numbers to give us warm but smelly hugs. And there would always be a hot sumptuous meal, even if we had arrived unannounced. It appeared, as if the family had not given up expecting us since our last visit there.

The monsoon was the worst time to travel. What used to be a dirt road would then become a perilous slippery path on which the bullock carts, tractors, and horse dung had wreaked havoc. Sometimes, Daddy could negotiate this only in the lower gears. First second, and then first. The engine would grunt and groan and Daddy would lean on the steering, as if putting his entire weight behind the wheel would get the engine to behave better. The car would swing dangerously on the swampy-mushy road, sometimes out of control, or come to a jerking halt with a rear wheel stuck in knee-deep clay.

I remember thinking, Daddy's mood's getting jerky as well.

By now, he would become just as temperamental as the car.

"Mani, why can't you be quiet!" he would yell at Mummy, who had generally not said anything yet.

To be sure, the backseat would be in muted silence, before Daddy could blow another gasket! We would sit still and try not to breathe. The situation would be further aggravated, if at that very moment the engine had stalled and had to be re-startled. Daddy would swiftly jump out in front, engage the handle into the hole just under the bonnet, give it a few vigorous twists and turns while instructing Mummy to step harder on the accelerator, thus jumping the engine back to life. We learned that the gearbox had to be in neutral to prevent the car from running over Daddy. He would then climb back into the driver's seat and simultaneously maneuver the accelerator, brake pad, gear handle, and steering wheel, all at once, with curses strewn in for variety and flippantly tossed at the rearview mirror. I knew that whenever I smelled burning rubber, I could smell trouble. Daddy must have ingeniously created resistance by strategically piling up logs under the slippery wheel. But we could all easily burn down together with the car! At other times, he would clear a pathway by shoveling away the dirt while eager farmhands stood watching on either side, with sludge packed under their soldering boots stuck in mud and curious faces lit up like fireflies by the lanterns they held. Always ready to help. We were helped by unknown souls that I would not recognize today. They wanted to be of assistance simply because they knew that we were the celebrated progeny of our illustrious grandfather. In my mind, everyone knew of Balram Yadav for at least a thousand miles in any direction.

How do these simple people even know us? I'd marvel.

It would feel like a lost battle if we would end up abandoning the car and walking by the light of the lanterns to the ancestral home, followed by a knot of scummy street urchins, with the sounds of the village navigating us in the dark. There were not as many lights in the village as there were stars in the sky.

We knew that we were close to home when we came upon the pond, where the village boys doused their bodies and played silly water games, before they bathed their buffaloes by guiding them into the water with crooked sticks. The animals would tread gingerly into the muddy pond between the floating lotuses choked by water weeds, with only their eyeballs above water level. And then I swear --- they would float!

Daddy said that all animals could swim when thrown into water.

"It's so much harder to drown," he would say. "Make sure," he would instruct the backseat occupants, "make sure you are like the lotus that rises to the surface out of the dirt, and not like the weeds twisted and stuck in the mud. Remember, just like that flower, each person finds his own water level in life. And make sure," he would add, "that you learn to swim back to the shore if you're ever thrown far out into the deep end."

And we would knowingly nod in unison. Even though, I did not quite endorse the notion of being thrown far out into the deep end of anything. Especially if that anything was a body of water.

The pond was the welcome sign put up by the village. Except on those wet nights, when the dirt around it, swollen by the rain, would tempt the car to go into its depths --- car, and us, and all.

I will never understand how, even at the height of the monsoon, we found our way in the dark through a maze of cornfields and cactus hedges invaded by dodder and our feet heavy with dirt and fatigue. We would pass by almost identical mud houses. Strangely, they all smelled faintly similar to the open clogged drains that circled them. This is where grime met with grime to become an open sewer. The viscous waters would lay still under a stagnant film for protection, so it could be saved from completely drying up by the sun. Sometimes, for reasons unknown, the drain would cross over to the other side of the path. We would leap back and forth over it disturbing the flies that seemed too preoccupied with heartily feasting on its contents to bother with us. At dusk, we would race after the dust raised by the carts loaded with brittle hay, or irritate a belligerent bull from the safe distance of a long stick, returning its gruff snorts with prolonged childish squeals of glee. It was hard to ignore the pancake-like patties made from cow dung, bottle to olive-green, laced with muddy-brown hay and slapped on the mud walls to bake in the sun until dry. They were then piled into pyramids of fuel cakes that spotted the fields alongside bales of hay. A sure way to keep a fire alive.

I'd reason, maybe that's why the *rotis* taste better here.

Everything tasted better here. Daddy said it had something to do with the fresh water from the hand pump and not that insipid processed water running through our taps in the large city.

At dawn, the smells and sounds of the village would come alive. The crackling sounds of burning wood and open fires accompanied the smell of freshly roasted polka-dotted rotis that swelled with pride just at the sight of us. Weary cows shuffled through more dung, chased by pie dogs adorning patchy skins with fleas chasing them both. The sounds of the koyal cuckooing into its glossy black plumage merged in with the mechanical grinding of the *chakki*, both fading out into the dusk as the haze settled in for the night. This is when the mindless chatter of the women kept the kitchen fires going, squatting on charpoys, their lives filled with mundane chores and dull gossip and nails curved back through the generations from vigorously scrubbing brass utensils with soot and ash. They would keep a veiled *purdah* as a token of respect for Daddy. Some of them had grotesque gaping earlobes, thunder thighs, and sagging breasts, which hung loosely down to their lumpy abdomens and bobbed with careless abandon under their tunic *kameez* like oblong oversized squashes. Made all the more noticeable, when they would spend the better part of a day shaking, rolling, tossing, and flipping wheat from the recent harvest on concave bamboo platters to separate the grain from the husk, while simultaneously pulling up a tunic to periodically nurse an infant. Women mired in their feudal past. Mothers were meant only to walk barefoot and always be pregnant.

It was strange how people in the village the same age as my parents had far more gray hair, and far fewer teeth. The whole village seemed to grow prematurely old together.

The children would be bundled off to bed early. We would climb up the super-steep staircase like the one I had read about in a science thriller, or the one I had seen in the movie, *The 39 Steps*. A staircase that could reach the sky. We would lay on cots lined up on the rooftop and be one with the stars.

Why, that was the same Big Bear that twinkled above the lawn of our beautiful bungalow overlooking the vast sea in Bombay! It reassured me that my city life would still be intact when I chose to return to it.

AND MORE DUST

I would wake up to the sounds of the entire village stirring in the morning, of passing hooves outside the window, the cracking of a whip, or someone's name being called out in a shrill voice. Then there were the animals. It was a special treat when I succeeded in coaxing one into being milked. Only the female category, of course. Every so often, I would take a stab at climbing onto a four-legged equal-opportunity creature, which tolerated giving up control to a naive rider of my ilk even for a few seconds.

Occasionally, I would find myself dragging cow dung on my slippers from a mile away, only guessing across how many fields it must have been stuck to my feet. I had to quiet the squishing between my toes until I got to the hand pump. It was quite a trick to alternately pump and quickly sidestep into the water stream, then jump and stomp in place in order to dislodge the gooey dung lodged between my toes. By now, I had practiced this routine to perfection. But it was a class act, almost of adult proportions, to lean over, cup my small palm, then attempt to sip water while simultaneously pumping along with the other hand made into a fist. I had to thrust the handle down hard and swift with my clean little city-slicker hand, and wait patiently to let the tepid water flow for a while until I could feel a regular stream of cooler water from down under. Daddy said that the earth has cooler water there.

Sometimes I'd muse, what'll happen if on one hot sunny day, the water inside the Earth gets totally finished and the pump dries out completely?

Daddy reassured me that there was enough water on Earth to last everyone a lifetime, and more. It took a few days to get used to this ground water. It tasted so different from city water. But the lentil *dal* cooked in it was quite another thing. Usually the men got to eat first, with a brigade of estrogen-soaked feminine gender in attendance. Except, of course, for our family. Daddy insisted that we all eat together.

Answering nature's call was often a chore, sometimes a feat, and usually an adventure. It was easy to speculate why my siblings and I would make a beeline for the fields, each carrying our own small pitcher of water along with some leftover modesty in our back pockets, way before the rising sun could burn out the morning mist and thus make our intentions even more obvious to an accidental onlooker. We would balance ourselves on the higher dirt ridges sloshing water as we walked along with other random cousins in a single file. Or why, on previous evenings, we customarily clipped off newspaper cuttings with name-that-politician-of-the-week from last year's *The Times of India* to smudge the thing with. From the corner of my eye, I would see speckled remains of the day alongside the naked drains. It was a tightrope act, this walking on the narrow mounds, so I would make sure that I stood straight and tall while keeping my eyes fixated straight and down. Sometimes, this would end up being a hop-step-and-jump game of skipping over landmines: on either side. As far as a casual unsuspecting eye could see, lay feces in varying degrees of aging and decay.

I'd pray that none of these piles of crap belonged to anyone in *my* family.

There's something weird about seeing your own family's shit.

Bullock cart rides were fun. So was sucking on sugarcane and playing Hansel and Gretel. We would make a trail of chewed pulp-nuggets so our parents could easily track us down, just in case we would ever get stranded or lost in a maze of fields.

Sanjay and I would wave our sugarcane sticks into a blurry image in each other's faces, and yell, "How many knots? Guess how many knots do I have? How many? Come on, tell me, how many?"

We would both win, since, by now, both of us had become experts in finding a more creative way to count between the clusters of rings at both ends.

I think of that brilliant monsoon mango season when the ripe-yellow fruit was kept cool and fresh in a bucket of water by the old well. I hated to bite off the bitter black goo on the mango knob, but loved sucking on the smooth sweet contents just beneath it. Simply suck, suck, suck. Delicious juice lay patiently in there, just waiting to be swallowed. By *me*. There was a technique in building up the juice in the fruit, as I worked my way up from the tip to the base, squishing the pulp with my eager little fingers as I went along. Sometimes, it would surprise me and squirt out from unintended places, running past my elbow and down my leg to become a sticky syrupy yellow trail that attracted flies in droves, some of which circled around me desperately in search for a landing strip. Somewhere. Just anywhere. On *my* body. In an emergency, those stupid insects even attempted to make a touchdown on my earlobes and inside my nostrils!

On every visit to the village paying homage to Dada's funerary monument was a must ritual. His ashes lay under the marble slabs in the mango grove by the tube well that fed the fields he had once owned and cultivated. Daddy would shut his eyes in reverence and be preoccupied in thought. But not in prayer.

What *is* Daddy thinking about? What am *I* supposed to say in my mind?

I would take cues from him and do the same, periodically squinting to peer through my eyelashes, just waiting for the green signal when I could open my eyes again. It was unthinkable to break the silence before Daddy did.

Then, back to the ancestral home where a meal would always be waiting for us. Past the threshold was a foot-high ridge to keep the animals from venturing in from under the swing door. The house was expansive, with a good-sized courtyard within. This is where everything happened. Where some visitors, who were not fit to be seated in the more formal *baithak*, were served jaggery sweetened tea in stainless steel glasses that scorched the lips at every sip. On the other side, a kitchen that could claim barely two walls to its name opened up. The patio was also where clothes were flung out to dry on the perpetually sagging lines between the bamboo poles. At night, the same poles were used to spread out wrinkled dust-laden mosquito nets over beds made from crisscrossed jute and pressed close against each other. Some of the beds rocked when I lay on them. This usually happens, when all four legs of the bedpost cannot quite figure out how to be on equal footing on uneven ground. Like in a dysfunctional family. The rocking would wake me up in the middle of the night, so I made sure that I did not move in my sleep. Even during scary dreams.

At the far end of the courtyard was where the bulls and buffaloes lived in disquiet harmony. They took turns to gulp water from concrete drains that ran the length of a mud wall, idly chewing on hay mixed with grain, and swatting flies against the sides of their abdomen with each swish of their tails. It was quite a sight! Animals kicking up dust, children playing peek-a-boo with their own shadow, and corn popping in frenzied rhythm as it emerged from the hot sand in the clay oven. I would be mesmerized from watching the *chakki* getting blurred with motion, and wonder whether the grain that was steadily fed by the handful into the central hole was the same one that was expelled at the exit vent in jerks of chalky warm powder. The one that was used to make crisp *rotis* later that evening.

Everything was slower here. It was like my very own pantomime. People moved around as if in slow motion. Animals were listlessly sluggish. Even the dust hung forever. It was as if time stood still.

Dada had been the first resident of Raipur to build a brick house, and the first landowner in the entire region to buy a tractor. When this great invention made its maiden journey up to the farm, a white man came along with it to demonstrate how it worked. And people came in droves to marvel, both at the tractor and the white man. Grandfather was also the first wealthy farmer in the entire district to own an Austin car. He had many other firsts. The first to sink a tube well: people gasped in stark disbelief at the miracle of pumping water from the ground with the aid of electricity! He was also the first to send a son abroad, when my father went to Australia.

"We're, after all, a special family," Daddy would constantly remind us, lest we forget.

Of course, it goes without saying that Daddy had a big hand in all of this. Dada was known to be frugal to a fault. Most likely, a dominant family gene with high penetration and a compelling need for immediate and direct self-expression. Grandfather could not bear to see money slip through his fingers. Paisa-pinching had become a way of life, even when there were enough rupees to go around. He saved today like there was no tomorrow. It was Daddy who was adamant that the farm be mechanized like it had been done in Stalin's Russia, which he had gleaned from the books on their revolution that he then started to read in college.

It was Daddy who insisted that his sisters be educated past the fifth standard. Or, was it the eighth?

"Of course, they could've married into far better families had Dada listened to me."

I'd often think, I wish Dada had listened more to Daddy. I wish *everybody* had listened more to Daddy.

Dadi, Daddy's mother, was weak and ignorant. She made sure her daughters hovered around to help with farm errands and household chores relating to their younger siblings. And, with more little ones on the way, there was always assistance needed at all odd hours of day and night. Mostly, because there were always more little ones on the way.

"How foolish of her," Daddy would say. "And, how very shortsighted of my father."

Nobody had the vision Daddy had. Dada should have stopped procreating, the way he kept "going at it, all the way into the sunset." He certainly did not know how to care for his increasing brood. Affording a fine education for his progeny entailed further spending, but money changing hands was a bold and preposterous idea.

"Education is the foundation of civilization," Daddy would pontificate. "Women are equal to men, and deserve the same education. Now, no one has the right to go on producing kids he cannot care for. It's so easy to bring children into this world, but so difficult to take responsibility for them."

This is why Daddy had a vasectomy after Mummy got pregnant with me, even though in those days this irrevocable intervention was still very new and scary. Friends would advise against it without being solicited first.

"Shiv, don't you want another son? And, what if you end up losing a child? By the way, haven't you heard that this operation is known to sap your vitality and makes you less male? In short, it's no different from being castrated!"

And I'd think, these stupid country folk. They don't have the courage to take even the first step out of the Dark Ages. Why don't they just go and live with *The Flintstones*!

It seemed to grow dark early in the village. At dusk, the dust of the day seemed to hang loose for a long time until the gas lanterns would eventually burn down. Then the wooden fires would come alive. I never understood what made the lanterns glow so, like shining miniature suns. That a bulbous net could produce so much light was pure magic! I would be afraid to touch it. Sanjay told me I could get burnt and easily lose a finger, or two. How I hated the idea of losing a finger, or two. Nonetheless, it was fun to pump the knob at the base and watch the flame grow with the glow, until it seemed dangerously close and all geared up to burst right in my super-enthusiastic face.

The largest room in the sprawling home stretched from one end of the house to the other. Over the years, the family must have continued to extend the far-end-wall farther and farther back as more and more children were born to Dadi. Inside, there were numerous pillars that supported the roof, with haphazardly rolled bedding, wooden hutches and everything-else-arbitrary stacked up against them as if to hold up the entire structure.

What's inside all these boxes? I'd wonder. To whom do they belong? And, who sleeps in *these* beds?

At night, the women would huddle by the kitchen fire cooking, chopping, and scrubbing dishes all at once, with at least one child perched on one hip (what wide hips they have, I thought), while a few young ones explored and poked at anything that came their way. Periodically, when the fire would start to die, a member of the kitchen female contingent would stoke the fire and blow through the metallic *phukni* (literally, 'to blow'), and get it swiftly ablaze all over again.

I remember thinking, what a shame that I have to dumb myself down for my country cousins. They all had chores. But, since we were from the city, and especially because we were our father's children, we just stood by and watched. Besides, we were obviously brighter and more educated. Or so it seemed. So we were permitted to sit along with Daddy's audience of older male relatives as he expounded on the philosophy of life, his travels, and the new world that was emerging beyond the boundary of this village, across this nation, and past the oceans. This certainly felt far more worthwhile and appealing, especially since Daddy would simultaneously throw in references about the academic achievements of all his three children. And I would return that with a bright and eager look to fittingly correlate with his boasts, just to prove Daddy right.

Despite all the continuous and noticeable attention on chores, housekeeping seemed to be generally lacking in the household. Uncle Shankar's wife ran the house, or, as Daddy would declare, the house ran itself. Clothes on the line continued to look limp and stained, kids' noses still ran shamelessly after a bath, and the courtyard generally appeared dusty and unkempt even after it had been swept back and forth at least half a dozen times earlier that morning. The purpose of the broom was mostly to raise dust, not to gather it. Disposing dirt properly was far too complicated.

"It's an art form," Daddy would say. "Spreading the dirt with the broom is easier than collecting it. Have you noticed, most people sweep the dirt out of their courtyard, and leave it in piles just by the neighbor's front door? In their juvenile minds, *if they don't see muck, it doesn't exist!* Now, how stupid is *that!*"

Uncle Shankar was essentially lazy, and never made anything out of his liberal arts education.

"He is a cog in his own wheel. The one that he himself is constantly tripping over. That's what happens when you're as stubborn as a mule. When you don't know a hole in the ground, from a hole in the ground. Or a tea leaf, from another tea leaf," Daddy would explain. "He prides himself in being a recalcitrant procrastinator. Don't you see? Life just *happened* to Shankar and his wife. Kids just *happened* to them. Nothing was planned. Nothing was ever thought through. Life's just passing him by. Now don't forget, he did get a First Division in M.A., while I barely scraped through B.A. And look where he is today, and how starkly different our lives have become! He has nothing. History is replete with stories about Princes who lost their entire kingdoms, simply because they spent their whole life looking forward to an inheritance. Or, should I say, looking backward at it. With ownership-filled eyes."

Daddy's so right, I'd think. This *does* explain everything about Uncle Shankar's pathetic existence.

Uncle had failed at every business venture. After graduating college, he came back to the farm with dreams of becoming a successful contractor.

"So, he decided to manage the donkeys and *Pathans* on the Afghan Frontier region, but only from the safe distance and the comfort of our father's home. Needless to say, both the lazy asses and

MY FATHER'S FATHER

There is a lot I can say about my grandfather, Balram Yadav. He was a powerful and well-respected man in the district but never more powerful than his own mother. Daddy sometimes spoke of his grandmother as if she were a female idol --- tall, fair, and strong. Her husband had died quietly, and rather suddenly, when he was still in his twenties, leaving behind a young widow with two children: a boy who would become my grandfather, and a girl, my great-aunt.

As was then the custom, my great-grandmother, Ma *ji*, was instructed to marry her brother-in-law. But she decided to face life on her own terms, and raise her two young children herself. Daddy would speak of her with reverence and awe. She was the super-boss of the entire extended joint family, a Dowager Queen; a woman with a commanding presence who controlled the entire clan, and anticipated and dictated everything that transpired within the four walls of the homestead and as far beyond it as her penetrating eyes could see. She would make it a point to be the first to taste the meal of the day in order to symbolically pronounce it as 'leftover.' Later, the random scraps from the kitchen were officially donated to the untouchables, who would not ever dare take a single step through the tired front door even though it did swing easily in both directions. So, they waited outside in their humility, stoically braving the elements, for food that had previously thus been made *jutha* by her.

There is an odd story of Ma *ji* indulging the younger male grandchildren including my father in nursing at her large fair breasts, then shooing them off to run along and play. It seems rather strange, because Daddy said that when his turn came she would ask him not to bite her --- so he must have had teeth. He must also have been old enough to remember. All her grandsons would literally line up for this special privilege of fleetingly putting a mouth to her nipples, and then scuffle each other to the ground in order to get their next rightful turn. In that same peculiar way, she would favor her youngest grandson,

Shiv, at this bizarre ritual. I have heard this story so many times, and as far back as I can remember. It feels odd now, for more reasons than one. However, growing up, the way Daddy narrated this practice in his blasé and humorous way, it did not seem too weird.

"They were beautiful breasts," he would reminisce with fondness, "large, soft, and white as milk."

When I was old enough to understand, Daddy would often say that I was the new Ma *ji* reincarnated into the family --- determined, beautiful and headstrong.

Dada had suffered a series of heart attacks, of which at least three were clinically identified. The last one, unfortunately, proved to be fatal. Grandfather had come for a visit at our cottage in Dalhousie before I was born, to recuperate from the first one.

"But of course, he had to be completely stressed," Daddy would say with his usual sense of authority on any subject. "His progeny was quickly going to the dogs. Believe me, it can be quite lethal to see your own offspring going down the drain. That's what killed him. I'm sorry to say, but the poor man actually died of a broken heart."

All of Dada's children, barring my father of course, had yet to be settled. The wayward son, Deshraj, who had voluntarily ended his education while still muddling through middle school, was assigned to take care of the growing farm. He had married young and then punctually produced a handful of rambunctious kids who romped around in the yard of his small rundown some-brick-but-mostly-mud house. In the ensuing years, the most deadbeat of them all would time his bender, usually credited entirely to moonshine, with every sundown. He favored one leg even when he was not totally smashed and would eventually earn the title, "Staggering Drunk." Uncle, who was quiet and soft-spoken, hardly made his presence known and even less his opinion. Furthermore, he was dominated by an older wife, who was just a few years younger than my grandmother and for that singular reason perpetually estranged from her for as long as they both could remember. Besides having a completely ill-defined waistline, this aunt of mine had no tolerance for ambiguity and but a thimbleful of patience. Except, of course, I never saw her use a thimble. Uncouth, uneducated and unkempt, with quick eyes, sharp features and a clever wit, Aunty was endowed with a super-shrill voice and an even sharper tongue. She could not resist the compulsion of speaking without invitation or a thought-filter in place to anybody within and outside her hearing range, about anything that triggered her rapidly-firing neurons.

"She's like a *belagam ghori*," was Daddy's ruling --- an untamed mare without reins.

Those were troubled years for Dada. His daughters had diligently neglected to seek further education and were yet to be married. Meanwhile, Daddy's other two brothers had also yet to define their occupational pursuits.

In a fit of rage, Daddy would often accuse his father. "Sir, I'm sorry to be the first one to tell you this. But, you love your money more than you love your children!"

Dada could easily have afforded private tutors for his three daughters. But with the curse of a tight fist that clutched hard and firm at currency notes intended solely to fatten his already bulging wallet, combined with my aunts' reluctance to learn, tutors never came. And suitors came and went. Obviously, there was a whole host of better educated girls to choose from other landed families similar to our own. There was a rumor, often hushed as most rumors go, that the two younger girls were going astray and were well on their way to becoming damaged goods. Whatever that meant. So very soon after Dada's death, the first order of the day was to protect them from any such eventual mishap that would most certainly bring dishonor to the family by having them married off in haste and in quick succession. Meanwhile, the farm had grown and flourished: all five hundred acres of it. It was spread out and needed much supervision. Something no male heir could provide, being bereft of both knowledge and inclination.

"In short, Grandfather left behind a family that was on the brink of total and absolute chaos," was Daddy's closing argument. "Indeed, it was a timely death," Daddy would go on to explain, "because your Dada was saved from having to witness his own dreams crumble to dust."

Dada was a tall man, but he stood taller because of how he was perceived by others. I remember coming upon old photos where he is seen standing in a row with some other British engineers in baggy pantaloons; prints of faded out misty-black, off-white and pearl-gray pictures, edges curled up, with at least a hundred people staring blankly into the camera as if they had just chanced upon a UFO. Some of these photographs had been pasted onto warped cardboard, blunted at the corners, yellowed by time and dusty upon touch, with names of unknown people from yesteryears etched in near-perfect calligraphy at the bottom. During Pre-Independence days, no one ever smiled in those picture frames. I suppose it is not customary to smile during a painful period in the life of a nation when it is on the brink of total tumult.

It has always fascinating to look at pictures from Colonial India. There is one of Daddy in tuxedo and bowtie, dancing a jig with British officers in the army club. He must have had an extraordinary life to feel so relaxed and at home in such superior company, when the rest of the country was still in the throes of feudalism. It seems that in those days, nobody traveled in the trains by first class. Except for the British and my father. As an officer of the Royal British Army he was treated like one of "them," hobnobbing over a glass of Scotch with *Pucca* English *Memsaabs*.

One of the several tales about Great-grandfather's premature demise was that he had accidentally stepped into cow dung with an open sore on his big toe, which became infected and killed him without further delay. So he died of tetanus, or sepsis, or both. Or whatever people with open infected toes died of in those days. That is how Ma *ji* became the family matriarch. Dada would shudder in her very presence, especially since, on more occasion than one, he had witnessed her fly into an unremitting rampage with little or no provocation. He would obey her every command, and be mindful of her every glance. Even when she was not looking at him.

Sometimes, I would think, had it not been for Ma *ji*, who knows in what degree of abject squalor of a back alley in a nameless backward village in UP would I still be squatting, under a dusty old banyan tree, dreaming up plain clueless dreams. She was considered to have wisdom far beyond her years and gender plus the foresight to educate her only son.

Daddy told us this story of how Dada proudly presented his first take-home salary to his mother after he was awarded his Engineering

HOW MUMMY BECAME MY MOTHER

I know little about my mother. And there is even less that I know of her, directly from her. Most of the stories of her childhood were also told by Daddy. Mummy hardly said anything and spoke even less about her childhood. I believe there are extended periods of her life that she has blocked out; huge chunks of time that are condensed into but a few lines. Daddy would recount stories about her growing up years with as much fervor as he did his own, and narrate them far better than she ever could. Daddy could even create a story about inconsequential non-events, and keep us all mesmerized.

Mummy was the middle child among four sisters and four brothers. She was the most attractive among the girls. Both she and her fraternal twin sister, Hem, who was married on the same day as my mother, were fair and pretty; the oldest two, Sundri and Chandri were not. Ironically, the word *sundri*, when translated literally into Hindi, means 'gorgeous,' where as *chandri* denotes the coyness of a new moon. Sundri was way past bad looks but eventually graduated high school, whilst Chandri was beyond insolent and almost as close to being uneducated as anyone could possibly get. That would make Mummy not only the most beautiful, but also the most educated in her family. A clout she would carry, and rightfully treasure, for the rest of her life. Chip on her shoulder. Mani's Badge of Honor.

Uncle Karan was the oldest in the sib-ship. He was always financially in trouble, though he never let that bother him, and emotionally dependent, which bothered him even less. Always wanting to please, never taking sides, he took it upon himself as a solemn undertaking never to take a stand on anything. Uncle was ever ready to give the last shirt off his back, barely having two rusty paisa rubbing against each other in his breast-pocket at any given time. The peacemaker in him would be tested over time, and, as you will see later in my story, he would pass with flying colors. All in all, a good chap, rather sickly, an eternal procrastinator; essentially well-meaning, but somewhat unlucky in love --- but that is another story, for another time. Black Sheep, Wounded Warrior, or White Knight? It goes without saying that Uncle Karan did not have the intestinal fortitude to stand up to my father. But then, I never met anyone who did.

When Mummy was twelve, she went to live with her uncle who had been appointed as a superintendent of schools in UP. He had a Master's degree, had been educated by the British, and spoke near-perfect King's English.

"Speaking flawless English is the only way to get ahead in life," Daddy confirmed.

That was the summer, which would change Mummy's life forever. She quickly discovered that her uncle's own daughters were excused from domestic chores simply because they had opted to go to school. This is how she started her education, and skipped all the way to class 7 in one year. Then she kept going, while the haughty female cousins she had thus far secretly envied took a midcourse sojourn. It was unconventional for girls to pursue an education for reasons other than as a pastime, or to marry up, but Mummy was headstrong and knew that she had her father on her side.

My maternal grandfather, Nana, was known to be a wise man. Even though he had never undergone formal education himself, Nana respected this asset in others and sincerely sponsored this pursuit in those of his children who cared. People would come to him from neighboring villages for advice and he seemed to have the right answers for they would come back for more. Mummy *would* get an education. Nana could predict the future, and education *was* her future.

I remember Mummy's father as a frail old man with an aquiline nose, very sparse hair and a small salt-and-pepper beard tied into a thumb-sized knot tucked neatly under his chin. He would suck at a hookah at varying interludes all day long in the small confines of his backyard, inhaling mind-altering stimulants that are so eager to cross the blood-brain barrier. After Partition, in a new Divided India, he had moved from his expansive farm in Pakistan into a miniature part-brick-part-mud house accessorized with a ramshackle thatched roof that leaked every year to announce the arrival of the monsoon season. I remember him often squatting on a crisscrossed jute cot that fell apologetically short for his tall frame, exuding quiet wisdom in the warm winter sun. He had a fierce conviction in equality, justice, and paybacks. Nana understood that fairness is the leading edge of freedom. Nothing comes from nothing. Nothing ever could. Never quite ambitious for himself, he was always able to channel it in those who had made a solemn promise to themselves to actualize their potential through combining risk with possibility.

It is a simple yet complicated story, and I am not entirely sure that I will get it quite right. It goes something like this: for some good reason, as most adoptions go, my maternal grandfather was raised by an uncle who was the patriarch of a family in Multan. To return the favor, for Nana believed in equity and righteousness, after the Partition of India, when in a single sweep of fate his entire extended family was displaced, he took this adopted family under his wing. I never heard Nana complain about what happened to him and his family because of Partition.

Now back to the hookah. I remember watching with fascination as Nana loaded the device each morning. Just the right-sized coal bits, pitch-black and shining fresh, carefully selected and waiting to perform, were gently hammered into bits, and ceremoniously stacked into the instrument over a layer of crushed coffee-brown tobacco that exuded a raw intoxicating smell. Then, with a single magical strike of a match, the black charcoal mound was lit. And to really get the blaze going nice and strong, Nana would begin to inhale like there was no tomorrow. These breathing exercises would send him into fits of short unremitting coughs on every inhale, interspersed with escalating high-pitched continuous wheezes on every exhale. I feared that he would never be able to speak again!

I had never heard anyone cough in this manner before, or since. Hesitant little coughs would build up into a crescendo of uninterrupted wheezing that seemed to come from far beyond his lungs, way past his gut, from some unnamed place deep inside his very being. His whole body would go into convulsions of coughing sprees that culminated in recurrent unrelenting retching. Just when I hoped that the commotion had finally subsided, it would resume again in fits and starts. By now, the hookah would be all ablaze and the coal a fiery-orange. Nana would make gurgling sounds as he sucked at the pipe, while Sanjay and I would stand by watching and waiting for him to momentarily look the other way so we could have a go at it ourselves. At the end of the day, the fire was abruptly put out with a quick splash and sizzle of water. While the steam curled out of the hookah, the remaining coal slowly simmered its way out into the night.

My grandparents on both sides had arranged marriages while they were still in their teens. And on both sides, they were perfectly mismatched. My maternal grandmother, Nani, looked just like any other old woman in the village. It pained me that I could not tell her apart. I wonder if Mummy was mortified by her own mother's rather rustic demeanor and shoddy appearance, because I certainly was. Sometimes, traveling halfway across the country on our way to my maternal village, we would come upon Nani with her rough hands and calloused feet lost in the straw and cow dung patties premix, squishing it with her industrious extremities to smoothen it just so, to coax it just into the right pancake shape fuel cakes to feed the kitchen fires.

Nani was a low-maintenance woman, a busybody immersed in simple daily chores of her simple daily life, never shy to target her abundant energy on the most menial of tasks. Her goal, it seemed, was to go through life entirely on autopilot and die only after completing all the errands she needed to accomplish for the day: the dinner cooked, the fire smothered, and the animals put to bed. She was incapable of malice and she was certainly impervious to the clutter bug. Small, energetic, and weather-beaten, she was completely incapable of carrying today's thought into tomorrow.

Having known her parents, I do believe Mummy must have been born an uncomplicated woman. I suppose marrying Daddy changed that.

Simpleminded but determined, Mummy aced her way through high school and went on to Lahore Women's College. There are stories about her student days that Daddy would relate, with Mummy occasionally adding a word, a nod, or a look, to authenticate his rendition. She resided in an all-girls dorm within a fortress built mostly to keep the boys out. In Muslim-dominated West Punjab, the custom of veiled *purdah* was universally practiced. The boarders would leave their laundry for the dhobi tied in a bundle at the door, with a list attached, so that they never had to lay their virgin eyes on the laundryman. For no other reason, except that he was a man ---

and they were still virgins. So Mummy saw very few men, other than those from. her immediate family. Even male cousins were abruptly struck off the attendance sheet. Hence, only her father could visit her at college, and even he had to identify himself at those lofty gates. Mummy said she never missed not being around men. All she wanted was to take a stab at higher education, in order to make something of her life. At one time, an older girl in the dorm came onto Mummy. Daddy told us about that. We would briefly chance upon her later in Bombay, quietly and happily married.

There is a vague mention of my parents being betrothed to each other and the arrangement being mysteriously called off and then curiously rekindled again. I have never wanted to know the details of this story-within-a-story.

I would never have been born had my parents not married each other!

Daddy loved to tease Mummy about their brief courtship after they were informally and mutually spoken-for. He would circle the high walls of her college on his bike, just to take one secret look at her, one glance at her beauty. Until his tires were worn down flat, since he was denied entry to her dorm every time the rubber hit the road.

When Mummy was in her final year of college, the country was going to split into three contiguous parts, all the universities across the land were forced to shut down, and the whole nation came to a halt. As such, it was only after Independence when she got a chance to finish up the remaining credits to get her diploma. Mummy would never let us forget how, because of the pandemonium around India's Freedom, she missed the deadline to apply to medical school.

August 15, 1947, was the day India became free. That was the day when the red, white and blue Union Jack came down the flag-post at the presidential Rashtrapathi Bhavan in New Delhi for the first time, and the Tricolor of saffron, green and white went up in every corner of this new nation. It was also the same day when the two arms of British India were chopped off. These would become East and West Pakistan.

1947 was also the year when many families were displaced and much blood would be shed. And as is commonly lamented, blood that would become a stain on the conscience of the subcontinent. I have heard that Mummy's family was more prosperous than Daddy's, before

Nana had to leave everything behind in Multan during the hurried scuttle to leave Pakistan for good. By everything, I mean *everything.* Land. Animals. Clothes. Jewelry. Friends. Even some family members. My parents were married in the "merry month of May" (like in the *Gunner's Song*) of '47, three months before Partition. By that summer, Mummy's family was scurrying around with other Hindu and Sikh neighbors to make arrangements to migrate across the border into a new India. On trains, horses, and bullock carts; in a cradle, on foot, or on somebody's back. Any which way they could travel, to put their history and hurt behind them. It makes me shudder to think of the carnage that ensued. There would be blood, tears, and pain. Then, more blood, more tears, and more pain. Blood that no tourniquet could hold back. A freaking bloodbath worse than death --- the likes of which was unknown in that region in recent living memory. One million people would be killed. Twelve million would lose their homes.

The India Exodus --- Just like Armageddon, Awakening, Apocalypse, or Anything-as-Horrendous. Like the atrocities of the Holocaust under the garb of ethnic cleansing. Always about religion and land. Life in exchange for a holy book. Families would be torn apart and other families would be brought together. Trains would come into town, silent with dead people. Complete villages would be plundered and burned to the ground, animals would be let loose and children lost forever. Hindu, Sikh, and Muslim girls would be raped, massacred, and disowned. Usually in that order. Homes were pillaged and entire harvests set ablaze. Fortunes would crumble, land would change hands to signify new beginnings, and trust would be dashed to pieces. Then new hope would emerge. Usually from nothing. There were winds of change that came and went, and came again, sweeping through the entire land. Nothing, and nobody, would ever be the same again. The only thing that stayed the same was change.

A lot has been written about the year India became free. People would wake up one day to discover that they had to move someplace else to escape the ravages of civil unrest, and find a new square-footage courtyard and four walls to call home. Families were broken up and sometimes lost, only to be found again in strange new places, under stranger newer circumstances. On both the far ends of the nation, people would start on a journey either eastward or westward bound, not knowing when, or where, it would end.

I'd wonder, how did they ever figure out that this is as far as they needed to go?

People got lingering sick on the way, or got way-too-sick and died. No time for the Last Rites. Even before the body was completely consumed by the flames, the grieving loved ones were forced to seek safety for themselves and move on leaving behind unmarked graves. Others lost hope and gave in to the Muslims, and died, or converted. Or converted and died anyway. Left to die where they fell. Yet, there were stories of Muslims who helped the Hindus and Sikhs, and vice-versa. It was all too confusing. It was confusion worse than death. Among horrid tales of deceit and embezzlement, there are heroic tales of saving lost souls. People took in strangers into their homes. Daddy said that some girls were lynched by their own relatives in order to save the family honor, before the innocent virgins would be inevitably raped by the looters.

Displaced families would now attain the status of refugee, to be poorly compensated by a new disorganized country, "That didn't know what to do with itself, now that it was free," was Daddy's expert commentary.

Refugee referred to a person who was alone and desperate, with absolutely nothing on his back and even less to his name. That is, if less than nothing is possible.

This is what happened to Mummy's family: a new life on a small patch of land, parts of which Nana was forced to sell at periodic intervals to educate his younger children, meager possessions, and rapidly dwindling resources.

Apparently Mummy's family was poorer now. Although as a child, for the life of me, I could not tell the difference between my grandparents' status, unless Daddy pointed it out. Both my parents' families lived in rambling sleepy villages near small dusty towns where the tar road ended in mud. The only discernible difference being that Daddy's ancestral home, even though just as dirty, was sprawling and dirty.

I used to think that everyone's parents fought. Ours did as well. It used to happen more often when we were little. As I got older, when Mummy learned to comply with Daddy's obviously more logical ways, of course it happened less.

Sometimes in a fit of rage, Daddy would yell at Mummy, "I picked you up from that filth and made you a Queen! You silly woman! You got everything on a silver platter! Never forget, even for a minute, that I can send you right back to the gutter again."

And I would wish Mummy would not displease him so, or we would all end up in that filthy gutter with her.

On occasion, Daddy would threaten to leave Mummy at the end of a fight. It was usually what ended the fight.

"Now, don't give me a reason to hit you again! You stupid woman! I'll send you packing back to your father's house! That's where you really belong. In that dirt!"

Immediately, I would picture a life without our comfortable house, well-stocked fridge and elegant car.

No. Nobody should make Daddy unhappy. It's so simple really, I'd conclude. Just do what he wants you to do. It'll be a better life that way. For all of us. Anything to prevent ourselves from joining the dumb-witted village brigade, who'd stare at us as if we'd descended from Mars!

How did life change my mother from a strong-willed, self-respecting, and opinionated woman, into a quieter, weaker, and self-absorbed person? Did she forget how to think for herself, as Daddy often complained? Was it because, somewhere along the way, she realized that she could not go through life alone with three young children to care for? Where *could* she go? Who *could* she turn to? Her own family had been abruptly dislodged and mercilessly displaced through Partition. Who *could* she trust? Besides, it was no rocket science that being on Daddy's good side made life quite comfortable really. So Mummy learned to forget how to think for herself, and how to live alone. And she never actually had to, until much later in her life.

It's not so difficult to please Daddy, after all, I'd coach myself. All you have to do is to believe in the same things Daddy does: not spend frivolously, not eat out --- greasy, fat-laden, salmonella-ridden food prepared by people who neglect to wash up after wiping their behinds, be mindful of Miss Manners and listen with rapt attention to his wonderful stories. Besides, they *are* so wonderful. And don't forget to study hard. Also, never pray to that entity other people call God.

And, especially never, I mean *never*, question Daddy.

Every now and again, Daddy would say he should have been our mother as well. He talked to us, connected with us, and was affectionate and protective of us. He was also the more sentimental parent of the two. Sometimes, something from a movie or novel would move him to cry.

"I've the heart of a woman," he would say. "I'm really very soft inside. If you can get to that part, you can make me do anything. I'll even move the Earth for you."

In reality, Daddy did move the Earth for us: he ran the household through Mummy, decided how time and money would be spent and chose who we could trust. Which was nobody.

As I got older both my parents had the same opinion on everything.

I remember some of the fights between my parents in those early years. Daddy would do all the talking, as he always did, even when they were not quarreling. He would raise his voice up several decibels, call her "a stupid, good-for-nothing woman," and without haste, allude to her being "loose and of low morals." Sometimes he would outright hit her and unceremoniously throw her out into the front yard.

Little wonder then, that she learned to think like him.

While they fought I would pretend that I was not there, steering clear of the war zone, hiding from Daddy's wrath. I would see my mother reduced to a non-being and fervently pray that she would not waste everybody's time, just cave in and quietly agree with him without further ado.

Sometimes, it scares me to think what I got from each parent: the grandiose fearlessness, or the quiet cowardice?

On occasion my father, and later the rest of my family, would insist that I was his clone. There was actually a period in my childhood when this felt like a well-intentioned compliment. As I got older, though, it would scare the daylights out of me and give me the creepy willies.

What if I'm *really* like him? I'd wonder.

The story will tell the story best.

Now back to the wedding day. From what I have heard from Daddy, Mummy did not really want to marry. She had set her heart on an education and felt secure in her new identity. When she saw the perils of Partition, her family broken and impoverished, and a future that had now suddenly become bleak and unpredictable, she agreed to marry after all. World War II had ended two years earlier, India would be free later that year, and, what nobody knew then, would break apart as it became free. And nothing and nobody would ever be the same again.

It was around this time that my parents came together in matrimony. True to his word, Daddy took no dowry.

"What's the use of all this education, I ask you? Dowry is an insult to manhood. It's no different than selling your son to the highest bidder. Mind you, I could've gotten anything had I asked for it."

As per Daddy's wishes, and much to the disappointment of his family only four people accompanied him in the *baraat*. The wedding party was made up of his father and three brothers.

"Big receptions are a total waste of time and money."

It was the first of May, Daddy would us with pride: a very hot first of May in Lahore. It was also Labor Day in the Communist world and therefore a perfect day to be married. Daddy came straight down from duty in the mountains for his wedding, still wearing his woolen army shirt, complete with the ribbon stripes of honor on his shoulder in tribute to the wars he had won, with enough room left over for the wars yet to be won by him. He was married in his uniform that day.

On the train ride back to the army base, in the finest first-class coupe, Daddy asked Mummy to remove the *purdah* from her face. She would never wear a veil again.

"Women are equal to men. Mani, you don't have to hide your face from anyone ever again," he instructed his new bride. "Especially, because you are so beautiful."

It was on their first day together when Daddy told his new wife, "From now on, my family will always come first. Remember this for all time. You come only after my three brothers and three sisters. So, bear in mind, you'll always be number seven in our family."

What *could* Mummy say? How *did* she feel? I will never know. But, what I do know is that she would always remember that.

My parents must have had some tumultuous early years in their marriage. Mummy came from a proud family, but she spoke English hesitantly. She was an introvert and uncomfortable in social settings.

She would now be called upon to entertain at home, attend dinners at the army club with impeccably laid out silverware that in those days was made of *real* silver, and a meal service that ran into several courses with a full brass band playing along.

Things would change in the army after the British left. Mess captains took the dinnerware home and made bedspreads from the curtains. They took anything they could lay their sticky fingers on and get away with.

"The Indian officers don't have an honest streak in them. It was daylight robbery! Downright stealing, I call it! Those low-lives! Those dirt-bags!" Daddy would complain.

The army club was stripped to its bare walls and soon lost its grandeur. The white-glove service was over. The clout of being an army officer was gone.

"What a bloody mess! The British should have never left. We were far better off when *they* ruled this dishonest and corrupt nation. I always maintain, that corruption is the side effect of democracy," Daddy would lament.

Daddy had some romantic stories about Mummy too. Early on in their marriage, he would strain his ears to the bathroom wall --- maybe, just maybe, his wife *could* sing! Her name Mani was, after all, derived from Harmon, short for harmonious maybe?

"Oh God! How I wished she would sing! But not a sound. Not even a single note!"

For everything that Daddy bought Mummy, he would buy an equal or identical item for each of his sisters. "Treat everyone with equal respect." This was the opening line of his first paragraph, on the first page in the first chapter, of his maiden publication on Fairness and Justice.

"You don't change simply because you are now married. You don't stop caring for the family you came from because you now have one of your own. I've met very few people who have stayed the same person after they got married. I can count them on my fingertips. Now, look at my brother Shankar. Why, on the very day he got married, I just had to take one look into his eyes to know that he was a changed man! This was not the same brother I had grown up with. That was the day when he gave up on using his marbles. You see, most men become slaves to their own wives, who trap them in a destiny that they themselves cannot escape."

How privileged am I to be born to these two people who are my Daddy and Mummy! I'd surmise. How different are they from all other parents. How knowledgeable and illustrious is my father! God must have been smiling down on me that day. The day when I first opened my eyes in Daddy's hands.

But then I remembered, I did not believe in God. Daddy said that there was no such thing.

The first few years into my parents' marriage played a bit like the movie, *Educating Rita*. Slowly, Mummy polished up her English and tried to learn some new society ways: how to needlepoint, cross-stitch, bake, and drive. Except that she could never learn how to drive.

"When you tell your mother to go left, she turns right," Daddy would laugh. "And then she goes straight for the tree trunk!" Daddy would go on, "Have you noticed children, Mummy must first say 'no' to everything. That's her default reaction. She can do that without thinking. She says that even in her sleep," Daddy would tease.

And Mummy would shake her head and smile to herself.

But even with her newly acquired ways, Mummy was more tongue-tied in English, more awkward socially, and would never have a chance to experience close, deep, or lasting friendships.

"She's my best friend," Daddy would say. "You see, she doesn't need anyone else. Remember Mani, that first year of our marriage when you wrote that love letter to me? When you told me how you felt like a fish out of water without me?" And he would chuckle to himself, and continue, "Children, your mother's an isolationist. If she didn't have to meet another person in her entire life, she'd be totally happy and content just being by my side."

So Mummy was totally happy and content with just being by Daddy's side, never trusting anyone else. She supported him in all his decisions: to educate their daughters, Anjali and me; to register Sanjay at the Sherwood School where only princely families go; and make English the chosen language in our dreams. If Mummy had any other ideas about how to raise us, we never heard them.

Sometimes Daddy would say he wished Mummy was smarter. At other times, in lighter moments, Daddy would tell us how grateful he felt that this was not true. "Or, I'm sure she would have left me a long time ago. It's so difficult to live with me. Very few people can. But, on the other hand, it's so simple really. There is no trick to it. All you have to do is think right."

Ever so often, Daddy would say he could not live without Mummy. "You'll all leave me one day," he would tell the three of us. "Only your mother will always be there for me forever." And again, he was right on the mark.

How proud Daddy felt when Mummy walked into a room! After all, she was not only his wife but she was a real head-turner at the club. What's more, she was the most artful haggler that ever bargained! It would embarrass me how she would confidently stride into a store, knowing fully-well that she was stepping into a den of thieves, then march straight out of a transaction and have the shopkeeper chase after her, begging her to close the deal. Even at less than her final offer! She would still walk away, head held up high.

While she haggled with petty tradesmen, Daddy would sit in the car waiting and watching both his wife and the other people in the bazaar.

"It's so interesting to observe other people," he would say. "Have you noticed that you can neither tell babies apart from each other, nor old people. You can't even guess their gender."

Sometimes, Daddy would predict what was happening in *their* lives. His premonitions about people and events appeared to be rather accurate, even though I had no opportunity to verify them. It seemed that he had a unique ability to understand and anticipate human behavior, like nobody else I knew.

"I would've been a vagabond had it not been for your mother. She has brought stability to our family," he would remind us.

I believe this part to be true.

How did Mummy feel to be so openly praised? I think I have some idea, because I loved it when it happened to me. For when he praised me, Daddy could never be too bad.

Mummy learned to put her hair up in curlers, carefully pleat her silk, nylon and chiffon saris, enjoy a couple of Booth's gin-'n'-tonic cocktails in the evening with my father and read Harold Robbins' *The Carpetbaggers* on the sly.

Mummy looked smashing, and Daddy spoke eloquently. No wonder at school, I wanted people to look at her, but listen to him.

My parents make me proud of where I came from, I'd often think. They make me proud of myself.

SNAKES AND LIES

Pathankot, in the Punjab, was the first army base that I remember from when I was about three. This mammoth military presence was in close proximity to the border with Pakistan for good reason, Daddy had informed us. It was also the place where I enrolled in nursery class, and then, like every other kid, automatically graduated to kindergarten. Nobody I knew ever failed nursery school. That is where children went before they started real school.

Pathankot has an army cantonment and we lived in the officers' garrison. All the houses on the street were identical. Our house was akin to a strip mall with all the rooms lined up in single file, as were similar cantt homes in other military settlements across the country. It was stretched out alongside a single lane road that led up to a bridge at one end through which only one vehicle could pass at a time, and to single-digit homes on the other side that I was now starting to learn how to count on my tiny fingertips. Our garden was no different from the other front yards on the street, with patches of lawn caught between bald earth, lined with orange and yellow marigolds that shrugged with each breeze to shoo off the bees.

On one side, stood the tallest mosaic of colorful hollyhocks in the land with blossoms growing in ascending order on the stem. It would make Jack's ascent so easy, if he ever chose to scramble up on this beanstalk. I remember wondering that if our house were ever to get divided into three parts, of course, I would rightfully be allotted the sitting room. It proudly displayed a Persian carpet boasting its intricate design and porcelain artifacts from Belgium and England sitting pretty on the teak coffee table. The carved Kashmiri wooden birds of varying sizes that hung in ascending order on the wall were most likely flying off in a perfect V-formation to an unknown destination far away. It is strange how children think about ascending orders. My parents were not dead yet, but that did not stop me from speculating about which third of their home was suitably owed to me. Even if I was the youngest. Especially, because I was the youngest.

Behind the house and beyond the sprawling banyan tree, was a deep and usually dry ditch. It was copiously lined with tall reed that ran up and down the entire length of the swale and tapered into fuzzy velvet bulbs. There was a swing gate posted right in the middle of the brick fence in front of the house. If left open, its hinges creaked in the wind as if it was haunted. Even several days after Diwali, the candle stubs remained silently plastered on the low wall --- with dirty-yellow, dusty-pink and vaguely-red teardrops of wax clinging to the bricks reminiscent of the joy of the season.

I remember playing hide-'n'-go-seek with other military brats in the neighborhood. I would lay low sitting on my haunches in the swale, or crouch behind the tall hedges and the plump potted pink-white dahlias and yellow-orange chrysanthemums that were regularly fertilized by the orderlies. If I ventured up to the bridge, I had gone too far. Mummy had dictated this geographic landmark to be categorically Out of Bounds. That is where, in the shadows of the trees, touch-me-not plants grew in sporadic abundance and were a sheer delight to play with. I would lightly graze my tiny pointer finger on those tender shy leaves, and they would immediately close up on me.

Even *they* seem to know me, I'd wonder.

When we grew tired of looking for each other in the most obvious of places, the kids would play highland-or-lowland, what-color-do-your-want, or hopscotch. Names of most children's games are self-explanatory. Usually, since I was the youngest of the group, I was the last one chosen to join in on seven-flat-stone *pithu*. That was just fine with me, since I hated *pithu*. Because it was such a *desi* Indian game, with a *desi* Indian-sounding name. Being the last one to be asked on a team made this sport even more unappealing.

When the juvenile enchantment with pop-out books got stale, we would generously spread Johnson & Johnson baby talcum powder on the carom-board in order to coax the chips to slide into the net, or simply blow on them so they would indeed tip over. Or furtively cheat at Ludo, and openly challenge each other at Snakes and Ladders. Fascinating, this dice thing. "Heads or Tails!" It was all about how artfully the dice was rolled. Sometimes we would create our own games, making up the rules as we went along. I was finding that it was generally getting harder to lose. Even at games that had no rules, where it was pretty tricky to identify a winner.

And I'd wonder, why do I always feel worse afterward?

I hate to admit, but we did what children all over the world indulge in: cruelly exclude those kids who are deemed, by some mysterious process of elimination, not to strictly belong to the 'in' crowd. They were often those who spoke a heavily-accented *desi* English or in snatches of tongues and or did not live on our street. But it was a carefree and innocent time --- adults still seemed to mean what they said, or did not say; children still seemed to have little ulterior motive in what they did, or did not do.

In those days, Mummy bathed us all. I do not remember when this practice ended, and we had to take this onerous task upon ourselves. She had strong hands, and knew how to separate skin from dirt. Sometimes, I used to think she took off a little too much skin. She would rub the sponge-shaped, seemingly benign-looking but super-rough pumice stone on the difficult spots --- the tricky crevices on my knuckles, elbows, and ankles where dirt loved to hide, attempting to smooth out their anatomical creases. Later, for some reason not very clear to me, she stopped bathing us together. She also stopped using the stone.

Good riddance! I'd think. It *is* backward and rustic. I've seen it being used in the village. Besides, it hurts so!

It felt good to be clean, but when stone rubs against skin it does sting and sometimes tickle. As the foam would gather, it got easier for Sanjay and I not to stare at each other's private parts. Only Mummy could build up this Lifebuoy soap into a frenzy, wash behind our ears, blow our noses clean, and dry us out in the sun.

This would soon become a family joke. Every time I wanted to fart, I would first ask permission from everyone seated for dinner.

"I need to pass gas *now*," I would warn all and sundry present in the room.

I would then be expeditiously excused from the dining table to go and hide behind the curtains. Safely away from public view, I would shut my eyes tight and relieve myself with "a big bang." Later, I would practice on holding it, or let out a whimper of a fart. I had decided that *if no one can see me, I do not exist.* Then the whole family would laugh, and I would laugh with them. I learned very early on that I could make other people happy. It sure felt good to see everyone relax. It would even distract us all for a little bit from table manners and such.

Periodically, the *kalai* man would descend upon our household. His job was to clean the brass utensils and make them shine like new. Even though, he himself was laden with grime. Everything would come out of the kitchen: a collection of pots, an assortment of pans and a spattering of pitchers; all tired looking, spotted brown, and scarred from abuse.

The *kalai* man's visit felt like our own private backyard magic show! First he would heat the subject utensil on the open coals. Then, holding the precious nickel string with a pair of tongs, he would make short quick flourishes inside the pan with its red-hot tip. Finally, he would finish it up by briskly rubbing the surfaces clean with a dirty-brown stained cloth. And voila! A shining metallic film appeared, as good as new, to perfectly coincide with my jaw dropping a few notches. I wonder now how much of that metal ended up later in Mummy's cooking. But at that moment, it did not matter. In fact, it hardly even crossed my mind. The show was all that I really cared about. It was a jolly good show and we did not have to leave home to have fun.

Every year we would spend the better half of a day on our family photo shoot. A professional photographer would dutifully arrive on our patio with a camera draped in a black velvet cloth and corresponding paraphernalia. He never ventured past the patio. Mummy had decided that the house was out of bounds for all strangers. Especially male-strangers.

Out of Bounds was becoming a familiar paradigm. Mummy rules!

I still remember posing for that mysterious black box. Daddy would ask us all to be still, and when a light flashed that nearly blinded me, I knew that it was over and I could breathe again. That spring the annual picture was taken against the brick wall with the creeper --- the one laden with purple flower bells, most popular with the bees. I swear, I could actually see them sucking drops of nectar from the buds!

Mummy had invariably been scolded about something earlier that day. This was not unusual. When something important like taking an annual family photograph was to happen, she would inevitably be chided because she did not "think ahead, or plan ahead." Maybe, that

looked like an ancient abandoned Greek ruin. The sinister shadows would grow long and the night dark. I would watch two fat lizards employ their erect tails to wrestle each other upside down on the ceiling by the ventilator overhead, and be petrified with the prospects of the slower one with the bigger belly losing the match and falling straight down on me!

I must keep my mouth shut tight, I'd remind myself, before I end up swallowing that horrible wriggly thing! And then it'll wiggle in my stomach for the rest of my life! Daddy *was* right. I must keep my mouth locked up at all times.

Sometimes I would play shadow boxing with the darkness drawing the curtain over the window to shut out the ghoulish world. I would pretend there was nobody else in the world outside. No one else inside the room except me and those two slithery lizards with their erect tails. I shuddered to make any sound, in case it might alert the intruder who must definitely be lurking in the shadows and would most certainly appear unannounced any minute now.

One evening after sunset, after Mummy had left on her errands and I was left alone with my reptile friends, a voice spoke from behind the curtain of the barred open window.

"Little girl," it spoke harshly. "Tell me, where has your mother gone?"

I froze with fear, and retreated even further behind the curtain.

"Hey girl," the voice was harsh now. "What's your name?"

When I did not reply, he said, "I'll shoot you if you don't answer!"

I could see the open barrel of the pistol pointing at me, but I could not see the face, and I certainly did not recognize the voice. I shrank back to the corner of the bed and stood still. I dared not breathe.

And then he laughed!

Gosh! I recognize the laugh!

It was Daddy of course. He was only testing me.

He had driven all day with Anjali and Sanjay to be with us over the weekend. Daddy later told me I had passed the test, because I did not disclose my name, or the whereabouts of my mother to an outsider.

"Nargis, you are so smart! You didn't trust a stranger."

I loved being praised for passing Daddy's tests. And, I promised myself, I would never ever trust a stranger for as long as I live.

For several years thereafter, I was teased about that night. I was such a coward. I could be so easily scared, even of my own shadow! Later, I would laugh every time Daddy would recap the story. It sounded more hilarious each time. I would forget how terrified I was when it had actually happened. I would never stop being the baby of the family. It felt special being the baby of the family: Someone who could be teased, spoiled and pampered.

I continued to be terrified of the dark. Later, Daddy would bribe me with small brass or nickel coins, to walk up to the gate at night and latch it so that the doors would stop creaking like a ghost. I must have cheated a few times, pretending to shut it on those nights when it was extra windy. Not to add more coins made from cheap alloy to my little stash as much as to avoid looking like a scared little fool!

Over winter holidays, Daddy visited Mummy and me at the Red Fort construction site driving down from Pathankot with my siblings sleeping in the backseat. I wonder what they did for meals while Mummy was away. It was around this time that my parents had just embarked on a one-way journey into health foods. In this latest single-minded quest to improve our minds, the last stop would be cod liver oil.

"That's why the Bengalis are so brilliant. It's because they eat fish, you know. How can we in landlocked UP ever match *their* IQ?" Daddy confirmed.

This time, the new fad would be live grapes swimming in several inches of caramelized sugarless cream. The trick of getting it into my stomach was to somehow get it past my throat. The fruit had arrived from Persia in large hampers. They must have had a bumper crop that year. We had grapes for breakfast, grapes for lunch, and grapes for dinner. And, for in-between snack time, too. All drowning in cream. Obviously, we had to finish them before they got stale. Mummy said that fruit has a tendency to get stale in a hurry.

During that break, Daddy and Mummy had fought bitterly. Sanjay and I were put away in the chicken coop for the rest of the day, to ponder on our lives while we trampled over fresh poultry droppings. I was shocked when at the end of the day we were given a choice to choose one parent.

Anjali and I decided to stay with Daddy. Sanjay said he would go away with Mummy.

"I'll live with her," he said innocently from the bottom of the spiral staircase, where he stood next to our mother. "I'll take care of Mummy."

That got Daddy to smile, and instantly broke up the fight. It was not always so easy to predict what would end the warring-sparring between our parents.

I remember very little of Anjali in those early years. She was somewhat plump and went through her cute toddler phase saying cute toddler things. Was she kept away by Mummy from the boys and men? That Out of Bounds rule? Or, did she not want to join Sanjay and me in the fun boy games?

I remember wishing Anjali were prettier, even though I enjoyed the attention I got when we were together. She was compared to Daddy's oldest sister, Aunty Balli who had the big Yadav behind. I always thought that was in such poor taste, especially because it so offended Mummy.

It was around Diwali that fall, when a strange thing happened that intrigued me a bunch and scared the rest of me stupid. In those days we would celebrate all the festivals. Even though they were religious festivals. That would be the last year Mummy would faithfully perform Lakshmi *puja* for the Hindu Goddess of wealth, before Daddy banished the deities Ram, Sita, and Lakshmi from our household forever.

There was an anticipation of excitement for Diwal. The festival of lights: when good triumphs over evil. That was also the day we remembered Mummy's birthday, because she was born sometime around that time of the year. She did not know her exact birth date so it fell on a different date every year, since, according to the Hindu calendar, the day when Diwali is celebrated changes from year to year.

"We Hindus will never get anything right. Not even our calendar! Why don't we follow the Christian year?" was Daddy's final comment on the subject.

It was sheer fun lighting the candles and earthen lamps with cotton wicks dipped in oil all around the house and veranda. Later at night we lit up the firecrackers, sparklers and bombs that had not lost their vitality from the humidity of the last monsoon. I would watch the little ones whizz around in circles before they finally burned down. As for the larger ones, I saw the light before I heard the bang.

"That's proof that light travels faster than sound," Daddy would say.

My first lesson in physics would be about breaking the sound barrier. A lesson well learned, and later put to test.

The stepladder crackers would travel all the way to our next door neighbor's house, and, one time even set his hedge on fire. The conical bombs sprouted fountains of burning-red, festive-orange, and god-awful papal-purple. One neighbor down the road was known to light up his stash only when he was sure that the entire street had pooped theirs, so he could wake everyone from their post-carnival slumber.

The day after Diwali felt strangely quiet: the sooty earthen lamps with glazed oil standing where the wicks had drowned; the half-burned ugly charred wicks sticking out like a sore thumb where the oil had been exhausted. The grunge marks on the driveway were a reminder of the revelry of the previous night.

That afternoon, Mummy was busy in the kitchen cooking yellow *dal* for lunch. I had fallen into the habit of making patterns on the wall, while secretly peeling paint with my fingernails at the far end of the side veranda near the neighbor's house. I managed to etch a girl, wearing a scarf casually wrapped around her neck, who smiled back at me. She looked completely like a Western girl and therefore a lot like me, I thought. It was also the same wall where Daddy would measure our heights, to confirm that I continued to be a couple of inches taller than my brother, and make it a point to remind his son that he still had a lot of catching up to do. I had started eating paint chips. But Mummy should never know, or she would certainly be super snippy-snappy. In those days she still used her fists to thoroughly box our ears when we got into trouble.

I turned around to hear someone call for me from across the neighbor's hedge. A scruffy orderly was beckoning. And, since I did not understand that I had a choice to refuse, I went over.

I do not know how I ended up alone in his tiny quarter with him. All those orderlies' quarters smelled the same --- that sickly stagnant servant smell. It was dark in there and very dingy. I could barely see anything. He was peeling an orange and gave me a few slices. As I sucked on the juicy fruit thinking this was not a fun game after all so it should be about time to leave, I do not know how, but he had taken a long dark object out of his pants.

"I'll give you another orange, Baby," he coaxed, "if you touch this."

He offered 'this' on the palm of his hand as if it was a stick of candy. Then he started to stroke it with his other hand as if it was a kitten.

I am sure that I did know what *this* was. After all, I had seen naked boys in the village.

But wait a minute, I thought. This looks like nothing I've ever seen before. So large. So dark. So ugly. So menacing? And, why does it throb in sync with the heartbeat that I hear coming from somewhere inside my chest?

Without thinking, I reached forward and touched it with my index finger, not knowing what to expect.

Do all adult men have this thing? I wondered.

I wonder whether Daddy --- I'll be damned if I ever let such a crazy thought enter my mind.

Think no further, Nargis --- This thing looks like a snake! And, it moves like a snake too!

Then I remembered what Daddy had always warned us about, "If you do something bad or if you lie, a snake will appear from nowhere!"

I've been a bad girl. I should've never gone over to the neighbor's house. I should've never touched that blasted thing! No wonder, Mummy would always make sure that I was never alone with male orderlies. Or male anybody. What a horrible thing to happen! I've been a bad girl. And --- bad things happen to bad girls.

Once again, the orderly offered to give me the rest of the orange if I would touch that thing a second time.

This is bad. Just bad. Bad. Bad. Bad. It's *my* fault that this happened in the first place. I should've never followed him. I should've never eaten that silly orange. I should've listened to Mummy. Time to run! I mustn't tell anyone about this. Not even Mummy. Especially not Mummy!

Thankfully, Mummy was calling out for lunch from across the fence. From across Out of Bounds. Happily, I escaped through a hole in the hedge to the safety of her kitchen and to the welcome smell of cumin and garlic *tardka* splashing and sizzling over delicious sticky-yellow lentil *dal*.

What'll she say if I tell her what just happened? I thought.

I dared not think any further.

I'll never do this again, I promised to myself. I'll never venture alone out of the house ever again. Phew! What a narrow escape! Daddy *was* right. Never trust anyone except for your own family.

I think it was after the hazy innocence of this phallic episode that a recurring dream of my childhood began. That was the Diwali that started the dream. It was a nightmare that happened periodically all the way into my teenage years and it tormented me whenever it did.

I am swinging on the front wooden gate of a house. It looks like that same Pathankot house. People keep coming at me in single file, wearing cheap patchy turbans. They are attempting to cut my neck with their swords, one at a time, while I keep wrapping towels around my neck to stop the knives from chopping my head off. My neck is now thick with towels. But not a drop of blood!

I am still alive, but I am frozen stupid.

Why don't I get off that creaky rotten gate and run? Why do I keep swinging to and fro, up and down, back and forth? For God's sake, why don't I run?

It never ever changed, this dream. It always ended up the same way every time. With me swinging on that gate, alone, fending off those turbaned fiends.

The school year was now over and Daddy told us that we would be moving soon.

It'll be good to leave behind all the bad things that have happened here, I thought.

For some reason, life did not seem simple and carefree anymore.

SOUR GREEN APPLES

It was that time again. To start piling our baggage on the truck. Time to move on.

We would be traveling to Dalhousie for the second time in my life. The first time I had arrived there was on the day that I was born. The day I took my first breath of that fresh mountain air. Obviously, I do not remember my first time there. Or, for that matter, the first year of my life when I lived in this mountainous terrain, abode to the deities and considered sacred by the Hindus.

I was about six when I embarked on a road trip into the heart of the Himalayan range, made famous by Lord Shiva and Mount Kailasa for some, and by Edmund Hillary and Mount Everest for others. My first journey to Dalhousie had been much shorter. I had to simply slide down my mother's birth-canal to get there.

"These are virgin mountains and valleys," Daddy educated the backseat occupants. "This means that no man has ever been here before."

These were indeed real mountains with tall forbidding peaks. Real valleys with mysterious deep ravines pierced by snake-like tunnels, some so long, dark and twisted that I could not see the other end.

What if the mountain decides to cave in just as we're driving through the middle of this tunnel-with-no-end-in-sight? Daddy, please, please press harder on the accelerator. For God's sake, let's hurry up now! I would say, but only to myself so that I was not confirmed a certified coward.

A silent sigh of relief would escape my lips when I could finally see the oval sky come through at the other end.

It was a long journey. We must have traveled for days through mountain ranges standing stoically through time, clad in thick wooded forests drenched with the smell of cedar and pine. When the rarified cooler air first filled my small eager lungs, it felt just mildly invigorating.

"It's got something to do with the lower oxygen content in the atmosphere at higher altitudes," Daddy explained.

Occasionally, Daddy would stop briefly to devise the best strategy to save the car from even a single fender-bender, ding, or dent, however minor, while driving around unforeseen landslides of rough loose boulders where the mountain had suddenly decided to crumble; or, while negotiating through the fast turbulent current of flash-flood riverbeds that could easily sweep the car clean off its wheels! And, needless to say, he always passed the test. We would unpack our lunch by scenic springs and gentle cascading waterfalls and wave to laboring lorries with the cheery greeting, 'OK TATA,' painted on their rear bumpers. Daddy was a terrific driver and he made sure that there was never another vehicle blocking our panoramic full-frontal view at any given time.

On the way, Daddy would tell us heroic stories, "From the good old days when my blood was still young and hot."

Once, while on duty in Colonial India, he was driving down a mountain road just like the one we were traveling on, both hands confidently gripping the steering wheel of an army jeep, merrily singing the *Gunner's Song*. Suddenly around a bend, he came upon another vehicle just in front of him driven by a British officer, who, unfortunately for both of them, would not let him pass.

"I came up close behind him and blew my horn. Then I steered left and right. And then left again. No luck this time. Then I slammed my brakes down hard and blasted my horn loud and long over and over and over again, but that son-of-a-gun wouldn't give way."

After this had happened more than half a dozen times, Daddy was eventually able to overtake the stubborn driver. Daddy jammed his brakes in front of the other jeep and both vehicles came to a screeching halt. Then he leaped out of his own, brandishing his officer's stick.

"I wanted to give this pale-face a piece of my mind. So, I fired out a mouthful of choice words that would make even his English ancestors shudder!"

No one ever dared to indulge in such an abysmal deed. No brown Indian ever dared to give a white British officer of the Raj a piece of his mind.

"Now, this was definitely asking for trouble. I could've been hauled in front of a military tribunal and risked losing my shirt on the way there. The stripes on my collar would've been immediately snipped off, in full view of the entire regiment in a public court-martial and I would've been dishonorably dismissed from the army."

But by then, the end was very near. The British knew that their days in India were numbered. So Daddy got away scot-free.

"Nobody has ever had the guts to mess with me," he ended, in his usual, cavalier, matter-of-fact way. "Or, for that matter, the gumption."

We all nodded in agreement from second row.

Another time, when he was a Second Lieutenant, enjoying an evening cocktail in the officers' mess, Daddy switched the radio to Indian music, even though, privately, he hated the dawdling miserable *gazals* that used to be aired all day and night on *All India Radio*.

"Melodies that put you into deep slumber and promise to take you right back to the Stone Age," he would often complain to us.

A British captain took another swig of his vodka tonic and walked up to the music box from the far end of the clubroom. He fiddled with the knob and turned it back to the *BBC World News*. Not one to hunker down so easily, Daddy jumped up from his chair at the other end of the room and dexterously switched it again to Talat Mahmood's silky-smooth voice singing a haunting song, *Sab Din Ek Samaan*. Next, the captain swiftly strode back as well, to fine-tune the knob and freeze it on Frank Sinatra's baritone, *And More, Much More Than This, I Did it My Way*.

"This merry-go-round went on a few more times. Naturally by now, my blood was past boiling over," Daddy explained.

Like a cheetah with Diwali firecrackers on its tail? I wondered.

"Who do they think they are, these British? How dare they insult us Indians! After all, we are a proud people with an honorable heritage that dates back to way before ten thousand BC, not slaves chained together at our feet to shuffle about in single file and be pushed around like this! It's no secret that I have never suffered fools kindly!" Daddy was indignant.

Daddy's fury knew no bounds --- and was rivaled only by his impulsiveness. So he hastily pulled out his gun and invited the officer to a duel outside the clubhouse to settle the matter once and for all. Daddy had decided to take the law in his own hands, and ended up shooting the officer in the thigh.

"The poor man fell to the ground face first, bleeding like a wounded dog!"

What followed was mayhem. Immediately, as if on cue, all the other officers in the mess scrambled for the nearest exit. They did not want to have anything to do with the matter. But Daddy stayed back. In fact, he was the last man left standing and was the one who eventually transported the wounded man to the base hospital in his jeep.

The British captain could have nearly died, the surgeon told Daddy. The bullet had narrowly missed his femoral artery by half an inch, or less. Had this incident happened even a few months earlier, Daddy would surely have been court-marshaled and sent home in disgrace.

But the Brits wanted to leave India quietly. Their heydays in the colony were over, and they did not want to ruffle too many feathers on their way out. So whole episode was played down. As a matter of fact, it was our brave father, who, with his benevolent heart, natural compassion and infinite wisdom, visited the officer at the hospital every day while he was recovering. The two of them would, in due course, even become good friends.

"Now remember this, children." It was generally understood that Daddy's stories always ended with a moral, which we were morally obliged to remember for the better part of our natural lives. "You must always stand up for what you believe is your *birthright*. But, at the same time, you must never forget to be kind and just. Remember, nicety-niceness pays in life."

Daddy's stories made traveling so much easier and so much more fun. It felt so special that our own father was unanimously declared a hero in each one of them. We never wanted him to lose. And he never let us down.

So we traveled on, five people related to each other and packed together, passing through lonely mountain roads. We had Daddy's anecdotes to cheer us on, along with a sporadic military convoy winding its way on the adjacent mountain range and headed for the Indo-Pak border to keep us safe. The sun would set so early here. The sky seemed colder and darker. At dusk, the fir trees loomed tall like silent giants making long shadows that swept silently into the valleys. The still of the night was broken only by the sound of a lone truck laboring uphill in growling guttural lower gears. Its engine would brake and stall and then rev up again.

It must be stuck in first or second gear, I thought. I hope that dimwitted truck driver has got enough brains to know what he's doing, like Daddy does. If that idiot's foot slips off the brake pedal even for half a second, his whole freaking truck could start rolling backwards!

I pictured the entire vehicle someplace overhead, loaded with pine logs and running on empty, spinning all the way back to clobber our car into a soap-dish and clean sweeping us all into the bottom of the gully with it.

To allay my fears, Daddy would make it a point to honk at every corner and was expectant and cautious at each one of them. So we were also expectant and cautious with him. Even before you could mouth "Jack Robinson!", a lumber truck could come lumbering down on us from the around the corner, and bulldoze our whole family into the bottomless pit of the dark ravine. Blindsided, sideswiped, T-boned and rear-ended. All at the same time. Fortunately, Daddy drove ever so vigilantly to prevent us from becoming a flattened tin-can, piled alongside other accident debris laying lifeless deep down in the gorges till the end of time.

There were welcoming signs along the way, etched in stone and painted over. Some said, 'Better Late Than Never.' We all chuckled when they read, 'Careful Around the Curves!'

Then Daddy and the three of us kids would break into song:

"There's butter, butter
Like the scrapings of a gutter
In the store--- in the store
There's butter, butter
Like the scrapings of a gutter
In the Quartermaster's store

My eyes are dim, I cannot see
I have not got my specs with me
I have, have
Not, not

Got my specs with me"

And on and on we sang, visualizing the diminishing and decaying supplies in the store, taking pity on the miserable plight of the dumb-witted, half-blind Quartermaster, and laughing at the punch lines over and over and over again.

I'd think, now, these scruffy country urchins, they'll never understand what this is all about.

Then we would sing along to,

"Hang down your head Tom Dooley
Hang down your head and cry ---"

And the song would take us to a place, far, far away.

Daddy would lead us into song, and all of us except Mummy of course, who would usually look worried sick and be on the lookout for oncoming traffic, would join in, singing lustily into the night until our voices got low and hoarse.

Sometimes I would glance through the window and think, here comes another military convoy on its way down to the plains. It sure makes me feel so safe and so much more at home. Thanks to the army, I'm sure we'll all arrive in one piece.

We were a great team together, the military and us. It was all so familiar, after all. We would wave with renewed frenzy as friendly unknown soldiers, riding on menacing Shaktiman trucks camouflaged in different shades of khaki and hunter-green, looking alert and battle-ready in army fatigue would cheer and wave back. The sight was enough to reassure us that India was still free, with her borders mostly secure.

Life's so good because we're a part of the military, I'd think.

"So organized, efficient, and cultured is the military," Daddy's commentary would continue, as if reading my mind. "Those civilians, those potbelly bribe-swapping dhoti-wearing petty businessmen, they've got no manners! They don't know how to eat properly at a dinner table, dress sharply for a cocktail party, or entertain in style. They simply haven't learnt how to live their lives without inviting confusion. And they absolutely refuse to think for themselves. Remember children, stupidity begins where thinking ends. When you stop engaging your mouth with your brain. Those brainless people in civvies? They have homes full of filth from floor to ceiling, and they are shamefully corrupt and devoid of any morals or sense of decency. And, have you noticed that they're never on time?"

I used to think, God forbid, if one day any one of us were to ever fall from grace and become a stinking civilian!

We knew we had arrived in Dalhousie, when we came upon dense rows of the popular poplar trees interspersed with stunning gulmohar trees lining the road leading up to Chamera Lake. For a brief period, we stayed in the home of our host military family until they were transferred out.

So once again, a new school, new friends and new uniforms. It was red woolen coats over bottle-green sweaters and gray corduroy pants at the Sacred Heart Convent. The school outfits must have cost a fortune. Strutting in my red coat I felt just like Little Red Riding Hood, had she opted to live in Dalhousie instead of within the stiff covers of my pop-out book.

But, beware of that *big bad wolf* lurking just *outside* our door!

Our coats were several sizes larger, as were most other clothes during my childhood. Mummy was pretty inventive when it came to stretching out hemlines. So much so that during my teenage years it would appear as if she had preferentially dressed me in miniskirts, even though that was certainly not her intent.

I am sure everyone remembers the name of that one special teacher from elementary school. By the way, I do too. Miss Jones had the prettiest of faces one could ever imagine, refined delicate hands with shapely fingernails painted a dusky-pink and the daintiest of feet that one could ever walk on. I was completely captivated and entirely blown away both by her face and by her feet. So, instead of paying attention to elementary math on the blackboard, I would spend all of class time just counting each time she would simultaneously blink her eyes and pinch her toes. I thought it was such a cute habit so I started to diligently practice it along with her in class and over and over again when I was alone by myself at home. Until one day, something dreadful happened. I have forgotten how I got into trouble. In front of the entire class, this pretty Miss Jones, whose very feet I felt so beholden to, spanked my outstretched hands. Then she proceeded to give me a sound hiding, using those same refined delicate hands. The ones I had admired so much. The ones with the dusky-pink nail polish. It was sheer pain. But more than the pain was the wretched embarrassment of it all.

When I came back home, I told no one about this. *It was becoming easier to keep secrets.* That was the day when I made a resolve: this would be the very last time anyone would spank me in public.

The very next morning, I stopped pinching my toes. Also, I started to hate Miss Jones. But for the rest of my life, in a weird way, I would find myself rather intrigued by the notion of anticipating behavior by correlating face with fingers and toes.

This incident did not prevent me from inviting more trouble. One day, Anjali, Sanjay and I decided to steal apples from the neighbor's orchard. We stayed up late on a moonless night and sneaked out into their yard like three free spirits. Before long, we had gathered a sack-full of hard green apples. Much to our misfortune, they were still raw and sour. For the next several weeks, every morning at breakfast Mummy insisted that we eat them until we had gone through the entire sack.

"That'll teach you all a lesson, children. That's your penalty for stealing," she said sternly.

The trip to Kalatop would dull the angst of our apple picking escapades, but start new trouble. Of course, there was always new trouble. On the gently undulating hills there stray patches of snow were still caught between the snow-capped mountains. Here glaciers chance to meet other glaciers and then inch their way down together, ever so slowly, through time immemorial. These colossal white sheets literally trickle at the snowline, to join other dribbling waters and eventually become mighty rivers like the Ganges. I was sure that beyond those peaks was the North Pole, where Santa lives.

We were accompanied by Daddy's boss, Colonel Harry (better known as Uncle Hairy, largely due to the hair shooting straight out of his nose like cannon balls), and his two sons and even went horseback riding with them. Though not exactly. My skittish four-legged not so sure-footed equestrian beast had to be walked by a guide, who gripped the reins for dear life, in order to hold back its enthusiasm. But Daddy reassured me, as usual, that I would be safe. The neighing mammal seemed to be in a super hurry to trot to a canter, and then gallop head-first into the valley, neighing, "Heeeee, Ha Ha!" all the way down. *With me.*

I fancied myself being in love with one of the sons.

I was in a Western movie, riding alone through a rugged terrain. A gang of bad guys had been hired to chase me down. A brave young lad would miraculously appear from nowhere to save me from eventual ruin and carry me off into the quiet sunset. That is how all the fairytales in my books were supposed to end: a young couple walking into a coral-pink sunset and fading out at the horizon.

It was so much more fun making up my own homespun stories in my mind. I could twist the fairytale any which way I wanted and no one else would ever find out. Not even Sanjay.

Sometimes, the ending would surprise even me.

Sanjay bet the two boys to a green chilies eating contest. We asked them to go first. Poor chaps! One of them got a little bit too sick with instant paprika-ingestion. And the three of us got into a little bit of big trouble. But this did not stop us from alternately exchanging glances and then silently chuckling to ourselves about the whole thing on the way home. Watching my diminutive and now rapidly paling hero throw up all the way back somehow squashed the fantasy of being saved by him.

There were rumblings of another transfer for Daddy. Before we finally left Dalhousie, I vaguely remember going past the house where I was born. It was a cute little cottage tucked away in an orchard of cherry and pear trees. It looked picture postcard perfect. I promised myself that one day I would surely come back again to see it.

But that was not to be. We were soon going to leave the mountains forever, this time for a place far away. It was called Bombay.

"COMIN' ROUND THE MOUNTAIN ..."

I was now seven years old. Daddy had received marching orders to move.

I cannot ever remember having a half-empty trunk to load on a truck.

Why's it that each time we pack there're more boxes to fill than the last time when we left town? They're always all filled to the brim, with just *our* stuff, I'd ponder.

It seemed that the only way to secure the latch was to first sit on it, to hold the lid down with the full weight of a human body. Especially after a full meal. Even the plump hold-alls would be bursting at the seams, threatening to spill out random contents along the way.

"It's called a hold-all, silly, because it holds all our belongings together," Daddy would coach.

It was critical not to leave anything behind, even if it had never been used --- especially if it had never been used. On the final day of the move, Mummy would bustle around to diligently check and recheck all the odd nooks and crannies to save that one last forgotten item, which we did not even know we owned, from being discovered by the new occupants of the house. We started this exercise way before "D-Day," as Daddy called it and chipped away a little bit every day. Like D-Day, it was imperative to conduct the exercise tactically and flawlessly in order to win.

"There's actually a method to this. The technique is to pack the kitchen at the very end."

Only Daddy knows how to do this right. Because Daddy *does everything right,* I'd say to myself.

Everything went, carefully packed between frayed newspapers and failed bed linen. I would hold my breath as I watched Daddy place the delicate porcelain English teapot with precision in the exact center of the trunk, lest it get cracked, chipped, or broken on the bumpy ride downhill.

These ignorant domesticated *sepoys!* I'd think. They don't know how to 'Handle Things With Care.' And, they certainly can't read FRAGILE, even when it's capitalized! Daddy's right about why education is so important. I swear, they'll never be able to decipher the English alphabet till the cows come home!

The woolies were stored in with mothballs arbitrarily strewn between the layers.

"If you eat one of those, you'll die in a jiffy," Sanjay had warned me.

So I would vigorously wash my hands if I accidentally happened to touch one. I was sure that I did not want to die. And if, perchance, that misfortune did come to pass, I certainly did not want to die in a jiffy.

As children our job was to help carry items belonging to the not-so-precious category to the trunk, bring in a new lot of old newspapers, watch safely from the sidelines and generally stay out of harm's way.

We were now coming down the winding roads of the Himalayan mountains, flanked by dusty tea-stalls that were erected by using unsteady poles, which swayed dangerously with every whiff of mountain breeze, accessorized with ragged jute that was chaotically spread out over them; past scantily-dressed mountain urchins who grinned at us through rotting teeth. I was sure that they must have been born somewhere between two corn fields.

These dimwitted kids! I'd think. Some of them even try to stroke our car as we pass by, leaving muddy fingerprints on the shining white metal with those grubby hands.

"Look," Daddy would point out, "I bet you that this shepherd will not budge until we actually come upon him."

The completely oblivious man, bent double with both age and ignorance, would periodically turn back to look at us through a pair of sunken pools and keep going, as if we would magically disappear by his just wishing it, while his sheep darted haphazardly all over the road. In a final moment of despair, when we would be almost ready to run them over, the four-legged fluffy creatures would scuttle helter-skelter.

He's just about as dumb as his sheep! Poor man, I thought. What'll happen to him if he's not able to gather them all!

We would never know. Thankfully for us, our world was starkly different from his and we were well on our way to a starkly different life. One to which he could never be privy. One that he could never imagine existed, even in his wildest dreams.

Daddy would point out the different elements of the landscape to us.

"This nation is made up of people who're so different from each other," he would elucidate, with real life examples thrown in to make his point.

It was always important that Daddy make a point and that his point be well understood right away.

"Now, look at that wrinkled mountain creature, carrying the weight of the world on her sagging shoulders. She looks a little bit like that woman from *The Good Earth*. See how she's adorned with metal bangles all the way up to her elbows, with her nose pierced in so many ways as if she was an animal and earlobes torn apart from having heavy metal earrings dangle there since birth."

What *is* her life like? What *does* she think about? Or dream about? Or, dare she dream? I'd wonder.

We had no time to reflect on the life of a woman with sallow complexion and keloid-ridden skin. Down the mountains we drove, stopping only at scenic vistas to unwrap Mummy's meticulously packed snacks of *aaloo puri* or mint-chutney tomato and cucumber sandwiches. Daddy would pull out the kerosene stove from the dickey and we would idly lounge on durries wolfing down munchies as we watched mountain goats and mules mulling through time. We never complained about anything. There was actually nothing to complain about.

Daddy would show us how to drive downhill with the engine turned off.

"This way, you can save on petrol. Now children, never try this yourselves. There are lots of things that you are *too young to attempt*. It can be very dangerous," he would caution. "You can lose control of the car and plunge headlong into the ditch."

Of course, only Daddy is the real expert, I'd think. Only *he* knows how to do things properly. Only he can save us from falling into a ravine. He can do *anything*. Experts generally can.

The mountains were now behind us. Just a backdrop looming in the distance, becoming smaller and greyer until they receded into and merged in with the horizon. Soon they would be gone, as if they had never existed in the first place.

"Out of sight. Out of mind," Daddy's favorite expression would come in quite handy to describe this.

At Pathankot, the car was loaded on a train and we boarded on as well. That was where trains switched to the wider gauge that would take us into the plains.

It was a long train ride through the warm dusty plains. Off came my little red riding hood coat, bottle-green sweater and gray corduroy woolen pants. Soon I started to get soot in my eyes, as I took in the passing and continually changing landscape. This inevitably happens when you keep a face pinned to a barred open window for too long, like I loved to do as to not miss anything. And how I hated to miss anything! Little coal particles would fly out of the steam engine up in front, smarten my eyes and stay there for the rest of the journey.

Now, that squat toilet was quite another thing.

What if I fall through this hole and am lost to my family forever? I'd wonder.

It was scary to see the tracks down under, rushing past me in the opposite direction. If I looked through the hole for too long, I would feel dizzy. You would see me walking out of there like a drunken soldier on a ship!

At night, I would drift off to the lullaby of softly clacking wheels. My siblings and I fought to sleep on the top bunks. Children the world over love those top bunks. The train seemed to stop every time it recognized a yellow-and-black signage on a platform. Little unknown towns with little nameless beggar kids coming up to the windows, their eyes loaded with yesterday's crusty scruff, wiping chronically running gunk with the back of their smeared little hands. Some had only stubs for arms, with a half-broken tin can dangling off an elbow. They would plead for a few paisa and apparently on the drop of a hat, demonstrate real tears. Tears-on-demand that would then promptly streak down those weather beaten faces, forming zigzag lines to expose bare skin on chapped sunken cheeks. "Emotionally-stubbed abominable delinquents, one and all!" Daddy said.

"Go away!" Daddy would yell at them. "Why don't you go to school? Go learn something, you lazy slugs! Go, get a job or something. Don't sell yourself short. Now, have some pride, you silly brats! At least, have some shame!" And finally, "I'll kick your little ASS if you don't leave NOW!"

They would scamper away grinning, but only after they heard Daddy holler 'ASS!' and 'NOW!' in Hindi.

Daddy would coach us, "Never give the beggars any alms. Don't steal their pride. Taking pity on them will definitely kill their soul. Besides, they'll always come back for more, and never leave you alone again. And you never know --- they probably had their arms and legs chopped off and their eyes gouged out by their keepers, just to get sympathy. You may not know this, but all beggar children have owners. It's a damn racket! If you allow them to get too close to you, they'll take *you* along with them. And before you know it, they'll chop your arms and legs off, gouge *your* eyes, and make you beg on the streets with them. Then we'll never be able to find you again."

So I stayed away from the beggars and made sure that I kept *my* arms and *my* legs to myself.

Those little train stations on the way, they all had names. When the train would start to slow down, we knew that we were approaching another obscure small town with another difficult-to-pronounce obscure Indian name. The engine would come to a halt, pull forward and backward a few times over and finally adjust its position against an imaginary line. Some people got off, others got on and the rest just shuffled about. Suddenly there were people everywhere, like at the end of a show.

It was quiet in our first class cabin. Mummy would get her thermos filled at the crowded stalls, or buy fennel tea served in little earthen cups through the barred window. The cups did smell of earth, but the tea was supremely delicious. Even I was allowed a sip. I would be afraid that she would run out of time and not be able to pay the stall owner, as he would frantically run alongside our cabin window with the train already starting to chug out of town. Using one hand, Mummy would take her own sweet time to rummage around in her purse to find the exact change with tea placidly steaming in a mug perfectly balanced in the other. But she always managed to pay for the mug. And not spill even a single drop.

"Mummy's addicted to tea at any time of day or night," Daddy would taunt, jokingly. "Now, children, never step out of the train unaccompanied by a parent. Sometimes, the engine takes off without warning. Then, *you'll* become a part of that wretched beggar team!"

So I made sure that I never took a single step out of the train alone.

We journeyed through dry land where the mud was cracked and sterile. Through fertile land where the carefree winds swayed encouragingly over lush paddies, across bridges that stood patiently through time, past grazing cows and nodding camels. The landscape was constantly evolving outside my window, as if *it* was whizzing past me in the opposite direction and I was stationary.

Then suddenly, there was water everywhere. As far as the eye could see. A mass of water so enormous that it ended only where the horizon met the sky. Daddy said that on flat land, the human eye can see an object as far away as thirty miles. Something to do with the Earth being a sphere. But this was like nothing I had ever seen before --- this wide majestic expanse of blue, the color of sky.

I'd think, now I can see it. And then --- as the train takes a turn --- now I can't. Where *has* it gone? And, what lies beyond it?

The water would always come back again, as if it was following us. It looked like it had been there forever.

That was how I saw the ocean for the first time. It appeared so calm, yet so intimidating. So peaceful, yet so daunting. In its mighty presence, Man must feel like a blade of grass in a tornado.

Where does it end, this water? Does it fall off the horizon?

"WHAT IF I'M REALLY A BOY?"

I always know when I am approaching a metropolis. At every new
bend in the road, there are more lorries, more cars, and more and
more people. Like busybody little ants coming out of a popular anthill.
Single and double-lanes, dotted with red, yellow, and green stoplights
where looming red double-decker buses bully miniature black-and-
yellow taxicabs, merge into triple-lanes contoured by boring-gray
multi-story flats that look straight into each other. That is how, I think,
voyeurism begins.

Why's everybody in such a hurry? Where *is* everyone going? I'd
wonder.

It appears, as if on a whim, Bombay city dwellers have decided to
exchange homes for at least half a day or two. As if they have abandoned
their houses to be out on the streets, all at the same time, looking quite
harried, like players during a game of musical chairs when the song
threatens to pause for that one last time. Gigantic movie posters lined
the roads, with beautiful buxom bejeweled women plastered with
garish makeup in every conceivable shade looking coyly into the eyes
of girly men; and actors, cheeks embellished with concentric circles
of rouge, with thick animal lips painted a gaudy-pink that peek from
under a hearty moustache.

The house we would live in for the next two years was a sprawling
English bungalow with at least six bedrooms, located on a hilltop at
the tip of Colaba, a peninsula, where the land sticks its neck out into
the Arabian Sea to catch a whiff of the first waves there. The military
exercises veto power over all national beaches. The entire area was
cordoned off to the general public. Especially to those civilians. We
stopped playing telephone with matchboxes and string because now
we had a real phone that sat on a side table against a wall. It hardly
rang, because most other people we knew did not own one. At the
entry gates to the base stood a sentry on guard, who saluted whenever
we passed by --- but only if Daddy was with us. The man would noisily

click his boots, raise his double-barreled rifle as far up in the air as his anatomy could allow, then strike it against his chest on the way down with respectful flamboyance before he would finally bring it to rest in a vertical position by his side. This completed the ritual and he could now once again stand at ease.

Past the gates was a large oval garden lined with coconut trees that competed with each other to reach the sky. A couple of times a year, a man would leapfrog up to the treetops that swayed in the ocean breeze dropping ripe rust-brown coconuts to the ground as he climbed. I would worry that one day the poor man would fall flat on his face on our hard blacktop driveway and arrive there before the coconuts did!

"Holy Moly! Watch out, Nargis! If a nut falls on *your* nut," Sanjay had warned me, "it can bust your face flat and crack your skull open."

"That's just not possible! Hold your horses, Sanju. Enough said about falling nuts!"

Privately though, I would look cautiously skyward to avoid randomly falling coconuts from busting my face flat and cracking my skull open. At the same time, I was extra vigilant of those laying on the ground that I might easily trip over, as I ran like the wind through the trees.

Then there were other frogmen, who would climb up the gaslight poles that lined the streets to light them up each night. At the time I used to think, that this must have been the only reason why they were born --- to light up ordinary street lamps every single day of their ordinary lives. I would watch them illuminate the street at dusk, shimmy up a pole and then freefall all the way to the ground only to dash up the next one in line.

As an artillery officer, Daddy was in charge of the naval guns. So now he had an entire battery under his command. Soon we would learn about rank, corps, and hierarchy in the military. Sometimes, I used to wonder what Daddy actually did after he left home. He looked pretty officious in his stiffly-starched greens proudly wearing his rank on his shoulder, with an assortment of vertical and horizontal ribbons neatly lined up on a badge just above his shirt pocket. I pictured him shuffling a few papers, taking the salute at March-Past, attending PT (Physical Training), making sure that his hair was just as perfectly parted as his shoes flawlessly brushed and ending the day with an inspection of the guns. He said he was lucky this time because he had no real boss to report to, who, he was sure, would most certainly scrutinize and criticize his every move as bosses love to do. This was particularly fortunate for Daddy, since he never got along with his superiors and responded rather poorly to both scrutiny and criticism.

"It's a universal truth. You have to butter up people to stay ahead," he would say. "It's a lousy coward's way to succeed in life. Kiss-up and kick-down. In the British army one was promoted on merit. But now, you have to bribe some Parliamentary goon or Minister nincompoop in Delhi, even for small favors. I refuse to do any hanky-panky. I joined the Military Academy with the singular goal to assist the Allies in defeating the Fascists. If you were to ask me, the most decorated soldier is also the biggest fatheaded person I know. He's honored for blindly following the ultimate irrational command: to kill a fellow human being. You've to be prophetically delusional and natural dumb to die for this country. What country, may I ask? The one made up of dishonest politicians and devious businessmen? As far as I am concerned, I'm just biding my time serving in the army to finish up my term, so I can provide for my family. Not to toot my own horn, but there are very few officers as honest and bright as me."

Only the big muckety-mucks, the real Generals admired Daddy. General Manekshaw was his first Commanding Officer. He would eventually be promoted to become Chief of the Armed Forces. General Raulley was another favorite.

"You can see why I was his blue-eyed boy. But it was way beneath my dignity to ask for special treatment."

That is why Daddy had a checkered career in the military, where promotions were so slow and far in between. Although, later in life, I learned that he had failed Staff College, which was why he was stuck being a colonel for most of my childhood. Privately, it would bother me that my father was not a general. But, I would rather be dead than found out.

In Bombay, Mummy got to be the leading lady on campus. As per some unrecorded protocol,she was unanimously elected to graciously give away prizes on regiment days as all First Ladies are supposed to do. That year, the three of us kids got top awards in potato in a spoon race, thread the needle race, sack race, and every other most stupid game known to mankind race. But Daddy made us give away the miniature shining trophies, the ones we clutched so close to our chest all the way back home, to the lowly NCO's (noncommissioned officer rank) kids who had come in second.

"You must lead by example," he explained later to comfort us. "Remember, you're more fortunate than the children of those poor soldiers."

By the front gates of the house was a fire-extinguisher that, thankfully, we had never seen used. Sanjay said it could cover your whole being with foam if activated.

"Holy cow! So much freaking foam, Nargis, that no one will be able to see your face through it!"

It goes without explanation that I never dared to touch that blasted device, and asked for no further free-for-all demonstration on how it worked.

At the far end of the oval garden was the officers' mess. Sometimes, I would see ruggedly handsome young men with super-close crew-cuts emerge from there. But Mummy had decided, seemingly in some arbitrary Mummy-fashion, that it was out of bounds for Anjali and me. By now, Mummy was becoming more creative in making up rules about where this imaginary border that separated us girls from the boys and men should lie. I noticed that very quickly this perimeter was shrinking closer and closer to home. And that the statutes were set in stone and becoming non-negotiable. So, I never ventured there.

Besides, hadn't Daddy always reminded us time after time that curiosity kills the cat?

Our sprawling bungalow came with its own old slanted tiled roof. What the original color of those tiles was intended to be is anybody's guess. There was a jamun tree by the side of our study. When the luscious rich-purple fruit was ready to be picked, the tree would bow under its own weight. After I had savored a bonus lunch made up of jamuns alone, my gums and teeth would become deep-wine for the rest of the day. Similar to when Sanjay and I would take a spoonful of Ovaltine and circumspectly spread it out evenly over our maxillary teeth usually made visible through a relaxed smile. That muddy-brown grin would even scare a dog!

During that first monsoon break, when the only jamuns left were the not so low-hanging ones, I crawled up on the old mossy tiled roof to gather some more.

"Nargis, your mouth is way bigger than your stomach. This child is just like you, Mani. She can live on fruit," Daddy would say.

Or, die for fruit?

My precipitous fall to the ground was broken only by the telephone wire dangling down the side of the house. It caught me in the crotch, and did it hurt! I could have easily fallen to the ground to lick the pavement. But we could never tell anyone when we got hurt. That too, in the crotch! Especially *our* parents! To be accident-prone was a secret curse! We would always end up getting scolded, if not thoroughly thrashed, for being so stupid as to get hurt in the first place. The spanking had the potential of hurting far more than the original injury. First, we would be smacked. And then, we would be spanked again because we had bawled out loud for being smacked.

That day I realized two things: First, Daddy had said there are some things that I'm too young for. Second, I don't do too well when Sanju's not by my side. Nargis, just grin and bear it.

Beyond the kitchen were easy back steps that led to the servant's quarters, as all easy back steps are supposed to do. This is where we raised rabbits that first year. Out of nowhere arrived countless baby bunnies, some as tiny as my small thumb. Little pink and naked bodies that wriggled, blinded by the trauma of birth, scrambling for their mother's milk in the darkness. *Even the runt of the litter managed to get some.* Beyond the servants' quarters was a water tank. That is where I started to store bones that I would discover on the beach, from previously deceased animals that had suddenly dropped dead.

I promise that when I grow up, I'll become a doctor, I told myself. I'll save people and stop them from suddenly dropping dead. For sure, that'll make Daddy proud.

I fancied myself as a bone specialist of national repute. One who would spend a lifetime reattaching amputated limbs of shell-shocked soldiers plagued with battle fatigue, who limped back home from wars they had won or more likely lost. I could not wait for the day when I would be able to tell the world, in my own humble way, that my expertise had blossomed out of a small stash of animal bones secretly hidden away on the top of a water tank.

On the other side of the house, just outside our study room, was the vast ocean; its soft waves weaving melodies, leaving behind salty froth naked on the shoreline. Since ours was the only house on the little hill, the unencumbered view of the ocean below us would now become our borrowed landscape. Usually the water would be royal-blue but at other times it would have blue-green, muddy-brown or gray-black hues. I could never predict what color it would be that day. At sunset it would take on coral and salmon tones. And then at night, it would shimmer like quick silver in the moonlight. Occasionally, from the bedroom that the three of us shared, I would hear a foghorn in the distance sounding faint against a backdrop of waves licking the rocks on the shore. There would always be a ship suspended on the horizon, moving ever so slowly, going off to distant lands: countries we read about in storybooks and dreamt about visiting --- England and America. I imagined that I was a stowaway on a ship heading far, far away to those distant lands. One day, I would be a miraculously found-'n'-saved castaway, while casually drifting on a raft by those foreign shores. It would certainly make the front page of *The Statesman*.

There was a lighthouse way off in the ocean and another one where the rocks would get completely submerged by the water at high tide. I would balance myself on those slippery boulders left exposed by the tide when it ebbed, jumping across them all the way to touch the lighthouse that was closer to the shoreline. From there, everything seemed so far away. Even home.

"It's called a lighthouse because it's a house with a light, silly," Daddy would pull my leg.

Now, why did I not think of that? Why is it that only Daddy's a know-it-all?

Then he would add, "Children, never be afraid to ask questions. Always be curious. It'll be much harder to show your ignorance when you're all grownup."

What's it like to live in a lighthouse? I'd wonder. It must be pretty lonely up there. And scary too. Who lights it up at night? What stops it from sinking to the bottom of the ocean? And, if that bulb ever fuses, who will save the ship from capsizing when it hits a hidden rock, or an iceberg? That's probably what happened to the Titanic. Maybe, a stupid bulb got fused.

Even though there were no visible icebergs in the Arabian Sea, Daddy had educated us about the reason why ice floats. He said that icebergs can be extremely dangerous, because at any given time seven-eighths of the entire structure is immersed in water. It had something to do with the density of ice and water.

"What's under the water is far bigger than what you see on top," he said. "It's a bit like how people reveal only a small part of their *real self* to others."

It all sounds a bit complicated, I thought. I'll be sure to pay more attention the next time Daddy explains this.

Further downhill, closer to the military base where the soldiers lived, was the graveyard.

"A graveyard is a yard full of graves," Sanjay explained knowledgeably, sounding just like Daddy.

Growing rampantly by the graves, were simple shrubs that turned into gigantic trees at the stroke of midnight. They had sweet-smelling white flowers hanging from the lower branches. When I plucked them, the sticky nectar would run down my elbows. For some mysterious reason, after the sun would disappear in the distance below the waterline, the same blossoms would begin to look like monster spider ghouls with spooky neon-white tentacles. I dared not loiter there during the witching hour.

Who's buried under there? I'd wonder. What happens to those dead people below the tombstones? It must be awfully dark under there. Does everyone die? Will I die too? What will happen to my body after I die? Will *it* also become a skeleton? No! Never! I don't want to die. I'll *never* die. I should get out of here quick! Run! Nargis, don't look back! Just run!

"Nargis, don't linger too long," Sanjay warned, sensing my fears. "There are lots of nameless ghosts floating around in white sheets at the graveyard. They like to come out after dark, looking for little girls like you. Especially on moonless nights. So, be careful! Their bare-bone skeletons will come running after you. Then they'll call for you by name, and take *you* away with them. Or the vampires definitely will, the ones with large canines dripping with blood. So remember, never go there without me. And, don't tell me later that I didn't warn you first," he went on, as we both ran home panting together, with me making sure I was not trailing too far behind never daring to look back even once to verify his superior firsthand knowledge on the subject.

On the hillside, tiny wild orange-red berries would hang on little bushes to tempt me. They tasted better than the plum-sized parrot-green ones Mummy bought in high season by the kilo, from roadside carts loaded with them in the bazaar. I always managed to pluck more than I could eat.

"Be careful, Nargis," Sanjay would caution. "Some of these berries are awfully poisonous. You can easily die if you swallow even a zillionth piece by fluke. You can ask me if you don't know the difference. Or else, your body might end up below ground level, lying motionless between two other skeletons in a grave. Remember, some of those people in the graveyard died from eating berries with black dots on them."

Sanjay could easily bulldoze my thoughts.

Maybe, Sanju *is* right this time. I must follow his instructions closely, I'd remind myself, or I'll be well on my way to becoming a skeleton myself!

I would make a quick indentation with my teeth and swiftly lick the juice. When I was sure that I had not quite died yet, I would go on to devour the rest of the wild *ber*. Once I was assured of their safety, I could easily make a meal of those sweet-sour berries.

To further indulge my insatiable appetite for sweet-'n'-sour, I would stop by the tamarind tree and gather some green-brown rind. It would, more often than not, fall to the ground usually not far from the tree. Just like apples do. If I ate too much, it made my teeth painfully raw and acidy for the rest of the day.

Wild grasses skirted the battery: a huge flat cemented platform, with tunnels running through it to form a crisscross of trapdoors and secret pathways. I loved trapdoors and secret pathways. This is where the army stored its ammunition. There was enough in there to blow up the whole city.

"Don't get tempted to tell anyone. Not even your friends. It's top-secret," Sanjay would say.

"Don't forget, mum's the word."

I would cross-my-heart-and-hope-to-die that I would keep this classified information close to my chest. I never broke my promise.

Especially because Daddy's in charge of it all.

By the battery was a pigsty with a corrugated tin-roof. Once, a pig was brought over to the house and asphyxiated in a tub-full of water. It was frothing at the mouth when it went into status epilepticus and died a miserable pig's-death, while we watched and cheered. Then it was artfully pickled, and we all got a piece to sample. The manner of death did not distract too much from the yummy taste of this delicacy.

That day, the three of us kids decided to steal the corrugated tin-roof of the pigsty and make our own little camp on a landing by the hillside. That is what all kids are supposed to do, just like the super smart ones on the cover of the Enid Blyton books we had started to read. Now that we had our own camp, we were bound to have our own wonderful adventures in it. It was going to be just for the three of us. You had to have a password to get in. So we put up a bold PRIVATE AND FORBIDDEN, TRESSPASS AT YOUR OWN PERIL sign at the entry flap of the tent, for all those who could read. This was actually unnecessary since there were no other kids around. And the few that strayed from the soldiers' quarters did not demonstrate any desire, or inclination, to comprehend the English alphabet. A central pole held the whole architectural wonder together. Every weekend, we would haul odds and ends from the house to this 'base camp' --- Archie, Jug Head and Peanuts, a hockey stick, hammer and nails, a BB gun to kill an approaching enemy and a slingshot to maim stray animals that dared to tread into forbidden territory. Next, we started bringing over tomato and cucumber sandwiches, the ones with a smidgeon of mouth-watering mint chutney, to eat at the campsite because they tasted better there. Everything tasted better there. Then we held high-level discussions about adventures that had still not happened and treasures that were waiting to be found. *Just by us.*

As we were arguing about how we should be equitably rewarded for successfully overthrowing the smugglers and who should be the rightful recipient of the loot, the central pole fell over. Down came the rest of the tin, creating dust and din. In the confusion that ensued, we did not notice a snake crawling out of the central hole where the pole had stood! Only Sanjay saw the slithering beast emerge and he went gallantly after it with hammer and hockey stick. Triumphantly, he killed the bloody thing and saved us all. He probably has a more embellished tale to tell of this conquest, as he usually does. On that day, we decided to abandon the camp scheme for good. Anyway, it was not my brilliant idea in the first place.

When we first came to Bombay, another family, the Simpsons, who used to live in that home before us, had not moved out. Sometimes, army families would briefly overlap in this manner. They had two sons who had English names (like in the books we read), and attended church (like in some other books we read). They were both tall and lanky and the older one had a girlfriend.

Who is a girlfriend? How is it different from having a girl for a friend? And why's it supposed to be all so hush-hush?

The younger Simpson boy, Chris, became friends with Sanjay and would exchange jokes with him. Afterwards, I would pester my brother to repeat them just for me. It felt pretty lousy to be excluded from this boy talk and be relegated hand-me-down gags.

One of the jokes went like this: there was a couple from the country who had just arrived in Bombay for the very first time. The poor man had never seen anything like this before: multi-story buildings; Marine Drive, also called the Queen's necklace; and Victoria Station, crowned with rounded cupolas. The guide asked him to observe the great domes around him. Instead, the villager starts to stare at his own wife's chest!

"Golly, I thought that *those* are the domes you're asking me to admire."

"Yeah, yeah, Sanju, I got the joke," I would insist. "Don't treat me like a kid."

Why do boys keep me out of their inner circle-of-trust?

I felt so shafted. I had begun to grudge that, more often than not, I was missing out. I was getting to experience only secondhand watered-down fun.

How I hate being a girl!

Later, when the army barber came to cut our hair, I urged him to chop mine up close 'n' personal to my scalp, insisting that he drag the instrument with that zigzag edge up and down the nape of my neck, until I could feel the bristles back there. Now *that* sure felt good.

Finally! Finally, I'm like a boy!

"People are hypocrites," Daddy would often say. "Is it not strange that even women pray to God for a son? Why, if their parents had begged the Almighty for the same favor, they themselves may never have been born! It's so true. I've seen this happen time and time again. The moment a male child comes into the family, people believe that they've achieved nirvana! They'll support only their son's education and rid themselves by marrying off their daughters in quick haste."

But Daddy, I'd think, he's different from all those fools. He treats his daughters equal to his son.He knows that I'm no different from Sanjay.

"Actually, girls often turn out smarter than boys anyway," Daddy would add, as if reading my thoughts.

Daddy made sure he did everything his father had not done and avoided other mistakes his father had made. Progeny the world over often strives to be different from their own parents.

Sometimes, Daddy would ask us to observe how people reacted to the query, "So, how many children do you have?"

And true to word, more often than not, the gardener or dhobi would respond unequivocally, "*Saab*, with God's grace, I've been blessed with three children," even though Daddy confirmed that the man had had the privilege of fathering at least seven daughters!

"By now, you've probably guessed it. It's the daughters who eventually take care of aging parents. Boys always end up becoming slaves to their wives. I've seen this happen more times than I care to count. And, while I'm on the subject of discrimination, there's no such thing as caste or creed. That's hogwash too! If you forget everything else I've ever said, remember this always: a girl can do anything a boy can. A girl can become anybody, if she sets her heart on it. I don't really care what you choose to be when you grow up. However--- there *is* a however. If you decide to become a shoeshine boy, or girl, by golly! Make sure you are the best shoeshine boy or girl in the entire country!"

But it's true, I'd reflect. Boys do have a better shot at doing wonderful boy feats --- find hidden treasures, tread into outlawed territory and even save damsels in distress.

This is why I started to climb the swing-set in front of the house, fast and furious. I worked extra hard at it every day after school. I would practice when no one was around, making sure I could do it faster than other boys. Or at least, faster than my brother. Like sliding belly first to get into first base!

Daddy would cheer me on, "Can't you see, Mani? I told you, she's determined, beautiful and headstrong --- just like Ma ji. She's our wonder child. She's better than the boys. I wish *she* were our son and Sanju our daughter."

And I would climb the rough rope harder and higher, until the bristles scraped my legs under my skirt and drew blood. I made sure that only I knew about the warm red drops trickling down the insides of my thighs and shins. I would scramble up to the top of the banyan tree and quickly feed a banana to the monkeys who lived there.

"You've to be extra careful with those animals. Sometimes, they're known to eat the hand that feeds them. They can get vicious and come at you for no reason," Sanjay would advise about those nasty creatures, who at any given time were less than half a genetic code removed from us humans.

Secretly, I was a little afraid of those wicked and impulsive beasts that could hydroplane with carefree abandon by curling their sinuous tails around the flexible hanging roots of the tree. So I let them be.

I was enrolled in the second standard at the Convent of Jesus and Mary, located just past the last bus stop in Colaba. My teacher was an Anglo who wore a pouf cancan skirt. When she turned around, I could see the netted frame that kept the skirt ballooned out and every so often, even expose a bit of thigh. It looked kind of sexy, although, I am sure that at the time, I could not confirm what this word precisely meant. Secretly, I wished that I could try on a cancan skirt just like hers, for my eyes only, just once, even if it were merely for a tenth of a millisecond. But I dared not ask Mummy for fancy cancan skirts. Or fancy anything. That same year, I transferred to the Military School to join Anjali and Sanjay and skipped the third standard. Thereafter, I would be in the same class as Sanjay for the rest of our lives.

Daddy lost no time in broadcasting the news, "Our Nargis, she's so bright, this wonder child!

She got a double promotion!"

Immediately, I would assume this super-intelligent look only super-intelligent kids are permitted to have. The ones who can skip a whole year in elementary school!

"Anjali and Sanju, why can't you both be more like Nargis?"

Bright or not, the three of us continued to endeavor at making our lives as adventurous as we possibly could. That is how the shell fights started. We would give each other enough time to gather shells on the sandy beach, do a recce of the grounds to check for camouflaged enemy posts. Then someone called the fight and we overwhelmed the opponent with our hidden stash. Who needed expensive toys to have fun? That year, Sanjay got a toolbox for his birthday. So Daddy got busy with both hammer and screwdriver, to hammer and screw things around the house.

For some reason we did not have a lot of kids visit with us at our home. One weekend, a pretty girl in my class came over wearing an elegantly frilled dress with fine lace peeping stylishly below the hemline. She had stain-free white nylon socks that stretched up to her knees and did not droop when she walked. Like ours did. Immediately, for that reason alone, we decided she must have an attitude. She boasted that she ate cheese only if it was manufactured abroad. We told her we had something far better than that. Not the Kraft cheese in circular tin cans that came off the ships, but real marmite from Great Britain. This was going to be a super-great extravagance. A special treat that she would definitely remember for the rest of her life.

"Take as much as you want," we coaxed her. "Eat it slowly. Relish each mouthful. Savor every bite," we coached, as we gave her a generous helping of the super-bitter marmite.

Then the mean spirit in us watched and waited, with bated breath. But not for long. She took one dainty bite and threw up instantly (and not so daintily) on her elegantly frilled dress with fine lace down to her stretched-out white nylon socks! She *would* remember it for the rest of her life. Needless to say, she never came back.

We used to walk together to school. Anjali would shield me from the slant of the monsoon with a trendy-pink rubber raincoat that Mummy had worn when she was in college. On the inside lapel, it boldly boasted that it had been 'Made in England.' I wished that I could wear it inside-out instead! But nothing could keep that Bombay rain out: not the English signage on the trendy-pink rubber raincoat, nor the apologetic 'Made in India' obscurely inscribed under the soles of the flimsy-brown rubber gumboots that would swish with rainwater or the clumsy *desi* plain-black umbrella. The one that would turn turtle each time the wind would change course.

The first day of the monsoon --- I could smell it for hours before it actually arrived. Down came large hail, the size of ping-pong balls, which fell straight down from the furious misty-gray skies. I would dart outside and bring in as many as my palms could hold, and lick them as I watched the rainstorm gather momentum from behind the safety of my rain-spattered windowpane.

Then the floodgates opened as if an entire ocean had leaked overhead, from where the skies had been torn apart by lightning. The haziness in the air made the world around me feel smaller. Then --- the welcome smell of wet bricks --- slimy unsure earthworms and slow hesitant slugs crawled between grass slumped over, while forgotten and unattended clotheslines weighed heavy with neglect.

Anjali also got Mummy's lady bike. It was different from a man's cycle, since it had no crossbar to accommodate the female anatomy between the legs. It was also, of course, Made in England. So was her purse, sewing machine and everything else that was, for that singular reason, carefully preserved by our family. They were obviously superior to the cheaper homegrown Indian merchandise of questionable quality and dubious antecedents.

My sister was starting to have problems at school. She had failed Math and distorted her marks on the report card. Once again, she got into serious trouble. Daddy later told us that he had similarly been a smart-aleck when he was in high school and was awarded no lesser corporal punishment. So out came the belt, the one with the spic-'n'-span brass buckle. I am sorry to report, she got it badly: messy lack-and-blue welts, a near-missed whiplash and all. She had now started to bite her nails, just like Mummy did. Later they were both able to stop, but very soon I would start and go on for a long, long time. Anjali had also gotten into the habit of picking at her pimples. I felt terrible for her because she had a dreadful case of preteen acne.

"If you pick at them, you'll have pockmarks on your face for the rest of your life, the size of smallpox and no man will ever want to marry you," Daddy would say cruelly.

I could picture her having craters on her face that would even make the moon shy away and turn pale. She would have no option but to marry this utterly useless good-for-nothing know-nothing guy, the likes of whom I had regularly seen in the village, squatting on a tattered homespun rug and swatting flies to count time.

Thank God, I never had those blasted things pop out on *my* face!

There was an issue about Anjali's walk.

"You must learn to walk like a lady, feet parallel to each other," Daddy would insist. "Like *this*," he would demonstrate with womanly panache. "And not like *this*," belittling her by imitating her wide-based gait.

Daddy would laugh and we would all laugh with him. Even Anjali did. It was only much later in life that I realized she had flat feet and could not help the way she walked.

At our co-ed school, Anjali was just starting to get into boys. She was also getting nifty at service-'n'-rally in ping-pong and would bunk class to play with the guys. I remember hearing one name mentioned by her more often than others. Ravi would become a close friend or boyfriend? As far as I was concerned, I was never good at any organized sport. And for that matter, I am proud to say that did not believe in any organized religion either. Daddy said studying was far more important than either of those pursuits, practiced individually or together.

Now my parents adopted another health frenzy with cult-like zeal. It was like a spiritual awakening of psychic proportions. Cod liver oil, followed by shark liver oil, to be downed by raw eggs lavishly sprinkled with salt and pepper. That fish oil? It looked like the brackish backwaters caught between the dark rocks ravaged by time, where crustaceans lived. And it tasted no better.

It must have been around this time when Anjali got her first period, although I learned about it much later. During her menarcheal phase, she became quieter and was playing less rough and tumble games. She started to use the spare bathroom at the far end of the house. It was certainly the best kept secret. Besides, I was too busy having fun playing fun boy games to worry about the changes a girl's body goes through. That year, Anjali suffered a swimming accident at the club while catapulting off the top-tier diving board. I thought that amply explained why she did not join us as often for weekend summersaults at the pool anymore.

Coincidentally or not, Mummy was also becoming more

paranoid. Anjali and I could not speak to boys for too long and could absolutely never be discovered alone with them. If Mummy found me talking to a person of the opposite sex, I was sure to feel guilty. Even if it had been an innocent encounter, which at the time it still was.

Mummy's rules were well on their way to becoming laws. No one dared challenge Mummy's laws.

Except Daddy.

KISSED BY A DOG

We had settled down quite nicely in Bombay, when our parents responded to a newspaper ad placed by a lesser-known actress of yesteryears. She was looking for a new abode for her dog, Daisy. So Daisy adopted us and came to our home --- a beautiful, dapper, pedigreed golden retriever. Her coat shone in the sun as she scampered to retrieve the ball and other stray objects to the command, "Fetch!" I used to wear a red headband, just like the girls on the cover of Enid Blyton books who made sure that they had no hair growing on their foreheads, on which Daisy tested her canines. With no less gusto, she chewed other things, too. In fact, much to Mummy's annoyance, soon this thoroughbred had chewed everything in sight.

On Daisy's birthday, this B-grade actress arrived with an A-grade bouquet of flowers, the largest I had ever seen, wrapped in cellophane and tied together with a magnificent pink bow that was way bigger than the bouquet itself! Needless to say, the flowers were for the dog. The birthday celebration had greater fanfare than any of ours ever did: Mummy would simply bake a corn-yellow sponge cake, remember to stick a candle in it and remind us in turn to make a wish before we blew it out. Daisy could not hold out too long with us though and went back to her glamorous and civilized, but aseptic, dog's life.

Other actors had started to visit us as well. In those days Bombay had been declared a dry city. Some prominent actors trooped over to our home for easy and legit military Old Monk rum and Gordon gin.

The moment they were seen off at the front steps leading down to the driveway, Daddy would advise us, "These film stars, they all lead superficial and synthetic lives. Never get too close to them, or you're bound to lose your own identity. Besides, they're so used to being catered to and they love freebies!"

Moreover, they were actors from Hindi films. So immediately, on those grounds alone they stopped having any significance for me. That year, *Ganga Jamuna* was one of the first Bollywood movies to be made in color. It was the same lame melodrama of dacoits riding untamed horses into a generic sleepy village, their hooves raising dust. The continuous high-pitched neighing implying that another innocent rustic beauty had lost her virginity, again. Cleavage thrust provocatively into the face of a lens during the proverbial raunchy item number and the eternal love triangle with overdressed men and underdressed women chasing each other in glorious, but strangely deserted, gardens.

Too far-out for me, I'd reflect.

Especially, since I could see *North by Northwest* and *Mutiny on the Bounty* at the Naval Club. Who wanted this sappy Indian stuff? Besides, in Western flicks, they showed protracted open mouth-to-mouth smooching while, concurrently, groping hands lingered over body parts that are usually supposed to be concealed by clothes. Even though such cheap thrills often came with a price tag: it did feel kind of odd to have my parents simultaneously watching this display of public intimacy, sitting quietly right behind me and literally breathing down my neck!

By now, our world had come alive with comics: *Flash Gordon*, *Superman*, and *Richie Rich*. Occasionally, I would lay my hands on a romantic one that I would read in secret alone. I did not want to be caught dead, or alive, with any one of those --- especially alive.

"These comics --- they'll ruin your language. All you'll ever learn from them is vulgar slang. Now tell me, how will reading trash ever get you into a top-class university?" Daddy would warn.

We could never dare string these words together, "Man, it's a bummer that we can't hang out for kicks with that bugger!"

Colloquial Bombay English was worse than slang. Because Daddy said so.

So we would catch up with our heroes in the comics on the sly, since we were supposed to study even during our ample weekend free-time. We had decided we knew better.

One Sunday, Sanjay was intently reading the Britannica Atlas in the study room, as if he was well on his way to becoming a geography scholar of national standing, furiously turning the pages within as he went along. As it turned out, Daddy caught him imbibing primitivism in the company of muscle-wielding *Tarzan* swinging with his Jane from tree to tree. At that very same moment, I was taking a private one-on-one tutorial on *Snoopy's* escapades, literally sitting on the edge of a toilet seat in the bathroom adjoining the study. I had forgotten that this room could also be accessed from another door in the courtyard, until Mummy came right through it and caught me red-handed. And my face too instantly turned red!

I realized then, sometimes, I don't do too well when I follow Sanju's example. I must be more careful with any *secret pastimes* in the future.

Now there were two of us in knee-deep shit. We were hauled in front of the highest authority in the land: Daddy. While I waited for him to deliver his verdict, I swear I could hear critters jump each time the paint dried up and peeled off the wall.

We were a disgrace to the family. We would never amount to anything. When will we ever learn? For sure, we would end up as beggars, starved and naked, with not a shirt on our back or a penny to our name, scavenging for fungus-ridden decaying leftovers from dustbins lined up by the curbside just outside the club gates on Sunday nights.

Daddy was now ready to announce his full decree. Sanjay was given Anjali's frock to wear for the day and I was given old clothes that were generally saved to be later donated to the servants' kids. Then the household help was dismissed "forever." And finally the bombshell! Sanjay and I were involuntarily dismissed from school. Also forever!

Forever? I panicked!

Both of us were given detailed instructions on our new household duties and corresponding downgraded status: sweep and mop floors, scour utensils with rough warm ash even though the maid preferred to use soap and eat off flat banana leaves --- that was actually fun. But we dared not mention the fun part.

For the rest of the day, Daddy was on a war path. While he was quietly incubating his anger in the study most likely robustly refuting Dr. Spock's thesis on child rearing, there was dense gloom that descended on our house thick like midnight smog. The silence was deafening. I could hear a pin drop --- if anyone dared to drop a pin. We wished we had relatives, however distant, who would pleasantly surprise us by knocking on the front door to break the spell. But they were far away in remote UP. So for that whole day we tried our utmost to staying out of harm's way, which, in essence meant, staying out of Daddy's way and not breaking character. The issue was not really the issue. It was the reaction to the issue that could get us into trouble.

A good time to talk to myself. Now, Nargis, don't get saucy! Be polite and subdued. Your job is to just sit and listen. Don't fidget. This could be a bad time to scratch a leg. Or yawn! And, never let on when you space out. Even a look can betray you. Just put on your polite-face. Be quiet and obedient. Speak only when spoken to. Never ask questions. Remember not to interrupt. And for heaven's sake, never counter back! So, keep your answers short. Better still, monosyllabic. Try to give some simple explanation, even if you've to make it up or else be sure to be doubly boxed on your ears. And, "I don't know" is a poor choice for an answer. He'll definitely blow his top! It'll just prolong the whole blasted thing and trigger a dozen more questions thrown at you. And you'll have to craft a different answer for each one of them. So be mute --- and still. Why does the human body have so many moving parts? Wouldn't it be better to just turn back into a pumpkin?

I'm afraid, I'll never get this prescribed behavior down pat. I'll flunk boot camp again and never be able to graduate from Daddy's obedience school, I told myself.

Nargis, now don't blank out, I would instruct myself. Just pretend you're hearing it all for the first time. And, since you've memorized it all so well, don't you ever get tempted to mouth the lecture under your breath in synchrony. *Even* if you think that's cute. Because cute spells T R O U B L E.

"One thing you must know about me --- is that I never stand for nonsense. And the other thing you must know about me is that I never stand for nonsense ---," and Daddy went on.

Daddy did all the scolding. Sometimes I would miss all the 'H' sounds in his words and at other times the ending of sentences or random parts of chapters, meanwhile looking only at his fingers and toes. And co-relating them with his face. And as he spoke, for some odd reason, his head became smaller and smaller, until finally, his eyes receded backward morphing along as they reversed all the way back into his skull. Whenever he was dreadfully angry with me, this apparition would somehow mysteriously take his place --- small head.

Pinocchio nose. Big body.

So on that day, our education was supposedly to end. On Monday, Anjali went to school alone and reported that both her siblings were sick.

"Sick together?" the other children asked.

Not to be educated any further?

Now that in and of itself was a scary prospect. I could picture Sanjay becoming an apprentice to a cobbler in the village, repairing metal stumps on the hooves of ailing cows and messing with smelly old leather in his general malaise.

But what about me?

To be sure, I would end up being married to this bumbling village idiot and spend the rest of my life dropping a pack of village litter. Alternately wiping snot off their faces and shit off their asses, with at least one kid on each hip and half a dozen trailing behind me! Or worse, become a permanent member of a rural professional bereavement brigade for hire, hitting my chest in chorus with earsplitting incessant wailing from behind my veil, only to interrupt the performance for brief interludes to alternately spew betel-juice loaded with saliva in the general direction of family mourners and furtively permit an occasional side grin. This was certainly a far worse outcome than missing school.

Then the day ended like it would end every time this happened. We would be summoned to Daddy's Supreme Court of Justice. Our parents had certainly perfected good-cop, bad-cop to a tee. Mummy would tell us to quietly go up to Daddy and ask for forgiveness without further delay. Sometimes, he was not quite ready to forgive us but it was a risk we would have to take. Often it meant going through, without intermission, a long tirade on 'good' and 'bad' behavior. As many words as a single breath could permit. The lectures went like clockwork. We already knew everything he had to say, even though we were not always so sure of the ending.

At the end of it all, Mummy would tell us to go up to Daddy, give him a hug and promise never to do it again. The only path to redemption was to make Daddy smile. Then all would be forgiven and forgotten --- until the next time.

There was always a next time. Our parents had gone out for another late night party. It was fun watching Mummy get dressed.

She would ensure that each pleat in her sari peeked out just so, ever so stylishly, exactly half an inch beyond the adjoining one. Mummy would use an ebony-black eyeliner with panache. Next, she would reach out for that deep-red lipstick to artistically color her full lips. She would then rub them against each other, up and down and side to side, repeat it a few times before demonstrating the final pout to approve the finished product. To complete the exercise, she would carefully apply the rest of her makeup and end up smelling of compact powder and Pond's Cream.

Secretly, I thought, maybe, it's just possible, that black eyeliner and red lipstick is not such a bad idea after all.

Mummy had started that new year by having her knee-length tresses chopped off at the ears for the first time in her life. Now she learned to strategically place three curlers parallel to each other on either side. She would pat her bouffant in place, while simultaneously checking to ensure that the sari's bottom edge did not sweep the ground to gather dirt.

Mummy looks simply ravishing! Daddy was right about paying attention to those two ends of your body: your head and your feet.

While our parents were away for dinner, the three of us kids got into a fight about something. I am sure it must have been over something quite trivial that deserved an innocent pillow fight. The outcome was not so trivial though. I ended up hitting Sanjay on the forehead with a hockey stick. After a short interval to survey the damage, he would have a small bump for a few days afterward, we were fighting again, now with shoes and fists. During the scuffle, somehow from the corner of my eye, I could see our parents standing in muted silence on the other side of the window screen looking at us and shaking their heads in cumulative disapproval. They had come back early and were intently watching us wrestle each other to the ground.

Gosh! How long have *they* been standing there? I was alarmed!

So immediately, I decided to become the peacemaker, pretending not to be a part of this hoopla and trying to get my brother and sister to stop. I ended up getting into more trouble than anyone else for my actions, which Daddy maintained smacked of trickery and deception. A thrashing that I would remember, when all hell breaks loose. A bit like when the panels on the dashboard suddenly light up all at the same time!

During in our stay in Bombay, we became acquainted with the Rawat family. They owned a foreign car, "Because, Uncle Inder took bribes under the table at the army supply division."

Are there any bribes ever taken *over* the table? I'd speculate.

Nonetheless, our families became good friends. Daddy and Uncle would drink together, get a tad sozzled and laugh at each other's jokes. Adults love to laugh at each other's jokes. It was good to see Daddy so relaxed. Uncle was also an army officer and it was somewhat reassuring to know another military family in Bombay. I found it a great challenge to explain at school what my father did for a living during those times when our nation was not at war.

Other families came over, too. One weekend, Mummy's friend arrived with her kin. I think she was the same one who had once come onto Mummy in college. So immediately, we did not like her children. Our kneejerk reactions had never failed us before. So Sanjay loaned her son our parachute bike and off he went downhill, down by the front stairs and past the oval garden. Obviously, we did not tell him that the brakes had failed. He would never know this, but they had never really worked for as long as we could remember owning this archaic mode of transportation. The poor boy's fall was broken only by the spikes around the fire-extinguisher by the sentry post. Now there were *real* bruises on his shins. And *real* blood on his chest. Hearing his wails, his parents came rushing out of the sitting room and his mother instantly fainted in Daddy's arms.

Just like in the movies, I thought to myself. I bet she'd planned it all along.

In short, once again we said *adios* to another set of friends forever.

Soon we discovered the Naval Club. We had to go past a shanty town on Dundee Road to get there. We would run down that road plugging our noses with our fingers and arrive sweaty and out of breath.

Sanjay swore, "It was on this very street that I saw, in cold blood, a woman pulling out a tapeworm the size of a hockey stick from a child's ass. You better believe this one, Nargis."

He told the story so many times that I was sure I must have seen it, too. So one day, I went back pinching my nose and looking askew, to verify if this phenomenal extraction was still going on in broad daylight like Sanjay had claimed.

Being unable to confirm Sanjay's tall tales once again, I took a detour to visit these strange folks who lived in the nearby naval flats. My brother had instructed me to stay away from their son.

"Mind you, he's a bit of a lunatic," he had informed me.

Today, I am sure the poor teenager must have been afflicted with schizophrenia. At the time though, to me he was just plain freaking crazy. The boy chased me around a dining table with his cockeyed glassy stare, threatening to plain kill me with a simple dinner fork. I never went back again.

It was a weekend treat, the movies at the club. They would start after dark, and transport us to places far away. The children would sit on durries liberally spread out on the grass in front of rows of chairs reserved for adults. This is how we kids got to see the big screen firsthand and up-close. In *The Longest Day*, I pictured myself jumping out of a landing craft along with the Allies and subsequently wading together onto the shore to embark on an amphibian invasion of Normandy Beach. It was I who told everyone to dive for cover when I heard a drone announce the threat of a blitz by enemy planes in a clear blue sky just before they came straight down at us! That is, before we shot them down, clipped their wings and forced them to belly-land, nose first, into the ocean. It was on that same day, when I helped change the course of history by ending the Nazi invasion of Europe. If you had paid enough attention, you would have also seen me in *The Ten Commandments,* walking alongside with the Israelites as they were being led by Moses to the Promised Land, just as the Red Sea continued to part like a blue curtain in front of my very eyes.

The army had apparently surmised that the minds of supposedly past-impressionable kids could not be contaminated any further, by showing them something they ostensibly knew about. So we were given a free run of uncensored A-rated movies. During the interval, we would fall on hedges simply to flatten them, trample on petunia flowerbeds and knock over potted dahlias, until the irate gardener would chase us away with a pair of hedge shears pointed directly at us. Then, we would reward ourselves with ice-cream bars from the carts --- chocolate covered vanilla, simply vanilla and oh-so-plain orange. Usually we ended up choosing the orange bars because they were only ten paisa each. The limits of our pocket money had to be acknowledged.

The movies did ignite our curiosity about sex. One of the stories that went around our elitist cool-kids circle was that sex happens when men and women pee straight into each other.

I would lay on the sandy beach, close my eyes and dream about new adventures. And it would appear like it was magically almost happening. One time, I do not remember how long I had lain there, but when I finally opened my eyes, the high tide had come up to my ears!

The previous day, some of us at school had gathered by the beach to see a body washed ashore. It was both strange and scary. It was all bloated up, skin partly peeled off to expose pink flesh underneath. It was a ghastly sight, made worse because it had started to smell.

What if I'd not woken up at all? What if I'd drowned and died? I was scared stiff.

I kept staring at the corpse --- curious and terrified. After that day, I did not care to lay on the sandy beach to dream alone.

Another time, we tried to drag our dreams out of the sea. Sanjay and I had seen an old barrel, bobbing up and down by the shore, coming closer with each wave. We were sure that it was loaded with hidden treasure; a fortune meant only for both of us to find. Finally, we were able to retrieve the barrel from the water. It was entangled in seaweed and was old with rust. But we were certain that it had enough gold and jewels stockpiled inside to last us a lifetime.

Or, since there're two of us, at least two lifetimes, I calculated quickly.

After a struggle to snip off the metal strips with handy pliers from Sanjay's birthday toolbox, we were finally able to crack it open. Out came more seawater! And, more seaweed!

Living in Bombay, or Bollywood as it is now fondly called, had a *filmi* impact on our parents. For no apparent clinical rationale, they had decided that learning Indian classical dance was a sure shot way to make us more civilized and cultured. We had no say in the matter. Before you could bet on our kismet, a dance teacher in a starched white dhoti was hired to teach Anjali and me *kathak*. He wore a necklace made of brown *rudraksh* temple beads that culminated in a sacred 'OM' sign made of gold, which dangled on his bare and ape-hairy chest and jumped every time he demonstrated his expertise. He also had flat amphibian web-feet and a confident smile that openly displayed pearly-white cultured teeth. To complete this scholarly persona, he had applied powdery white ash on his forehead. I could not take my eyes off that ghostly powdery white ash and those ghostly amphibian web-feet. Face and toes. Toes and face. I wondered whether he would look less cerebral and civilized without the three horizontal white lines on his forehead, which would become visibly jagged every time he raised his eyebrows at my lack of proficiency. He could never gain our respect with the dhoti, ash and all. On the second lesson, spearheaded by my siblings, we sheepishly offered him super-duper toffee, which we had previously neatly cut out of brown laundry soap and cleverly wrapped in silver foil. Then we watched with bated breath as he sank his pearly-white cultured teeth into a cube of soap! Like other people before him, he never came back.

The best thing we kids had decided, therefore, was to just hang out with each other. By now, we had lost Daisy but gained Bullet. He was a lean-machine pie-dog that had chased after Sanjay who was on his way home through shanty town during a rainstorm. Bullet was a crazy little fellow, mostly playful, but always hungry. Actually, crazy and hungry. He would eat anything in sight, which came in quite handy since he would sit like a phantom under the dining table to devour the meals we could not finish. In the months ahead, Bullet would became a chunky chubby fellow.

"You must always finish everything on your plate," Daddy would instruct us. "Never waste food. Remember, there are millions of people on Earth who're starving. Especially in Africa. They'd give their right arm to have *your* life."

I'd wonder, what do parents in Africa tell *their* kids?

Bullet was a complete hero with a split personality: the saddest and most droopy eyes a dog can have, combined with the widest and most impish grin possible in an animal. He was as dogged as a dog with a bone can get. A creature of habit, he would stop for a short break to take a quick leak at every tree trunk to mark his territory, so he would not forget his way back home. Bullet did not want to be ever lost again. He could easily out-bark his little dog lungs at other animal that strayed on the property, then whimper as he retreated backwards wagging his bony tail in apology. Sometimes, he ended up barking up the wrong tree! He was also rather overfriendly and kind of rough with visitors and had to be held back from expressing undue familiarity. Tired from holding down his enthusiasm to leap way beyond his physical capabilities could permit when he was animated, Daddy exiled him to Oyster Rock, a rocky island in the bay. I had heard that there was so much ammunition and gunpowder stored there that you could never light a match on the island. It would most certainly blow up the whole nation! When we went to renew our solidarity with Bullet, he was so excited to be reunited with us that his skeletal tail went off energetically in salutation. If necessary, I was confident that he was ready to fly straight off the island and leap into the ocean. Just for us!

Like all other families, we made trips to the zoo, the aquarium and the planetarium; boring museums that proudly displayed mostly-chipped tablets and half-broken relics recovered from excavations of ruins that existed B.C. And like all other kids born in A.D., who have been shaken out of deep slumber on early Saturday mornings to expand their horizons, we hated it. One day we went to Elephanta Caves. It was a terribly rocky boat ride that made me supremely squeamish. I was sure we would be swallowed by the swells into the depths of the sea and become a fossil over time, like those I had seen encased at the museums. I remember clinging to Mummy to stop the boat from rocking.

That year, 1961, Russia had sent the first man into space. There was a replica of the Sputnik in the museum, so Daddy insisted we go to see it. An American reporter from Life Magazine was taking pictures. He spotted our family, as Daddy was spiritedly explaining to us about the stars, the moon, and the universe and about everything else we needed to know on the subject. Soon other visitors joined in and his audience of enquiring minds rapidly grew. I wonder if that photo ever got printed. I could visualize our family on the cover of Life, looking so modern and sophisticated.

This is what the world really needs to see: a refined family like ours from India. Not those poor children with megalocephalic heads, potbelly middles and spindle-shaped legs that the camera lens of Western journalists always managed to sharp-focus on for the indiscriminate American reader.

This was also the year the Portuguese colony of Goa became a part of India. There was going to be a major military celebration and of course, Daddy was in charge of it. He would tell the story of how two dhoti-clad Banias came to bribe him with wads of cash, so he would order the fireworks for the commemoration from *their* factories.

Daddy always told the story with naked pride. Initially, he led on the weasel-faced businessmen and watched them calmly as they nodded up and down like a pair of twin Chinese dolls, agreeing with everything he said and grinning from side to side at all his jokes, however lame, while basking in the prospects of a huge order from the military.

"They looked like hungry dogs waiting for someone to throw them a bone, saliva dripping from both sides of their mouths to form huge puddles. Obviously, they were expecting to drown in doodles of money! Their greed knew no bounds," Daddy would narrate.

When they had pretty much sunk to the depths of their immorality and were busy drooling on their chins and groveling at his feet, suddenly, Daddy went ballistic! That is when he took out his belt!

"I should've killed them both, those bastards! Those bandits! Those turncoats! And I was fighting those dangerous wars for *them*? And putting my life on the line for *them*? They want to sell this country. *Our* country. Traitors, one and all! Fit to be killed for treason! But they did not know this --- no one can ever buy *me*. No one can even dare!"

To add insult to injury, he did not stop whipping them until they fell on their wobbly crooked knees begging for mercy, crawling backwards all the way through the front door and down the front steps.

Why, Daddy had fought for those very principles with *his* father and had killed to save the world from the Fascists. He would never let illegal money corrupt him. He would never let temptation change who he was and what he stood for.

I remember very little of my mother in those years. She had started to take art classes using bird feathers, colorful beads, nylon string and etched glass. But, of course, not all at the same time. Next, she moved on to tinker with exotic foods. This is when our family became part of a double-blind controlled study and was subjected to sampling her newly inspired baking experiments from her latest culinary class. They tasted horrid, even though they had foreign-sounding names. That year, she baked Anjali a birthday cake shaped like a heart.

"It's so simple. You make a square cake and a round cake. You slice the round one in the middle and put it all together," she explained, demonstrating the geometry perfectly. "Like this."

None of this interested me. I could never immerse my life in such trivial mundane X-chromosome pastimes. Anjali had gotten her ears pierced, but I had refused. Not because of the primitive practice of employing the sharp end of a twig from a new broom for the purpose. I was getting into drainpipes and collared shirts, which would look dreadfully untrendy when accessorized with dangly earrings.

I cannot move on from Bombay without telling the dog story --- also better known as the-dog-who-kissed-Nargis story.

Our parents had forbidden us from stopping at anyone's house on the way to school.

"Don't you children ever go to a friend's house. You know better than to trust anyone. One never knows what kind of family they come from. Remember, birds of a feather --- And, make sure you're never alone," was the dictum.

I am not sure why, but on that day I had decided to dodge the cliché and take a detour. Some rules, I suppose, are made to be broken. I left Anjali and Sanjay and went up to my friend's house to accompany her to school instead. She was still getting dressed, so I waited outside in the sitting room petting her dog. It was a monstrous Alsatian with sharp wicked teeth. Until then, I used to think that all dogs liked to be stroked. Like elegant Daisy and heroic Bullet. This one though, was quite different. It jumped up to my face and went straight for my lip. That is how it became a family joke: I was once kissed by a dog. I think Sanjay started it.

So now there was this snarling dog and frightened me, both dripping with blood from our respective mouths. *My blood.*

I was not scared of the blood. I was not scared of the pain. But what scared the daylights out of me was what would happen if Daddy found out? I could feel sand shifting under my feet in every direction. Even though I was not on a beach.

But this was certainly no picnic. My friend's parents drove me to the naval hospital and left me there. I remember the doctor asking me if I liked balloons. Then he told me that he would push down on a black balloon as we both counted down from ten. He said he would pump one time for each time we counted together. I think that I did not go past the number six. He did.

When I woke up, my lip had been stitched and my parents were there.

How on earth did they even get *here*? How do they manage to get *everywhere*? I was stunned!

I feared the predictable we-told-you-so, followed by a thorough thrashing even more hideous than the possibility of a permanent disfigurement to my face. Daddy did say "I told you so," but there was no thrashing. This had happened before. And would happen again. Sometimes, outlandish as it may sound, he could be "very calm in a storm."

"I can get excited about little things, but in a calamity I'm like a rock," he would tell us.

We drove back home together, with Daddy joking all the way there narrating comical dog stories from his childhood. I was sure that the spanking was being saved for an opportune time after I had healed. But there was no spanking this time.

For some obviously sound medical reason, the army had decided that all dogs are potentially rabid, so I was escorted back to the hospital for anti-rabies injections in my abdomen. The male nurse would circumspectly pinch my abdominal wall and then swiftly plunge the contents of the syringe into it. I had to go back fourteen times to complete the course. Sanjay could not stop teasing me. He swore that after the last one, I would wake up the next morning and start barking like a dog! By now, I knew better than to take him literally. For a whole month, I walked around with a bandage for a mustache. There is even a picture with that wretched thing on my face. I look like a kid who had to get her mouth taped shut because she talked too much.

There was a family trip to Ajanta and Ellora caves to see nude people in weird naked poses carved on the temple walls. To me, some of these poses appeared to be just not anatomically feasible. There were a few American tourists taking pictures. Daddy, was, as usual, explaining something animatedly to Mummy. It was all too boring and monotonous for me. Just like those mind-numbing trips to the museum to look at half-broken multiple-chipped B.C. objet d'art.

In 1962, a sex scandal had broken out in England involving a famous politician and Christine Keeler. I heard snatches of conversations between my parents whenever they would discuss the matter with each other, about how this abysmal gossip had shaken the entire British Parliament. They would switch to hushed tones whenever we kids were within hearing range, especially, every time Daddy used the word 'paramour.'

Meanwhile, India was at war with China. Daddy took out a map and explained our military strategy in great detail.

"We mustn't lose even an inch of our land to that chinky nation," he declared. "India has a chance at winning, only if our politicians don't screw up."

Our politicians did screw up. It was a brief war and India lost.

Thank God, Bombay is safe and sound, I consoled myself. Our home is so far away from the northern border. Daddy will keep us safe.

I have a faint memory about a picnic by a lake. Daddy had pulled out his binoculars and was watching a scantily-clad, white, hippie couple in the distance behind the bushes. He was explaining something to Mummy and asking her to look through the lens as well. From what I understood from a vantage point that I did not much care for, the couple was apparently doing something that happens in the movies when the camera stops rolling. Daddy's interest in them made me vaguely uncomfortable. But it was a brief moment and was soon forgotten.

Before long, we were getting ready to leave Bombay.

I do not remember how this began, but I had started to go to my parents' bedroom to sleep between them. Was it bad dreams that woke me up in the wee hours of the morning, or did I wake up before my siblings did to get more attention? Sometimes, I would go there on my own. At other times, Daddy would call for me. I would nestle between my parents and catch another hour of sleep, before it was time to get ready for the day with the rest of the family.

My back always felt itchy and Daddy would give me backrubs. Daddy always gave the best backrubs. I would put my head on his shoulders. His chest felt warm and comfortable. His armpits had this nice Daddy smell. It felt so good to circle my arm around his broad shoulders and feel his love. Later, he started to loop his leg around me as well, and I would return the favor. Soon it became a leisurely pastime --- he would roll me over himself to one side and then roll me back. He would then roll me back again. It was our own private game. Then he would circle my body with his strong legs and hold me there for a while.

It felt special to be held like that. So close. So safe. Nothing could *bother* me here. Nobody could hurt me now. I was alone. Alone with Daddy. It was our special time together. It was meant only for me.

It was around this time, I think, when I first started to bite my nails. It was also around this time, I now know, that innocence ended for me. Forever.

I had just turned nine.

UN-INNOCENCE

JUST ME, THE MIRROR, AND MY BODY

We did not know then, but the next year we would be moving twice.

It was a long train ride across vast lands, chugging straight up northwest from Bombay, past slumbering countryside where life seemed to slow down to a near halt. Even the cows seemed to masticate ever so slowly as if they were either dazed to see us, doped from chewing weed, or both.

This time Daddy was posted to an obscure military base near Jodhpur. When we first arrived, as per the prescribed protocol, we briefly shared a house with another army officer's family who had lingered on for a bit after their posting out of town had been announced. Since they had older children Mummy was protective, guarding us from any chance vice or option of immorality. A mother hen is known to fluff out her feathers to gather her gullible chicklings close under her wings to prevent them from harm. She makes sure that they do not stray far from her but walk in step with her, just under her, at all times.

"Girls, if anyone even tries to bother you, tell me immediately," she would warn every now and then, shaking a finger at us to make her point.

A mother is a person who stands guard between you and the rest of the world. Someone who mothers and smothers at the same time.

I know Mummy means well, but I wish she'd say it nicely.

At a little over nine years old, I understood bothering as a boy laying a finger, even if by sheer chance or accident, on a part of my body where no wandering finger should ever reach. Not even my own. I must confess that I never entirely understood the full extent of my mother's paranoia. You see, she had never completely explained it. As for myself, I felt abject guilt in even giving a hint of curiosity on the matter. Periodically, she would check in with me by looking straight at me, through me, with her prying eyes and attempt to ascertain whether anyone had bothered me. I would put on what I hoped was an innocent-enough face and quickly assure her that nothing bad had happened. At least, nothing dire that I myself was aware of at the time. Nothing bad and dire actually happened. In my heart, I would pray she would believe me right away and leave me alone for good. I am not sure Mummy believed me right away. And she sure made certain that she never left me alone for good. In fact, I would hurry out of a room if there were only boys present, mostly to avoid the volley of questions that would surely follow me until I reached Mummy's safe haven. This certainly contributed to my somewhat awkward behavior around prospective love interests later in my teenage years.

While Daddy was allotted a house in the cantonment, the pre-eminent girls school, St. Anne's Convent, was located a couple of hours away. So in order to stay close to school, we ended up renting a small two-room flat on the first floor on a humdrum little street in small-town Jodhpur. I hated humdrum little streets in obscure small towns! Daddy would drive home on weekends from his digs in cantt to be with us. It took a little getting used to this new arrangement.

I missed the sprawling bungalow circled by cool vacant verandas on our own adorable little hill in Bombay, the freedom of ample open spaces and the vastness of the ocean!

Has our family fallen on bad times? I wondered.

Jodhpur is a dry, dirty and utterly disgusting Rajasthani town not dissimilar from other dry, dirty and utterly disgusting towns I had seen on our travels across India. On either side of dust-laden roads Neem trees grew in dense abundance, loaded with clusters of stone-hard and quinine-bitter yellow berries that swell at the end of sturdy twigs. The surrounding low hills were mostly stony and rugged, dotted with crouching bumble bushes that seemed to make an ever so feeble attempt at covering the visibly cracked earth underneath. On weekends, our family would go on hikes in the nearby hills. I was clearly winded as I reached the top, with sweat gathering in my underarms and trickling all the way down into my shoes thus impeding my ascent. The city looked less dirty from up there. I tried to convince myself that from the highest summit it actually even managed to look somewhat picturesque.

Once again --- a brand new school and brand new friends in brand new uniforms.

I do not remember any of my teachers. I do not remember being interested in school. I do not remember being interested in anything. I hated being a small-town girl in this filthy small town, with its narrow winding streets and dusty crowded bazaars teeming with scruffy tobacco-chewing and beetle-spewing common folk. While trekking on those hill trails, for a few moments I would imagine that this terrain could be a wonderful setting for a Western flick with handsome, hardy cowboys thrown in for good measure. They were all John Wayne lookalikes with a sturdy wide gait, who tipped their hats whenever they passed me by. Except for this fantasy, life was rather dull.

I do not remember this period of my life, perhaps, because I did not like where we lived anymore.

What I do remember, though, was that my body was starting to change. For one, there were these two tiny bumps that just happened to sprout symmetrically on my upper chest. It bothered me, because they seemed to have a resolve of their own. Yet, for some reason I did not entirely understand, they fascinated me.

How big will they eventually grow? I'd wonder. When that happens, will Daddy stop calling me a tomboy? Will I no longer be his little girl, the one who can be pampered and spoiled?

One day, when I was alone and bored at home as even little girls with miniature bumps sprouting on their upper chest can tend to be, I took off all my clothes and started to examine my body in its entire nakedness and splendor in the full-length mirror of the bedroom. Then I swayed my hips from side to side to see how that looked. This is what those scantily-clad heroines in see-through negligees seemed to have mastered, indulging in this wonderful time-pass in the A-rated movies.

I ended up dancing in front of the mirror. This was kind of fun: just me, the mirror, and my body. And my swaying hips.

I must have been preening like this for a while and had just turned around to see if my body looked even more exciting in a side-view profile, when I saw Mummy's stern face in the mirror. She was standing by the open door, appearing quite cross.

And just behind her, was Daddy!

Gosh! How long have *they* been watching me? I was frozen. How do they find the right --- I mean, the *wrong* time to show up?

Was I embarrassed! I felt my face turning beet-red. Sweat started to gush out of every hair follicle on my scalp. I had done something dreadfully sinful and forbidden. I had become the bad girl my parents had warned me to stay away from.

How reassuring it was when Daddy laughed! Actually, it surprised me that I was not punished. Then, or later.

Daddy said something like, "That's okay, Mani. Don't be upset. Nargis is finally growing up."

Mercifully, it was never mentioned again and I was spared any further embarrassment. Nevertheless, I was still left with the feeling that I had done something vile and loathsome. I had descended to the depths of abysmal immorality. Crawling out of there just by myself could easily take a lifetime. Or if I am lucky, a better part of the rest of my life.

That evening, Daddy's boss, Colonel Hairy and his wife were invited for dinner. First, they came to our puny flat for cocktails served with roasted nuts and crusty *samosas*. Mummy would put out cashew nuts only for special guests, so it must have been a special night. Soon the adults were all convivially inebriated and we all merrily drove down to Quality restaurant. Our guests must never know, but this was the first time I would dine at a restaurant. *Our* family? We never dined at restaurants.

Daddy had regularly cautioned us, "The food in cafes is perpetually dripping in cheap fat-rich ghee that'll most certainly clog your arteries with lard. Now, let me tell you something about the cooks. They all live huddled together in absolute and total squalor, in dirty back alleys with no flushing toilets or running water. As you've probably guessed, they never wash their hands after they're done with cleaning their behinds. And the owners have the audacity to charge you an arm and a leg for *that!*"

Nonetheless, we washed down the artery-clogging, bacteria-ridden, delicious dinner with the super-soft, individually wrapped, untainted Kwality Tooti-Fruity ice-cream. The real one. The one that used to melt in my mouth even before it had a chance to reach my tongue.

I thought that the evening was a lot of fun. Later that night, Daddy was a tad drunk and thus in a jolly good mood. He had gone through a few stiff drinks and as he narrated hilarious anecdotes from his life, his humor was even more spontaneous and free-flowing than ever. Just like the stiff Red Knight whiskey-sodas. As an aside, it was largely reassuring that not only did he actually get along with his boss on that night, but that none of us were found blue and dead the next morning from an overdose of fat-laden, germ-infested, gastronomic extravagances.

It was quite late when we got back home. As usual, I crept between both my parents in bed.

I remember Daddy rubbing my back as usual, as I faced away from where he lay beside me, feeling his rapid breath behind me, his body warm against mine. And as usual, it felt so good. So relaxing. For a while he continued to massage my shoulders. Then he moved his soothing hands purposefully, to rub the nape of my neck. Also, just as usual.

But what was about to happen next was not just as usual. His hands started to move forward. Then he began to fondle the front of my chest, gently playing with and titillating my budding breasts. Or whatever they were supposed to be called at the time. He was stroking them tenderly, one at a time, circling my nipples with his long tapering fingers. This felt strangely odd and novel, fun but scary, good and bad, all at once.

I was feeling sensations that I did not know until then even existed. Then it happened again. And again. I kept my eyes closed throughout.

When I close my eyes, I cease to be. When I can't see anything, it's not happening to me. It's actually happening to *someone else*, I imagined.

I remember feeling there was something wrong about the whole thing. But for some reason, it still felt exciting and special. Then it was all over as suddenly as it had begun and we both went to sleep.

My first thought the next morning was, Mummy should never know. She would surely automatically assume that I'm a *bad* girl. That it's all *my* fault. *Nobody* should ever know. This is something between just Daddy and me.

It'll never happen again, I told myself. It *must* never happen again. It's just possible, that it never even happened in the first place. Maybe, it was just a bad dream.

Like that nightmare I still experienced from time to time, of being attacked by turbaned fiends while swinging on that creaky rickety gate in Pathankot. And warding off their ghosts.

Then the moment passed and all was forgotten. I cannot remember if it happened again in Jodhpur.

We were going away again and I was running a low-grade fever. Usually, we dealt with all routine illnesses at home. Daddy would give us an aspirin or two for all random fevers and a handful or so for raging ones. But Mummy was busy packing and the house was a total mess. So I was sent away to the base hospital for a few days.

This was the first time I remember being away from my family. I was all alone in a hospital room. Occasionally, a nurse or medical orderly would give me a hurried sponge bath, then abruptly stick a thermometer under my armpit. I would crane my neck to watch the mercury go past the red line, which meant that my discharge date had to be postponed again. The food was moderately insipid and, as I would later discover, is the same served in hospitals the world over. There was nothing to do all day. So I spent my abundant spare time reading storybooks, or dreaming up little girl fantasies. One day, I pretended that I even had a baby of my own and the pillow tip was its head. I remember attempting to nurse the pillow. Nobody saw me do that.

But the nights still felt lonely, dark, and endless.

I was happy when my family finally came for me. The house was taking longer to pack every time we moved, but it was all done and we were ready to go. Except for Anjali, who came to St. Anne's Convent as a boarder for the next few years to finish up high school.

Our family was on the road again. Off to a new destination and newer adventures.

By now I had started to discover that whenever I move to a new place, I can leave the past behind.

It's happened before. I'm sure, it'll happen again.

I would start life on a clean new slate. The rest would surely be left behind and forgotten.

And hopefully, forgotten forever.

LITTLE STREAM
TURNS INTO A ROARING WATERFALL

This time the whole regiment was moving by railroad, led by jovial, larger-than-life Colonel Hairy. It did not matter where we were going. It was simply fun to be a part of an entourage of military khaki and green. All I had heard about the new town, Indore, located in the huge state of MP, was that it was another small but strategic military base, bang in the middle of the country. I had not done too well at St. Anne's Convent, so I was thankful for an opportunity to start over.

That's the best thing about the military, I reflected. It sure gives you a clean break to start over. That's probably why you get moved around so much.

There was always that one incident I had desperately wanted to erase from living memory about each and every place that I had lived at so far. I did not know then, but this trend would pursue me in all subsequent moves as well.

The entire train carried only our regiment on board. So, it felt like it was just our train. During the whole duration of the ride, Daddy was second in command. So by proxy, this would automatically anoint Sanjay and me with second in command status. We were curious about how a steam engine runs, so to the steam engine we were taken. It felt like having first row seats at a school play. A few grisly men, with grimy hands the color of soot, were shoveling coal with rapid fire into a massive stark-red flame. It was unbearably hot. Every time they would open the latch to this blazing inferno, I could see the fire roaring unrelentingly within the guts of the engine. The chief engineer was trying to explain to us how the engine converts water into steam, which in turn propels the engine forward.

"That's the basic law in physics," Daddy explained. "There're five types of energy, and each one of them can transform from one form to the next. It's true. Our whole world is fluid. Nothing is stagnant in our universe. As an example, energy and matter are interchangeable.

Even people are never the same. Let me explain, how Einstein --- power --- mass --- famous formula ---," I could hardly hear what he continued to say, above the din, "--- Japanese --- Pearl Harbor --- atomic bomb --- Hiroshima ---energy --- proton --- cancer ---"

But I nodded anyway. It felt good enough just to be chosen to see the insides of this mammoth machine, with its huge pistons and colossal furnace. No girl ever went there. Only Daddy made this possible for me.

Later at one of the stops, the driver released piping hot water from the engine through an exhaust pipe on the side. Mummy immediately refilled her time-traveled thermos and threw in a perfect proportion of dirty-green Lipton and muddy-brown Brooke Bond Darjeeling tea leaves.

"Mummy sure needs her tea. Have you noticed, children, that your mother doesn't utter a single word in the morning unless she's taken her first sip of tea for the day?" Daddy laughed.

Daddy told us that the water from the engine was safe to drink. No bacteria could survive at that temperature. That was a basic rule in biology.

Daddy sure knows all the basic rules in every science, I thought.

Indore cantt was a single street military settlement. There were only a handful of homes. Everyone lived in barracks, both the officers and the soldiers; the only difference being that the officers' families were assigned a whole barrack to themselves. Down the street from our home were PT grounds for morning drills. There was one flag-post for the national tricolor proudly displayed a 24-spoke wheel in the center and another one for the regiment colors that was hoisted separately. Both always on full mast. Unless there was a national tragedy. Like a Prime Minister's death or another lost war, both of which were pretty infrequent. There was the officers' mess and a MI room --- short for military infirmary. Here we were examined for random minor ailments at leisure, by an indiscriminating compounder with an empathic but lazy eye. Down the road was the clubhouse and the Quartermaster's store --- well-stocked with supplies that sadly took turns to get stale, just like in the song we used to sing. All the homes ran parallel to each other, complete with front lawns and bilateral symmetrical vegetable patches of pointy parrot-green lady-finger, rounded deep-mauve brinjal and dented pale-golden squash.

In the summer months, the ground would become so excruciatingly scorching hot and dry that I could not walk barefoot. The perpetually sweating smelly *sepoys* would load water for the gardens on military trucks in large black leather bags that jostled around and leaked on the bumpy ride all the way to their final destination.

Uncle Hairy got first preference simply because he was the colonel of the regiment. No questions asked. He had the best row of multicolor sweet peas in the land that bloomed elegantly against a cane grid. His was also the most well-tended vegetable garden where fat pumpkins swelled silently crushing the diminutive mounds they rested on. Even his corn rose tall and thick over his high fence, to signify that he was the uncontested and uncrowned top-gun of the entire regiment.

The officers' mess was uphill from where we lived. I had heard that some of the younger officers who lived there were bachelors. Just like those Junior Officers from our Bombay days, I was intrigued by these dashing close-shaven young men who roared in and out of there on their mo-bikes, looking an impartial mix of preppy and official. One of them, who we nicknamed Second Lieutenant Dandy, looked like a carbon-copy of my then heartthrob, Clint Eastwood. Mummy had forbidden me from speaking with carbon-copy or heartthrob anyone. It had been officially certified by Mother, signed and sealed on gooey molten wax, as 'Taboo!'

We lived in the second to last house on the lane. The housing arrangement was in ascending order of hierarchy, which is an art the army has mastered over the ages since British times. Uncle Hairy, of course, occupied the last house on the street. The family down the pecking order below ours was the Narulas. Their father had to salute *our* father whenever they happened to pass each other, however casually. There is nothing casual about the military. This was just adequate information for us to declare his children as good-for-nothing. We started calling them 'copycat Narulas.' They would imitate us at everything we did even in matters that did not deserve plagiarism: Like planting double zinnias, raising spotted English hens, and even buying a secondhand car just like ours. Only theirs was completely ragtag and rinky-dink.

All the kids in the neighborhood were military brats. I had heard that both of Uncle Hairy's sons were away at boarding school in the hills. In my mind, I was sure that one of them would have a crush on me. Even though we had met only once. That too, more than a couple of years ago. By now, I had even forgotten what any of those boys actually looked like.

The house we lived in was just another run-of-the-mill home, like the other nondescript dwellings on the street, somewhat similar to the Pathankot house. That year, we had a bountiful crop of summer blooms skirting our rectangular front lawn: on two sides grew mammoth zinnias with rows of concentric petals, the biggest and brightest I had ever seen. They were different hues of pretty-pink, golden-yellow, brick-orange, and burning-red. At the end of the summer the flowers would become so huge that the whole plant would bend over as if to salute their beauty. On the other two sides were outsized daisies, deep-amethyst and innocent-white, which swayed in the breeze, caught between mellow-yellow eager snapdragons. Carefree saffron butterflies with tortuous black veins fanning their wings would flirt from flower to flower, and earnest little sparrows would descend on them and industriously peck for nectar, while plump eager bees hovered around buzzing sweet-nothings to each other --- too busy to hassle with me.

"Bees will never harm you, if you don't try to *bother* them first," Daddy would always manage to explain. "That's the rule of the world. Now, this is true for both man and beast. Left to their own devices, they usually leave each other alone."

It was a wall of color and life. When I lay on the soft grass, I could see nothing but the flowers around me. And the rectangular sky overhead. Like the soft sandy beach in Bombay, this would become an easy place to dream. And dream alone.

After summer break, it was time to start school again. Anjali was sent back to St. Anne's Convent as a boarder. Daddy had decided that because of his frequent transfers, it would be best for her to stay there to finish up high school. It is rather sad that I do not remember feeling sad after she left.

Now I had Sanjay all to myself. I would attend St. Raphael's Convent and he was admitted to St. Paul's in Indore, another D-grade city in the B-to-F category of filthy little towns I hated. Where F stood for Foul. My school building was at the end of a long driveway that was lined with trees festooned with weighty bundles of fragrant yellow bell-shaped flowers, which dangled loosely from the branches. In the height of the season they drooped down low enough to sweep the ground. Later in the year they would turn into long and twisted dust-brown pea pods that we would use for hockey sticks.

The army kids used to be transported to school on a military truck that had been converted into a van with cushioned seats placed across from each other. It would take us take us to our respective gender coded schools about an hour away from cantt. There were some older rowdy, testosterone-laden boys on the van. Sometimes they would tease me provocatively or just stare, as older rowdy boys of that age and ilk tend to do. The banter would typically include sexual undertones, mercifully, not all of which I completely understood or even cared to comprehend at the time. Even Sanjay looked the other way. I would never complain to Mummy. Because it would either be my slip up to begin with, or sheer negligence on my part for not retorting back in quick order and thus stop it from happening in the first place. Neither of these outcomes was acceptable to me.

Either way it's my fault, since I can never open my stupid trap on time, I thought.

Besides, by now I had learned that if I look the other way, I do not hear anything. If I simply block it out, *nothing has never happened.* That seemed the easier way to deal with these crude and vulgar innuendos. After a while, it ceased to bother me. The moment I got off the van, the impropriety of the ride to and from school was all over and forgotten. And I did want to forget it all, because the rest of my life was becoming fun again.

What was fun was the outdoors. There were vast lands past the cantonment where wild berries grew. Sanjay and I would go hunting with Daddy in the wilderness to shoot birds and other animals in their natural habitat. Those wild partridges tasted far better than the flabby tame chicken, fattened on coarse grain that had been inadvertently sprayed with DDT and laced with pesticides, which Mummy usually cooked on weekends. The hunting trips were a special treat since I was the only girl who went. Sanjay would tease me whenever the recoil of the gun would startle my shoulder, so I would try to distract him with a poorly delivered PJ (Poor Joke) whenever that happened. We would shoot anything that moved --- idle pigeons, hopping rabbits and busy squirrels. After sunset, the deer would get immobilized when caught in the headlights of our jeep. And not just figuratively.

I imagined that I was in a Western movie on a recce in the wilderness. I was riding with a bunch of tough Yankees wearing wild broad-rimmed cowboy hats, digging their boots into the rump of hardy horses as they galloped fearlessly through the deep canyon. We would plan a surprise attack on an imaginary foe. We were gallant and fearless and always the first to slay the enemy. Later, the reverie would take on a different turn. Someday, a tall, handsome and not so dark cowboy would miraculously arrive from nowhere to save me from the dragon --- the one that lives in the deep dark dungeon and belches fire from its mouth --- and sweep me off my feet. Then together, we would ride into the sunset. It always ended with us riding together into the sunset, with me clinging to the cowboy and dust rising behind us at fade-out.

Once, I do not remember how Sanjay got to go hunting without me. When he returned with Victory! inscribed boldly all over his face, he swore he had seen a real live python . He reported, his chest swelling with pride with each syllable that he had been the first to spot the reptile slithering in the tall dry grass right in front of the jeep --- all forty feet of it! He was also the only one to witness this monstrous snake swallow a whole deer in one large gulp. He claimed he had even heard a dreadful crushing sound, when the bones of that unfortunate creature were turned into pulp inside the python's abdomen, as the viper was winding itself up on a tree trunk for that very intent.

Sanju and his tall tales! But, I do feel terrible for having been left behind.

Beyond the army base were the wild open spaces where hesitant little streams twisted between a shock of wild flowers caught betwixt swaying grasses, which stood taller than me at all times and through every season. These were the streams where Sanjay and I would gently launch our paper boats into the water, then nudge them to go faster by coaxing the water forward with the palm of our hands. The rivulet would become bone-dry at the end of the summer, when the water would slow down to a near trickle and the desiccated grass around it would easily crack when bent. A short walk away were the railroad tracks, where trains would seldom run. When that rare occurrence happened, Sanjay and I would nod our heads in sync to count the bogies under our breath, just as the extra-long goods trains would pass through our line of vision. Obviously, most times, we would each end up with a different number and argue that we were both correct.

I used to think that those train tracks led to nowhere. My brother and I would search our pockets for a handful of chump change and pick out the most faded-out *khota* paisa --- the one that could not buy us any more bait. The one that we did not have half a chance of accurately deciphering the number on the face. Or, for that matter, the face of the Head of State.

I bet it's a man's face, I'd imagine.

We would take turns to carefully and strategically place our respectively owned coin on opposite rails, then put our ear to the track and crouch close by, waiting for a train to run over them. I could hear the rumbling sound from a mile away. When we were sure that the engine was almost upon us, we would quickly dart to the side. Afterwards, we would crawl back to retrieve what was left of the coins.

"Heads or tails?" we would both ask.

Together, of course.

The coins was now larger, flatter, and warmer. They would shine as good as new and we would save them for keepsake. It was even more fun with the old-paisa, the one with a hole in it. By now there were very few left of those circulating around. Later we would compare our coins to see whose had become bigger. As always, we both claimed we had won.

One day, we imagined that we were stranded on an island. We were tired of living on dry roots, devouring raw fish and ingesting live crabs. Desperately needing to eat that one last hot meal to stay alive we gathered dry sticks, and, after some initial snags, were even able to start a fire by striking two stones against each other. Daddy had taught us how to do this. He said it would come in handy if we ever got lost. Like on an island.

"Nature's there to help us. You just have to look around. *Survival* is a *natural instinct* in all living creatures great and small. Including human beings," Daddy would advise.

Later that day, we tried to hold down a wild goat to milk it for real. We did survive this one. It kicked us with its sturdy hind legs, also for real! That was enough to bring us speedily back to the shore. So no more real or imagined island adventures for a bit.

When the monsoon arrived, everything in our new wild world changed overnight. The leaves on the trees glistened in the sun anew, whenever it stole a moment to peek through the thick dark clouds. The grass turned fresh and supple again and the streams swelled up. That July, it had rained for days and we were cooped up on lazy summer afternoons playing carom with Uncle Hairy's sons who were home on break. When the sky finally cleared, we all walked to our old haunts by the pond where Sanjay had taught me how to thread a worm up the curled hook, then fling it far out in the water and wait for a nibble before a fish was harpooned through its heart.

"Nargis, remember the order: Hook, line, and sinker."

As we approached the fishing site, a humming sound grew louder and louder. We were walking faster now.

What's happening? I wondered. What *is* all that noise? Is it an earthquake?

We started to run. We scampered past the miniature berry bushes in search of the modest little stream that used to feebly join another lazy little brook to become a tiny zigzag rivulet. But, where was my own meandering little stream that used to fall ever so gently over the rocks? And look, whatever happened to our small placid pond where I used to be able to trick those dumb and mute fish with stale squirmy earthworms?

It had become a thundering waterfall, washing away everything that came in its path! The innocence of our little stream was gone --- the cascade came straight down, menacing and brutal. The power of the column of water crashing down against the rocks scared me. Both Sanjay and I could have easily been swept away in it! Downstream. *Together.*

Now that we could neither steer our flimsy paper boats nor safely cast a line in this violent torrent, we walked back home in silence totally crestfallen. Sanjay took a shortcut and I found myself hiking back with Uncle Hairy's younger son. We sauntered together rather awkwardly, barely speaking to each other.

Suddenly, he asked, "Do you want to fuck?"

As if, he was inviting me to play ball.

I was stumped! I did not look at him but kept walking, my eyes pinned to the ground. I pretended that I had not heard him. Even if he thought I had taken notice, I wanted him to know that I did not completely understand the word, which was partly true. I knew that this was something men and women did when they are all grownup and alone. This was how babies are born. But this was not the boy I had a crush on, even though that did not matter just then. When standing tall in his casual loafers, he could barely reach my chin!

For heaven sakes, why is it taking so long to reach home? I asked myself.

I ran the rest of the way, not minding the nettles and thorns on the bushes that scratched my shins.

When I saw him on the next school break, it was hard to look my diminutive but bold suitor in the face. I successfully concealed this embarrassing foray from everyone. I dared not even tell Sanjay.

He would laugh at me, "Shucks, Nargis. You know something? You're off your rocker. No, actually, I take that back. You're just plain daft!"

That was his favorite word for the season. That, and POS, for Piece of Shit!

Sanjay had failed his first attempt at the entrance exam to Sherwood School. By now, he had also started to put on weight and as was customary in our family, most of it was on the behind. He had to endure putdowns by Daddy about his knickers getting tighter. The pencil marks on that wall in the veranda where Daddy regularly measured our heights continued to confirm that I was still at least an inch taller than him. Daddy had become even more stern about our lengthening exercises. We had to stand backed up against the wall, slowly breathe in, stretch our bodies far beyond our natural frame, then slowly breathe out. Every time we reached a new level on the wall, Daddy would once again raise the bar. I believed that if stretching ever failed me, deep measured breathing certainly held enough promise to help me grow taller. I would hold my breath at inhale until I almost felt faint. Daddy reminded us that we had but a handful of inches left to reach our adult height and but a handful of years left to excel in school as well. So Sanjay had to deal with not being strong enough, not being smart enough, and now not even being tall enough. Daddy would make him run all the way uphill to the officers' mess. Once Sanjay got caught, and subsequently punished, for stopping for a breath-break on the other side of the hill. You could never stop for a breath-break.

I do not know how I managed to be thrashed less than my older two siblings. I did not stop to reason this. During that period in my life, there were not a lot of things I would stop to reason about.

That summer, for some unknown reason, the skin on my face suddenly became blotchy and pale. To the regiment dispensary I was escorted, back to that godforsaken MI room. The compounder, like some of the other conditions he had successfully treated thus far, had obviously never seen anything remotely similar to my presenting malady. Treating accidental coughs, sporadic colds and relentless sniffles were the limits of his expertise. The bandages he would apply on our limbs made the wounds look a hundred times as large, after he would first generously dab the injury with tincture iodine, making us look like forlorn soldiers coming home from a lost battle. Before I knew it, he had painted my whole freaking face with that violet liquid! Did it sting! Over the next few days, the skin on my face started to peel in the most obvious places --- the ones his brush had previously highlighted. For a while it was a little scary.

How *would* I look without the skin on my face? Like those nameless ghosts Sanju had warned me about that float around in flimsy white sheets in the graveyard? Or like that pink skinless dead body that'd floated by the shore in Bombay?

Finally, petite and freckled Aunty Nutty saved the day. She advised Mummy to apply freshly-churned soft butter on my raw skin. Slowly, all would be well again. And I got my face back.

That summer Dadi came to visit us from Daddy's village. Mummy was given strict instructions on how to treat his mother and what she could say to her. And especially, what she must never dare utter, by some minor slip or lame omission, even under her breath. Heaven help her if she ever tried to make an attempt at mouthing a single wrong syllable! During those days, I remember my parents fighting more than usual.

"There's a reason why you are given two ears, two eyes and one mouth, woman! Now don't you muck around with me, or I'll send you right back to the village where you came from. I'll send you right back with *her,*" pointing to his mother who was sitting silently, hunched over.

What a terrible thing to happen! I thought. Who'll run the house without Mummy? What'll happen to us? What'll happen to *me*? Mummy, please don't get too smart for Daddy. Don't think too hard. Maybe --- perhaps --- only for now --- don't think *at all*. Just do what he says.

On the last day when we drove Dadi back to the train station, Mummy had forgotten the five hundred rupee note at home that was intended for Dadi's return journey back to UP.

Daddy was hopping mad. Just like a cheetah on a hot tin-roof! I imagined.

"I could've predicted this. I know you forgot it on purpose, you good-for-nothing woman!" he was shouting, followed by a seamless litany of collateral expletives from his arsenal. "You never wanted to give my mother any money. I knew all along that you never even wanted her here with us in the first place. Don't look at me as if I've grown horns! Now, don't you get too clever with me," he warned. "You lousy woman! You can't fool me. Nobody can. So don't even try. Damn you!"

And all at once he slapped her. In front of all of us. And Dadi. All Mummy could do was blink rapidly. She did not have another option in the matter.

It was all quiet and still as death. Dadi said nothing and neither did we. Neither *could* we. She departed quietly, smiling weakly and waving feebly as the train slowly pulled away.

It was around this time, I began to notice that Daddy was starting to pad on some more pounds. He had always been heavyset as far back as I can remember. Now he was also developing a paunch. He had weighty man-breasts, a condition that I later learned was anatomically termed gynecomastia. Sometimes he would laugh about it, saying that this was proof that he was more of a woman. He would have made a much better mommy than Mummy. Not only because he was the more emotional and demonstrative of the two, but that his body was like a woman's as well.

"In my next life, I want to come back as a woman. You'll agree, they've a much easier life than us men. They don't have to fight wars, or be killed in battle."

One day at the club, a child came up to him and pointed at Daddy's chest.

"What're those two things?" he asked innocently.

For once in his life Daddy must have been embarrassed, because he just laughed it off.

As was the case in Bombay, the club was where we got to watch films we should never have seen at our age. Or at any other age for that matter. Among others, movies like Fanny. We were shown the uncensored version too, with a lot of skin rubbing against skin. Later we would see *Twelve Angry Men and A Nun's Story*. The staff used an archaic projector, probably a throwback to colonial days. When those zigzag lines that stung my eyes and made me blink incessantly suddenly flashed on the screen, I knew we had reached the end of a spool. I had to remember where the story had been cut off, while I patiently waited for them to load on the next one. On occasion, we would be inadvertently shown the end of the movie just as we were walking in, maneuvering our way in the crowd to take prime seats upfront and mid-center. At other times, we had to piece it together in our minds to figure out the crux of the story, when a missing reel from another film was erroneously thrown in for our random entertainment.

The second time he tried, Sanjay was accepted at the Sherwood School. So finally, off with the stretched-out St. Paul's half-pants and goodbye to the Velcro striped tie. For the next five years, he would be gone to faraway Nainital in the Himalayas. My brother would soon be inducted into the big league and one day belong to an Old Boys' Club. When I saw him off at the train station, suitcase in hand and looking rather lost, I choked back a tear. I knew that the house would feel empty without him.

Now it was just my parents and I left at home. I did miss Sanjay terribly. It became dreadfully lonely. Even the outdoors did not seem fun anymore, especially since I had no one to accompany me there, except me, myself, and I. And Mummy would never let me go alone. So I took on a little fluffy chicken under my wing for a pet. One day, while chasing it in the front lawn, I accidentally stepped on it and its guts spilled out all over the driveway. Mummy cooked it for dinner that night.

It feels kind of weird when you eat your *own* pet for dinner.

I was always tall for my stated age which ended at some point. I had also developed early which would also stop shortly. I remember looking at those little growths on my chest, wondering if one day they would become as large as those that Mummy neatly tucked away behind her blouse.

Let a lightning bolt strike me dead instantly! This very minute! I was aghast. If I ever think such awful thoughts again!

It felt awkward when I ran because these swellings had started to bounce. One day, when my parents were having their usual afternoon siesta, I crept secretly into the bathroom to try on Mummy's Maiden Form bra. For a few minutes, I felt all grownup, just like Mummy, especially since the apparatus was several sizes larger. I pushed my chest protuberances together to see if they would fill it up. It felt sexy. But scary, too. So I took it off just as hurriedly.

The next day, something super strange happened. I do not think that I was quite ten years old yet. I had just returned from school and I was playing alone on the swing-set in the front yard, when Mummy called me to come indoors "NOW!" I would obey right away whenever Mummy used capital letters in that particular tone and that too with an exclamation mark. She was saying something about the clothes that I had left behind after a bath and alluding to them being unusually dirty and soiled.

"Nargis, did you know you had blood in your underwear this morning?" she asked.

My first thought was, I must've done something wrong. What? *Again?*

Did this happen because of yesterday's bathroom-bra scenario?

My second thought was, I must've accidentally hurt myself on the swings. Maybe, that's why Mummy sounds so serious.

But Daddy was also there and he lost no time in reassuring me that it was "all okay."

"Nargis, this is what happens to a girl's body when she grows up," he explained calmly.

Then he gave a rather long and tedious lecture on how a girl's anatomy changes as she prepares to become a woman.

"Every month, the womb gets ready to receive a fetus. When no baby is conceived, it bleeds to shed the bed of nutrition that the mother's body has prepared for the embryo. Until the next month, it's time, for --- it happens again, when --- the cycle goes on, because ---"

I remember spacing out through most of it. That was the only way to deal with uncomfortable conversations with a father about a woman's body.

"Mani, you should be telling her about this," he ended, after he was done explaining it all.

I'll ask my science teacher about this tomorrow. Wait. Maybe, I don't really want to know the gory details, I concluded.

Later, Mummy told me not to tell Sanjay anything about this. It was a little girl's own little secret. It had happened to Anjali when we were living in Bombay. Knowing that I was not the first one in my family to be afflicted with this dreadful female malady was somewhat comforting. Mummy taught me how to manage the monthly with pads.

I could never really manage it. How I hated this period thing! Suddenly my life had changed for the worse. First Sanjay left me. Now this stupid monthly kept me from the outdoors. Or what was left of them. Also, Mummy had become even more paranoid, if that is possible, when I was around boys.

Those were long hot summer nights. At sunset, the orderlies would lay out our beds next to each others in the front lawn, complete with green-and-brown army mosquito nets hanging loosely from crisscrossed bamboo poles, between the flowerbeds of daisies and zinnias wild in their cacophony of colors. There was a technique of getting into bed, ever so speedily, to keep those wretched insects out. Even if a single one managed to get in, be sure to suffer yet another sleepless night. It would buzz around my face for a while, enter through my ears and then keep on buzzing right in there for the rest of the night. When it was silent, I knew that it was only taking a short breath-break from drawing blood from my bare extremities exposed past my pajama-suit.

I don't know how these miserable creatures manage to suck and buzz at the same time. Tomorrow, during science class, I must remember to ask my teacher, I thought.

After sundown, the breeze would cool things off just a bit. It would become even more comfortable when the lawn had been watered after dusk. The smell of pollen sprayed by the wind rising up to my nostrils was ever so refreshing. The smell of earth and grass. Sometimes in the middle of the night, it would suddenly start to rain. When I would feel the first raindrops pitter-patter softly on my face, it was usually a gentle reminder of things more ominous. I would pretend that it was not rain coming down, but just the sprinkler left on. I was getting good at make-believe. Then slowly the tiny drops would gather momentum. Finally, when the cloud would burst right in my face somewhere just overhead and lightning would pierce straight through my mosquito net, chased by another round of thunderous applause, I would run indoors abandoning my bed on the lawn. Daddy and Mummy would gather up the bed linens and follow me.

Sometimes, Daddy would ask me if I was sleeping yet.

"Nargis, come let me rub your back. Come and get some love from Daddy," he would say, and beckon me into his bed.

I would leave my own cot, and quietly slip into his from under the mosquito nets that separated us, throwing caution to the winds. There I would lay, my head on his strong shoulder, my arm around his male chest. Soon this became a nightly event.

At other times, Mummy would encourage me to go to Daddy's bed, "Go beta, get some love from your father."

And I would creep over into Daddy's bed crawling past both our nets. And way past any prudence or sagacity between us.

Now the backrubs went on for longer, the hugging was harder and closer and the caressing more involved Daddy would start to fondle my body and chest. Strange sensations that I remembered from the first time this had occurred were happening again. They were exciting and enjoyable, even though the whole situation felt odd and scary. I would keep my eyes closed throughout until I fell asleep.

Somehow, this made it less odd and scary.

When I woke up after dawn, it felt as if nothing had happened. My day and night were now a world apart. They were like night and day. So diurnal. So different. Because they were so different. So disconnected. It was a tough act to straddle between the two.

Which one is real? They both can't be real at the same time, I reasoned.

During the day it was all about solving rigorous math sums at school, muddling through mindless afterschool sports, discreetly staying away from the boys and of course, biting my nails with renewed vigor. At night, it would become a world of fondling and secretive strange sensations. The Pathankot dream was also recurring periodically, the one with me desperately trying to ward off an entire army of sword-wielding turbaned fiends.

I am certain I knew that the night world was all wrong. It was wrong to feel these pleasurable sensations. It was wrong to allow my body to be aroused in this manner. It was especially wrong to have these feelings with Daddy. It was wrong for Daddy to do this to me.

But most of all, it was wrong that I enjoyed it and did not make any attempt to stop it. Not only did I not want to end it, but I started looking forward to being in bed with Daddy.

My body was not supposed to respond in this way. So how could I complain to anyone, when it was actually *my* fault to begin with? Nobody would ever believe me now. Even I would find it hard to believe me now.

Do I really want it to stop? I asked myself.

When Sanjay and Anjali came home for winter break, the days were once again filled with carefree fun with hunting, fishing and playing rounder's-'n-cricket with the Narula kids. The nights continued to be secretive, pleasurable and guilt-ridden all at once.

Does Mummy know what's going on? I'd wonder.

I dared not ask. I prayed Mummy would never bring it up. She had always been somewhat distant and rather engrossed in cooking, knitting and sewing. Besides, she had no power over Daddy.

And Anjali and Sanju --- what can *they* do? Besides, I *am* Daddy's favorite.

The break was over, both my siblings had left for their respective boarding schools in different states far away from home.

Would I not lose my special place if this ended? *Never!* I told myself. I'm not ready to give it all up yet.

I started to feel specialness in a new way. Through this bond with Daddy, I started to feel his strength, his intelligence and his control ---

and everything else that he was. I was becoming him. Nobody could bully me or push me around anymore.

Being secretive also became easier than ever. As simple as throwing away the jelly that tasted like glue into the potted plant at Uncle Hairy's party.

So life went on. As was customary, all national religious festivals were regularly celebrated by the righteously secular Indian army. It was *Janmashtami* this time, the birth of Lord Krishna. Everybody went, except Daddy. He was staying away, more than ever before, from anything religious. Besides the chorus of the repetitive hymn, *Hare Rama, Hare Krishna*, I did not know the songs or understand the chanting. But it felt good to be a part of the celebrations even though I did not have any inkling what all this mumbo-jumbo really meant. The crowd was singing praise to the multicolor idol representing the blue-blooded God with a baby face --- the same one, in whose presence simple common people were known to lunge prostrate in the sporadic Hindi films I would chance upon at the club.

When I looked around me through the smoke rising from the incense sticks surrounding the deities and curling up to the ceiling, I saw simple common people sitting cross-legged on the durries. They were swaying rhythmically together and reciting mantras in a singsong cult-like manner, with eyes closed in abject reverence and palms held together in hopeless prayer. As the hymns became louder and louder, the temple bells more hurried and the clapping more rhythmical, the crowd seemed to be getting into a trance of heightened communal frenzy.

It's funny, how people close their eyes only when they're praying. Or when they're having sex, I thought.

At that moment, I realized that the world around me was quite different from what my own had now become.

BUDDHA AND CHRIST

Word came that we were moving to Calcutta. Sanjay had taught me this limerick:

"There was an old lady from Calcutta
Who found her shit in a gutter
The rays of the sun
Fell on her bum
And turned her shit into butter"

"This time we'll be traveling northeast as the crow flies," Daddy told us.

Anjali and Sanjay joined us on this long road trip, since they were home from boarding school for the summer.

We drove by day and slept at wayside army rest-houses at night, which were managed by slow sleepy watchmen. Poor chaps, they could barely see their own shadows in the poor lighting! En route, we detoured into Varanasi, where so many Hindu souls regularly volunteered to be collectively cleansed of all sin, eventually sinking to their final resting place deep down in the muddy waters of the Ganges.

During a brief stop, Daddy donated one thousand and one rupees for a marble brick inscribed with Dada's name at a local temple. The priest muttered a short ceremonial prayer before the Yadav name became a part of the holy shrine wall forever. Daddy reverently closed his eyes in memory of his dead father. And, as expected we did as well.

Then we stopped at Bodh Gaya, where Daddy wanted us to see firsthand the monumental ruins from centuries ago that had been built in memory of one of the wisest men who ever lived: Buddha.

"Now children, let me tell you a little bit about Buddha in order to capture the gestalt about his teachings. He lived about five hundred years before Christ. He was born a wealthy Hindu Prince, but died a lonely Buddhist pauper. One day, when he was sitting cross-legged under a banyan tree right here in Bodh Gaya, eyes closed in deep meditation, he got so-called Enlightenment. So, he decided to seek truth through *sannyas*, leaving his entire Kingdom for good and taking off for the forest. That's how a new religion was born. And that's when he discovered the Wise Mind. 'Stay in the moment,' was his sermon. 'Forget about yesterday and don't think about tomorrow,' was his counsel. But, as you and I know, we do learn from yesterday's mistakes and must plan for tomorrow's future. I must tell you that there are many gaffes in his teachings, but, in my opinion, there are two that glaringly stand out: Reincarnation and Renunciation. Buddha believed that we live as well as the dead, since the human spirit never dies. It's reborn and actually comes back on Earth to reside in the bodies of dogs and cats. The human body, he declared, is just a temporary home for the spirit. Buddha believed that he had rightfully earned a Ph.D. on the condition of the human spirit. He alleged that the soul slips easily in and out of living bodies of all creatures, including plants. The cycle goes on and on. Now, how unwise is that! He also preached that the only way to end all suffering is not only to eliminate all needs but also rid oneself of all greed. He taught us that the only path to salvation is through giving up attachment for all objects and worldly possessions, whether dead or alive. He even urged his zealots to renounce sex. Now, how fanatical is *that!* It's not only utterly impossible, but, as you can see, it's also totally impractical. You cannot skirt around logic. How will life on Earth continue, if man stops procreating?" Daddy explained. "We're humans after all, not robots. Man will never stop being a man."

As we passed through the town, I noticed statues of Buddha in different poses. In every park and at every crossroad. Hands folded in acknowledgement of the world --- Smiling Buddha, Standing Buddha, Sleeping Buddha and Simply Buddha.

Later, we stopped at Patna and visited a famous Gurdwara. This is where, in the seventeenth century, Guru Gobind Singh camped to gather some strength after fleeing from Muslim invaders. He was the tenth and last Guru who established a legacy by founding the religion: Sikhism.

"Have you noticed that all religions are born out of tumult? That's because religion distracts people from their pain. Now let me tell you about this tenth Guru. Poor man! Did you know that he was on the run most of his adult life? And people pray to him as if *he* is God himself!

As a matter of fact, he even saw two of his own sons buried alive in a wall in front of his very eyes? Yes, sir! Layer by layer, and brick by brick. And the remaining two were killed in a useless futile battle. If you were to ask me, all battles are useless and futile. They're a result of man's ego. Wars divide the world into North and South nations, and cut off the East from the West. That's when simple commoners get caught in the crossfire and others learn their geography. What a terrible life this Guru must've lived. Wouldn't you agree? Why, he spent an entire lifetime running away from life itself!"

The next day we woke up to the reports that Prime Minister Nehru had died. Daddy was the one who broke the news to us. For several days afterwards all the newspapers in the nation vied with each other to carry front-page headlines about a man who was born with a silver spoon in his mouth, but instead chose to be jailed with Gandhi to make India free.

"A Light is Out!" the newspaper hawkers shouted in the crowded streets.

This illustrious son of the soil had unexpectedly collapsed. There was even some speculation of a tertiary aortic aneurysm going bust. It was sudden and final, as death sometimes is. A great man born to a great nation had taken a step through that forbidden door.

"This country will implode on itself. It'll never be the same again," Daddy bemoaned the loss, along with the rest of the nation. "It's impossible to rule chaos. I don't know of anyone who can. This is certainly the end of our freedom. And death to our democracy. What democracy, I ask you? The one handed over to us on a silver platter? The one our chronically crooked and constitutionally dishonest citizens don't deserve to enjoy? If you were to ask me, there's only one solution to all the problems in this country. And that is to establish military rule in India."

The whole nation went into mourning. But there was no military rule.

Now when I look back to the events of the time, it is interesting to observe that President Kennedy, the other famous politician from the trio on those village calendars, had also died just six months before Nehru passed away. JFK's assassination shocked the world. He left behind a beautiful widow who wore pearl necklaces and looked the picture of grace in grief at the funeral.

"Shame on the West!" was Daddy's cryptic comment on the matter.

Onward eastward we went. At one time, the car had to be transported onto a large raft to cross the Ganges, which was now over a mile wide. I was sure the boat would drown midstream and take us all down with it, into the nothingness at the bottom of this great holy river, where the cumulative ash from millions of deceased Hindus lay piously to rest in peace for the rest of eternity.

We stopped briefly at Shantiniketan for a few hours. Indira Gandhi had once studied there. It was a great institution and had produced great minds. A school founded by Nobel Laureate Tagore's father, where classes were held in Bengali and English with special focus on the ancient Indian language of Sanskrit.

I wish that it were Latin instead, I remember thinking.

"Nargis, let's decide whether we should register you here," Daddy suggested, reading my mind. "In this school, they don't teach in traditional classrooms confined within four walls," Daddy explained. "The premise is that one should get every opportunity to open up one's mind and think freely."

I could almost picture myself studying under the dense shadows of the peepal trees, reclining in the soft green grasses with the coral bougainvillea bushes for a fortress and listening to the soft sounds of peacocks fanning their tails as I pored over Socrates, Plato, and Kant. I was quite excited by the prospect of an outdoor, free-flowing, free-thinking education, until we came upon the dhoti-clad Principal. He was dressed in a fairly informal flowing *kurta* with cheap floppy *chappals* exposing his rather relaxed and freely-liberated toes; complete with a *jhola* casually slung over his slouched philosophical shoulder; all made from discounted coarse yarn and a throwback to the Gandhi *Swadeshi* homespun movement.

"I don't agree with everything Gandhi did, but, I must admit, his economic strategy to boycott all British goods in the non-violent struggle for India's freedom was quite ingenious. That's why great leaders like Martin Luther King followed his example," Daddy believed.

This did it for me. The dhoti, *kurta, chappals* and *jhola* were all probably bought at seriously discounted prices from super-bazaar,

Khadi Bhandar. This was not a finishing school befitting a sophisticated young girl like myself.

So we traveled on. The land on the sides of the road was slowly becoming greener and flatter, as the majestic Ganges flowed on with immeasurable might to meet the ocean at the Bay of Bengal.

"So children, do you know why older villages are built on higher ground?" I heard Daddy quiz.

"Because, over time, the ancient houses turn into a heap of rubble. Then newer homes are built on the mound left in their place and the cycle goes on." As usual, I was quick to chime in before anyone else did.

"Mani, I told you she's brilliant!" Daddy nodded with pride.

I'm not sure my answer is correct, I thought, but for now, I'll take the credit anyway. Actually, when you stop to think hard about it, my answer does make a lot of sense.

We arrived at our new home quite late at night. In the old days, Barrackpore was a little Kingdom on the outskirts of Calcutta. Also in the good ole days, it boasted of its own good old little King. And it was this lesser known King's not so little palace that would become our new residence. It was huge and spread out, so we used only a small part of the living quarters. I believe a Raja had rented out this stately mansion to the military long ago, sometime after Independence, when the privy purses had dried out and he had fallen on desperate times.

Daddy said that there was a lesson to be learned: "The poor chap never learned how to earn a livelihood, having relied all his life on the labor of his subjects and the fat of the land. That's why Kingdoms come and Kingdoms go. History is replete with examples of lost riches and fallen empires. When princely progeny frit away an entire inheritance and end up as rickshaw pullers. Now, you all saw what happened to Dada's offspring? So my dear children, you *must* work hard. And you *must* learn to be independent."

The long driveway to the palace was symmetrically lined with tall coconut trees. On one side stood the cemented water feature that once could have been a fine swimming pool, but now was riddled with weeds strangled between fallen coconut leaves. I pictured the inept, lazy, good-for-nothing King, wading there in the midst of multiple exotic women-in-waiting while languishing in their wet tresses and bemoaning his losses. Daddy said that attending to multiple exotic paramours was another reason why Kingdoms were vanquished.

There was a separate muddy commonplace pond by the gate, for the commoners to use.

"Every home in Bengal must have access to the local pond." Daddy knew everything.

Bengali women would first wash their everyday utensils in the pond, then their daily laundry and after giving their mouths a thoroughly noisy swish-and-rinse they would finally emerge with shiny, wet, straight, black hair: The Bengali Pride. They would then air both their copious hair and their abundant arrogance for the rest of the day, as they went about their dull chores.

"Watch how that woman treads into the pond fully attired," Daddy would urge us to observe with him. "Now, see how she carefully takes off one article of clothing at a time while still submerged in the water, without getting any of her clothes wet. Notice how, throughout the act, her thick bountiful hair is discreetly covering her entire body. It's a miracle!"

"Bengalis have the brightest minds in the nation, except perhaps the Madrasis," Daddy would remind us. "And how they hate to concede to second place! But let me remind you that the Bengalis are also the filthiest community known to mankind. They sweep the dirt out of their homes and simply pile it up in front of the neighbor's fence, which they've previously spat on with a mouth-full of dirty-maroon *paan* juice! People from the great state of Bengal claim that they come from God's own country. As if they're descendants of Lord Rama himself! They also believe that they're the most cultured and literary society in our nation. And, they'll never let you forget that Tagore was one of their own."

There were huge gardens within the high walls surrounding the house, spread over several acres of dense forest with even thicker underbrush. The pathways into the wooded areas seemed forbidding and were strewn with coconut, nutmeg, mango, and leechi trees. Over break, Sanjay and I tried to climb the trees and even made a feeble attempt to cross the lotus pond on a raft made from crisscrossing fallen coconut leaves. The raft came apart somewhere in the middle and unhappily capsized, so we had to quickly swim ashore and abandon the project all-together. Long green snakes came hissing in our general direction slithering up and down the trees, daringly shooing us away with their constantly protruding forked tongues.

Daddy said that green snakes are harmless.

"They'll never bite you unless you *bother* them first. That's true of all the creatures in the animal kingdom. It is *man* who's the culprit. He's the one who's insecure and attacks them first."

The monsoon in Calcutta is the heaviest I have ever seen. It starts in Australia traveling northwest, as it slowly gathers moisture and strength over the Indian Ocean, until it reaches the Indian peninsula to pound the entire nation with its full might. When it rains, it pours torrents. That too, horizontally, with the wind. As if a tsunami had been brewing in the sky all year. You cannot see the sun for days.

"Whatever happens next, Nargis, you must remember one thing. These are the most important years in your life. So pay heed to your studies. Nothing else should matter. And I mean, *nothing*. Your performance over the next five years will decide whether you'll end up as a Prince or a pauper, a Raja or a rickshaw puller. After that, your fate is sealed."

It was decided, because Daddy had decided. And I was packed off to boarding school for the first time in my life.

Anjali had already been there for a year. So she knew the ropes and took charge of me right away without asking me first, reminding me with escalating frequency about all the do's and don'ts of the institution. At times, I felt that she ordered me around a bit too much, instructing me to do things just right. I did not always eagerly respond to her directions. As a matter of fact, sometimes I openly resented her seemingly dictatorial regime. She appeared to be more acrimoniously authoritarian than I ever remembered her at home.

One day during study hall, Anjali and I had argued about something. I remember feeling she was pushing me around, again. I was sitting in the last row simmering with pent up rage, most likely writing an essay on *Totalitarian Rule by Aurangzeb, The Last Mogul King*. I decided to suddenly bring down my desktop with a bang. I was so mad at her and that was the only logical and impulsive comeback that occurred to me at the moment. Immediately, everybody in the room turned around to look at me.

I stormed out of the classroom, howling uncontrollably as I ran, ripping off my school tie. I cried my heart out all the way to the gigantic front gates of the school.

It's a damn lousy place and coming to this school was a damn lousy idea! I told myself.

"I'm going home!" I bawled. "I won't stay here another minute! Daddy, Mummy, take me home!" I yelled to the hot air. "Where *are* you when I need you? Come and get me. *Now!*"

A couple of nuns in flying habits chased me in hot pursuit and dragged me to the Principal's office. I prayed that I would not be dishonored by having to adorn a dunce cap in full view of the school at tomorrow's assembly. It took another couple of penguins to intervene and calm me down. I was getting quite frantic. This was the first, but certainly not the last time that I would get hysterical in my life. Sadly, this would also not be my last trip to a principal's office.

I think my parents got wind of it later, but, strangely enough, they never asked me to explain my behavior. For the life of me, I still cannot remember what the whole fight was all about in the first place.

In uppity St. Anne's Convent, there were special uniforms for every conceivable occasion --- sports uniform for squash, walking uniform for museum treks, concert uniform for elocution, swanky uniform for formals and God only knows which ones I have forgotten. My parents were now supporting all three of us in boarding schools at the same time. All this must have cost a pretty penny, and entailed spending most of Daddy's salary on our education. Being an armchair gentleman farmer from halfway across the country, supplementary funds trickling in from Daddy's share of the largely mismanaged ancestral farm were not only meager, but also frequently delayed by the Indian Postal Services. So no frills for us; no yummy Cadbury's almond-covered chocolate stuffed in oval tins, chewy Wrigley bubblegum in individually wrapped packs, or other treats from the tuck-shop like most other kids got to routinely enjoy.

"First of all, chewing gum is probably the worst Western habit you could ever pick up. Secondly, education is what's more important," Daddy insisted. "Mushy chocolate that's deceitfully wrapped in colorful bright foil and jam-packed in dainty tins will not get you admitted to a top university. Besides, it's all sugar, and therefore not healthy for you."

The boarders would sleep in a large dormitory with curtains drawn around our beds for privacy. We had a small drawer on one side where we folded and stacked bloomers that had our initials sewn on them, along with other nameless odds and ends. There was no safe place to keep a diary, so I never wrote in one.

Periodically, the nuns would go into Retreat and walk around for days without talking, or smiling. They hardly smiled even when they were not in Retreat. Their habits looked kind of cute and they looked quite busy and authoritative, gliding up and down in the hallways in their black and white outfits, telling us what to do with merely a quick nod or look. Or mostly, what not to do. They seemed to be important people, who did important things.

It sounds like a damn good idea, I thought to myself. Maybe, I too will become a nun one day.

I wanted so desperately to believe in a God like everyone else did, so I started to go to the chapel that was located at the far end of the school compound. Sometimes, I would go there alone. As I walked up those pristine steps, I felt as if I was leaving all my troubles and sins behind. Especially my troubled-sins. I would go up to the altar and look up at Jesus, his arms outstretched on the cross and palms bleeding for the crimes of the world. He would gaze down at me with his soft-blue eyes, ever so gentle and forgiving, with his head hanging to one side. As if to say, "Praise the Lord, my child. I *understand*. Remember always, *Jesus* understands."

I would imagine that God was watching me the entire time I was in the chapel. Most likely, He would be peering through the stained glass to size up my sins, with his nose pressed against the pane, ready to walk me down to Humble Park.

Wait a minute, I told myself. I've never seen Him. Nor has anybody else. And does He really have a nose? Or a face? But then, the whole world *does* pray to Him. Even the nuns do. Everybody can't be mistaken. Maybe, it's Daddy who's got it all wrong, after all.

I did not know what to utter, so I would kneel at the pew, fold my hands, close my eyes, and repeat under my breath, "Our Father, who art in Heaven ---," over, and over, and over again. I imagined each wrongdoing being pardoned, immediately, at the end of every prayer.

And each sin being forgiven, instantly, every time I uttered, "Amen." That was the only prayer I would ever know.

It was time now for the annual play. I was not selected for any part. That year the performance was from *A Midsummer Night's Dream*. Or was it *The Tempest*? I was not chosen to be a fairy, even just for dress-up sake. Most parents came for the play. But not ours. I had heard that some actors from Bollywood, like Pran the perennial villain of Indian films, had come all the way from Bombay to watch their daughters' perform. Obviously, *those* girls had, by some stroke of luck mysteriously passed the audition. Somebody pointed out the actor, seated in the front row. I swear that I could not recognize him without his pockmarked rapist face on.

I spent the entire semester at St. Anne's without making a single friend. I was rather unhappy there since nobody singled me out even as a pal, leave alone as a buddy. I am not sure that I missed home either. I hated all my classes. I do not remember any of my teachers. I do not remember much else either. It was overall a blah period in my life.

"Nothing to write home about," as Daddy would have said.

No adventures, no outdoors. No Sanju, no fun.

I was quite relieved when my parents eventually decided to pull me out of St. Anne's. I would have a chance at making a fresh start elsewhere. It is possible that they had heard of my frenzied outburst at the school gates. Besides, Anjali would soon graduate high school and start college in Dehradun, so it made no sense in my being left alone in the vast desert state of Rajasthan, For some reason, my parents had decided that I would not do too well if I was left alone, all by myself, in any vast state of any country.

In the next few years Daddy, now Colonel Yadav, would be coming close to the end of his army career. My parents would then settle down in their Dehradun home, the Red Fort, as they had planned all along. It was more logical, therefore, that I should start boarding school in that very city.

The rest of the family would inevitably join me in a few years and we would all be together again.

But, will we all *ever* be together again? I remember wondering.

"THAT DAMN TWIG!"

When we first arrived in Dehradun, I did not know that I was going to be the only boarder at the all girls' school, Convent of Jesus and Mary. I had passed my eleventh birthday and would enroll in the eighth standard. God only knows how Daddy was able to convince Mother Superior to take me in. She told him that they had conducted this experiment once before and it had not quite worked for either party. To make his point well understood, Daddy had to go into excruciating details about the extenuating circumstances in our family. He always excelled at making a point, especially when backed into a wall. You could never know whether you were killed by Daddy's words, or his charm.

"Look, Mother Superior," he started. "We're a family of five and isn't it an appalling shame that at the present time we're all living in four different cities? Even God would not have wanted it to be this way. Especially for a self-respecting family like ours. Now, I must tell you this. I've been a good soldier all my life. My duty to defend this great nation of ours has always come first, even way ahead of my responsibility as a father. So, it is now the duty of this nation to take care of my family. If you accept my daughter as a boarder, I'll have at least two children residing in the same city at the same time. Nargis is an outstanding student and you'll never regret it. In fact, you might even start a boarding school after having had a successful trial run with her. You might even make her a nun," he joked with her. "And by the way, I'll have no problem with that!"

Daddy could make quite an impression on his listeners. Using his silver tongue, he always managed to tell a compelling story. He had an innate knack to sound both sensitive and genuine, persuasive and chiding, all at the same time; a skill that I have hardly ever seen in anyone else so precisely perfected to the nth degree. And quite unbeknownst to the audience, he knew when to flawlessly time his act of simultaneously tugging at their emotions as well. Ever so gently. Rather uniquely endowed was Daddy. At other times, I had seen him cajole, humor, plead, or manipulate to get things done. Whatever worked. In whichever sequence. Daddy was not one to hunker down so easily. If the person still did not agree with him, he would resort to unleashing his rage lavishly sprinkled with expletives and simply browbeat the poor unfortunate man into submission. This "brainless" individual was now classified as, "a useless, worthless, and incompetent bloody fool." Daddy would threaten to report the "injustice" to the man's superiors and have him fired posthaste. Once, when I had accompanied Daddy to a government office, security had to be called in and he was unceremoniously shown the exit door because he had threatened an IAS (Indian Administrative Service) officer. I had no choice but to leave with him. It can be quite humiliating to be the last one to leave a room under such circumstances, hoping that the door does not hit you on your way out.

"I'm sick of your shenanigans!" Daddy had shouted at the stunned man sitting behind the desk in suit and tie, even as he himself was being escorted out. "It's because of officers like you, you bungling file-pushers, that this country is going to the dogs! It's because of bureaucrats like you that India has become a breeding ground for dynasties of corruption! What a bloody shame! You know every trick in the book. Trickster is what I call you! You sign papers with one hand, while with the other one you accept bribes under the table! Thug is your middle name! The red-tape, monkey business and money-laundering in this country will bring us all down together. Yes, both you and me," pointing with his finger. "We'll both go down together. Now, don't look at me like I've descended from outer space. You stupid man! You're utterly incapable of respecting a genuine request. I know all your antics. You claim that you must go by the policies in the book. *What* book, may I ask? You change rules on a whim. *Your* whim, I must add. I can predict with cent percent certainty that you don't even *know* the rules. Legends in your own mind! You're totally inept and completely incapable of thinking for yourself. If you were to ask me, fools like you should be disqualified from running this nation and you should be forced out of this job immediately! And, by the way, if you had any self-respect left, you'd just resign without any ceremony and of your own accord."

It was bad enough to be shown the door. It was downright humiliating though, to see my own father reduced to nothing.

None of that happened this time in the negotiations with Mother Superior. Simply because she had readily agreed with Daddy and eagerly acquiesced to his request. It was a happy ending all the way round. The nuns were quite taken in with his emotional plea and they took me in. So this is how I became the only boarder at Convent of Jesus and Mary.

Initially, it was rather strange. All the other children rode their bikes home, or were picked up at the end of the day. I, meanwhile, would walk across the road to a bungalow, where, during the day, little nursery school kids chanted little nursery school rhymes. I had my own private room there. The nuns lived in the house next door, which was off limits for me. I could not venture past their parlor. I hated it.

It felt special to be singled out, but having to give explanations was quite something else.

Once again, I felt alone. I remember carrying heavy tomes of the Encyclopedia Britannica from the school library back to my room and spending many an evening by myself, poring over their contents. I read about everything --- Prehistoric Man, the Steam Engine, Great Inventions, the Beginning of the Universe and the Center of the Earth. It was so easy to recognize the old maps where two-thirds of the world was painted a bold-pink to connote the power and expanse of the great British Empire. All this was quite interesting for a while. I was sure that one day I will know everything there is to know about everything and in that process inevitably become rich and famous.

Maybe, I'll end up even inventing something all by myself!

Soon I was tired of skimming through encyclopedias. I could never memorize the bottomless fund of knowledge stored between the hardcover covers of those fat tomes. Besides, spending time reading about inconsequential factoids that did not pertain to my daily life was starting to feel rather pointless.

I started to circumspectly notice the other girls in my class. Hema was the one with the nice long legs and therefore immediately deemed groovy. Her uniforms were always fresh and impeccably starched. When it came to final exams, the lunches prepared by her resourceful cook and packed by her ever-indulging mother became even more elaborate and her grades even more pathetic.

Bublee, true to her name, was a bubbly, fair and freckled girl with long chestnut-brown hair that her parents would never allow her to chop off since she was a Sikh. Being a proud Elvis fan, she had life-size posters of his iconic mousse-pouf hair gracing his sexy baby-face adorning her bedroom walls. I believe she had once visited Paris, which instantly made her cool beyond a reasonable doubt. She had movie-handsome brothers in the armed services, but, of course, I was scared stupid to even say *bonjour* to them.

Usha was a sweet, soft-spoken girl. Her brother, unfortunately, was stricken with Down's Syndrome. When she kissed his face, with drool trickling down under his collar, I could not look at them. Together, or apart.

Thank God, Sanju's genetic code has been saved from such a terrible mix-up!

Shashi, a General's daughter, had oil dripping from her thick braided hair. An absolute throwback to medieval times. That was enough reason to ignore her instantly and completely. From top to bottom. From head to toe. Even her middle name spelled 'UN-COOL.' Jaya meanwhile, who was a pretty, petite and uncomplicated girl, was easy to talk to. Fortunately, some people are. Later, her mother would die of breast cancer.

It's too damn scary when parents die, I was saddened. No, I shouldn't think about such awful things. Cancer will never happen to anyone in *my* family.

Finally, there was Pollyannaish Pearl. The smartest one of them all. The one I could never hold a candle to. Her grades were always several notches higher than mine and I could never bridge the gap from second place. I would usually lie, claiming that I did not need to study too hard after school.

Or else, she might think I'm a damn knucklehead. Didn't Daddy say that white lies are harmless?

Close to exam time, strange things had started to happen in our class. Somebody was stealing notes from the brighter students. That day, it was dumb Hema's turn to find math homework missing from her desk.

You've to be real thick to steal *her* notes, I thought. It's common knowledge that she barely has the attention span of a fruit fly!

The whole class was summoned by our math teacher, Miss Sen. She had a quiet commanding presence and was assigned to identify the real culprit. We were told that she had to take just one quick look at you, to find out if you are indeed the guilty party.

There was a hush in the classroom. Nobody said a word. It was quite eerie actually. And strangely paranoid. Everyone was suspect. I do not know why, but somehow I had decided that everybody must automatically infer, by some implicit code of elimination, that I am the criminal.

I remember wondering, why do I even think that I'm a prime suspect, when this is the first time I'm hearing about this godforsaken theft myself? How can I prove my innocence when confronted? Will I sound too hollow, for trying too hard? Why's guilt such a natural go-to feeling for me?

I was deathly afraid. And sweating, too. I felt an abdominal migraine coming on from somewhere below. Somewhere, from the depths of my being. Surely, Miss Sen would see guilt written all over my face. It would not be long before I would be found out. And of course, punished. Punished and ridiculed. Ridiculed and scorned.

A storm was brewing outside. There were hot summer winds blowing past the dusty classroom window that could easily have blown Mary Poppins into self-orbit. Soon the dull-gray sky was turning sickly-yellow and then it quickly became pale-orange to acknowledge the solstice. The fig trees swayed dangerously in the wind with their long branches appearing like outstretched fingers, alternately pointing accusingly at the wretched sky and at wretched me. Downcast leaves flew around trying to speak for me racing to meet their reflection in the rainwater puddles --- only to sink in them.

Suddenly, there was dust everywhere --- over the pencil-scratched beige desktops, on the ink-smudged brown book covers and between my perfect pearly-white teeth. It seemed as if there was an earthquake way off-the-charts on the Richter's scale just waiting to explode right in my face. And I was standing just over the tectonic Fault Line. I could swear that I saw a planet larger than Earth, looking a little like that Jupiter from the encyclopedia, hurling toward the school building with full force. It would instantly strike us with full might and that would be the end of everything as we know it. We would all implode together. The whole freaking school building, my classmates, Mrs. Sen, and I.

Inside the classroom it was deathly still. It seemed as if every particle of dust suspended in that very still air was loaded. Loaded with tension. And scrutiny. Miss Sen had brought a dry twig from the peepal tree by the bike-stand. Then she asked each girl to come up, one by one, to where she stood by the blackboard, straight and tall.

"Hold the twig in your hands and pray," she instructed firmly, staring at us with ice in her eyes. "Hold it carefully now. And don't be cavalier about it either. If you're guilty, the twig will automatically break," she added knowingly.

Is there a hint of a smile on her otherwise stern face? I was too afraid to confirm.

It was my turn now. I felt as if I was crawling on broken glass as I came up to where Mrs. Sen stood. The pain in my face was palpable. The pupils in my eyes felt bigger than my eyeballs. I was sure that the twig would instantly crack in my guilt-ridden hands, which by now were trembling uncontrollably. I was shaking like a leaf myself! I could feel my cheeks burning, as I was working up a panic. There was sweat erupting above my lip, over the bridge of my nose and across my brow. My armpits and chest felt moist and heavy. It felt as if my heart was pounding out sweat to every part of my body, down to my very toes. Pumping out pure, sticky, clammy, godforsaken sweat.

A myriad of terrifying outcomes flashed in my mind. I was sure that I would become a laughing stock amongst my peers. During the next break, my sullied reputation would be sold for a lark in the crowded school hallways.

Miss Sen was looking quizzically at me.

"Nargis, it's your turn now," she said, her voice sounding like the static from nails grating on a chalkboard, making my teeth hurt.

As much as I tried, I could not look straight back at her. I stretched out my hand hesitantly to hold the twig, my face flushed crimson. I felt like a hamster caught in a wheel. A hamster that was quickly running out of Joules of Energy. Running on empty.

"Nargis, hold this twig firmly in your hands, and let's say a prayer together," she said brusquely.

I should at least *try* to look her squarely in the face, I told myself.

Or else, she'll surely presume that I'm guilty. But then, why do I *feel* so guilty?

I could not look at anybody, or anything, except at that stupid lonesome twig in my hands. The twig that would decide my fate. *Very soon.* I held it tightly just like she had instructed me to do. Maybe --- too tightly.

Then the damn twig broke! It was all over. Just like that.

And I'm finished! It didn't have to go down this way. *Nobody will ever believe me now.* Everyone'll think I'm a thief, a liar and a cheat, all in one. Soon the whole world will know. It'll spread like wildfire. The girls will never stop talking about this, lingering on by the bike-stand, huddled together. I'll never be able to back-paddle out of this creek. Nobody will ever forget what just happened. I'll never forget what just happened.

I felt guilt and shame of glacial magnitude rapidly gaining might to become an avalanche of climactic proportions, which would come crashing down into an ocean to become bobbing icebergs named: Disgrace and Dishonor.

Before I had a chance to feel anything else, I was swiftly escorted by Miss Sen to the office of Principal, Sister Maria, where I had no option but to plead guilty and apologize for something that I had not done. I wished the earth would swallow me up right away, now and forever.

I do not know how I ever survived the twig episode. After that unsavory experience, every now and then I would sense some of the 'snitch-bitches' smiling sick pathetic smiles in my presence, or grinning quick hideous smirks behind my back as they spoke in audible whispers, reveling in the randomness of a rush to snap judgment. I would conjecture they were passing snide remarks about me. That, I believe, is generally the purpose of audible whispers.

But nobody talked about it again --- or at least, nobody talked about it again with me. And I pretended it had never happened.

By now, I knew the litany all too well: if you don't talk about it, it *hasn't* happened.

I must burn out my bad karma, I mused.

This is when I discovered the joy of candy and went through jars gorging on toffees and sweets by the mouthful. I could easily polish off an entire container and then throw up from challenging the anatomical boundaries of my stomach. Most likely, I escaped an eating disorder DSM IV diagnosis by a few extraneous symptoms.

The nuns had assigned an ayah to me, a young dark buxom South Indian woman, who was troubled because she was of marriageable age and yet not married. She would launder my clothes, wash my hair and bring dinner trays for me from the nuns' kitchen.

I cannot remember how the fondling started between the ayah and me. Like with Daddy, it was forbidden, secretive and pleasurable. Of course, it was always after school. My days and nights took on the familiar dichotomy. While at school, I was learning about Newton's Laws of Motion, King Henry the Eighth, and the comprehensive anatomical detail of the reproductive system of a cockroach. Then back in my room with the ayah, it would become a different kind of study. Maybe she was found out, because she was replaced by an older, stern and heavyset woman whose cheek muscles never sanctioned a smile. I was left to my own devices for a while.

Before long, it was winter break and time to go home. It was close to midnight, when a nun accompanied me to a desolate railway station from where I would catch the Howrah Express, which used to travel daily all the way east across the country's width to Calcutta.

I do not remember feeling even a hint of trepidation that I was traveling alone. It was actually fun to be away from school for a while and finally on my own. At the very first station, I exchanged all my pocket money for the proud ownership of half a dozen comics, including *Young Romance* and *Forbidden Love*. For the rest of the journey, traveling on word balloons would make the ride much more erudite and smooth. And marvelously romantic.

There were a few older girls in my compartment from another boarding school in the hills who were also going home for winter holidays. I was embarrassed to tell them that I was still only in the eighth standard. I looked so much older.

Without a doubt, they must conclude right away that I must be totally dense. And that I must've failed at least a couple of grades.

So I decided to dial-up my abilities. I was in the ninth standard, just for them. Just until the train reached Calcutta. Soon they started exchanging notes about Einstein's Theory of Relativity and Mendeleev's periodic table. Very quickly I realized, that the scope of my knowledge was not going to last the entire duration of the two-day train ride. It was rapidly becoming a steeper uphill course to keep up with them. So I unloaded my comics on this seemingly scholarly crowd. This put an end to questions about a curriculum that I did not have even the faintest notion about. Also, I reminded myself, this way I will not be caught red-handed when I arrive home, my sticky fingers tainted with comic-strip trash.

It's Daddy who taught me how to kill two birds with one stone.

Two nights and one day later, the train pulled into Howrah Station. It is a super busy station with throngs of people bustling about, chasing after coolies in close pursuit just in case they might run away with their baggage, kids trailing behind them so they do not lose sight of their parents chasing after those coolies. The station boasts of servicing at least a million people on any single day.

My parents had instructed me not to talk to anyone and *never* to trust a stranger. I quickly got off the train. Then I briefly looked left and right. I did not see my parents, so I kept on walking.

I was certain that Daddy was watching me from a strategic place, testing to see how I might react to this novel situation of not finding my family. There was no chance of his ever being late. Daddy was never late. For *anything*.

It's simple. I just have to use my brain and do the next right thing, I thought. I must follow his advice to the letter. Like he's always coached me to do.

"Remember, you must never stop to talk to anyone. It can be dangerous. So just keep walking."

So I did not stop to talk to anyone and just kept walking.

I had now reached an exit sign at the station. I followed an older, almost toothless woman to the local train station to catch the next train to Barrackpore. I was sure that I could trust an older, almost toothless woman. I must have looked kind of lost because a policeman came up to me to offer assistance. I told him rather confidently that my parents were waiting for me just around the corner and my father was a top army officer. I was positive that the man was a part of the mob and was just impersonating a cop. He would surely kidnap me without further warning and, with a pimp's dubious intentions, initiate me into the Red Light area just like my parents had frequently warned.

I got off at Barrackpore and took a rickshaw home.

"Remember, never take a taxi. The cabby will lock the door and you'll be trapped in the backseat and never be able to jump off and escape," was sound parental advice.

Why does 'trapped in the backseat' sound so familiar?

I arrived at the small King's palace uneventfully. I asked the rickshaw puller to drop me off at the front gate.

"Remember, never let strangers go past the front entrance of the house."

When I was sure that the man had merrily paddled out of sight and had no immediate plans of abducting me for an undisclosed ransom, I walked with suitcase in hand down the driveway lined with coconut trees. Then I rang the doorbell.

No answer.

I've followed all Daddy's instructions to the letter. But, where *has* everybody gone? I was puzzled.

I was sitting on the front steps of the house busy snapping groundnut shells that the nuns had packed for the journey, when Mummy and Anjali finally arrived. They were worn out and emotionally drained from the events of the day. Daddy had been held up at work and my mother and sister had arrived as the train was just coming in. But the predictably unpredictable Indian Railways had once again changed the arrival platform at the last minute. They must have missed me by just a few seconds. And by several heartbeats. Mummy had me repeatedly paged overhead through the entire vast Howrah Station.

"Looking for an eleven-year-old girl with a bob-cut and red headband, who goes by the name of Nargis."

Finally giving up hope, both of them turned back to go home crestfallen and heartbroken. For sure, I had been brutally assaulted, sold for a lark and lost to the family forever.

Mummy was crying silently when she saw me. She was sure that the next time she would see my face, it would be looking sadly back at her from the Missing Person section of *The Telegraph*. Emaciated frame, deep sunken eyes. Hollow cheeks, no smile.

Under the photo, 'Girl from boarding school abducted at pointblank and lost to the underworld. Preferred language: English.

Looks older than eleven. Name before being kidnapped: Nargis.'

For a long time after this episode, Mummy would tell me that she would get goose bumps whenever she would think of what could have happened to me that day at Howrah Station. This was the first time I ever remember Mummy having such strong feelings for me.

When I returned to school after vacation, the war had started. Pakistan was attacking Amritsar in the West and Barrackpore in the East.

Is that not just a stone's-throw-away from where Daddy and Mummy live? I was worried.

Sometimes, I would wonder if I would wake up tomorrow to the dreadful news that my parents had been killed in the bombing. But I did not spend too much time thinking about such gloomy tidings. Long trenches had been dug out in the school grounds, and in preparation for the air raids the students were subjected to war drills at all odd hours. Sometimes, we had to suddenly stop in the middle of a chapter on the Great Lakes Waterway, Ivan the Terrible, or a quadratic equation, and run for the trenches to crawl in there with our heads pinned to the ground. I was sure that very soon the school yard would be littered with bombshell craters and we would all be captured as POWs. You would come upon our entire class in next week's national newsreel, hands shackled behind us, shuffling along chained together at our feet, trudging through sludge made soft and mushy with our own sweat and marching in single file to the sound of 'Squish, Mush, Squish.' Then we would all be lined up against the school fence, instructed to crouch with our heads between our thighs, and simply shot to death.

Obviously, we were able to escape this dastardly finale.

No real bombs ever fell. The skirmishes were contained at the border towns. India won the war.

Soon, I was well on my way to attaining the distinction of being the class clown. I had discovered that this was another way to become popular in a hurry. One day, when our science teacher, Miss Anne, was late, I went up to the blackboard in her place. To entertain myself, but mostly to amuse the rest of the class, I drew a picture of Principal, Sister Maria. Except, this Sister Maria had no clothes on. Save for a black and white headgear with a rosary and cross dangling between her hanging breasts. The whole class went up in a roar of laughter so deafening that we did not notice Sister Maria walking in!

So, back to the principal's office this court jester was hauled, to spend all of lunch break painstakingly working on my calligraphy: '*It is a sin to disrespect our teachers.*' I had to write it all of six thousand times, only to be saved by the bell.

One day when I grow up, I'll buy this whole damn fucking school! I consoled myself.

This seemed the only legit way to get back at misrepresented authority.

I was starting to fear that I was becoming the bad company my parents had often warned me to stay away from.

Aunty Tara came to visit one Sunday afternoon, with her muffin-top flowing middle draped in quasi-village attire. I was plain mortified to see her. She looked, perhaps, just marginally better dressed than my dumpy ayah and she spoke only in monosyllabic and heavily-accented English. It was sheer torture to be with her in the same room.

And to admit that she's related to me? *Never!*

Suffice is to say, it was a short visit.

There would be another boarder to share my room. She was older than me, and for some reason I have forgotten her name. Sometimes we would talk about sex and giggle together. I told her that boys get periods just like us girls, except theirs seep out white blood corpuscles instead of red and it happens only once a year instead of every month. It felt good to be more knowledgeable about male physiology than an older girl, even if I had to make it all up as I went along.

And who knows, I thought, maybe this *does* happen to boys.

There was a brief period of fondling between us. I do not remember how it started. But I do remember sometimes taking the lead. However, soon it would end when one day my roommate abruptly packed her bags and left school. I was alone again.

By now I had decided that only the church could save my soul.

Please God, I prayed, save the sinner in me. Only *you* can do it. Only you can help me become a better person. Starting today. How about, starting *now*.

So one Sunday at the school chapel, I stood in line for confession. I would tell God everything. Yes, *everything*. Someone pulled me aside.

No, I could not do that. This was meant only for Christians. I felt as if I had been kicked to the curb.

Why *am* I different? Why am I not a Christian? Why can't I do things other people can? I *have* to find a way to straighten up and give up my bad ways. But, what *can* I do?

That is when I turned to books and discovered my passion for reading. With each leaf I turned in the book, I imagined as if I was turning over a new leaf in my life. With each chapter I ended, I was closing another chapter of my past that I wanted so desperately to forget. *Forever.* I had an insatiable appetite for the written word and would read everything in sight. There were no visitors in the evenings or on weekends, so I would escape into a magical world of places far away. I read Shakespeare, Dickens, Hardy, the Bronte sisters and Austen. I soaked it all in and still had room for more. Reading was a perfect way to forget all the bad things I had done, and the bad things that had been done to me. One day, I promised myself, I would travel to those faraway places and start a new life there. When I finally grow up, I was sure that I would travel to England, or America, and live there happily ever after.

At the end of the school year, Daddy and Mummy came to get me. I feared that the nuns had told them *all*. Mother Superior recommended that I go back with my family and become a day scholar, like the rest of the children. More than an experiment, it had been a gamble --- this boarding school thing. The one I had failed at a second time over.

Daddy even alluded to it being, "The right time for Nargis to come back home, or she'll soon get into bad ways."

I wondered whether my parents knew of all my follies and foibles of this past year.

Do they know more than they're telling me? Will I be called on the carpet? I panicked.

I was never called on the carpet. Nothing was ever said about my year as a boarder. It would soon be over and forgotten, like some other events in my life that had long since been over. And forgotten.

I had passed my twelfth birthday.

FOR NOW, JUST THE TWO OF US

For the next three years it would be just Mummy and me living together in Dehradun. Daddy stayed on in Calcutta to finish up his posting, and my siblings continued at their respective boarding schools. Our own rambling house, the Red Fort, had been rented out to the military to help defray the cost of our education. So we lived in a tiny two room annexes of a larger home in a nice uppity neighborhood. Sanjay christened our living quarters Lilliputian house, for reasons that nobody could dispute.

How small was Lilliputian house? It was so tiny that I could hear our landlord's toilet flush on the other side of our wall, like the crashing sounds of Niagara Falls across state lines!

We shared our new home with a captain and his wife. Before I had a chance to meet them, I had pictured him to be a Dustin Hoffman lookalike. Much to my dismay, he looked more like a tired Santa Claus on Boxing Day and had been retired for some time.

The front room of our section was used as my study. On one side was a simple desk positioned below a bookshelf in the wall. This would now become *my* desk. And this would be the bookshelf where Quantum Mechanics, Magnetism, Arthropods, Entropy, Invariants, and *Julius Caesar* lived together in peaceful harmony with *Great Expectations*. Against the adjacent wall lay a long trunk cushioned with a mattress and accessorized with throw pillows, where an extra guest sometimes slept during a brief layover. The only window in the room was flanked by two easy wicker-in-teak armchairs since according to Mummy's Rules only two visitors were allowed into the house at any given time. This would become my window to the world and this study would be the place that would eventually shape the rest of my life.

The back room had a single large king-sized bed with high posts, where Mummy and I slept. That is the same bed where, every night, she would insist that I put my arm around her to confirm my presence.

The door to the kitchen, where Mummy diligently cooked meals just for the two of us, could only let one person pass through at a time. That was just fine with me, since it was an affront to my intelligence to venture into such domesticated spaces unaccompanied. The old English radio, His Master's Voice, was kept on a low rickety table. I would bend over to fiddle with its knob and catch a spluttering over the static of the *BBC World Service, Forces Requests*, or *A Date with You*. After homework, I was allowed to sing and swing along with The Beatles, The Beach Boys and Herman's Hermits. Growing up without television broadcasting, music and books would become the sole means of easy and fun distraction for the next three years. Today, I am certain that reading saved me from both a Padded Cell and Life Interrupted.

Yet again, I had to deal with a situation in my life that I felt compelled to explain: why do we live so miserably, when our family indeed owns a massive and stunning home just a few streets away?

"This place is quite big enough for just Mummy and me --- and it's temporary, you know --- Anyway, we'll eventually live in the Red Fort when Daddy retires --- It's an awesome home, with ten to twelve bedrooms and matching bathrooms, plus a huge library upstairs --- and Daddy lives in a humungous old palace in Calcutta --- and my brother goes to Sherwood School ---" my voice would trail off.

After a while I stopped giving an explanation, simply because nobody actually ever asked me for one. I still hated living in Lilliputian house, though.

I never talked about that previous year in boarding school and luckily for me, Mummy never alluded to it either. There was once a vague mention of the nuns regretfully shaking their heads about my falling into bad company.

Or, did they mean *I* was that bad company?

Initially, I had some power struggles with Mummy as most prepubescent pre-teens the whole world over are supposed to have and once even got a thorough spanking. I believe some house rules are made just to be broken. That would be the last corporeal punishment I would ever receive at Mummy's hands. Or, so I thought.

"I'm sorry to inform you that for all practical purposes, starting from this very moment, I don't need you in my life," I told Mummy defiantly, as I walked in a huff into the kitchen for the very first time.

"I don't need *anyone* to help me. I can very well live on my own. And by the way you may not know this, but I can take pretty good care of Nargis."

To prove my point I ended up cooking dinner for myself, comprised of haphazardly shaved hard-boiled potatoes doused in boiling water with raw spotted turmeric floating on top. It was yellow and bitter! And Mummy made me eat it as a penalty.

Very soon we settled into a healthy coexistent relationship, which would be the best we would ever have, then and since. Mummy took charge of our home and of me. She woke up before dawn and firmly instructed me to wash the sleep stuck between my eyes before I sat down at my desk. She would fetch fresh milk from UP Dairy booth, start the stove to prepare a meal that always managed to fit snugly in my lunchbox, watch over me as I swallowed a raw egg with an intact yolk sprinkled over with salt and pepper and washed it down with sweetened lukewarm milk in one huge gulp and send me off to school.

In the winter months, Mummy would get the coal clay oven started. When fully ablaze, the earthenware stove would boast glowing red-hot embers. The antiquated device sure simmered black lentil *dal* to perfection, heated water for our baths and roasted groundnut shells to a crisp smoke-kissed finish. When the last coals died down with the sun to turn ash-gray, we knew then that the day was done.

Anjali failed her first year of B.S. in college and the anticipated, but totally annoying and distressing, gloom-doom scenario set in the house. There were many rounds of "I told you so," by Daddy with predictable and escalating frequency that month.

What'll ever become of poor Anjali? I worried.

I was beginning to accept the hopelessness of the situation, albeit reluctantly, until one day we heard that Anjali was accepted at a Home Science College in Kanpur. The entire family breathed a sigh of cumulative relief. One that could have blown away at least half of an entire continent! If anyone was in trouble in our family, it always felt that all three of us kids were sinking in quicksand all at the same time. And holding hands all the way down.

Mummy and I continued to live a Spartan existence, but I had learned a long time ago not to complain. Most of the girls at school, unlike me, wore a fresh uniform every day. In the summer, it was a light-blue pinafore to pin down pubescent breasts, and a preppy-white collared shirt accessorized with a deep-blue and white striped tie. During the winter semester, it would be a somber-gray skirt with a navy-blue blazer. Same shirt, same tie. From uniform straight into my night-suit and back at my desk. It was expected of me mostly by myself to despise all Indian apparel, so I hated all Indian attire

"I'll never be caught dead, or alive, in those rustic *kameez, chunni,* and *churidar* outfits!" I would warn Mummy.

No countryside-inspired stretched-out shapeless tunics, bucolic scarves, and ill-fitting sagging PJ-lookalikes for me.

Mummy did not really care, as long as I did not lift a single eyeball off my textbooks. Even in her absence. Not to sweat the small stuff, on weekends she kept me looking hip in skirts and collared shirts. She had to bring down my hems, so that my frocks could still cover me fairly modestly for another couple of years, or so.

Soon I learned to drive a scooter. A year before I would officially be called a teenager, I had unlawfully acquired a drivers license through Uncle Karan's connections. I discovered quite early in my life that in the country of my birth it is fairly effortless and customary to circumvent laws. Especially, if you have the right connections. So now I could drive Mummy everywhere as she went about her chores: to the wholesale bazaar for top-tier fruits and vegetables bought in bulk at bottom-rung prices; to the *chakki* for warm freshly-ground wheat flour; to the *Bania's* shop, for pulses and spices. Whenever Mummy arrived, he would give her a special discount for being his first customer of the day. I would drop her off and watch from a respectable distance: golden apples from Kashmir being meticulously polished with a muslin cloth, oranges from Nagpur being obsessively lined up to form a pyramid and mangoes from Lucknow turning sweet-yellow snug tight against each other. Mummy would methodically inspect the apples and turn them over one by one to rule out concealed worm tunnels, pinch the oranges in the second layer from the top looking for stale mushy spots and palpate the mangoes to ascertain if they had been ripened with artificial light. I would hope bystanders did not conclude that Mummy and I had arrived together!

This was not for me. I was meant for a different life. None of this boring shopping or cooking, sewing or cross-stitching and other ordinary chores meant mostly for other ordinary people.

I had settled into a comfortable routine. Every morning, like clockwork, my friends Naina and Lara would bike up to my house on their way to school.

"NAAAAAARGIS," they would holler at my gate, ringing those little bells on their bicycle handles.

I am sure that the neighbors adjusted their watches whenever they heard my name yelled out loud. The three of us would bike down together to school. Sometimes, dirty old men would follow us on their rusty old bikes, attempting to undress us with their leery looks and lascivious annotations.

Do I have "Jerk Magnet" written on my forehead? I was livid!

I would pretend that I did not understand their lingo and would paddle even harder, imagining that they were phantom people in a dumb Halloween movie, as I chased the shadows of the clouds on the road and my imaginary dreams in the sky.

The nuns had set the gold standard, "Now remember girls, don't chase after the first pair of pants you see. And don't you ever get crushed by the first crush in your life."

There must not exist a girl who grew up in the sixties in India who has not had a bottom pinched on the streets by some beyond-despicable hoodlum, who also intermittently dared to flash an appendage as she passed him by. I loathed it when this happened to me and despised those lowly creatures, but I would never complain to Mummy. She would almost certainly blame it on me for not getting away in time, so I kept her out of the loop. It was always easier to keep her out of the loop, since Mummy was already amply paranoid, at any given time and without any rational reason. By now, I had accepted that this was her natural state. If perchance I had to stay back at the school lab to finish up a chemistry experiment, Mummy automatically decided that I had been run over, or abducted, or both. I would find her fuming and way out of breath at the laboratory door, or well on her way there. She was always very stern and upset on such occasions and I remember coming back home with that sick feeling in my stomach that I had done something terribly wrong. Especially when helicopter-mom would look at me with that let's-get-to-the-bottom-of-this face. She would discourage me from going to friends' homes after school, or on weekends --- especially if they had older brothers, which they usually did. On the few occasions when I would go over to Lara's place, even if only to verify homework assignments, I would be surely riddled with at least half a million questions afterward all in rapid fire. Not to mention the admonishment, "For heaven's sake, Nargis, why did you forget your homework?!" It was easier just to stay at home. To complicate things further, I had started to develop something of a pre-teen bust. Finally, it was Anjali who implored Mummy to fit me with a bra because I bounced so when I ran. It is electrifying, yet embarrassing, to be fitted with a bra for the first time.

Slowly, we started to get used to our new neighborhood. The Guptas, who lived across the street from us had three children. Rakesh was in engineering school and considered quite brilliant. Sunita, a medical student, initiated us into swiping grossly overpriced Christmas cards from a store, owned by a *Bania* who wore cheap metal-rimmed spectacles made of the thickest glass possible with Diopters way off the charts. The youngest one, Neena, was at a boarding school in Simla and was a free spirit. Mummy called her 'that flirty trashy tramp.'

Sour grapes, or forbidden fruit? I wondered.

"She's too much into boys," Mummy would warn. "She'll never amount to anything. Nargis, make sure that you never become like her."

Uncle Gupta was mostly balding and therefore obviously supremely wise. He was also one-hundred percent a *Bania* and therefore evidently super shrewd. He would exchange notes with Daddy about mutual and globally prevalent problems in families.

I remember uncle quoting, "Relatives make imperfect relationships --- they're like blazing coals. When they're too close to each other they burn with jealousy --- and when they're too far away, they smolder with longing."

"That's the universal truth about families," Daddy would zealously agree. "Relatives are never happy to see you doing well. If they cannot become your friends, they will just remain biological accidents. It's no secret that they're constantly waiting in the wings to see you fall flat on your face."

The Guptas had some wild tailgate parties too. Trendy teenagers in faded-out, patched-up and thread-worn blue jeans would emerge from their gate, sometimes flagrantly holding hands as they lingered by my fence, with music following them as it blared in through the open window of my study way into the night. I could hear them giggling to adult jokes and reciting love poetry to each other, most likely, strung together from discarded Hallmark cards. I imagined that they must be dancing together, holding each other tight and whispering sweet-nothings as they swayed like a single body to *Jailhouse Rock* and *A Hard Day's Night*. Meanwhile, right across the road, *I* was the one having a *real* hard day's night in Mummy's lockup, busting my bum with a tortuous physics numerical to calculate unit-g of the gravitational pull of the Earth, wondering instead, what Newtonian force of adolescent attraction they must be experiencing in which I could never partake. I knew that Mummy would never let me go. "Nose to the grindstone," she would say, without even bothering to look up at me from her needle-point. I would feel guilty and naked just for asking. And, how I hated feeling guilty and naked!

That winter, when Daddy came home from Calcutta for his two month annual leave, he showed Mummy a photograph of an American woman he had met in an ancient temple located by a beach in Puri.

"Have you noticed that the pundits intentionally erect the doorway to the temple very low, so you end up bowing to the deities as you enter? It's a damn trick to get you to pray, even if that's not your intention," Daddy complained, with obvious authority on the subject.

It was kind of strange, but it was a photo just of the woman's hands. White skin, elegant fingers. Polished nails, no ring. I remember wondering about the whole thing. But, like other times when such questions would crop up in my mind, I let it be. Besides, Mummy seemed to be quite okay with it herself. Was it weird then, that I never wondered about my parents being in bed together?

Do other children think such crazy thoughts? Stop it, Nargis! You must never think about such stupid matters, I told myself.

Once, during that visit, I remember Daddy asking Mummy, "Mani, do you feel like it?"

All three of us used to sleep in the large bed together. They must have thought I was asleep. I tried not to stay awake for her answer, although I could swear I heard her say, "No."

Didn't Daddy often say that Mummy said "No" to everything? I reminded myself.

I am sure Daddy must have fondled me during that visit, just to get caught up. I remember it rather vaguely. Some of the events from this period in my life are still a blur and seem to be condensed into a compacted kernel of memory. I accidentally came upon a Harold Robbins romantic novel, *A Stone for Danny Fisher*, which Mummy was reading at the time. So now I discovered a whole new genre of writing that excited me. I did not understand everything, but it was fun, especially, because it was forbidden and exciting.

When Sanjay came home during school break, once again we read enthusiastically all summer long. We managed to carry an entire consignment of authors on the backseats our bikes from the library, all on top of each other, all in one load --- Sir Arthur Conan Doyle, James Hadley Chase, Agatha Christie, and Perry Mason, along with PG Wodehouse, George Bernard Shaw, and Oscar Wilde. And everyone else remotely legendary on whom we could lay our impatient hands. I had developed a writing style that earned me accolades from my English teacher, Sister Elizabeth, at school and from Daddy at home. On weekends, he would have me read my essays aloud to any wandering visitor who happened to descend upon our household.

"One day, Nargis will write the history of our family," he would boast to them with conviction and pride.

Those who do not have an exit strategy are termed captive audience. It felt vaguely uncomfortable, but distinctly flattering at the same time.

Studying was becoming easier than ever. Mummy would shake me out of bed at the crack of dawn so I could practice test papers in All Major Subjects (translation: All Subjects) on cheap rough books bought by the dozen. They soaked in ink like desert sand, until my fingers were smeared in the black liquid for days afterward. I never let my math teacher discover that the reason I aced each test was because I was playing out arithmetic symphonies even in my dreams! Excelling in Miss Sen's class was a perfect way to get back at her, since just a little over year ago, with a sham-show of that damn twig, she had singlehandedly declared me as the undisputed culprit of a crime I had never committed. I would strain my ears to listen in from the sidelines whenever she would boast to other students and teachers alike: "Nobody can complete a trigonometry paper as quickly and accurately as Nargis." And I would bite my nails down to their very roots as I crammed way into the night.

Despite my super human efforts, at report-card time, I still could not beat Pearl. My parents seemed to believe that the teachers favored her and I said nothing to challenge that notion. Even though in my heart, I was not sure that this was entirely true.

That summer, beautiful, buxom and blonde Aunty Kate walked through our front door. Daddy's handsome brother, Uncle Paul, had migrated to America several years ago and married there. I was thrilled to have an American for an aunt and was certain that one day I would also immigrate to that great country. Uncle would admonish Sanjay for calling her 'Kate' instead of 'Aunty.' It was around this time that Sanjay was going through his own teenage hormonal burst. He would ride the scooter with a new abandon, rounding off the curves on the road. Especially when his curvaceous Kate sat on the pillion seat behind him, holding on to him for dear life!

One day during this visit uncle asked Mummy about the family's stash of gold. The one that had been missing for so many years. Mummy became quite upset.

"Are you accusing us of stealing?" she replied angrily.

We did not see either Uncle Paul or Aunty Kate for the remainder of the trip.

Daddy was now transferred to the Punjab. There had been some talk about his retirement. With the three of us children still in school, he decided to serve for another couple of years. He took over as NCC (National Cadet Corp) officer in Bhatinda and was promoted to Brigadier. Both the promotion and the transfer were considered a copout by the military and there was no hope of another elevation in rank. Besides, because of eating spicy food from a roadside *dhaba* in Barrackpore, he had developed an ulcer on his tongue that refused to heal.

For a long time, I remember feeling that this was all my fault.

If only I'd been a good kid in boarding school, Mummy wouldn't have had to come and live with me in Lilliputian house and Daddy would've had wholesome home-cooked meals. Good God, Nargis! If only --- if only, you'd been a better child, I kept admonishing myself.

A year later, the ulcer became malignant and Daddy had to undergo surgery to excise a part of his tongue that was struck by the Big C. When caught in the act the mutated cells decided not to wander into the rest of his body. The surgeon was able to save the glands on his patient's neck that had escaped metastases. Daddy was all ready to become clean-shaven for the surgeon's scalpel. That would be a good excuse to get rid of his close-cropped moustache which he had anyway been somewhat ambivalent about all along. The verdict was complete remission.

After the surgery, for the rest of his life, Daddy would speak with a lisp that would soften his Ds, Ts and Js. Even when he was angry.

"People who envy us are saying I *thalk thoo* much, and *thath's* why *thhis* curse has *happenedh tho* me," he would say. "As you all know, people have always been *dhealous* of our family."

I think he means jealous, I'd decipher.

Initially it was hard to understand everything Daddy said. Slowly, I would get used to the soft consonants. Like I had gotten used to the rest of him.

It would become a part of him --- like the rest of him --- the good, and the bad.

ONCE BITTEN, TWICE SHY —
THIS DOG, TOO, MUST DIE

The summer vacation of my thirteenth year was a good-bad summer. Our whole family was together with Daddy in Bhatinda. That is where we met that Evil Temptress, NCC Captain Mohandeep. She was a petite but ugly woman, unusually affectionate but sexually uninhibited, with a history of minor transgressions that followed her in and out of other people's homes, where she would surreptitiously find her way in to becoming a part of a family unit. Like in *our* home. And *our* family. She would dispassionately fawn on all of us and help Mummy with every conceivable planned or accidental chore. Very quickly, she attained the stature of a general hanger-on in our household. The woman gave long clingy hugs, but after she had the nerve to pinch my breasts at least a couple of times I learned to keep this wiccan at arm's length. And I mean, not just figuratively. A couple of years later, she was transferred to nearby Tehri in the hills. It was rumored that this consummate philanderer continued to play charades with other women's husbands and even dared to have an affair with the colonel there. She had never failed the practiced strategy: Bait and switch, switch and bait. Thenceforth, in our house, she was referred to as 'that loose woman.'

June is probably the hottest month in Bhatinda. A steamy scorcher, the likes of which are commonly experienced in idling Turkish baths. When the dog-day afternoons alternate between painful sweltering heat through raging dust storms and pervasive sticky humidity during unrelenting downpours. Even the bugs look stressed from bugging you all summer long.

This was when Sanjay and I decided that we had finally found our calling: we would become prolific writers. That too, in a super-great hurry. Not like the ones who die from living like packrats in wobbly damp cardboard boxes and feeding on thin soggy crackers. But the ones who would, with due process, be awarded the Pulitzer

200 · Bulbul Bahuguna

Prize and overnight become world famous the entire globe over. We wrote vigorously all summer long, and would hide our masterpiece manuscripts from each other --- lest we should give away our ideas prematurely, or succumb to blatant plagiarism. Sanjay's protagonist was named Golden Tooth, a stocky pigeon-chested Napoleon lookalike army officer with lewd beady eyes who flashed precious heavy metal in every smile to foist his presence. He would come over to our house unannounced, stand in the doorway shifting in place, look straight past us with his shifty gaze and sheepishly suggest that we all have fresh lime sodas to celebrate life! When, what he actually fancied was a cool glass of refreshing frothy Golden Eagle beer! He had a couple of wimpy kids who accidentally fell out of the backseat from his rickety car on a bumpy country road. The dumb man did not realize that he lost his progeny until he had finally reached the next town! When he eventually drove back on a near-empty tank to look for them, they had found a new life. I, meanwhile, was writing about an orphan girl who bounced from family to foster homes, through back alleys to deserted bus stops, from abandoned barns to country inns, in an attempt to find her real parents. Strangely though, in that process, she becomes a recluse and gets lost herself.

It took a better part of that summer for us to realize that we would probably never become adequately famous this way in a super-great hurry. So we went to Plan B, and took to target shooting with Daddy's point 22 rifle. This is how I picked up from where I had left off in Indore, when I had first learned to hunt. We shot pigeons, crows, and sparrows. We shot every being in the animal kingdom that flew, hopped, or crawled. One day, by the old well near the house, we came upon a horrifically gaunt ill-looking dog with his shriveled tongue dripping sick saliva, his pokey bones protruding precariously through his ribcage, and his long and emaciated guts trailing behind him as he walked toward Death.

Poor creature, I thought. No one deserves to live such a miserable life.

"Shoot first, ask later," Daddy had often coached.

In order to curtail his misery, I shot the dog a few times over. It was a clean bulls-eye every time! I riddled his dead corpse with a volley of bullets and emptied the entire cartridge into his body as it jumped with each shot. Then he flipped up high, rolled over, and croaked! I felt a few inches taller. I had become a Savior. I had saved a terminally ill animal from an inevitable and painfully drawn-out death. Sanjay never stopped broadcasting about his little sister's first attempt at euthanasia.

"You should've seen the poor dog take off when he kicked the bucket! All the way to his heavenly abode!" he bragged to everyone.

My brother had started to develop Daddy's wit and told the story with his usual Sanju-flair, punctuated only with our laughs and my sense of pomposity.

That summer, Daddy called me to his bed every night. Nobody questioned it. Least of all me. Not only was I his favorite and the best-looking among his children, but I was also becoming the topnotch student at school. As usual, Mummy was often in bed with us.

I hope she's asleep, I remember thinking. I hope she hasn't seen or heard anything, I was cautious.

I learned to slide off my bra over my shoulders under the sheets, then close my eyes and wait. As usual, my body was there, but my mind had left through the back door. A few times Daddy even tried to kiss me on my mouth, but I would not let him. Somehow, that seemed all too gross and would make it all too real. Besides, his mousse-primed moustache would prick my lips.

It was around this time when we visited Mummy's sister, Aunty Hem, at her farmhouse in Namgarh, famous for loud mouths, crass jokes and raucous feasting. This is where a portly distant male relative lived, who was renowned in the entire region for his expertise in chopping off roosters' heads. First, he would skin the entire fluttering bird using but two fingers, with feathers flying into his open mouth as he laughed tirelessly. Then in one clean sweep, he would crack open the frantic bird's chest and arrogantly reveal a dying heart that was still fretfully beating. He was visibly proud of this simple country feat. *Jaats* are known to take visible pride in such simple country feats.

This is also where I got into a milk-chugging contest with my male cousins, Sunny and Guddoo, better known for their well-practiced udder-squeezing technique by employing a thumb and forefinger to squeeze the teats in alternating rhythm in order to direct the stream of fresh warm milk straight into their open mouths! I wanted so desperately to win, to be the best at everything. I was certain that I would beat those poor country bumpkins. Daddy would shower me with praise and whenever the tale would be told and retold over the ensuing years, it would gather steam and continue to be polished and embellished in my favor as did most other stories about anyone from our family.

This time it was not to be. I lost miserably to my country cousins and threw up my arrogance for a long time afterward.

What a stupid country sport! I concluded.

There was talk about Mummy's widowed sister, Aunty Chandri, getting out of hand.

There was a vague mention by Daddy, "I've seen her acting fresh with some male relatives without any qualms or reservations. It looks like Chandri is going astray and will surely bring shame to us all."

I do not know what actually happened. Maybe, nobody does. It is a strange macabre story and as strange macabre stories go, her death is shrouded in mystery. I have heard a few versions, but something foul probably occurred that night in Namgarh.

Something foul *did* occur that night in Namgarh.

Nobody knows the truth except Aunty Chandri. But she is not here to confirm it. Her loud mouth was silenced forever. Daddy said that she had gulped down some Old Monk rum spiked with poison on the previous night and woke up dead.

"In *our* family, we kill girls who become loose. We get rid of them. We bury them alive," Daddy told us with authority and pride, while I squirmed inside wondering if this would ever happen to me.

I had also heard somewhat vaguely that Nana, in all probability, not only knew about these events as they were unfolding but also approved the final decree in order to bury the family dishonor. It is just possible that he might even have secretly solicited the murder of his own daughter. Nobody confirmed or denied the story. Nobody was caught. Nobody talks about it anymore. It is an inconvenient truth that went up with the flames at her hurried, sparsely-attended funeral.

The one other event, which also happened on that same night in Namgarh, I will remember till my dying day. But unlike Aunty Chandri, I woke up alive.

Daddy had had a few drinks and asked me to come to his bed.

million red blood corpuscles, the ones I had been studying about in biology.

Daddy lost no opportunity in commending me on my performance in final exams.

"Think of the lotus flower," he would say over and over again lest, of course, I should forget yet one more time. "Its roots are stuck in muck and sludge deep down in the muddy waters, but eventually it rises to the surface and blooms to become this stunning flower. Make sure you grow up to be this beautiful blossom. Make sure you emerge way above water level and leave the dirt behind. *You know what I'm talking about.* I know you have it in you, Nargis. I know you can do it. If anyone can, *you* can."

I would look wide-eyed at Daddy and take in his praises, along with everything else he uttered. Daddy believed in me. In return, I believed in everything Daddy did.

"And remember my dear, *nobody* knows you better than I do," he would add, quickly and purposefully.

Instantly, I would look away. I could never openly acknowledge the truth about our relationship.

Returning his glance would make everything too real

"Nargis, you can become anybody you want to be. Remember, you live only once. There are a lot of slips between the cup and the lip. Believe me, you're a happier person when you can enjoy old age with the least number of regrets. You will agree, I know a lot about life. Look, my hair did not turn gray overnight. Rome was not built in one day. Mani, my dear, I'm confident that there'll come a day when this girl will make us both proud. I know she'll live up to everything we've dreamed about for her. I've an excellent understanding of human behavior. And *nobody* understands our daughter, Nargis, better than me."

And in how many ways!

With this weekly reminder, I plugged on. My nails got shorter, the cuticles more bloody.

"The gates to success start closing down on you without a warning," he would caution. "Only a few people are allowed in, you know. Make sure you're the first to go through those Golden Gates. Remember, they garland only the foremost person who enters through them."

I would picture myself sailing through the Golden Gates smiling and waving with casual abandon, with marigold garlands hanging copiously around my neck all the way down to the ground and trailing behind me.

Since we were in the same standard, Sanjay and I studied together during the holidays. I pushed him around, because I believed I learned faster than he did and mostly because he let me. He did not seem to mind my assuming the role of his coach, which I took on with great zeal and a new sense of responsibility toward both of us. Most likely, Sanjay acquiesced to my unspoken authority because he thought that this was an acceptable price to pay for improving his scores. Especially after that last report card, when his teacher called him a 'floundering square peg in a round hole!' Besides, I had Daddy on my side. A few years later, one of our private tutors would even name his daughter after me.

Daddy retired from the military and was now spending his plentiful spare time expounding on the meaning of life and the essence of god. I would sit in on these discourses generally meant for the general public, or anyone who mistakenly chanced to wander into our home and happened to be remotely within --- or just past --- hearing range. Even if that person did not have the time, or the inclination, to participate.

Daddy knew when he had a completely caged audience and was never in a great hurry to get his point across. He expressed his largely unfiltered and unadulterated beliefs in a long-winded circuitous manner with grand candor and absolute truthiness. It was critical to enrich the lives of the common populace with his well-thought-through and finessed-to-perfection philosophy of life. Daddy did not do too well with interruptions either. And even less with a difference of opinion.

Daddy's philosophy of life deserves a separate chapter.

GODLINESS AND GODLESSNESS

"I pity those who believe in God. They are weak and selfish: weak because they don't believe in themselves and selfish because they always want something from God for themselves. From dawn to dusk, the petty shopkeeper *Bania*, that glib salesman, conjures up a cock-and-bull story, about wares that are typically suspect or fake, thus cheating other people and swindling the government of monies owed to both with black lies and white lies. Lies of omission and lies of commission. He has mastered them all. First he fabricates a story about his merchandise, then he butters up your wife and sweet-talks her into buying a substandard bill of goods. Before you know what hit you, he's ripped you off! Remember, it's the crooked finger that can scoop the most ghee out of the canister.

"Then, every single night, this charlatan broker folds his hands, closes his eyes and prays looking skyward. As if God is somewhere up there hiding behind the clouds. The conman abandons his conscience at the temple door and bows down to lay prostrate on the floor before a mute and motionless stone idol he calls God. That would be Ganesh, the one who has an elephant's head with its trunk swaying on an overflowing potbelly. The money launderer begs Lord Ganesh to forgive him, save his spirit and redeem his soul. Forgive him in one clean sweep. Just like that! Con artist! Scumbag! After all, man is the most important creation of God, so obviously God must want to forgive him. Poor, dumb, foolish man! He believes that no one has the power to save him, except the Almighty. Another fellow being would just stiff him up.

"Then, the very next morning, guess what? The Ponzi artist, this creature of habit goes through the entire routine again, of deceiving and double-crossing his fellow beings and lining his pockets with OPM --- Other People's Money. So, now here's another new day to ask for forgiveness. And another new day to wipe that slate clean for tomorrow. That damn slate has to be wiped clean at the end of every single day of his life. It's quite a job, as you can tell. Then to crown his duplicity, he prays for a son. When he's thus blessed, he feels as if none other than Lord Krishna's avatar has stepped into his house. A son did not happen by divine intervention, my dear friends. It was just by sheer luck, chance, and coincidence. Then back to the half-truths, hogwash, and hyperbole --- The cycle never ends.

"But, as science teaches us, there's no such thing as a spirit and there's certainly no such bunkum as an afterlife. My friends, I'm sorry to be the first one to inform you that after you die, your lifeless carbon atoms will instantly return to dust. In a pantheon way, the best way to explain this is that there's nothing beyond the beyond. Ostensibly, death is mysterious and final. Now it's simply impossible for the human mind to comprehend the end of life. Or accept its irreversibility. So rebirth is another grand myth man creates, simply, because he's afraid of death. As you all know, the greatest fear is fear itself. Reincarnation makes man as omnipresent as the God he has himself created. But, as I'm sure you're well aware, man is an intelligent being. He tries to stay on the right side of reason. But he's also known to be a fool by choice. So in order to cope with the finality of death, he extrapolates from manufactured and mismatched facts and creates the concept of life after death. It's total religious hokum! I must also tell you that there is no such thing as Heaven and Hell. Or Hell, Fire, and Damnation. As you can see, the very concept of death is an insult to man's intelligence.

"And that Darwin? The man was a pure genius. 'It's all about survival of the fittest,' he told the world. And the Christian church went up in arms! He taught us that the living cells have evolved through the millenniums of time. We all came from the apes. You and I. And our dog Noodles! Now people say God made the world a perfect place. But we all know there's enough chaos around us. Even human cells are subjected to the frailty of sickness, old age, and death. Cancer does happen, when a cell becomes its own evil twin. And shit does fall. With gravity. Even God cannot reverse that. Knowledge is power. And reasoning is freeing. That's what makes us different from the animals.

"So let me ask you the quintessential question: Who created whom first? Cause or effect? Did God create man, or did man create God in his own likeness and image? To me, it sounds like circular logic. When there're gaps in the gap. Pray may I ask, do you know why God is a man and not an animal, plant, or lifeless object? And then, why's he a white man who looks like other white Christians in the Western World? Why is he not Oriental, black, or homo? Not to belabor the point, but each faith has its own image of God. And by the way, we Hindus excel at this by far. We have countless Gods and Goddesses. As if we're buying an option on God himself!

"If God is Truth, then what's the truth about God? Is God an It, Him, Her, Them, or They? How do you know which one is the real one? I've never met two people who've the same concept of God and His Prophets, or the Devil and other demonic entities. Or for that matter the same idea about the soul, the spirit, or afterlife. Truth be told, reincarnation is another clever myth created by man. Even cats don't have nine lives! Every person has his own brand of spirituality and his own way to bastardize spiritual preaching and wisdom from the sages. And how I detest those who wear their religion on their sleeve! It's the new *maulvi* fresh out of the *Madrassa* who says the loudest prayer. Now let me tell you what I think of the agnostics amongst us. In my mind, they're atheists without balls! But jokes aside, I must ask you this. Why is God not a woman? I see that you are quiet. You don't have an answer. Never mind, I'm not surprised. Then, let *me* tell you why. When man first created God, people lived in a primitive patriarchal society where man was physically stronger and therefore more privileged than a woman. He could overpower her, even in lust. And I'm not being facetious about it either. Have you ever heard of consenting rape or a man getting sexually violated by the opposite sex? Man is an animal. So man created God to tame his own animal lust."

There was not a chance of anyone getting in a single word edgeways.

"Now, don't get me wrong. Those wise men who we call God probably did exist. Jesus, Mohammad, and Moses were probably real people with real flesh and blood like yours and mine. They also lived and laughed, struggled and died, just like other real people. Let me ask you this. Why did Jesus have to die on a cross to save the world? Did people stop sinning after his crucifixion?

"Then let's talk about Lord Ram. From mythology, we all know the popular story about how he abandoned his wife for seven long years simply on a whim. And he wants to teach *us* about the sanctity of marriage and the concept of forgiveness? Yes, these sages did come at difficult times in history, to create societal laws so that people could coexist more peacefully. For example, 'love thy neighbor,' and 'don't covet thy neighbor's wife' became very useful in creating harmony in families and preventing conflict or war.

"As an aside, you and I know of the countless useless wars that have been fought over religion. Brave, fearless, and able-bodied men have led naive and simpleminded people into battle over a holy book. Look at the three blood brothers, the Christians, the Jews, and the Muslims, feuding over their mother's milk! And those poor Israelites! They've suffered enough stark injustice to last them a lifetime! Hounded and hunted down, persecuted and wronged, generation after generation after generation. For centuries, they've been running from pillar to post looking for a home. God knows, they've been denied even the smallest of sanctuaries on Earth. As you know, I've always been a champion for the underdog."

Daddy would pause only to taken another swig of Red Knight whiskey with a dash of soda.

"Based on what was relevant for those ancient times, wise men, not Messiahs, created rules for people to abide by in order to simplify their lives and better the society of that time. The Jews were told not to eat pork because pigs live in dirt and squalor and carry a host of life-threatening diseases that kill man. Mohammed told Muslim men that they could have four wives at a given time, because there were very few men left after the battles to care for the multitude of war widows. Guru Gobind Singh told the Sikhs to wear their hair long, so they could easily identify each other when they fought the Muslims. The Hindus don't eat beef because cows produce milk, which is a form of excellent animal protein. As you can see, these laws were relevant for the times when they were created. They have no relevance in today's world."

All this makes a lot of sense, I'd consider. Daddy has always been ahead of the times.

"Now, if you look at them closely, all religious are almost equal. No religion sanctifies the killing of other people. No religion tells you to lie, steal, or rape. Man assigned God as the Creator of all rules, so people would take Him seriously. Besides, man is essentially a weak being and has a need to be led. He's enslaved by the very notion of slavery. He creates a Being more powerful than himself, who he can follow blindly and turn to in times of trouble. Even if this Pied Piper leads him into Ridiculous River! Thus, belief in God has become the best coping skill known to mankind and also the most profitable business enterprise on Earth."

Daddy would punctuate his monologue by alternately stroking his man-breasts on either side. He would twirl his otherwise rigid mousse-styled moustache and coax it into pointed ends so they would indeed horizontally face away from each other.

"Now, I do have some questions for this person you call God. First of all, I'd like to say to Him, 'If you're there, come out and show me! If you're listening, give me a sign! Like thunder. Or lightning. Or something!' Now, if He's indeed a good God like you say He is, why then does He tolerate the evil that goes on in the world? Why does He suffer poverty, suffering, disease and death among the gentlest and holiest of people? Why does he tolerate the premature demise of innocent children, who do not even know right from wrong?

"You tell me, 'He does that to test man.'

"Well, if He's indeed the Almighty benign God, like you say you believe, why can't He find a better way to test man in a manner so nobody gets hurt? And, if He's indeed an intelligent God, again, like you say He is, and knows how you'll react by reading your innermost thoughts, like you say He can, then why does He have to test you in the first place?

"You tell me, 'To teach people a lesson.'"

Daddy loves to ask questions and then answer them himself.

"Why, then He's a mean and evil God, who does mean and evil things to human beings just because He wants to get a rise out of testing them! I'm sure, you get the drift. After all, you're a smart person with a brain that can think for itself.

"You say three billion believers around the world couldn't be wrong. To that I say, 'There's enough insanity on this planet.' You say, 'He's a secure God.' 'Why then,' I ask, 'does He demand that you proclaim His name and sing His praises? And proselytize to spread His teachings? And sacrifice in His name?' You also say, 'He's all powerful.' Why then, in the name of reason, can't He do all these things Himself since He's indeed omnipotent? If you were to ask me, He's a jealous and selfish God who cannot tolerate if you pray to another one. He is in fact the anti-nemesis of God."

Time to shake the drink and make the ice cubes joggle in agreement.

"You say God keeps track of each and every human being's deeds on Earth. So, if He's such a busy person, why's He interested in a humble person like myself who's merely performing his duty of raising a good family and protecting his country from foes? I've seen men killed in war and when I went to examine their bodies, to my utter shock and dismay, I found that a bullet had gone right through the pocket-version of the holy *Bible, Koran,* or *Gutka* lying safe and sound in a breast-pocket. The irony of it all is that just behind that sacred book the poor soldier had saved photos of his innocent children. As luck would have it, the bullet went straight through their smiling faces, too! *Why do bad things happen to good people?*

"After I die, I want to meet this man you call God. If He does exist, I'm sure that I'll be the first one He will want to garland. Not those God-fearing black-marketers, *Banias,* politicians and hypocrites! He must know a good man when he sees one. What do you think He'll say to me when we finally meet? But you can bet that there are a lot of questions I've saved up for Him.

"From your faces, I can tell that you have a lot of questions, too. It's so wonderful to have an enquiring mind. That's what promotes the progress of mankind and makes us different from animals. As you can see my daughter, Nargis, is never afraid to ask questions."

Usually the audience would have no questions. At least none that they felt confident enough to ask openly or assured enough of getting an unbiased answer. So they would put on an appearance of listening with unremitting rapt attention, even if they did not understand some of the words because of Daddy's lisp.

"We hardly know anything about our own Milky Way," Daddy would continue. "We don't even know how the neurons in our mind actually fire or what lies beyond the fireball at the center of our Earth. We certainly don't know what exists beyond the boundaries of our universe. Where does our universe start? Where does it end? Or does it end? There's a lot we know nothing about. So, how do we know so much about God, someone we cannot see, hear, touch, smell or feel?

Pray may I ask, how did we become such a high authority on this subject in such quick order? But religious conviction has an answer for everything, doesn't it? So the cleric comes up with the notion that God is an amorphous Being. He's shapeless, formless, faceless and nameless.

"We think everything must have a beginning and an end, don't we? Like every story and fable we've ever heard has a beginning and an end. Like birth and death. We were born to somebody and that somebody was born to somebody else, who in turn was created by another somebody else. This is the cycle of life. This is how our simple minds think. Just to make it easier on ourselves, we say that everyone was created by this same somebody. We call that somebody God. Such is the limitation of our human mind. We believe that He is the ultimate Creator and that no one created *Him*. God is an answer to our ignorance. Lenin rightly said, 'Religion is an opium for the masses.'

"Some people have told me that belief in God will keep man meek and humble. That's both a myth and a fallacy. As far as *I'm* concerned, the vastness of the Universe and the smallness of man keeps our grandiosity in check. I'm sorry to inform you, my dear friends, that man is just a microscopic speck in this Universe of ours, and God doesn't care a hoot!"

How spot on! Nobody can say it better than Daddy, I'd conclude.

"Other people insist that there must be a God, because, 'Look at the order and purpose in the universe,' they say. 'Look at the order in each molecule and the purpose of each human cell. Everything has a reason,' they claim. 'What order? What purpose?' I ask them. The same order that causes meteors to crash into Earth? The same order that causes earthquakes to swallow thousands of innocent people? The same order that causes the DNA of a single cell to go berserk and become cancerous. I call that *disorder*."

Daddy could easily ignore the fact that he was repeating himself and smile at his own eloquence.

"Some people think they're holier than thou because they've a hotline to God --- those immoral priests, pundits and *maulvies*. They're all hypocrites, one and all! That obsession with idolatry! If they're indeed better human beings than you and me, then why should you bow to them? And please, educate me. Why must they wear those special clothes, purple, white, or saffron in color? Why must they sit on adult highchairs that are elevated way above us simple people? In my opinion, they should set an example and *sit* with you, wash *your* feet and serve *you* --- and not vice versa. Only then will they be truly God's men.

"Allow me to recapitulate. I've seen many religious leaders chanting in God's name, rocking their bodies back and forth like programmed robots. They're all a bunch of crock! Loathsome holy men with fat bellies who hide their deceitful faces and dubious intentions behind flowing white beards while they prey on the congregation. Not P-R-A-Y for the congregation. Mark the difference in my words! Do you think this devout preacher really understands everything that he's chanting about? I've often caught him looking askance from the corner of his pious eyes to keep track of the *dakshana* collections for the day, or trying to ascertain who's the most attractive woman amongst the flock. Most times, these holy men are indeed the worst sex offenders in society. Those predators! Those child molesters! If there is a God, He should have the power to stop their hearts right during the act!

"And those soothsayers and astrologers? That's a bunch of hocus-pocus as well. When they can't even predict their own death, how can they foretell *your* future? It's rather pathetic that the human mind is so feeble and frail. And so easily fooled.

"Nargis, can you bring down Bertrand Russell's book titled, *Why I Am Not a Christian* from our library and read a few important paragraphs that I've underlined for the benefit of everyone here?"

After I would dutifully read a few pages in real earnest, feeling at least half as intelligent as my father, Daddy could resume his Sunday sermon.

"By the way, I'm willing to learn. I've always wanted to enrich my life with new ideas. As you know, I do have an open mind. Now if there's any part of this you didn't understand, I'll be happy to go over it again with you."

Usually, most people in the audience readily claimed that they got it the first time and politely declined a recap.

After he had exhausted the topic on God, Daddy would go on to educate his listeners about the principles of Marxism and the underpinnings of a superior economic and social system. The ones detailed in the *Communist Manifesto*: a perfect society through a logical and equitable redistribution of wealth.

It all made sense: 'From each based on his capability, to each based on his need.' It seemed so humane. So just. So right. Even more so when Daddy would spend an entire afternoon playing to the gallery.

"Mark my words. One day, the whole world will become Communist. It's inevitable. It *has* to. Look at the multitudes of the underprivileged with a wolf waiting at the threshold of their huts. It's strange that the moneyed continue to gather more wealth both in good economic times and in bad. The rich simply cannot go on existing peacefully on their lonely islands of bounty totally oblivious to the sea of poverty around them rising with each wave. Soon, we'll all be totally submerged and drown in it together! In our society, even today, we're simply mortified to breathe in the same air as the untouchables. It's a goddamn shame! Did you know that the first to touch The Constitution of India was an untouchable? Because he is the one who wrote it! You've all heard of Ambedkar, haven't you? I'm sure you've noticed that whenever a pundit performs a prayer service, he leaves his shoes at your doorstep. That is a signal for the untouchables to wait outside. The holy man must be sniffing salts! I do believe that the day is not far off when our house will be taken over by honest citizens of society, those sweating and toiling peasants, rickshaw pullers and *dhobis*. If you were to ask me, this Red Fort really belongs to the common man. Frankly, our family of five should be allotted just one room in this mansion. Now, I'm not being disingenuous. I really do mean this. I'll be the first one to greet the masses with open arms. That, my dear friends, is the absolute truth."

Sitting in on these discourses, I started to imbibe most of Daddy's ideas, which he elaborated with occasional real life examples thrown in with a touch of sarcasm and rhetoric license. Although, I am not entirely sure that I quite relished the thought of our entire family being all crammed up in just a single room of the Red Fort, with street urchins romping around by the dozen; squatting around with their emaciated bodies draped in tattered rags; fixating their ownership-glazed eyes on our shiny Kota-stone veranda and sliding synchronously up and down our finely polished teak staircase banister --- the one decorated with metallic musical notes --- by hugging it with their spindly legs.

When he fell short of words, which was pretty rare, I would carry on the discussion where Daddy had left off supporting his arguments and vision for a better world. He could go on for hours. All he needed was half an audience, albeit with nominal attention.

Sometimes on weekends, Daddy would trap me on long walks that I could not easily abort.

"A penny for your thoughts, Nargis," he would say usually somewhere at midpoint, catching me completely off guard.

For the lesser half of a second, I would stop in my tracks. Then as if on cue, I would continue the lecture where he had ended it last week. At other times, the topic would shift to the opposite gender.

I was always stumped by this next curveball, "Nargis, tell me, what kind of boys do *you* like?"

I would stumble on a pebble in my path and mumble something nondescript under my breath. This would usually not stop Daddy from continuing on this sore topic, which always made me squeamish and uncomfortable

"Nargis, you know, it'll be hard for you to find someone who can match your beauty and brains. If you were to ask me, the only young men I really respect who are truly worthy of you are those who are entirely self-made. Men who have made something of their lives by sheer hard work and intellect. Not those, who've twiddled their toes and fritted away an inheritance passed down by generations of exploiters. By the way, there's nothing wrong in staying single. I agree with you. A lot of famous women in history couldn't have achieved what they did during their lifetime had they gotten married."

"No Daddy, I don't like *any* boy. Not a single one. And, by the way, I will *never* marry," I would say hurriedly. "Believe me, I just want to study hard, be successful and make something of my life. Something that will make Mummy and you proud. That's all what I really care about."

Somehow, this seemed to satisfy Daddy. At least, for just then.

Why are parents the easiest people to fool?

It would give Daddy an opportunity to continue his ramblings on his belief system --- one that was slowly also becoming mine.

FINAL CURTAIN CALL

I was now developing bold new ideas on Economics, Society, and God, most of which were not quite popular at school. I remember talking about my father with classmates, portraying him as a supremely intelligent man with an infinite vision. Different from all other fathers. As if he was God himself.

In my new found boldness, I tested other waters too. My parents had zeroed in on a *Jaat* physician with academic promise from a nice family quite like our own for Anjali to marry. He came complete with a unibrow, an unruly moustache drooping over crowded crooked teeth with no wiggle room, and a beard neatly trimmed to make a statement under his chin, et al.

"He's too much of a *Jaat*," was my brief commentary on the matter.

Anjali's heart was spoken for. She was dating Anil, a neighbor's son, who would casually strum *I Saw Her Standing There* on his guitar every time he saw her standing there, just behind our fence. When he ventured past the doorway of Lilliputian house for the first time asking for her hand in marriage, carrying his besotted bleeding heart in his *Bania* hands, the poor soul did not know that he was walking straight into Father's Den. Daddy reflexively slapped this eager and credulous suitor at least twice!

"I don't believe in this hocus-pocus caste system," was Daddy's succinct explanation. "But, you must know that any man who'll marry any daughter of mine must be stellar!"

The proposed union was definitely a betrayal of our family. Most of all, it was a betrayal of Daddy and of everything that he believed. There was nothing right about this ill-fated *Bania* and there was nothing redeeming about his family either, even though his father was a wealthy merchant. The union would surely stall the ascendancy of our family forever. There was no other way to think about it. At least, no other way that made sense.

In the midst of the tumult that ensued, Daddy called Anjali a slut, a whore and a barrage of similar epithets. She had no place in his house. She was setting a terrible example for her younger brother and sister, who, due to our unspoken empathy for her as is universally expected of the relationship, were also thrown out of the house into the front yard during a pesky rain shower. There, in full public view, we collectively licked our wounds in the presence of unknown but dazed passersby. It was a miserable scene all the way round, with collateral damage saved only by the sunset. The three of us crept back into the house, hoping against hope that on the path to our beds we would not accosted by Daddy in another sequel of rage. An inevitable preamble to a painfully memorized should've-could've-would've lecture with no end in sight on how his children would amount to nothing and nobody.

The next day, I wore the only *salwar-kameez* from my skimpy wardrobe. On an impulse, I drove my scooter to meet the parents of Dr. Unibrow Crooked Teeth, pretending to be Anjali.

Without losing any time, after a cursory but abrupt *Namaste* greeting, I blurted out, "I'm sorry to inform you, but I refuse to marry your son because I'm in love with someone else!"

They looked stunned, as if they had been shot in their bellies by a passing sniper with a stun gun! At least, a few times over! Reeling from sheer hemorrhaging shock, they did not even consider inviting me to take a seat in their drawing room for the purpose of verifying my identity.

Needless to say, we never heard from that nice *Jaat* family again. I had taken a risk that Daddy would never find out. I was right. Daddy never did find out. Actually, nobody did. Not even my sister.

My only motive was to protect Anjali. Even though she was older, I felt an unspoken responsibility and loyalty to support her in her forbidden love. There is something heroic about rooting for an underdog. I was starting to feel empowered in my ability to challenge Daddy, even if not directly. I was becoming strong again. I could do anything. *And* get away with it. Furthermore, in my last year in high school, I was elected by the faculty to become a Prefect and Assistant Head Girl. Much to my chagrin, Pearl was chosen to be the Head Girl.

Things seemed to be evolving rapidly for our family. This is when

Daddy did the unthinkable and unpardonable act of betrayal to the legacy of our *Jaat* heritage by initiating the sale of parcels of the land passed down by his ancestors.

"*Jaats* have been landlords for centuries before us. We never sell ancestral land. It's worse than selling your son."

Why's selling a son the second-worst thing? I'll never understand the connection.

This turned out to be the best advice Daddy would ever accept. Buying a lucrative limestone quarry in the foothills, an hour away from Dehradun, would change the financial standing of our family forever. Not only that, Daddy ended up making Uncle Gupta his business partner.

"These *Banias*, they *understand* money. They *breathe* money. They know everything there is to know about how to invest wisely. Only Gupta is clever enough to advise me, because of the generations of shrewd business acumen that runs in his blood," Daddy would concede, albeit a tad reluctantly. "This real estate is real," he confirmed. "Believe me, this will be a sound foundation for our family for generations to come," Daddy predicted.

Daddy was right. He named the mine Terra Firma.

During summer break, I started to regularly go over to the quarry site to hose down the newly laid concrete foundation of worker's sheds in order to firm it up, just like Sanjay did. I was like a son. Nobody dared stop me. I did not need a payback. The exhilaration of being like a son was intoxicating enough.

"Look, my children have no qualms about working shoulder to shoulder with the labor class," Daddy would tell family and friends with pride. "That's how I've raised them. I wish the whole world would do the same. We must not look down on the unfortunate underclass, simply because they're poor manual workers. A class society never lasts. It's just not economically practical. Look what happened to feudalism. It fell flat on its face. That's why capitalism will also fail," he would predict with certainty.

I supported Daddy in his big ideas. And he let me rule my little world.

Our assortment of cousins had not done quite as well. Everything I knew about them spelled ORDINARY. One in particular, slovenly, morbidly obese and slow on the uptake was Orlick, who had discovered the joys of dabbling in bootlegging! Sanjay had christened him after the loutish Dickensian character with a similar name and a shoddier reputation. Daddy was known to extrapolate the truth from observing a person's face. He would put Orlick on the spot, literally forcing him to fabricate a yarn in order to save face. Daddy pointed out how our cousin had stepped into his own labyrinth of lies just as he was still not quite done weaving it.

"He should stop digging himself in a hole, when he has reached the bottom of the pit!" was Daddy's sound advice.

Just because we're cousins doesn't mean we're related to each other! I convinced myself.

Senior Cambridge exams came and went. I studied into the wee hours of the morning, until I would feel lightheaded from my frontal lobes throbbing with an overload of knowledge and shriveling from a depletion of neurotransmitters. For good luck, Mummy would give me a spoonful of sugar before I took each exam. When the results were announced both Pearl and I got 5 points, but I beat her in the overall percentage! So finally, Pearl was fading into the debris of my past.

Maybe, my parents were right. Maybe our teachers *did* favor her, after all! I managed to persuade myself.

The impossible had finally happened! I topped the Indian School Certificate examination from the entire state! I felt on top of the world! People from the great state of UP often think UP *is* the world. I was flying high as a kite and gulping helium by the quantum as I ascended, turning cartwheels in a sky with no ceiling. Nothing could hold me down. Not even my past.

Life is sweet, sweet, sweet! I can do anything now. I'll never go back to being second best, I told myself, again, and again, and yet again.

Around the same time, I was offered a scholarship to pursue Literature at the University of Cambridge in England.

"This means taking a huge risk," Daddy advised. "You can never be assured of making a decent livelihood as a writer. After all, everyone has a story to tell. Now, I'm sure you must've heard of the countless unpublished writers who've died in their attics, unknown and unsung. They're often found slumped over their own manuscripts that never made it past the slush pile. And there are millions of poets who've been buried in a pauper's grave."

Besides, truth be told, our family would have to pitch in towards the tuition.

"It's much safer to pursue medicine," Daddy suggested. "That's definitely the best career for women in India today."

As always, Daddy's right, I quickly agreed.

The admission procedure for the premedical program at the Women's College could commence only after I had officially accepted the first spot there. As I approached the college boundary wall I imagined that I was seeing those Golden Gates, the same ones that Daddy used to talk about during all my years growing up, opening up only for me. Without my even having to press the buzzer!

Before Sanjay and I started the one year pre-medical program, he attended the local Men's College, our family moved into the Red Fort. We finally settled in this beautiful and expansive home, yet I can hardly remember enjoying my time there since all my brother and I did was cram that entire year long. We would start long before sunrise and go way past sunset. We owned only one set of textbooks, so naturally we studied together. This was not only easy on the pocket but also the sensible thing to do since I had voluntarily, obviously without due process, assumed the role of Sanjay's tutor. Simply because it was expected of me to do no less.

One morning, after Mummy woke me up at three in the morning, and I, in turn, had shaken Sanjay out of bed, much to my dismay I discovered that he had forgotten our shared chemistry textbook at his friend Johnny's house. I insisted he retrieve it immediately. And I mean *now*!

Poor Sanju. He rode his scooter to Johnny's home in the darkness of the cold thick fog. Sucking in his pride he gingerly rang the doorbell, only to be chased by an untamed angry pit bull that had been rudely shaken out of a deep snooze!

When Sanjay finally returned home, somewhat shook up but textbook firmly in hand, my wrath was bubbling over. In a fit of rage, I instantly tore the chemistry book in half!

"Jeez, Sanju! How *could* you? How could you be so careless? Do you want my marks to tank like yours?" I was livid! "Here, you take

Organic Chemistry and I'll keep the Inorganic portion for now!"

My brother had wasted my precious morning study time. My grades would suffer because of his irresponsible behavior. He did not deserve my well intentioned guidance. From now on, he would have to fend for himself and suffer his grades alone and in silence, with Daddy's shadow lurking not too far behind him!

Nobody questioned me anymore. Even our parents did not think that I was being unreasonable. After all, was I not the more conscientious one between the two of us?

The events of that morning are now chalked up to another funny little story of our childhood. Besides, Sanjay and I did patch up the next day. Even today, he relates it with a splash of spice and a dash of humor.

We were, after all, buddies who would walk around the house chanting in sib-ship synchrony:

"Friends, Romans, countrymen ---
The evil that men do lives after them:
The good is oft interred with their bones."

At the end of the year, I swept away all the awards on Prize Day, with my parents gloating over me right up in front row. I had my picture taken with the Governor's wife, just like Daddy had had his photograph clicked in the honorable presence of another Governor at another time, so many years ago. My 'good name' was published in *The Indian Express* and I was accepted to all the five medical schools where I had applied. It was my privilege to reject four of them.

The Golden Gates were indeed opening up in front of me. Ever so eagerly and elegantly. Just for me.

I should remember to be gracious as I hold my head up high, I told myself.

I chose to attend the most selective medical school in India, universally accepted as one of the top medical schools in the world. It is known as an incubator of future leaders in medicine. *The* Institute, as it is fondly called by the elitist group that walks its great corridors, selects thirty five applicants on open-merit from the entire country.

What a rare honor! I've made my family proud. I've made *Daddy* proud. It's ironic, I thought, that Dadi used to ask only about Sanju's grades when we would visit her at the ancestral village home.

Forget Dadi, I quickly told myself, Nargis, you've no time to waste on negative thoughts now. Don't sweat the small stuff!

Thankfully, that same month, my brother was taken off the wait list and accepted into the Indian Military Academy.

Barely two months after starting my first term at The Institute, after surviving that awful hazing, a wire from the Ministry of Education in New Delhi arrived at the front door of the Red Fort. Similar to the telegram that had arrived at the swing door of the ancestral home so many years ago, with the news of Daddy's selection to attend the World Scout Jamboree in Perth. This time, it announced that I had been chosen for a Full-Merit government exchange scholarship to study medicine in Moscow, USSR. I had inscribed the name of that university on my bookshelf four years ago in Lilliputian house. Only two candidates from our entire nation were selected to attend the First Medical Institute.

It's so much more fun competing with an entire nation! I could have walked on water!

In the interview conducted by a distinguished panel of experts in New Delhi, I was asked to explain a physics concept designated as 'mew.'

"It sounds Greek to me," I replied confidently with a smile.

The selection committee loved me immediately! The rest of the interview was a cinch! I walked out feeling several inches taller. Even without Daddy's breathing exercises. But of course, I was breathing rarefied air now. Drunk on power. Inebriated with pride. I felt, as if I had discovered a whole new continent. All by myself!

If only I could shout from every mountain top, "Look at me! I did it! I did it! Look at me!"

The whole world was opening up in front of me. I was walking on cotton balls way past those Golden Gates just as Daddy had envisioned. In my humility, I must remember to bow my head when garlanded.

Europe! This was where I had always imagined that I would eventually live. This is the continent that I had dreamed about when I would lay in the warm welcoming drizzle as it would wash over my face on the beach in Bombay so many years ago. When I would attempt to make some sense of the complex patterns in the clouds overhead way past the sky.

Nothing would stop Daddy from incessantly singing my praises. Soon, either people already knew what honors had been bestowed on me, or Daddy would certainly make sure they did.

"I told you that she'll be our wonder child," Daddy kept telling Mummy over and over and over again, without waiting for her response. "Mani, this child of ours can do anything. She has incredible will power. Believe me, *I know*. When she sets her heart on something, she makes it a point to make it happen. Remember Nargis, you've to give credit to your mother," he would add. "Even though she herself missed an opportunity to apply to medical school because of Partition, she made sure you would become a doctor. As you can see, her efforts have paid off."

Mummy smiled. She had nothing to say. As usual, Daddy had acknowledged her and therefore said everything for both of them. And for all of us.

What'll tomorrow bring? I took a brief moment to reflect.

Those watershed moments in life --- One thing that I *was* certain about was that my life would never be the same again.

And I thought to myself, *I'll* never be the same again.

CHECK POST INDIA

My dream of going to Europe was unfolding before my very eyes. Never mind that the destination was going to be Moscow and not London. Never mind that the Iron Curtain was considered only second best to the West. All that mattered was that I was special again and this time in a new and special way.

I was going to a faraway land, to an advanced country that had been inducted into the Superpower Hall of Fame. A nation that had successfully challenged the Third Reich. A nation that was the first to send man into space. A nation comprised of a people that Daddy admired: home to the Proletariat and haven for the downtrodden. A place where you are assured a loaf of hearty wholesome bread on the table; where sanitary childbirth is a birthright, along with mandatory education and suitable employment that best matches your Mojo; and where a sturdy shingled roof over your head to ward off raw elements is not a chance occurrence. But most of all, a country where you are guaranteed respect. This is where everyone is born equal and will die as an equal member of a social order.

It's all about human value and social order. From each according to his abilities, to each according to his needs. The whole world must opt to adopt and follow this dictum to the letter. Daddy said that one day this would surely happen.

This was the same country where Daddy's attempt at being smuggled into had been foiled so many years ago. I would go in his stead.

Daddy immediately arranged for an audience with the director at The Institute.

"Brigadier Yadav, I'm not sure about the standards of medicine in that country," the director remarked rather candidly.

"Now tell me, Dr. Swami," Daddy asked. "Would you have sent your own daughter to Russia, had she had the privilege of being accepted to such a fine university?"

"The short answer is 'no,'" he replied, quickly and unabashedly.

I do not think Daddy heard him. I do not think he wanted to hear him. By the way, neither did I. Indecision cannot be the decision. When we left his office, both our minds were made.

Maybe, he's plain jealous. I bet he doesn't have a daughter as brilliant as me, I concluded.

Anjali came home from college for the weekend.

"Don't send Nargis to Russia," she pleaded. "It'll be a huge mistake," she warned, shaking her head worriedly all the way from the Red Fort gates to the front door past Daddy's prize roses, most likely named Ace of Diamonds and Cloud Nine.

Maybe, she's worried that she'll lose my support in sponsoring her love interests.

Daddy stopped asking other people for their opinion on the matter. Of course, it was generally understood that Mummy thought the same way that Daddy did. So the decision was made. I *would* go.

I will never forget the days leading up to my departure. The feeling of specialness and euphoria permeated through every living cell in my body. My ecstasy knew no bounds. It really did not seem to matter to me that I was going to be so far away from home for the next six years. It did not even cross my mind that I would not see my family for extended periods of time. The notion of being on my own was exciting enough. But leaving the country at seventeen, just like Daddy had done so many years before me, was both daunting and exhilarating. The only difference was that he was abroad for six months --- I would be gone for six years. I was sure that everyone we knew would soon hear about my selection into excellence. One day, I would come back home and remember to tell them all about it. Humbly, of course.

The travel arrangements were made expeditiously by the Ministry of Education at Shastri Bhavan, in New Delhi. By special invitation, the select scholars were ushered into an auditorium within the confines of this Ministry. Over ice-diluted Coca Cola and generous helpings of mildly stale raw cashew nuts we were instructed to watch a movie on a large screen showing the grand and idyllic Moscow landscape: the Gothic architecture, the Parisian style rooftops, the mishmash of flyovers strewn like spaghetti throughout the modern parts of the city, the museum-quality Metro stations adorned with epically historic sculptures standing perfectly erect in near operation-theatre cleanliness, and finally, Vysotki, the seven mighty towers of Stalin tapering into the majestic Communist night sky. There was order and purpose in every frame, juxtaposed to Indian crowded streets generally blindsided with debris in varying degrees of decay where breaking wind while jaywalking is a national pastime! No shanty towns ridden with fetid open-sewer potholes and putrid PWD (Public Works Department) manholes, where you have to hop-step-and-jump at random to save yourself from a freefall into a cesspool of excrement. No hungry-eyed scruffy panhandlers, who take time off from scratching their gonads in public to boldly stretching out their palms, scrounging for *bakshish* at every street corner. What a shame! They put on a show of abject deprivation, then openly snicker to themselves after straightening a sham limp just past my car window, unbeknownst to them, still within my field of vision.

Freeloaders all! Russia is where I really belong.

The orientation papers instructed us, this group of elitist National Scholars, to carry an abundant supply of toothpaste, chewing gum and other sundries. I did not stop even for a moment to think that this lack of mundane toiletries sounded a bit of a paradox for such a Supreme Superpower as the great Soviet Union. I did not want my thoughts to be distracted with such irrelevant detail that interfered with the much grander scheme of things to come. If the Soviets can launch a Sputnik into the unknown and beyond, surely in comparison, squeezing toothpaste into a tube is an inconsequential feat!

For reasons I still cannot fully understand to this day, on that last morning at the Red Fort, I took time off from my unremitting reverie to make a recording on our Made in America six-channel tape-recorder.

"This is Nargis, checking in from Chicago," I said into the mike with my newly assumed poise, imitating rather poorly a Texan drawl. "I love it here, and miss y'all back home. I'll be sure to return soon. Good bye, Yadav Family! Toodle-loo, India!"

Why an American accent? And why Chicago?

Then I took one last sweeping look at the elegant sitting room: the luxurious Persian rug spread between the stylish sofas, upholstered in rich-maroon velvet, sitting against the backdrop of a golden hue of flowing silk drapes standing guard by delicate cream lace curtains.

A confident and scholarly Nargis smiled back at me in a black and white photo sitting securely right in the middle of the mantelpiece where she belonged. In that final sweeping glance, I briefly pondered about everything that had transpired in this room thus far: Daddy's wonderful lectures on life and the world, his incessant praises about my intellect, the five of us sitting together as one family and Mummy hovering over us passing around *samosas* with tamarind-mint chutney, with tea still quietly brewing under the tea cozy embroidered with dainty daisies frozen in cross-stitch. Life is made up of many last looks, some of which have remained indelibly etched in my memory. Those fleeting last looks: of rooms and spaces, of people and faces.

Soon it was time to leave.

It was now my last day in India. The month of September is known to bring change in the lives of students the world over. I arrived at the New Delhi aerodrome all packed and ready to go, with a pair of newly-acquired bellbottoms from Karol Bagh and a stash of photos hurriedly snatched from family albums, clutching my new unstamped passport with a picture of my eager face stamped with quiet pride. The Aeroflot flight to Moscow was as expected on time. Daddy, Mummy and Anjali rode with me to Palam Airport to see me off. Sanjay had just joined the Military Academy and could not come. I was so engrossed in this sudden rush of nostalgic memories and exhilarating dreams that were both competing for my attention, so I had no time to miss him.

I remember feeling super excited about a journey that I knew would change my life forever. I was about to take my first steps into this rarefied stratosphere. I pictured myself catapulting into outer space. The one that the Soviets knew so much about.

We laughed all the way on the ride the airport, while Daddy, as usual, drove with precision, talking about the rustic custom of garlanding all foreign-bound travelers with double strings of yellow and gold marigolds.

No garlands for me, thank you! I assumed the posture of being a poised and savvy traveler.

I was now at the security checkpoint at immigration. Since that moment, I have been at this very place at the very same airport many times again in my life, but I will always remember that first time.

There were twenty one students traveling in our group and I was the only girl.

It's rather unfortunate, I thought, that this lot of twenty boys looks kind of nerdy, clueless and undernourished, so they don't deserve a second look. The moment I cross over national boundaries, I'll most certainly have more promising beaus in store for me. I looked straight ahead, past the security line to a place beyond, where a new life was waiting for me.

I remember we quickly hugged as a family. I felt like crying, but the tears would not come. Daddy was saying something about the three fundamental rules I must live by: first, always remember what kind of family you come from. Second, keep in mind that family always comes first. And third, never forget the first two rules.

As I walked past security, I turned around to look back at the three of them one last time: Anjali appeared vulnerable, Mummy seemed kind of unsure of herself and Daddy looked proud. Then they were all lost in the crowd.

A tiny gasp escaped my lips. Then it died down just as suddenly.

Perhaps for the same reason, a tear appeared somewhere in the corner of my eye. I did not want anyone to see it. It was brief and sudden and even took me unawares. After I wiped that one away, there were no other tears to follow. Or so I thought.

In the first letter from home, Daddy wrote that they had all lingered on in the airport lounge until my plane had finally disappeared into the northwest sky.

"That's where Nargis went," he told Mummy, pointing in that general direction.

"We'd go to your room and smell some of the clothes you had left behind and hug and cry together thinking of you," he wrote. "Mummy and I miss you terribly. But we know that you'll study hard and make us all proud, like you always have. We know you'll live up to our family honor and name and come back a winner."

It's always critical to live up to the family honor and come back a winner.

I did not realize then, that this would be the moment in my life when I would begin to learn to be by myself. It would also be that moment in my life when I would start the journey of *being* myself.

What I also did not realize was that the young man, who would soon totally blow me away, sat just behind me on the same flight that glorious September day --- the day I left my country, my family, and my father.

SIMPLY LOVE

THE PRAVDA ABOUT RUSSIA

It was a long flight. It felt uncomfortably cold and dark in the plane. I was afraid to ask for a blanket because I did not have the nerve to bother the white air hostess. Especially, because she was white. Besides, I certainly did not want to relay my naiveté on the PA system. Having deemed my fellow male counterparts as a bit too scholarly for my taste from that preliminary perfunctory look in their general direction at Palam Airport, I made no attempt to connect with them during the flight. Most people understand subliminal messages, so they left me to my own devices. I suffered my superior attitude and facade of savoir-faire in solitude. I endured the chill alone in the dim cabin wondering what tomorrow will bring, as the plane pierced into the endless sky.

Before we landed, we were served the quintessential Russian sticks of candy. They were quite hard and unwelcoming and certainly not as tasty as the colorfully wrapped soft toffees back home in India.

But, never mind the impenetrable tooth-pulverizing candy and the insipid herb-bashful food, I thought to myself. And ignore the thick English accent and the universal apathy of the stodgy cabin crew, branded the world over for a proclivity for BO resulting from gross negligence and a candid contempt for antiperspirants.

For the first time in my life, I was about to land in Europe! I felt a sudden rush of thrill and anticipation. A tingling sensation ran through every nerve ending in my body as we descended past the thick clouds into my brave new world.

We landed at Sheremetyevo Airport in Moscow on a cold gray September afternoon in 1970. The sparsely-populated, sterile airport was managed by the Russian Gestapo. At Immigration, I realized for the first time that I now carried the new label of foreigner similar to the term commonly used for Caucasians who travel to India, as did the twenty boys on my flight. But I steered away from them. They were from the old world and I certainly did not want to be confused with *their* lot.

We were hustled onto a bus that would take us to the university. I found it rather novel and striking to see white people working at mind-numbing menial jobs as porters and drivers. Apparently, not all Caucasians are high powered corporate moguls like the Rockefellers, Weinberg's and Fords, or handsome movie stars like Robert Redford, Paul Newman and Peter O'Toole!

We drove past dense birch forests burning in a blaze of golden-yellow, down Leninsky Prospect with its eight-lane regimented traffic. It was lined with larger than life portraits of the century's great Russian leaders marked by glaring bold-red signage: Proletariats of the World Unite!; Brezhnev appeared grim and surly in his stiff military jacket and Stalin looked rather boorish, his shrewd smile hidden behind his walrus moustache. There were statues of Lenin and Marx at all important crossroads --- of life. Even the crows did shy away from insulting them with random droppings. World famous thought-leaders that had one arm stretched out in the general direction of the horizon and a finger pointed unequivocally to the future, as if to show the rest of the world the only sure path to deliverance.

Finally, we arrived at the dorm. An obese matronly *dzhurnaya* sullenly checked us off on her list and supplied us with clean and starched white bed linen --- sheets that had been laundered by comrades, for comrades. I suspected this country ran on checked off lists. We quickly learned that for just five kopecks we could travel anywhere in the city Metro; that the price of a loaf of bread had been frozen since the great Russian Revolution at thirteen kopecks. Lenin had indisputably declared that inflation sucks the air out of the underprivileged class. Why, in the name of reason, did the rest of the world not adopt communism? It struck me as a fair, logical and perfect system: a panacea for all incurable economic maladies on this planet.

The first few months were the biggest adventure, adjustment and challenge that I would ever experience in my life. I wished my other Indian comrades belonged to my genre of cool people. Clearly they must be inordinately bright, otherwise they would not have been a part of my entourage. To my total disappointment, their preferred lingua franca was Hindi and at the drop of a Soviet *shapka*, they would burst into primordial Bollywood songs from the Raj Kapoor era. I realized that most of them came from humble families.

I felt that I had to apologize for my family's comparable wealth. It was easier not to talk about it. An art I had practiced well --- never to allude to things that make me uncomfortable.

Initially, I resisted joining my other peers from the motherland, including a female contingent comprised mostly of a Bucolic Brigade. I preferred to bond with the obviously more gentrified student body from other countries such as Cyprus and Argentina and had started to regularly seek them out. But I was enthusiastically guarded and not sure this was a perfect fit either. In my quest for attaining instant cool-dom, one weekend I even bought a pack of cigarettes. I sadly thought then and thankfully realize now, I could never learn how to inhale. Similar to those precious little stubs carelessly discarded by Uncle Kapoor in our Pathankot home.

No Sanju by my side to give blow by blow instructions.

Before the long Russian winter finally set in, through mutual acquaintances I had met a senior medical student, Salim, who was an Indian Muslim and had been raised in Moscow.

I thought to myself, since he's an atheist who knows everything there is to know about communism, I'm sure Daddy would approve.

Our dating lasted all of a couple of weeks, when it dawned upon me that Salim was at least a couple of inches shorter than me! The only thing redeeming about him was that he was an expert kisser! Indeed, a connoisseur in that art form.

This'll not work. This'll never work. Nothing to write home

about, as Daddy would've said.

This, was new territory. And a horrific quandary. Being so green around the gills, I did not know quite how to end the relationship. You see, I had never ended one before. That first winter break, I was part of a student entourage selected to perform a Western song and dance routine at an annual concert in a university in East Berlin. As the train was chugging out of Moscow Central, after a brief PC peck on the cheek, I hurriedly waved *Ciao* to Comrade Salim.

Over the noise of the engine, hoping nobody could hear me --- not even myself --- I shouted to the wind, "GTH!"

"What does that mean?" he yelled back, as the engine was gathering steam and pulling away.

"That means, GO TO HELL!" I shrieked, quite shocked at what I had just done. Sanjay had taught me the acronym in the seventh standard.

For a long time afterward, I was quite embarrassed at the absurdity of it all. I heard that Salim was quite broken up. My embarrassment would cause me to quicken my pace whenever I passed him by in the hallways of our university hugging the wall and barely able to make eye contact. Strangely, the corridors appeared longer, narrower and more vacant than ever before. Thankfully, for both of us, he had a new girlfriend the following year and soon married her.

That first year of Preparatory Faculty entailed speedy acquisition of a rich and poetic language --- the one used in *The Brothers Karamazov* and *Crime and Punishment*, instant exposure to a Superior Economic Order of Communist proportions, and covert indoctrination parceled off as education. There were trips to Lenin's Mausoleum --- Is that really *him*? And, is he *really* dead?; the Bolshoi Theatre, where perfectly harmonized anorexic ballerinas twirled flawlessly to Tchaikovsky; and GUM, the famous all-embracing shopping bonanza in the USSR boasting a pathetic display of second-rate wares from sister-class Soviet bloc nations. Prada and Chanel would invade this mall soon after the Berlin Wall came down post Glasnost and Perestroika. At the May Day Parade, I enthusiastically joining in with the lustily cheering masses to celebrate the victory of the working-class common man. A grand military show culminating with a display of sturdy MIGs gliding smoothly on stretched-out floats, followed by a string of consummately threatening missiles, Tsiklon and Taifun, all pointing accurately, ready and waiting to annihilate the West, being wheeled through Red Square --- It's not really *red,* is it? All that abundantly demonstrated the muscle, authority and dominance of this Communist frontrunner.

Privately though, I was painfully aware that living the life of a working-class common man, or woman, being rudely jolted about in public transportation and dragging my feet in line for over an hour for a miserable bag of potatoes or a wretched loaf of bread in the long Russian winter was not such a supreme feat after all. In my heart, I missed the hierarchy that I had hitherto enjoyed as my birthright coming from a respectable family and hated having to apologize for India's poverty and starving millions. For, in my newly adopted 'ism', everyone was equal; comrades stood equally patiently slouched over and bundled-up in untrendy oversized *paltos*, lighting up as they dragged their feet in long queues that snaked around dull buildings outside the dismally bare grocery stores, hoping to partake in their rightful share of vigilantly rationed meager supplies portioned out by obese and usually loutish attendants. Or worse, waiting their turn to be mandatorily autopsied by tubby morticians, whose chubby chins wiggled as they chiseled through cadaver skulls, with fragments of fat globules from fellow comrades flying into their eyes. Or still worse, being interviewed as patients, spontaneously diagnosed with schizophrenia, who until then had been political prisoners, staring blankly with a fixed medicated gaze.

The popular joke was that the longest lines were the ones most sought after by the Proletariat; the longer the wait, the greater the chance of acquiring something special at the end of the line --- kidney beans from Bulgaria, dark beer from Czechoslovakia, or lead crystal from Poland. The name of the product would speed up and down through the chain of shuffling prospective shoppers like Chinese whispers. Risk-taking in this economy entailed taking a chance that the prize product would not be exhausted before one's rightful turn. The ultimate entrepreneur even bought an 'option' from a lawful owner of *his* place in the queue, to generate a market for a place in the line, rather than for the product on sale. He was labeled by the establishment as a Traitor to The Cause. Very quickly, I learned that in this economic order 'ownership' was an acrimonious and forbidden word.

It was indeed a Utopian society. During the next six years, I would never see what a tuition invoice looked like and could only wonder how many commas and zeros must follow the digits on the actual statement: probably countless, since the ruble was not doing so well in the world currency markets. To top it all, every student would receive a stipend for buying meals, books and supplies, just for announcing an intent to attend school. Some of us scrupulously saved all year long from sparse funds in hard currency, intended for seminars and such, that was vigilantly dispensed by the Government of India, so we could travel to Western Europe during summer break. The West was cast as an Evil Empire: A world of corruption, bribery and deceit, where the only way to succeed in life was to deviously take iniquitous advantage of those who are less fortunate.

Despite the order and purpose in this new world, I missed my family, the comfort of the Red Fort and Mummy's cooking. On weekends, I would step on home soil at the Indian Embassy after changing a couple of Metro and tram rides. There I would skim through *The Times of India* from last month and watch old Bollywood movies from the fifties with now gradually diminishing ambivalence. I would also retrieve limp, crumpled and occasionally visibly intercepted letters from home mailed through the diplomatic post that would arrive erratically by the invariably delayed Air India Boeing 707.

I wrote long letters home, describing how beautiful Moscow was. And how perfect was this State-ism just like Daddy had depicted all along. I would not forget to PS about my *otlichno* grades at school, which would surely make any parent gloat. Coming to the Soviet Union for higher education was the best decision Daddy and I had ever made. In turn, he would read my wordy essays on Communism over and over again to whomsoever showed even the faintest interest, or had accidentally ventured into the house with no ready plea bargain. Daddy would write back every time, about how proud I had made the family and PS: "You should never ever forget what kind of family you come from."

At the end of his letters he would often add, "Write back soon, Nargis, before we start missing you too much," and save enough room for barely two lines from Mummy.

Dear Nargis,
It's good to hear you're doing so well. Keep it up.
Love, Mummy

That first winter, Anjali wrote some of the most tender letters I would ever receive from her. I wish I had saved those loving notes that were written on a collage of faded birds and bees printed on chic fashionably crinkled capitalistic stationery, to remind myself in later years of her more nurturing maternal side. She wrote about how our parents continued to reject her love for Anil and openly frown upon any possibility of a union between them. Undeterred, she continued to carry on with him in a clandestine manner. It saddened me to read about her ongoing and threatening to be rather unending struggle to consummate her love. I enthusiastically supported her efforts through our mutual Secret Sister Society, but being so far away, felt helpless on the matter. Helplessness has never been an easy feeling for me.

My peers had nicknamed me slip and slide Nargis because of my chronic imbalance on the black ice concealed under the white stuff on the pavements. In March, around the time when the snow finally merged with the slush, the graceful willowy birch tree outside the window of my dorm had started to suggest a hint of green.

For a whole week my entire being shook with raging fever, which was synchronized with unrelenting headaches and projectile vomiting. Then a menacing cherry-red rash the size of a five kopeck coin spread like wildfire all over my body. If I were to add up all the coins on my limbs I would surely be quite rich!

I became terrified when I could not move my neck.

Immediately, with Soviet precision, I was evacuated to the Institute of Infectious Diseases located on the outskirts of the city. A gray-haired be-spectacled specialist would periodically stop by my bedside, then tap my knees with a little hammer, looking alternately at his hammer and at my knees. He appeared visibly triumphant when my symptoms perfectly matched his diagnosis, performing an investigative interrogation for the benefit of an archetypal cluster of easily impressed but visibly intimidated medical students in tow.

When I become a specialist, I promised myself, I must make it a point to celebrate in establishing a cure, and not just on honing in on a diagnosis. I must remember, at a minimum, to at least look at the patient who, already half-crazed with anticipatory anxiety, gasps when he first hears the name of his syndrome. And Nargis, do take a polite pause, while the poor guy is memorizing the word and mouthing it under his breath to practice the pronunciation of his disorder that is most likely named after the four European experts with hyphenated names who first discovered it.

From where I lay drenched in my own fever, India seemed farther away than it had ever been.

Why are infirmary beds such lonely places? Why do hospital rooms have only one exit door?

After two weeks of solitary confinement and generous doses of acetaminophen administered in bulk, I was nourished back to health with watered down *shee* soup which I obediently gulped. I emerged from total seclusion, completely cured from a violent but textbook-perfect case of meningococcal meningitis.

What if I had died?

When you are young, it is easier not to dwell on such dire outcomes.

So now, I not only owe my education to the Soviets but also my life.

SPRING FEVER IN MOSCOW

I am quite sure that by now you are probably wondering about the twenty boys in the geek-squad on that fateful flight from Palam to Sheremetyevo Airport. In my mind, they were a bunch of nerds in a herd' --- average age seventeen, with a standard deviation of 0.5; average GPA, a whopping three point recurring nine with a standard deviation nearing zero! Quite a bit like Arjun Sharma, who was my senior by a year in medical school. Obviously, *he* saw me before I ever laid eyes on him. I am not sure he bothered to remember me because of my high-brow isolationist behavior on that flight to Moscow, when he was returning to campus after summer vacation. Actually, it was kind of mutual, because I certainly did not care to think of him either.

Our paths were destined to cross again. And again. And yet again. We were both chosen by two older Indian boys, to start a rock band. In the early seventies, being selected to join in a band was the surest way into the inner circle of the coolest kids on campus. As usual, it was fun being the only girl.

By now, the only girl paradigm for so many exciting situations had become a fairly predictable theme.

Our band leader's father, in an apparent fit of Communist nostalgia, had named him Stalin. Arjun, the guy with the Jack Nicholson quizzical eyebrows below his funky hat, had played marching drums during sporting events in high school. He was automatically anointed as our drummer. Scraggly Arun, probably the only bona fide talent, strung gently at base, while I muddled through playing lead on a Spanish guitar having had sketchy training in the ninth standard. Meanwhile, Stalin wildly and violently beat the rhythm out of his guitar. If it was at all possible to single out someone for this distinction, he was also the worst singer among us. He did take his leadership seriously and also insisted on keeping his thick lips glued to a mike that was cranked up to the max at all times during the act, as the four of us belted out *Yellow Submarine!*

We opened with *Ob la di, Ob la da* and ended in a glorious crescendo with *Back to the USSR*, for a Russian audience that had an insatiable appetite to ape anything even remotely Western. Arjun had intuitively christened our band, *The Was That Never.* Our band was destined to be doomed, as our name suggested. We were almost equally untalented, although our leader was by far more delusional than the rest of us. But thank the Lord, we all knew when to quit.

Consequently, the band abruptly disbanded. Scraggly Arun was expelled from school for inhaling contaminated weed. Swollen headed Stalin, who was better known for habitually getting hammered before curtain rise, barely dodged the cannabis bullet but was forced to retreat back to the dorm defeated and unknown. Arjun and I narrowly escaped, crushed and crestfallen, but largely sober.

Those were long tram rides with Arjun on the way back from weekly jam sessions. We hardly spoke to each other, and I --- I barely looked at him. To my utter dismay, he had the audacity to pass me by the stairwell after class without offering an iota of sympathy as I was crying my heart out, hopelessly indignant after getting a C in Scientific Communism. A grade that stuck out like a sore thumb in an honorable slew of A-pluses on my report card.

Scientific what? Come again? What an oxymoron for a subject! I consoled myself.

Much to my annoyance, I imagined that Arjun, most likely, spiced up that story with a generous splash of unadulterated one hundred and twenty percent Absolut vodka at the boys' dorm that night.

That first summer break, Arjun and I, along with thirty other freshmen and sophomores, were thrown together at a *Pioneersky Laager* in Sochi, on the Black Sea coast. The landscape was stunning beyond beautiful. Our living quarters were on the top of a hill akin to the Bombay home, with the ocean waves below us rushing to meet the low knolls. It was not the best beach for swimming, since there was an abundance of impatient and overly friendly jellyfish by the beach that swarmed up to me whenever I ventured into the sea.

We Indians hung out together as minorities on campuses around the world tend to do even today and steered clear from those eager young local comrades proudly wearing red scarves in a Marxist knot around their necks. The language in our indigenous group was newly acquired Russian, with a smattering of Hindi and Punjabi thrown in for color. Being so far away from the motherland, I had no option but to finally resign to my new reality: I could no longer escape these Indian languages, their enriched verbiage and crass colloquialism.

One evening, sitting with friends by a roaring bonfire at a camp social, I saw Arjun dancing rather up close and personal with my roommate, Ludmilla, a top-heavy and buxom --- high center of gravity, to use Arjun's all-embracing physics jargon--- bouncy bubbly Russian girl. Later that night, my roommate and I were chatting, as we lay in our bunk beds star-gazing through an open window in our room. The sounds of the grand finale, *Kalinka* and *Podmoskovniye Vechera* were still playing in the distance. A perfect time to confide in a roommate. She told me that she had "the hots for that Indian boy with the cute boyish face."

"Is he not the most *sympatichni* and *seksy* in the bunch?" she pointed out.

I did not answer, but I think the wheels had started to turn. I started to observe Arjun in the ways boys and girls examine each other on the sly. When they think they cannot get enough, and are absolutely certain only about one thing: they want more.

In that brief moment, I had started to see what Ludmilla saw in Arjun.

Is this what happens when you're smitten?

We spent the rest of that summer Tom Sawyered into picking cherries, stealing corn and being chased off the *kolkhoz* by toothless babushkas.

Back at school, Arjun and I were now a part of the same nerdy group of friends, which by virtue of my inclusion had suddenly taken on the distinction of being the *in* crowd.

I had heard that the dorm room Arjun shared with two other classmates was unanimously known on campus as *the den*. This is where vodka flowed as wildly as the river Volga and the air was thick with tobacco fumes accentuated by the spoils of violent hormonal surges. It was a thoroughfare of both a regular nerd and a chance wayward . Nobody could actually identify the original legit occupants of the den. Not even the original legit occupants! Arjun had a reputation of being a physics whiz, his handsome boyish face buried in his homework, oblivious to the chaos that surrounded him; not caring to raise his head from the oversized topographical anatomy textbook even once, to size up the contours of the rowdy girls who would trespass through. I will never know if the challenge of getting his attention added to his charisma and to my mounting desire to be in the same space with him.

I started to feel only Arjun's presence in a room full of people.

But, he must never know. *Nobody* should ever know.

By spring, I was stricken with spring fever. Even the bright-eyed dandelions by the sidewalk had never looked unhappier being weeds!

One day, Arjun's roommate Ramesh surprised me when he came over to my dorm room and asked me out on a date, as had other boys before him whom I had uniformly and heartlessly turned down. I hated the just friends platonic scenario, which invariably led to agonizing over a friendship gone awry when it changed course midstream. Ramesh though, was persistent.

"Nargis, I cannot take 'no' for an answer. You have to tell me why we can't go out together," he insisted, as I continued to shake my head. "There *has* to be a good reason." He made it harder for me when he added, "I will not leave your room until you've given me a good explanation."

Ramesh was a perfect gentleman with a long hooked nose that abundantly betrayed his mushy inner core.

Overcome with the fear of never realizing my love and with a surging compulsion to share my innermost secret desires, I finally blurted, "Don't you know? It's because I'm in love with Arjun! Promise me," I pleaded quickly. "Promise me you'll never tell him. Swear by your own God that you'll never let anyone else know about this either. Arjun should never hear a word. Not a sound. Not even a whisper! It has to be hush-hush. Promise me now!"

Now that my secret was out, it felt even more real and consuming.

Ramesh, this kind gentle soul, readily retreated from his own pursuit and instead became my confidant as we both embarked on a stealth mission. Most people who knew Arjun thought he was pretty intelligent, but he never figured this one out! How both he and I were thrown together in the most unexpected places: traveling to class on the same bus number 144, waiting at the school cafeteria with a tray of tough *azuu* and bland peas pilaf in the same line, or checking out textbooks at the very same section of the library during a matching and seemingly unplanned break time. I even bunked class just to ride the tram back to the dorms with him. We had some random awkward conversations that I do not remember today and even more uncomfortable chance moments together that would make me tongue-tied and fidgety. If only he knew how desperately I wanted to be with him! Just to be held in his arms! Just this one time! Instead of sitting uneasily across the aisle on an otherwise quiet and smooth tram ride to class, pretending not to look at him.

By now, I had figured out that I made Arjun ill at ease, but I did not know quite what to make of it. After all, he did raise his Jack Nicholson eyebrows every time he saw me!

Does he know that I'm torn apart when we cannot meet up? Does his heart also defy those normal conduction pathways that my physiology professor swears by? Is it just possible that Arjun also feels the same way about me? Or, heaven forbid! Does Mr. Physics Buff have the nerve to think that I'm stalking him!

One day, I had Ramesh steal Arjun's student ID, the one with his nerdy buzz-cut headshot. That night, back in my dorm room, I put it under my pillow and made a wish.

What felt like a lifetime of waiting and wanting, actually transpired in just three weeks. Finally, one sunny March day, when Arjun was twenty one and I was still two years younger, unbeknownst to both of us Ramesh invited me to the den. It was just the three of us.

"This has been going on for too long now," Ramesh started, in his soft voice. "Both of you are intelligent people. And both of you know what this is all about," he added in a matter of fact manner. "So from this moment on, you're on your own. You don't need me anymore," he ended, and without further delay, left us with a bottle of champagne and a bowl of sweet, warm and squishy holy *halwa* between us.

We could barely look at each other!

Sobered and buzzed at the same time, we walked back to my dorm where I showed Arjun pictures from my family album. Nothing would scare him now!

As for myself, I did not stop even for a moment to think about his family. They must be wonderful people to have produced such a brilliant son like Arjun.

So our dating began.

On our first date, while I stirred tea leaves, the physics buff tried to impress me with a long and boring one-on-one tutorial on centrifugal force.

"It's about --- acceleration --- Earth --- objects --- surface --- gravitational pull ---"

I did not hear a word he was saying. I was certain, what he really wanted to talk about was the attraction between us!

By the next date, I noticed that he had nicks on his chin, where he seemed to have tried extra hard to shave. There was hardly anything there!

On the third date --- abbreviated version --- kiss, kiss, kiss! They were long, wet and clumsy. My lips were sore for a few days afterwards.

The next time we were supposed to meet, the unthinkable happened! Arjun stood me up! He stayed back with the boys, as he was detained by a surprise delivery of special Czech beer at the school cafeteria. Twenty years prior to the invention of mobile phones, I had to wait for over fifty hours before he found out how mad I was. Fifty hours can be a long time to weather a lover's spat.

A few dates later, Arjun took me out on a movie date. All Russian movies are about wars. And there is a good reason for this. Not too many people around the world know this fact except, of course, for the Russians and maybe the Germans: twenty million Soviet soldiers died in the Second World War. Every family lost a son, husband, or father. The movie opens with Sasha crouching in a trench, hiding out from the Fascists. He is grimy and cold, with tire marks on his uniform and a gaping wound crying out for attention on his forehead oozing with blood. Overhead, he sees tanks exchanging rapid fire, cannon balls exploding midair, body parts flying asunder and the enemy being dismembered beyond recognition. At the end of the battle, he trudges back home in his heavy boots knee-deep in snow. He cannot wait to be back in the arms of the lover he had left behind before the war started. All he can see in the gathering ice storm is Galya's hair, her smile, and her eyes. And the way she had turned her head back that one last time to look at him. When they finally meet, he sweeps her off the floor as they kiss passionately. And then he carries her off to bed.

I miss the he-carries-her-off-to-bed part, because Arjun and I were also kissing. That too, wildly.

When Arjun walked me back to my dorm, we were still smooching on the street, locked-in, totally oblivious to late night stragglers and the rest of the world. I told Arjun that we would have two children. And, if I had my way, they would both be girls.

We ventured to explore each other on the mattress in the stairwell, shooing away the cats that had cuddled and nuzzled there before us. By simply closing my eyes, it seemed so easy to block out the past. Our hormones exchanged rapid fire in successive quantum of pleasurable pulsating energy. It was instant combustion.

"Now girls, remember, never go all the way," the nuns had warned me so many years ago.

I did follow their command. To the letter.

Within a few weeks, I convinced Arjun of my brilliant idea of pooling our scholarship money, so I could manage it for both of us. Soon, I lost track of what he owed toward our grocery budget, which I had kept diligent track of until then.

A few months later, I noticed that he had grown another inch. Taller!

Our dating became a habit neither one of us wanted to give up on. I realized that I would have to talk to the folks about Arjun. So talk to the folks I did. I wrote home briefly, ending with a tiny footnote about how I had met this brilliant boy at school, who I would love for my parents to meet one day. I was confident that they would be just as proud of him as they were of me. While he came from humble beginnings, he was a person of substance, a self made man in the making and a stellar student, the kind that Daddy had taught me to admire. At the end of the letter I meekly suggested that the next time I came home on vacation, would it not be a great idea that we could all meet together?

That was not to be. In the next diplomatic mailbag, a stiff letter from Dehradun was waiting for me. It started with a curt and stern warning.

"Stay away from *that* boy," Daddy wrote back tersely. "It behooves you to only focus on your studies. Remember, that's why you were sent to Russia in the first place. And I don't expect any less from you. Nargis, always remember what kind of family you come from. Always.

NEVER forget that."

Needless to say, it was a short letter.

So I stopped writing home about that boy. My parents wanted to believe that it was over between us, so it would have been rather imprudent on my part to give them any reason to think otherwise. Life was so much easier this way with them not knowing how, over the next three years, the love between Arjun and me would blossom into a wonderful friendship.

And how, for the rest of our time together in Russia, we had become inseparable.

A WHIFF OF CHANGE

During my six years in Moscow, I would learn more and more, about how to make do with less and less. Another household Communist maxim --- *less is more*. This was not too difficult for me, since I have always been a fast learner.

I became accustomed to a scarcity of routine provisions and basic amenities that I had never thus far experienced. Although I did miss some of the essential comforts from back home, which I had thus far taken for granted, I do not remember ever resenting the responsibility of having to manage this new life on my own. I felt so singularly proud of having the privilege of being inducted into the Hall of Fame of self-made people, the kind that Daddy had instilled in me to admire. In comparison, everyday comforts came in way past last place. I loved the freedom of being an independent young girl who had the right of making independent young adult decisions.

While I struggled with episodic and by now fairly predictable roommate standoffs that happened like clockwork, due, in large part, to an innate inability to express my needs honestly --- the adolescent brew-and-stew maladaptive coping over roommate PDA --- my relationship with Arjun became even more trusting and intimate. We learned to cook together, using rusty sawdust curry powder smuggled past airport customs saved from the keen eyes and sharp noses of prying officials as well as prowling hounds. I would keep a running tab of our conjoint funds and what my boyfriend was supposed to contribute --- without any visible protest, or having to raise that eyebrow --- toward our shared budget. But soon that would get blurred. His account was usually in the red anyway! Other boundaries between us began to blur as well and very soon we were doing almost everything together. Except, of course, shacking up, in our last feeble attempt to have some semblance of propriety for the benefit of our otherwise nerdy fellowship. So that we did not fall from grace.

It was in the privacy of the top stairwell landing in my dorm where we generally explored each other on a discarded mattress, feeling a rush of sensations: urgent, heady, and pulsating. Freeing and liberating. I would wear collared shirts for days afterward, only this time, in order to hide my weekend hickeys.

I shared the excitement of my childhood escapades with Sanjay, hunting in the wild grasses of Indore for deer literally frozen in the headlights, retrieving treasure from a barrel of seaweed on the sandy beaches in Bombay and having the guts to save a dog who was walking toward Death by shooting straight into its frail guts in Bhatinda; Daddy's great adventures in Australia, heroic exploits in World War II and his gallant courage to stand up to the British; Mummy's fine education, Anjali's tenuous love affair and how special my family was. So it was indeed a shock to Arjun when one day, rather unprompted, interspersed with bursts of incoherent sobbing, I told him in a couple of sentences, or less, that Daddy used to touch me in all the wrong places when I was a child. It took all of two sentences to say the words.

Arjun held me very close, as I gulped in hot thin air to choke back my tears. He did not say anything. He did not have to say anything.

We never talked about it again. Our life was so carefree and fun in every other way, I did not want to complicate it. Also, I am not sure either of us fully understood what molestation really means. For that matter, even today it does not all make sense. For but a moment, however brief, I remember feeling that I had betrayed my family. Eventually, even that would pass.

It would take me the better part of two years to take the huge risk when I asked Arjun to meet my parents on his next trip to India. And meet the folks he did, while I was out of harm's way, at least fifty thousand light years away in Moscow. As a twenty three year old young man, he certainly mustered up enough courage to enter through the gates of the Red Fort for the very first time, probably past the roses, Daring Red and Double Delight, and introduce himself as a Nargis' friend. He thought he was leaving my parents guessing.

"I had to eyeball him just once and I figured him out right away," Daddy told me later of the visit. "The boy simply couldn't take his eyes off your photograph on the mantelpiece!"

My parents' version of that first summit meeting appropriately titled, "Let's-Get-To-Know-Each-Other Politely." Daddy bragged about how he had tested Arjun by offering him another round of Peter Scot whiskey, within the first ten minutes of that fateful encounter!

"And he had the nerve to accept it right away!"

Poor Arjun. Of course, he was nervous --- and promptly failed the litmus test! He was rather naive and totally oblivious to the inevitable no-confidence vote. One hundred percent precast, nonnegotiable and set-in-stone. The physics buff insisted that first drink was rather pale-yellow, since Daddy was hell bent on vigilantly measuring out the hard liquor as if through a pipette while simultaneously removing parallax!

The other odd grievance against Arjun was the apparent anatomical aberration of his "small hands." He could never be a "strong, broad-shouldered and able-bodied *Jaat* stud like the other men in our family." Moreover, being a Brahmin boy of humble beginnings, he could never be a part of us. Sticking points that Arjun could never shake off. In Daddy's Book of Rules: "Three strikes, and you're out!" And be sure to be thrown way out of the ballpark!

My parents wanted so frantically to believe that it was over between me and "that poor Brahmin boy with small hands and a predilection for alcohol, who, for those reasons alone and a million others not even worth mentioning, can never live up to our family image." Consequently, it took very little manipulation on my part to restore their confidence in me. I had seen Anjali perfect the same strategy over the last several years to handle her own love life with Anil, so I adopted an identical line of attack."We must learn from our elders," Daddy had coached us well.

"You were right all along," I reassured them all too quickly, "You're absolutely correct about 'that boy.' Of course he's just not worthy of me. Actually, nobody really is. I don't even speak to him anymore."

I also started referring to Arjun as that boy.

Most parents love being told they were right all along. Furthermore, I was getting good at lying through my teeth, boldly and unflinchingly. If you repeat the same lie often enough, you start believing it to be true.

Nothing was mentioned again about what's his name during my next trip home except privately with Anjali and Sanjay, as they conspired with my love story like siblings are expected to do. In fact, I remember bonding with Anjali through shared secrets of our respective forbidden love interests. Sharing secrets is an excellent way to bond with a sibling. That was the closest our relationship would ever be, before and since. She even proudly introduced me to a couple of her physician girlfriends, as her brilliant foreign returned sister.

I remember making a total ass of myself. As it turns out, I did not appear to comprehend either the basic pharmacological rationale of narcoleptics, or the fundamental biochemical principle of the Krebs Cycle, using my now unintelligible Latin-Russian hybrid medical terminology poorly translated into English on the fly. But I was able to argue without the help of punctuation marks, like a wound-up energizer bunny with a backup set of Eveready batteries packed in its abdomen, employing eloquent and emotionally-loaded verbiage, about the demise of all capital markets and the eventual and inevitable victory of Communism over both hemispheres. Reading them my Self-Righteous Act, I condemned these members of the Capitalism Club comprised of America-bound doctors for aspiring to embrace an "unfair, integrally flawed and chaotic free-market economic system that is bound for collapse. And Hail to Lenin!"

Privately, I remember wondering about if going to medical school in Russia such a brilliant idea, after all? Why do I sound so dumb? I hate sounding dumb.

All these thoughts were quite confusing. You can be confused only if you think too hard. So I stopped pondering on the matter altogether.

It was not so easy to ignore the diary episode though. Daddy and I were expounding on the merits of the Communist regime in the lounge at the Red Fort within the confines of our mutual admiration society, with Mummy listening and agreeing with both of us at the same time. And, also as usual, sipping tea. It had been raining cats and dogs for the last several days. Mummy had fried ground chick peas flour sprinkled with aniseed and served with cilantro chutney. Crispy sweet *pakoras* taste best served indoors at teatime on long rainy afternoons.

Somewhere midstream in our discourse on the ultimate rise of the Proletariat, Daddy took the wind out of my sails. Suddenly, out of the blue, he sprung this at me. A little bit like a magician does. Daddy was known to pull rabbits out of a hat.

"Nargis, do you remember, you had left your diary in a trunk in the staircase attic before you had left for Moscow that first time? By the way, my dear, I *did* go through it," he said simply, as if he was reading the subtitles of a movie. One syllable at a time. Aloud.

Daddy was looking straight at me. Through me. It got deathly quiet. Even the rain had suddenly stopped to listen to him. The air was thick and humid. You could have sliced it with a knife.

Does Mummy know what he's talking about? I wondered. Did he read it to her, too? How did he explain the contents? I *have* to stop thinking about this. And we *must* stop talking about this. This very minute. *Now!*

As for myself, I prayed that I would disappear into my toes. Even today, I am not sure what I mumbled in response. Mercifully, it was never brought up again. At least, it would not be brought up again for a long time.

I tend to mix up the next couple of years. I was back in Moscow when I received the news of Anjali's wedding. In a last desperate attempt, she had grabbed a kitchen knife and held it to her chest. She threatened that she would indeed stab herself this very instant and immediately bleed to her death if my parents did not acquiesce, without further delay and no strings attached, to her desire to be married to Anil. Evidently, Daddy's heart melted and after some heated exchanges, alternating with mending fences, over intricate and tricky negotiations with the neighbor *Bania* out-laws, Anjali was married in a simple ceremony in the backyard of the Red Fort. No priest. No pomp. No pretensions.

Apparently, the two families could not wait another three months for my next trip home during summer break. It is possible that Anjali was afraid Daddy might change his mind on a dime. He had been known to do so on prior occasions. One could not chance anything by flipping a coin. No heads or tails. *Not with Daddy.* So clearly, it was best to be married right away. I think she acted wisely, but I do remember feeling left out. Left out and letdown. It felt strange to think that my family could make such an important decision without asking me first.

I'm not even in the wedding photos, I thought. It's just the four of them. Just like in that photograph from before I was born. As if, I'm not even born!

I realized, though, that it would not be fair to the specialness of this auspicious occasion for me to complain about feeling invisible. A feeling that would follow me into my adult life. A feeling that would always make me squirm. So, I said nothing.

Instead, on her wedding day, I spent an entire month's stipend shouting monosyllabic felicitations over an inaudible scratchy line from a lonely and claustrophobic phone booth in Moscow, feeling as lost and miserable.

"Will the groom be coming on a horse?" I shouted into the phone.

"No, Nargis, it's not a farce," she yelled back.

"How about flowers on the groom's car?"

"No, there's no war either," she replied, quite perplexed.

"Forget it. I'll just write all about it in a letter."

"Who's better?"

And then, more, "Who? Who? Who?"

I sounded like an owl. That was when I gave up.

My sister and I have had periods of sketchy communication. Even on clear telephone lines. Today, though, I am not ready to give up on it so easily.

I had the same feeling of being an outsider looking in when the next year rolled around and I came home to visit with Anjali just before the birth of my first niece. The new parents-to-be were unabashedly cuddling with each other and ignoring me completely. I noticed that Anjali was becoming more and more involved with her in-laws, a wealthy silver merchant *Bania* joint-family.

Have things changed at home so much? Or, is it *I* who am now so different? I asked myself.

I believe, change is usually proof that time is passing by.

My relationship with Sanjay was still unchanged probably since he was still single. I visited the stunning Vishnu Temple in Hardwar with my brother. Poised by the ripples of the sacred Ganges, the tapering domes glistened in the clear blue sky, as soulful soothing music emerged from its walls to greet us. I embarrassed Sanjay beyond mortification when I refused to wade through rather murky water in order to ceremoniously cleanse my feet before entering that stunning shrine. The priest would not allow me to skirt this purifying ritual and lost no time in chastising me when I did not follow his strict instructions to simultaneously cover my head.

I've never heard anything so retarded! I comforted myself. There's no sense in wasting my time in explaining to this stupid man that if God does exist, why would He consider my rejection of that silly head cover as a mark of defiance and disrespect? Besides, most intelligent people will agree that the naked head is certainly more vital and divine than a flimsy piece of cloth. There's a reason why it's usually the first part of the body to emerge at childbirth. But this dumb pundit, he'll never get it!

"If you're truly a saintly man," I said aloud, "you should be paying more attention to the scriptures rather than ogling at my bare head. And for God's sake, why are you looking up from your holy book to stare at my face? You're a priest, aren't you? Your job is to keep reading," I told the stupefied man. "Think only about God. And don't stop!"

Without further ado, mostly to save himself from any further humiliation, Sanjay quietly escorted me out. Later that evening, he wanted to see a newly-released Bollywood flick, *Bobby*. He told me that he had a crush on the emerging actress, Dimple, a teenage sure-shot heartthrob. In those days, most Hindi movies continued to be infantile and sophomoric.

But I'll go anyway. Just to do Sanju a favor and make up for embarrassing him at the temple earlier today.

During intermission, I found sufficient time to assault a hooligan as he was aimlessly wandering through the aisle. He had been sitting in front of us wearing a gold chain that dangled on a hairy chest, abundantly displayed through his wide-open buttoned shirt. The cheap gaper had the audacity to keep turning back periodically to stare at me during the entire show while simultaneously sticking out his tongue in viper-like fashion in my general direction. Similar to those ruffians on rickety bikes, who used to eve-tease me on my way to and from high school. This was enough to make me livid. So the first chance I got, I jumped out of my seat and hammered him on his upper torso with my clenched fists. Hairy chest, gold chain, and all.

"The movie behind me is even better than the one on the screen!" the rogue had dared to utter.

The attack was followed by a prolonged gaper's delay. This is when Sanjay decided that his sister had not changed. She was the same Nargis he always knew: brash and hoity-toity. So, without further delay, he took me home.

At home, too, I realized that things had started to change. For one, my parents were now living in a better manner than I had ever experienced growing up. Retirement and Terra Firma had measured up to the promised good life for them.

Too much of bourgeois decadence for my taste, I remember thinking.

During the same trip, Daddy mentioned, in passing, that only Sanjay would have a direct and major share in the title of Terra Firma and other movable and immovable assets owned by the Yadav family. Daddy proceeded to inform us that upon marriage, both Anjali and I would be relinquishing all claims to the Red Fort as well.

"You see, only Sanju will carry the Yadav name," Daddy explained.

It is always uncomfortable to hear a parent talk about your inheritance. For therein is implied the anticipated death of a parent and obvious benefit from their demise. I refuse to pawn off my self-respect in these cheap back alleys for even a flicker of a display of self-indulgence and greed.

I hope that they don't think I can't wait for them to die, was my inaudible soliloquy. And this family name thing? What a lame concept! What utter baloney and bull crap! Is it that I've become more advanced, or has Daddy gone backward?

The result in and of itself, of being thus excluded from our family's mounting assets hardly seemed to bother me at the time. By now, in my more sophisticated lexicon, the word ownership had been relegated to the glossary of lesser than a moron. Unless, it alluded to Marx's collective ownership. What I did not realize then was that Daddy's decision on property distribution would periodically gnaw at me during the more difficult and financially unstable years later in my life. For some unearthly reason, I am ashamed to admit, I would feel shorted even during the times when I thought I felt more secure. No Entry to the Lucky Sperm Club.

The next summer vacation, I did a double take: Sanjay's confident graduation photograph from the Military Academy had mysteriously appeared on the mantelpiece in the sitting room alongside my parents'. Just next to where, so far, only mine had proudly stood between theirs.

I felt like how a dwarf must experience, when he sees himself in a full-length mirror for the very first time.

LONDON, HERE WE COME!

Back in Moscow, Arjun and I were getting rather comfortable in our relationship. So much so that we would no longer hesitate, for more than a few milliseconds, to even divulge the scores on our respective report cards to each other! Generally, the self-disclosure was painless since both of us always got top grades anyway.

When I came up with the joint plan of sponsoring Sanjay's travel to Moscow from India, so that he could chaperone me through Western Europe during summer holidays, Mr. Physics Buff did not even bat an oscillating eyelid. To accomplish this lofty goal, Arjun and I would not only have to eke out rubles and kopecks from our monthly stipend but also deplete the small stash of Western currency from our now seamless funds, which were now under my superior management. This would result in gravely endangering the paltry rations of our usually bone bare pantry. Sanjay would become my accomplice, since the name Arjun was an unspoken virulent antigen to which my parents reacted so violently. With a brother by my side, they would not have to agonize about my traveling seemingly alone on a two month long trip to the West. To that Continent of Peril.

"What a brilliant idea, Nargis!" Daddy wrote back.

Daddy, content with living vicariously through his children's successes and adventures, in a moment of generosity, however brief, even parted with some much needed British pounds to pad our slim wallets in order to ease our otherwise no-frill travel. Sanjay had to go through painfully drawn-out red tape as an officer-cadet to secure a release from the Ministry of Defense for an extended overseas trip abroad.

The plan was simple. In those days, Arjun would readily agree with me about everything that mattered and about everything that did not. I was now twenty years old and this voyage was going to be a great adventure to properly ring in the next exciting decade of my life.

I was so thrilled at the prospects of sharing my new world with

Sanjay. I was equally vigilant about ensuring that Sanjay and Arjun got along with each other and that they did so without further delay. My brother loved his maiden debut into the Western Hemisphere. He was quite content licking peanut flakes sprinkled on vanilla *morozhenoe* bought from roadside kiosks and shouting, "Awesome! Fantabulous! *Ostorozhno! Dveri Zakrevioutsa,*" as he jumped in and out of the Moscow Metro. He looked like a little kid in a candy store!

Preparing for the travels ahead was at least half the fun, similar to the trips to the ancestral home in our childhood and most expeditions through history.

In short order and with very little resistance, I was able to impose on my two boys turned men the bright idea of helping me vigorously knead and flatten dough, then roll and fry, stack and pack enough *puris* for the entire journey, in an effort to diligently anticipate, monitor, and control our expenses. Especially control. I was painfully aware that we were traveling on a shoestring budget, but even that hardly seemed to make a dent in our spirits. Without much opposition, I had taken over as chief comptroller for the entire duration of our trip. I was fair and reasonable, but firm. Even today, both Arjun and Sanjay will admit, albeit tongue in cheek, that we would have never been able to come back in one piece had it not been for my tight wallet and sometimes tricky parleys every step of the way. Especially with Sanju. The previously fluffed *puris*, however, curled up with fungus before our train arrived into Warsaw.

Traveling by Soviet train, dipping low density, butter rich *pechene* in weak Russian tea prepared by a plump, sluggish and generally indisposed *dzhurnaya*, whizzing past the lush expanse of thick *kolkhoznick* corn in Belarus, we crossed into Poland. This subpar, sister-block nation seemed to be a less regimented and watered-down stepsister version of communism, so we were eager to travel on.

In East Berlin, I developed an ingrown toe nail that got infected and threatened to cause more trouble. This would certainly slow down the progress of my impatient fellow travelers. The clinic recommended I be instantly hospitalized for no less than a week to attend to this grave medical emergency. The treatment would not have cost me anything, but would agonizingly erode several precious days in our meticulously planned journey. Unanimously, the three of us agreed we could not

260 • Bulbul Bahuguna

afford to lose a single day.

Sitting me on the curbside of a bridge --- Arjun whipped out a razor blade. In full view of curious passersby he proceeded to make an incision, precisely on the ailing toe and deep enough so it hurt. *Healing usually begins with hurt.* First he drew blood, then he let out pus and finally, with an "Aaaah!" and a flourish, he dabbed the wound with a dash of stinging Old Spice. The curbside consultation did the trick. Onward on our journey we went, with me wearing open-toe shoes to air the operation site. Needless to say, my foot healed well.

As we approached Western Europe it was hard not to observe, what appeared to be, a ludicrously extravagant range of processed cheeses, high-fashion miniskirts and psychedelic neon lights. We must have traveled by the subway under that infamous Berlin Wall back and forth several times, before we finally crossed over that one last time and arrived into the Wicked West. A piece of that historic, graffiti-ridden wall that used to separate estranged German cousins now adorns my bookshelf. This was the first time I had seen a Mercedes taxi, that too, driven by a well endowed blonde. Sanjay took an instant liking, both to the fancy car and to the endowed woman. He did not want the ride to end, until I had to gently remind him about our budgetary constraints. Future reminders would not be as gentle.

It was quite dark when we arrived at a deserted train station in West Berlin, next to a honky-tonk bar. There were a few graveyard shift workers and late night stragglers in the now rapidly thinning crowd when a bunch of rugged hoodlums with disheveled punk hair came upon us in the underpass, reeking of stale cigarettes. They were dressed in ragged oversized faded jeans with gaping holes in odd places large enough to expose tattoos of anchors and snakeheads and kicking empty Heineken cans to guide them along, while spitting defiantly at the wild graffiti on the walls.

Suddenly, I had become a liability to my male companions. To add to my annoyance, they both insisted that I roll up my straight long hair under a cap so I would look like one of them. I just quietly snuck up between my two watchdogs. We were all quite relieved when we finally arrived safely at our gender-specific youth hostels. Sadly for Arjun and me, we had to go our separate ways.

By our next city stop, we found ourselves standing outside the youth hostel in Amsterdam looking rather lost. We had arrived just after the doors had been locked up for the day and did not know where to spend the night. To our good fortune two elderly ladies from the house next door saw our plight, took pity on us and took us in. They were both loyal Gandhians. We hastily agreed with their political affiliations and took deferential interest in their philosophical leanings in exchange for a sumptuous helping of salami sandwiches and red wine, followed by a breathtaking jaunt in the country the next day. They insisted though, much to my disappointment, that I occupy a room separate from the boys. On our last day in their home we washed and buffed down their Skoda car until we could see our eager faces in the metal, since, in spite of our sincere intentions, they had refused to accept any money for room and board. I am sure that had Gandhi been in our shoes, he would have done no less. But then, after he became famous, he had given up on wearing shoes.

Onward to Rotterdam we went. On the deck of the choppy ferry ride to the British Islands I stole time for some clandestine rocking under the blanket with Arjun, quite mindful of Sanjay's keen, protective and increasingly watchful eyes. The rough waters certainly did charitably contribute to the rocking.

When we finally arrived at Harwich --- I did not know how to feel. For the first time in my life I had stepped onto British soil! This was the country of Shakespeare and Hamlet, of P G Wodehouse and Jeeves, and of Churchill and the Queen. This was the same country that I used to dream about all those years in my childhood when I would lay on the sandy beach in Colaba, or float in the pool at the Jodhpur school trying to see past the sky.

I was quiet on the train ride into London absorbing it all and trying to savor this special moment, which I had fantasized about so my times in so many different ways. I was finally living my dream.

We were taken in by a family friend and gorged on butter chicken and *parathas* that our now constantly groaning stomachs heartily welcomed. Thanks to the inevitably delayed mail, I was able to risk that my parents would not hear anytime soon from our hospitable host family about the other boy who had accompanied Sanjay and me on the trip. I was sure that it would take the Indian Postal Services several weeks to sift through, decipher and sort out the assortment of currencies printed on foreign stamps.

What if, through his clever sleuthing practices, Daddy finds out that the other boy is actually that boy, the one he had given me strict and explicit instructions to expel from my life forever? I'll be dead in the water! And, God be my witness, lotus flower or not, I'll never be able to float back up to the surface again!

The next morning, our hosts were gracious enough not to call us on the carpet. The upstairs floorboards had creaked in the middle of the night when Arjun had secretly come up to my room to spend some fleeting private moments together, which by now we both desperately craved.

Over the next several days, I reluctantly gave up absolute authority, but only an inch at a time, when we tripped over our budget at Marks and Spencer and C&A. We gawked at Buckingham Palace from a respectful distance. From where I stood, I wondered what it would be like to live behind those high walls secured by toy guards in fuzzy top hats. We stood in awe at Westminster, where so many world decisions had been made. This was the place where scores of countries had been systematically colonized and later haphazardly freed, some at the stroke of midnight. Countries like India.

Just like other tourists in London, we became a part of the throng of humanity weaving in and out of the Tube, thumbing a ride, gallivanting on Oxford Street, feeding the tubby hungry pigeons at Trafalgar Square and pretending to be one with the stiff glass-eyed wax dignitaries at Madame Tussauds. For a final hurrah, we took a daytrip to South Hall and in a nostalgic moment of weakness for the crispy crunch of *panipuri*, indulged in hygienically altered street *chaat* served with plastic gloves. It was not quite like the real thing.

I was sorry when we had to leave London, the generosity of our host family and the obvious comfort of their home. I would have bet my last bottom penny that one day I would return to visit this city of my dreams.

From London we sailed over the English Channel to France. Fatigued from the journey and soon going broke, we lounged on the lawns by the Eiffel Tower, only to be shooed away by the French police. We had saved up enough francs to take a tour of Paris along Champs-Elysees. The bus took multiple pit stops at cute cafes that smelled of gourmet coffee and French croissants, most of which we could not afford. We were so sleep deprived that we slumbered through the entire tour!

Onward and down the Italian shoe we traveled. In Pisa, I looked down from the top of the leaning tower, where Galileo had stood so many centuries ago, to prove that Aristotle was mistaken about the speed of falling cannonballs. I, meanwhile, was mistaken for a local. An Italian asked me for directions and in spite of my defunct Italian, the poor man followed us on the train all the way into Rome, home to the Sistine Chapel and The Coliseum.

Venice deserves the name Quaint City. In no other town in the world is it such pleasure in being lost. We *were* indeed lost. At every street corner one can see the ocean rising up to the footsteps of ancient buildings that appear to bob up and down the waterline, while garlanded gondolas negotiate twisted canal ways. With now rapidly dwindling funds, the smell of seaweed became even more sickening! This is when I vetoed that Sanjay forego his daily allowance, since he had repetitively and heedlessly fritted it away on his continually emerging fashion needs. He was forced to spend an entire night sleeping on Italian newspapers, spread out on a hard iron bench by the train station, because he so desperately wanted to have Elvis tattooed on his upper arm at the flea market!

By the time we arrived in Zurich, we were weary from roughing it out, pinching pennies and sleeping in sitting cars. I was tired of slapping stale mint on limp cucumber sandwiches, doling out long out of fizz Coke from supersize dented plastic bottles and rationing flaccid chips bought in bulk to my now begrudging and progressively complaining fellow travelers. This is when Sanjay and I got into an argument as he had frivolously bought fancy leather boots earlier that day totally unmindful of my stringent budget guidelines. In order to end the dispute, I flung his most recent acquisition into a street fountain. Flinging objects is a sure way to end a squabble. An act I would perfect over time.

We were soon coming to the end of our journey. Both of us siblings wanted to forget this minor misgiving and put it behind us. Like the other minor misgivings that we had been so easily able to put behind us in the past.

Three weary travelers with backpacks full of memories were now heading back into the Communist world. At the Czech border, the guards poked under our berths for fleeing defectors, forbidden copies of *Playboy* and *Hustler*, records of *Lara's Theme* and other corrupting merchandise procured in the Evil West.

Finally, the train rolled into the grand Moscow Central. I did not remember the city looking so drab and dreary when we had left for our European rendezvous two months ago.

Sanjay was going back to India. While I would miss him, I am sorry to say that I was more than slightly relieved to have Arjun all to myself again.

Little did I know, but the following year something horrific would come between me and the rest of my world ---

THE BACILLUS BITES THE DUST

You have a cavity in your left lung, the size of a walnut," the pulmonologist's words kept ringing in my ears, "and you *will* die if you don't get help."

"Nargis, you can beat *anything*," Daddy had said.

I looked out of my window in the TB sanatorium located on the outskirts of Moscow and through the haze of the blizzard saw my ancestral village, Raipur, in the distance ---

In the winter months the fields would turn spring-green. As far as the eye could see, swaying in the cool breeze was a golden carpet made of bright-yellow mustard flowers.

Mustard. Its young innocent stem bent weakly in my fingers, but did not break apart even between my teeth. A sea of tongues made of a million petals, licking the vacant air, waiting for the wind to spread fine yellow dust on the grass, the dirt roads and the mud banks. Before sunrise, dense flowers bathed in dew tickled my neck when I walked through. From the mud huts smoke would rise, curling up to meet the sky, while the mist would hang close hugging the ground.

It's so easy to get lost in these green fields and forget all my black pain.

During the last six months while recovering from tuberculosis, all I could think of was how to close that wretched cavity that had threatened to take over my entire being and be back in Arjun's arms again. My body and spirit were both on my side, as I was steadily nursed back to health.

It was as if God was saying, "Life? Or death? Let's give Nargis life, after all!"

The cavity did give up and eventually close down on itself, hardly leaving a scar. Some scars, thankfully, do eventually fade over time. It would be necessary to comply with a complex medication regimen for another two years to prevent relapse. I now looked the picture of health, gaining back more weight than I had originally lost, on generous doses of steroids. In the ensuing months, I was well on my way to becoming the plus-size *Jaat* girl who would make my parents proud.

I stifled a sob when I said goodbye to my roommates at the sanatorium. The ones who had taught me about the two phases of recovery. Wait. And Hope. I knew that I would never see them again. I feel terrible that I cannot even remember their names today.

I have not forgotten though, the love given to me by total strangers in a country that I can never call my own.

YOU WIN SOME, YOU LOSE SOME

There is a reason why it was called the Iron Curtain. Nothing came through without being filtered. Nothing went past without being distorted. The consummate spin zone.

When I left that nation, the one with the hammer juxtaposed with a sickle, it felt like being released from Central Jail. Similar to how a Bollywood movie often begins. A gray-haired protagonist with an overgrown stubble is standing outside the prison gates, suitcase in hand, creased street clothes hanging loose on his lean body, squinting at the stark sunlight, waiting to tell the world that he was indeed innocent all along. It was not he, but his twin who had actually committed the murder for which he had been wrongfully sentenced to life term. That evil, evil, twin. The same one who had been found and raised by simple peasants after he had drifted downstream in a wicker basket, where their unwed mother had left him, naked and crying, somewhere between the water and the stars and given him up for dead. Poor people often drift downstream. Abandoned babies are usually given up for dead. The protagonist looks at the people who have come to take him home from prison, feeling bewildered and lost. He cannot recognize anyone anymore.

So much has changed in the last thirty years since the prisoner first entered through the gates of Sing Sing. An ideal setup to tell a story between its covers. A perfect way to make a point with a flashback?

This is how I felt when I left the Soviet Union. In the last six years, a lot had changed in the world and much had changed in India as well. Coming back to the motherland, I was the embodiment of Heinlein's stranger in a strange land. I did not realize how much I had missed out on, until I Googled that period for the purpose of telling my story. The word did not exist at the time.

In the Middle East: The oil embargo leads to stagflation and chokes the world economy. In subsequent years, oil would become a currency that would be repeatedly misused, bartered, negotiated, exploited and held hostage.

In Africa: Asians and Europeans flee from Uganda to escape the genocide masterminded by dictator Idi Amin. Similar to the forced exodus of millions of innocent people that has occurred throughout history. Like the one my maternal relatives suffered during Partition.

In Russia: Mikhail Baryshnikov defects to the West. In a major coup d'état over communism, Alexander Solzhenitsyn wins the Nobel Prize in Literature. The news item is mentioned as a small footnote in the Russian newspaper, Pravda, ironically named Truth.

In the U.S.: Bra burning spreads like wild fire on the streets of Washington, DC., and Roe versus Wade establishes a woman's right over her own body. A right, I also believe, to the sovereignty a woman has over who can touch it. The Sears Tower is completed in Chicago becoming the tallest building in the world. Seven years later, my home would be ten miles from that imposing edifice. America takes the lead to open up new frontiers by initiating a détente with China's Gang of Four through the ping-pong policy. The Vietnamization of America results in the mistrust of the Imperial Presidency. Which, in turn, leads to the embarrassment of Watergate, Nixon's resignation and farewell, "Only if you have been in the deepest valley can you ever know how magnificent it is to be on the highest mountain." He could have easily run out of the White House in Nike shoes, since the company was founded around the same time. But he chooses to leave with dignity, when he waves to the nation for one last time before he enters through the door of Air Force One.

Famous lines in Hollywood: "Leave the gun, take the cannoli," from *The Godfather*. Nurse Ratched from *One Flew Over the Cuckoo's Nest*, "Your hand is staining my window." And from *The Exorcist*, "If you can't control it, it'll control you."

In the music world: The heartbreaking breakup of The Beatles, and the launch of The Jackson Five. A Grammy win for *Bridge Over Troubled Water*, and *For Killing Me Softly with His Song*.

In Europe: The nonstarter bravado at the Munich Olympics, which are hijacked by Palestinian supporters Black September. Margaret Thatcher becomes the head of the Conservative Party in Britain. Woman power. In Stockholm, the Nobel Prize in Medicine is announced for the discovery of the chemical structure of human antibodies to antidotes and not for their psychological configuration.

In India: Blockbuster *Sholey* is released, the largest grosser in Bollywood, when good triumphs over evil. Again. New business houses are established, some of which, like the Ambani Group, will eventually enter the world stage in later years. The Bangladesh war ends: India instruments the dismemberment of Pakistan and releases the largest number of POWs since the Second World War. Much to the consternation of the West, India tests its first nuclear device, Pokhran, with a code name of Smiling Buddha.

In the summer of 1976, I left a totalitarian regime to come back home to a new India. Prime Minister Indira Gandhi instruments a State of Emergency, which leads to a temporary loss of democracy. The press is muffled, prominent opposition leaders are arrested, and the rules are forged to make compulsory birth control a law. Mrs. Gandhi would be assassinated eight years later.

It felt as if I was waking up from a long sleep. Like something a modern day Rip Van Winkle might have felt when he finally wakes up to rub his eyes: when his pupils are dilated just enough for his surroundings to be visible again.

BACK TO THE MOTHERLAND, AND MORE

I had graduated with my class. In fact, I graduated with High Honors, like Daddy had predicted I would.

I came back to India at the age of twenty-three, complete with signed and sealed diploma in hand, at least several pounds heavier from gorging on *khleb, kartoshko* and generous doses of steroids; dragging bags laden with gifts of curios and replicas of landscapes by famous Russian artists for my family, and a heart heavy with longing to feel safe in Arjun's arms again. A new and improved version of *From Russia with Love*.

Coming back to India, as I have repeated so many times in the years before and since, has always been a hugely emotional experience --- a sense of belonging as the plane first flies into the Indian sky and the wheels first touchdown on Indian soil. It is all so familiar: The heat as it rises off the runway and the smells of India as they seep through into the cabin; the gusts of hot humid winds swirling overhead; the bored and sleep deprived faces of the immigration officers, and the rude awakening of milling with throngs of brown people, a sea of humanity that has little concern for conserving personal space and even less for dispensing body odor, scurrying around chatting like magpies as they wigwag with complete abandon --- the color, the dust, and the din.

When we met in New Delhi, I clung to Arjun and sobbed. In that moment, the pain of the year-long separation and the despair of my protracted illness were gone. As I lay in his arms for a few fleeting hours in a hotel room during that brief layover, I worried myself sick thinking that Daddy must have surely followed me there, militantly incognito. All the way from the gangway, past the security and customs at Palam Airport, through Connaught Place, and finally to Hotel President where Old Delhi meets New Delhi. Where old love was being rekindled into new love. I imagined Daddy was waiting outside the door to nab me cold, with at least one finger on the trigger of his well-oiled point 22 rifle and both open barrels pointing straight at me. Ready and loaded.

Arjun and I decided to go our separate ways, until the opportune moment arose to be reunited again. I took the next train to Dehradun and went home to live with my parents. In my heart, I prayed that the stay would not be long.

The Red Fort felt big and empty. Anjali's family had moved to Surat in Gujarat, to become the leading diamond merchants in that state. Sanjay, meanwhile, having been awarded the coveted Sword of Honor upon graduation from the Indian Military Academy, was rapidly promoted and posted out to NEFA (North East Frontier Agency). Even Daddy could not chide him now!

All I could think of was how to marry Arjun. Yesterday. Immediately. Now. We were living over two hundred miles and many more heartbeats apart, except during those stealthy trips that he made to visit with me, when I was on night-call at the City Hospital where I interned. We were starting to get bolder, as we casually strolled in the Botanical Garden, cozying up behind the rosebushes somewhere between Angel Face, Bewitched, and All That Jazz, trying to steal a moment of the much missed intimacy with each other. One day, we just missed my parents by a hair-breadth and had to duck for cover, when they almost walked through the middle of the movie screen! Fight. Flight. Freeze.

I was also starting to feel desperate, as I fended off matrimonial proposals of suitable boy' who came from other respectable *Jaat* families like ours.

"Who'll marry me, a girl recovering from TB?" I would plead, to deflect my parents' perseverance. Or, "Please, leave me alone for now. I really want to focus on my career," I would counter, to end all discussions on the matter, a copout universally employed by many young adults similarly cornered before and since my time.

Daddy would periodically ask me about that boy. He would ambush me on long walks, prying into what genre of boys would I give a second thought. In order to escape such queries, I had no other choice but to continue to practice my manipulative ways. Daddy was so eager to believe that it was all over between us, that I did not really have to work too hard at convincing him that I had no clue where Arjun presently lived.

"For all you know, he may still be in Europe," I lied, gritting my teeth. "Or living in some godforsaken place like Timbuktu! Most likely, he's already married. Or dead --- or both!"

My voice sounds strange, even to myself. Our families are so different. The dots are so far apart. Sigh! I'll never be able to draw a straight line through them.

During that year, I was able to hoodwink my parents the few times I slipped up and accidentally referred to Sanjay as Arjun. Their names sounded rather similar. But it was 'Arjun' who was on my lips. And in my heart.

Nargis, just be patient. You survived last year and came home with flying colors You can do it again. Remember, nothing can be as bad as last year.

Anjali was engrossed with responsibilities towards her growing family. Sanjay was busy leading stealth military operations at the Indo-China border and could not be reached for months at a time. I knew then that I was left to my own devices.

So one day I invited Arjun, accompanied by his close friend, a professor at Delhi University, to the Red Fort. My parents were away on their routine evening stroll, most likely, discussing, "how to rope Nargis into marrying a boy of our choice, from an established family."

In that instant, I had decided that this was the moment to take charge of my destiny. My wishes were so orthogonal to my parents' desires for me. I was fed up of this whole thing. I was sick of lying. And I was tired of hiding out and living apart from Arjun.

I must run away and I must do it *now!*

Quickly, I packed a small bag with a change of clothes, along with my passport, diploma and some family photographs. I was ready. I was ready to leave my family forever. They would never agree to this. They would never give me their blessings to marry Arjun. I had lost all hope and I was tired of waiting. If I did not act now, I would end up being a disgruntled old maid living in this stupid Red Fort!

Arjun was becoming rather impatient as well. In those days, he used to agree to most of my plans. However crazy they might be. He would smuggle me out of my parents' fortress, we would run away together and have a shotgun wedding. I would never have to see my parents again and never have to explain anything to anybody. Ever again. Or, at least, anytime soon.

The professor being older and wiser than either one of us, prevailed on our better senses to abort the plan. This was not the proper manner to do things. There must be a better way. There must be a way to reason with reason. He reassured me that they would come back together again some other time, to persuade my father.

Did you say persuade? Do you really mean *persuade?*

Crestfallen and utterly heartbroken, I was nervously unpacking a tote-bag in my bedroom when my parents rang the doorbell. My mind was going like a fast freight train on converging tracks. That too, downhill! Smart as he was, Daddy would have never guessed that when they entered through the front door, my heart was pounding in my mouth and my stomach was doing a summersault in my throat! Sweat was running all the way down my legs to my toes and doing a squish-squish in the Bata flip-flops that I had been planning to run away in. I had missed the proverbial bullet by barely a tenth of a minute. Actually, I was sweating bullets!

A few months later, I devised a newer and better plan. Newer plans are usually better plans. I convinced my parents that I should intern at a New Delhi hospital, where I would have far more advanced training than in rusty old Dehradun. My intentions sounded so obvious that it totally befuddles me how I got away with it so easily. Was I really able to dupe Daddy? Or, could he see through my poorly devised plan and still let go of me? I will never know.

I was now staying at the Y and interning at Lady Hardinge Hospital in New Delhi. It took all of one week for Arjun and me to put up the banns at the local courthouse. The law required for us to wait a full month in case anyone had any objection to the union. That was the longest month of my life. I would imagine Daddy storming into the courthouse, whisking away the blasted document from under my eyes even before the ink could run dry and tearing it into shreds in front of the very judge! However Honorable he might be. It would be all over and done with even before it started. A flash in the pan. Nipped in the bud. Killed in situ. And all would be lost.

Arjun made all the arrangements. His family had expressed some concern about our coming together in the eyes of the law, which, when translated in any language, means that they did not stand in our way. All the court needed of us was to drum up two garlands, two witnesses, two signatures and one pen. And of course, two eager and willing participants. That would be us.

Do I look tense in our wedding photographs! I was doing shoulder checks as I signed on the dotted line, in case Daddy would walk in that very minute and end it all!

No bells! No whistles! If anyone were to ask me today, I cannot even remember the weather on my wedding day.

I was married in Mummy's Banarsi silk sari, which I had borrowed for a hospital Diwali party on my last trip home. I dressed my hair in a bun and placed a large round crimson-red *bindi* squarely in the middle of my forehead like I had seen on the actress Rekha. Then I dabbed a spot of Coco Chanel on my wrists and touched it lightly behind my ears. Just for Arjun.

At the reception that night, I barely knew anybody, except for Arjun and two of his buddies from work. Arjun was all who I really needed to know.

A few days before the wedding, we had rented and hurriedly furnished a small second floor flat in the home of a traditional Sikh family. We flabbergasted them when we conjured up a story of traveling for ten hours back and forth from Delhi to Dehradun that same day, to be married with sound parental blessings. In deference to us, they did not ask us for details we could never provide. After all, we were a newlywed couple, and it is considered highly improper to ask a newlywed couple a lot of newlywed awkward questions. Besides, we had paid two month's rent in advance!

I learned much later that totally unbeknownst to me, on our wedding day my local guardian, Uncle Inder from the Bombay days, made a surprise visit to the hospital where I worked. He had wanted me to join his family for a home cooked dinner. To his complete shock, he was told that Dr. Nargis Yadav had taken the entire week off for her wedding!

Immediately, he called up Daddy in Dehradun.

"I know you've very advanced ideas, Shiv," he complained. "But I'm terribly offended that you did not even inform us about your daughter's wedding, leave alone invite us to such an auspicious occasion. Now, how many years have our families known each other? And we call ourselves bosom buddies? God help you, my friend, for you must come up with a good explanation."

I can only throw a dart in the dark to guess how Daddy handled this. Or what color rabbit or dove he must have pulled out of his hat this time! I cannot even picture what Daddy and Mummy must have said to each other.

As in all times of crisis, Daddy must have been a rock.

"Inder, you know my daughter is super obstinate," he probably explained, calming his voice. "She's got some new and bold ideas. Believe it or not, some of them are too modern even for my taste. That's what happens when you've lived abroad for so long. That's what also happens when you've had too much education, like she does. As you know, Nargis doesn't believe in big weddings. It's her explicit wish to have just Mani and myself present for this special day in her life. You know, my friend, in some ways she's just like me. She has a distaste for wasteful pomp and show. As per her instructions, we've arranged for a small reception on the lawns of the Swiss Embassy. Just for the two families. I'm terribly sorry, Brother, but it has to be this way. I know that you'll understand. And I promise, we'll make it up to you the next time we meet and drink a double-scotch together."

I'll never understand the Swiss Embassy part.

It took my parents the better part of three months to partially recover from the shock of it all. Three miserable months for Daddy to devise an immaculate plan for the benefit of the extended family to properly arrange the wedding of his youngest, most doggedly-tenacious child. My parents sequestered themselves in their own home for three full days not accepting any phone calls, answering the doorbell, or venturing past the front door even to pick up the mail. Three copies of *The Indian Express* dotted the lush lawn lined with prize rosebushes, probably bang between Bold Red and Defiant Pink. Daddy made it generally known that they had gone to New Delhi to marry off their pigheaded daughter in a style that she had dictated. At the end of this self-imposed exile, they emerged from their home assuming exaggerated jubilance, and distributed *laddoos* and *barfi* sweets to friends and family to announce the union.

After the festivities of the reception dinner attended by largely unknown but mostly well meaning guests, we drove back to our flat hardly talking on the way. I wanted to remember everything that had happened that day.

Arjun looked at me with his bedroom eyes as he carried me up the flight of steps to our first home together. After five long years since we had shared our first kiss laced with champagne and *halwa* on that fateful spring evening in Moscow, it was finally just the two of us. Together. For the rest of our lives. I do not remember ever being happier in my life.

I belong here. Right here with Arjun. Only in his arms, I whispered to myself.

When Arjun shut the bedroom door to the outside world for the first time, we were finally ready to exchange bodily fluids. We made passionate love like never before. Then he penetrated me and we became one.

That was the night I was surprised to discover that up until that moment I had still been a virgin. Why this was so important to me I will never fully understand.

What I also did not know then, was that this was also the same week when I got pregnant with Mandy.

"MADE FOR EACH OTHER"

It was sheer bliss to be together with Arjun at last. I liken the first few months of our married life to how the sweet taste of clear sparkling bubbly replaces the bitter taste of dark frothy beer. It was super exciting to have our own small place together, sleep between our own bed linen bought at the Rajasthan Emporium and entertain friends with our very first china dinner set made in Calcutta. We could now define life on *our* terms and forge new lasting friendships together. Everything was more fun now. Even sex.

I was equally eager and ready to shed my Yadav surname. We had been all but married in the years we had dated, except that now I was finally Mrs. Arjun Sharma and we had real sex after spur of the moment foreplay. Heady, giddy, sex. Then my husband would hold me close to his body, while I slept soundly in his warm and fuzzy bear hug. And nothing mattered anymore. Not even time.

We made an attempt to take on the responsibility of managing a budget; decorate our bookshelves with knick-knacks from Janpath, pottery from Jaipur, with Russian artifacts thrown in for good measure; and stumble through spontaneously planning our lives as couples all over the world have done, before and since our time. This was now *our* place. And we had *our* stuff in it.

In my weaker moments, I was painfully aware of that wolf lurking at the doorstep from having no support outside the walls of our little home. We put on a brave front of handling our lives on our own, wherever they were headed, because we had hardly a clue. I muddled through trying to negotiate a polite and cordial relationship with Arjun's family. Like most newlyweds, I would admit only much later in life that I wish I had done a better job. In spite some of the good intentions on both sides being lost in translation, the association evolved into a good working relationship.

I still did not believe in God. Secretly, I wished that I did. Faith would certainly help answer a lot of questions posthaste, and ease life's tribulations instantly. Even if for just a little bit. I learned, though, to respect other faiths, including Arjun's who remained a practicing Hindu. And he made no attempt to convert me either. We had enough faith in each other to put this matter to rest.

In my new life, arguments over money, mother-in-law and having to make do with less were starting to crop up. But, even in those difficult moments, we were fairly confident that we could get through such thorny issues on our own. I do not remember ever second guessing the choices I had made. We could hardly wait to be with each other. It was sheer bliss to go to sleep in Arjun's arms and wake up together in the same bed.

By January of the new year, I realized that I did, on occasion, miss my family and the comforts of the Red Fort. Sometimes, I would open up my photo album to look at their faces and wonder what they might be doing at the same time.

In my mind, my family could never be the same without me. With my new life heading in a direction so alien to the way my parents thought, and with the passage of time, any chance of reconciliation was becoming a hazy mirage.

There was no communication with my parents. One morning, while riding on a bus on my way to the hospital, I was completely stunned when I found myself retching. This is how I discovered that I was pregnant. At the age of twenty four, it was a complete shock!

How in the world did *this* happen? Surely, it could not be happening to *me*! I thought. To *my* body. Inside my body. Not *now!* What'll Daddy and Mummy say when *they* find out?

I was sure that I had done something terribly immoral.

Without a doubt, after today I'll never be able face them again! I lamented. I'll never be able face *anyone* ever again!

And then crept in the nagging self-doubts. Self-doubts are often known to nag.

What a dreadful blunder I've made! How'll I ever be able to take care of a baby? I feel too young to be a mother. I'm still a child myself! Did that doctor make a mistake? Am I *really* pregnant?

I am not sure why, but it was around this time when I decided to write a letter to my parents. A little bit like what Daddy had written to his father so many years ago.

Dear, Daddy and Mummy

I know that you'll never accept me because of my decision to marry Arjun. I'm happy to tell you that we have a wonderful life together. It saddens me that I can never imagine either one of you ever being happy for me.

I am now pregnant and soon will be having a family of my own.

I've only one request. Please take me off your will and testament with immediate effect, so I can end all ties with you and with anything you own. With this, I end my relationship with both of you. Now and Forever.

This has been a difficult decision, as I now say goodbye.

I need nothing from you. Not even a reply to this letter.

Your daughter,

Nargis

P.S. By the way, can you send my typewriter over to Uncle Inder's place?

I never did get a reply. A few days later, as per my instructions, uncle had my typewriter expeditiously delivered to our flat. The instrument that represented the freedom to express myself. I could now go on with the rest of my life without wondering whether Daddy would suddenly barge into our home, screaming expletives and demanding explanations.

By now Arjun and I had happily settled into a young couple's routine, working by day and partying with friends at night: overflowing ashtrays left unattended, empty Kingfisher beer bottles forgotten under the sofas and blaring music that annoyed our neighbors at all odd hours. We had little thought about what the future might bring.

I was now getting bigger, and my body was starting to change. There was a new beginning happening inside me. A new life. In *my* body. One night, I was woken up by strange little movements. Soft tiny kicks. They reminded me that I was not alone anymore. Even when sometimes I felt alone.

I must feed my baby, I thought, as I voraciously ate corn-on-the-cob roasted on orange hot coals by the roadside on my way to and from work, juicy plump kernels smeared with pepper, salt, and lime.

It was Independence Day weekend when Mummy's brother,

Uncle Karan, flew in from New Zealand to visit with Arjun and me.

"Nargis, I can't believe this is happening!" he exclaimed, as he entered through the door. "You know, my father, your Nana had the wisdom to predict this. That one day both you and your sister would marry of your own choice because of how your father was raising you girls. This is a result of his modern ideas. He never had the courage to talk to your father about this eventuality. As you know, nobody could ever confront *Bhai Saab* Shiv about anything."

I believe the last line to be true. When two people agree, it generally becomes a truth.

"This is not right, Nargis," Uncle went on. "You're soon going to have a baby. It's unacceptable not be talking to your parents. Leave it to me. I can arrange for you to go home with me. Now don't say 'No'. Trust me Nargis, you'll be *totally* safe with me."

In my heart, I think I was ready to go home. Even though I was deathly scared. I was ready to apologize for my wrongdoings, for excluding my parents from my life, for getting pregnant and for anything else they wanted me to also express regret over. Just to get one chance to make things right again, the way it had always been between us. I was petrified with the thought that Daddy might lash out and employ choice curses --- whore, slut; or hurl a shoe --- the spit-'n'-shine one. He might even pull out his belt --- with that spic-'n'-span brass buckle and throw Arjun and me out of the house lock, stock, and barrel! With the neighbors watching and wondering about it all, from a safe distance across our fence!

Most people will agree, it is usually far less embarrassing leaving of your own accord.

But, what if Daddy pulls out his old point 22 rifle? Is it really fair to subject Arjun to this risk?

Thankfully, I did not think too hard. I do not know why, but I was willing to chance any outcome. For all three of us: Arjun, baby, and me.

The next morning, Arjun and I drove to Dehradun with Uncle Karan by my side, holding my cold and clammy hand. It was tense in the taxi all the way there. Uncle attempted to make small talk and some lighthearted comments, about how he had learned over the years to work his way into *Bhai Saab's* heart.

"Nargis, you do know that your Daddy loves you," he consoled me. "He's always been so very proud of you and hasn't stopped talking about your achievements. He's really a good man and you know that he has the heart of a woman. Don't worry. I'll be there with you at all times. So rest assured, you'll come to no harm," he winked. "Or we'll all go down together!"

Uncle dictated the plan and I had no option but to acquiesce. Especially, since I had exhausted all my bright ideas, and, for once, had no real plan of my own.

According to the plan, Arjun would wait at the sari store on the market street just around the bend from the Red Fort, until the coast was clear.

How I mustered up courage to waddle into my parents' house just one week before I was to give birth to our first daughter is anybody's guess. Including my own. Uncle walked in first and I followed closely behind.

Uncle wants to be the hero. And I've no fight with that, I thought to myself.

"*Bhai Saab*," he announced himself. "Look who I brought with me."

Then he moved to the side. There was now nothing between my parents and me, except for some very still air and my very large tummy.

For what felt like an eternity, it was deathly still --- but it was probably just a second, or two. Then Daddy and Mummy walked up to where I stood and together they put their arms around me. I cried. And they cried. We all hugged together and cried together. Obviously it could not be a very close hug, because there was now a baby between us.

It was like a happy ending to a Bollywood movie! Rich girl meets poor boy, runs away to get married, gets pregnant --- on film, usually in reverse order; objecting and hostile parents turn into indulging and obsequious grandparents and they all live happily ever after ---?

In that moment all was forgiven. And forgotten. My parents never asked about the circumstances around my runaway wedding and I was grateful to be never put on the spot. It was never brought up again, as if it had never happened. Just like other things that had happened before in my life that were never brought up, as if they had never happened.

Then we were all laughing and joking all at once. For a little while, we almost forgot about poor Arjun who was still waiting at the sari store. When he was escorted home by Uncle Karan, Daddy gave him a huge hug and a firm pat on the shoulder.

"Come son, fix me a real drink. I've saved this special bottle of Royal Salute just for you. We must drink together to celebrate!" Daddy exclaimed, thrusting his empty glass in his outstretched hand toward his until a few minutes ago completely estranged son-in-law, while simultaneously looking away.

"Arjun," Daddy continued, "you've come just in time to drive us down to General Panduri's house, whose daughter we think is a perfect match for Sanju. I'm so delighted that you're here to help us make this very important decision, since you're now a very important member of our family. I must say, you Brahmins have the wisest minds. There's a reason why so many of our nation's leaders have been Brahmins, including some of our prime ministers. We cannot make this decision without you, son."

Privately, I could not believe that this was happening! But I said nothing, in case that would break the spell.

That night when I went to sleep in the Red Fort with my husband for the first time, it felt rather strange. There is something weird about sleeping with a man for the first time in your parents' home.

I still think about that day. I marveled at my parents for this triple-digit degree turn. Daddy would always say that in a time of crisis, he was like a rock. As for myself, I pretended that last year never happened and prayed that I would never have to revert back to that year long standoff.

But standoffs are a part of my *Jaat* heritage. We make the best of friends, but also the worst of enemies. Little did I know then that later in my life, it would happen again. And that in Round Two, it would last for six years.

I went back to our flat in New Delhi feeling more relaxed than I remembered feeling that previous year. This was opportune, because one week later Mandy was born.

The monsoon had lingered on and it had poured for days. The rain washed away all the pain and suffering of that last year. The leaves looked fresh and green, bringing the joy of a new life into our lives.

They say that the pain of childbirth ends with the first cry of the newborn. This is so true.

A new life was placed in my waiting arms. She looked up at me, asking me to pick her up, coo with her and nurse her. She looked so tiny. So innocent. So *mine*.

Finally, I have a family that I can call my own.

I wondered how my parents managed to explain the birth of a healthy full-term baby to friends and family, who had heard the wonderful news of my wedding only five months prior. I do not think that even Daddy could have straightened out the math.

Was it not his mantra, "When you tell one lie, you've to tell many more to cover up for it?"

A month later, on the next trip home I took Mandy to the Red Fort for the first time. Past the stunning roses, Pink Paradise and Perpetual Bliss.

Greeting us in the doorway, Daddy exclaimed, "She's such a precious baby! Mani, see what a wonderful gift Nargis and Arjun have given us!"

From day one, Daddy treated Arjun special. Like he had treated me special. Daddy knew how to appeal to anyone's narcissism. Like he had appealed to mine.

"Mani and I couldn't have picked a better boy than Arjun for our daughter," he would boast. "Nargis could only have married someone as brilliant as herself!"

Flattered but completely mystified, I could hardly believe my ears when Daddy added, "And let me tell you, they are made for each other."

THE AGONY OF HATE

WILL WORK HARD, HAVE A DREAM

The last six years after our marriage had been both easy and difficult for us. Easy, because Arjun and I had finally made a decision to immigrate to America to start a new life and take a stab at owning our destiny. And difficult? Also for the same reason.

"A land of milk and honey," Sanjay had warned, "where the cow still kicks, and the bee still stings."

The best worst thing that happened to me in India was that my career was stuck in the mud. With each passing day, I was becoming more and more restless with the brutal reality of working for a pittance. Some of my cousins who had migrated to North America would come home on vacation laden with gifts like Santa Claus. For me, these homecomings glaringly amplified the depravity of life in the Third World. After every family reunion, I became even more painfully aware of everything that I so desperately wanted but hopelessly lacked. Family reunions are known to do that. I was afraid to acknowledge my mounting feelings of uneasiness because of my growing financial dependence on my parents. The nagging and gnawing notion of self-doubt had started to creep in, reminiscent of the faintly stale smell of leftover fish from yesterday's dinner.

I am so utterly miscast for this part, I lamented.

Sometimes disquiet can be an opportune distress. It has been known to be a great motivator.

It would certainly sound presumptuous on my part if I were to proclaim that the idea of immigrating to the U.S. was an epiphany that happened on another hot and humid Indian summer night, simply because it was hot and humid. One could have bet on it and easily won hands down. The leaves had just started to change to shades of yellow, gold, and rust when we arrived on a Greyhound bus across the Canadian border into the U.S., after meeting with Arjun's cousins at their home in Calgary.

1983 was the year I arrived in a country that would become my home for the rest of my life. The year of Reaganomics, Star Wars and trickledown economics. The year Sally Ride was the first woman to ride into space, and Vanessa Williams the first black woman to be crowned Miss America. The year Martin Luther King, Jr. Day would become a national holiday. It was also the year when Michael Jackson swept away the awards at the Grammys for *Thriller* and *Beat It*, and the movie *Gandhi* did likewise at the Oscars. A success story about minorities is always a good sell. A story about freedom becomes a blockbuster. Especially in nations around the world, as in the one I adopted, which pride in democracy and self-determination.

It was on a crisp September morning of that year, thirteen years after I had first landed in Moscow, when my Indian passport was stamped by U.S. Immigration at Noyes, Minnesota. I hear it is a ghost town today and even the duty free shop has been forced to bring down its shutters. Arjun and I traveled on with our two bundles of joy, Mandy and Natasha and everything else we owned stuffed in four travel bags, through the Midwestern states to settle down in resident graduate housing at the University of Chicago in Hyde Park, a southern suburb of Chicago, Illinois. The Land of Lincoln. The birthplace of democracy.

It's rather uncanny that so many years ago and just a few days before leaving for Moscow, I had bragged into the tape recorder at the Red Fort drawing room, "This is Nargis, checking in from Chicago!"

America was a new country for us and Chicago a new place to call home --- Deep Dish Pizza and Chicago Hot Dog. Hometown to McDonalds, which had introduced the Mc Nugget that same year.

Lake Michigan, the Loop and the Magnificent Mile. The Sears Tower, Adler Planetarium and the John Hancock Center. I never knew, until then, that John Hancock is also a metaphor for a person's signature.

In our new homeland, we would begin to write and speak English in a new and different way: 'Lift' would be replaced by 'elevator', 'scent' would imply 'perfume', 'queue' would equate to 'line', 'weighing machine' would spell 'SCALE', and 'torch' would be 'flashlight'. The worst offense? To call an 'eraser' --- a 'rubber'! The list goes on and on. We would make on the spot immigrant decisions about what part of ourselves we should retain and what we must discard. Immediately. Without further ado. Some of these choices we would later regret, since, as is universally acknowledged, one can never perfectly balance the two. It took considerable effort to get accustomed to open-mid central unrounded vowels, and practice rolling my Rrrrs and sharpening my Vs. Rounding up Ws would take some 'Wwwwork.' I consoled myself with the thought that the American pronunciation would present as a formidable challenge even for "'enry 'iggins!" In the months to come, I would be able to experience firsthand the sheer cadence of direct and explicit American metaphors, which sounded lyrical to my ears.

"It's a 'Double whammy,' 'Smart Alec!' 'Break a leg!' Or, 'Take a rain check' and 'Eat crow,' 'There ain't no such thing as a free lunch!'"

The concept of personal space was also new. Direct eye contact would take some getting used to. Initially it felt faintly violating and intrusive, but in the country of my adoption it conveyed attention and respect. Handshakes are also confident, firm, and strong.

I love it! Everything in America is direct, self-assured and powerful.

Back to the red, white and blue. But different from the Union Jack. This time the stripes came with stars.

The Star Spangled Banner, Memorial Day and Thanksgiving. Football Madness. Happy Hour. Supersize. The melting pot and the fruit basket --- I took it all in.

America! Wonderful America!

I remember the festive starry night sky on the Hyde Park beach, sprayed by shooting stars of red, white, and blue on the Fourth of July, with our two toddlers in tow. For the rest of our lives, this holiday would have a special meaning for all of us.

The onerous task of starting over, turning around a winding cul-de-sac, backing out of Wrong Way, coming to an abrupt halt at a truncated Dead End, keeping the weary cylinders firing full throttle in spite of audible grunts over a hidden Speed Bump was challenging enough. But having to explain myself, again, and again, and yet again, was becoming rather tedious and frustrating. Like rolling spaghetti uphill on a wet slope.

Notwithstanding their naiveté', I did find most Americans to be generally honest and genuine. A trusting and hardworking bunch. A magnanimous race with an unmatched love for freedom. For Arjun and me, a chance to enjoy the colors of this great nation --- no pun intended --- was truly invigorating. The opportunity to be finally gainfully employed, pursue excellence, experience self-determination and dare to dream in the most powerful nation on Earth was as exhilarating as a heady double-vodka cosmopolitan.

All our life savings were swiftly exhausted with no regrets, after traveling to the U.S. and setting up house. After writing that last fat check, we were left with very little --- except for a rather skinny wallet and a will to make something of our lives for ourselves and for our two little daughters who depended on us for everything: from baby formula to baby smiles.

Right from the start Arjun and I worked as a team. And as is offhandedly and mostly colloquially mentioned back home, we left no stone unturned. During the first year of Arjun's residency in surgery and mine in psychiatry at the University of Chicago, I would come back to our condo at the end of a workday feeling like a rag doll. The weekends were no different. The word fatigue would be dropped from my Thesaurus forever.

During the next couple of years, in an attempt to cope with drastic change, acute want and harsh uncertainty, I would make blunders in judgment that included, but were not limited to, whacking, smacking and latch-keying the kids; maladaptive coping through hysteria especially around the inevitable monthly hormonal disruptions, and episodic mood dysregulation when estrogen would be warring with progesterone.

A couple of years later, one day I drove little Mandy to Beach Park

Woods, not far from our two-bedroom swanky condo in Hyde Park. I was going to punish her for something she had done or not done. I cannot remember what it was, but I am sure it must have been quite trivial as are most deeds of little children thus callously punished. I threatened to leave her there in the rain to brave the lions in the woods. Mercifully, we got locked out of our new Honda Accord, with rain beating down on its shiny metal and its headlights illuminating the trees in the woods that appeared to be shaking their heads violently in silent disapproval. When we walked a few blocks back to our home, cold and drenched, she was crying and I was fuming. The punishment doled out to me was to trudge back to the park to retrieve the car, angry and alone, soaked up to my socks in the torrential downpour!

"Tut, Tut, Nargis. You just followed Daddy's stupid example. Surely, you can do better than that!" I said to myself all the way home.

Meanwhile, depending on my siblings gave me new insights on some of the unspoken simmering dysfunction we had shared growing up, which was now amplified in our adulthood. A bit like those trick mirrors at country fairs where the nose appears grotesquely magnified and the ears monstrous and misshapen. Sanjay and Anjali had never seen me more vulnerable. While my brother was declared Best Cadet at Staff College, my sister's family had become prominent diamond exporters in Antwerp.

A new relationship with my siblings would emerge that was starkly different from what I had previously experienced during my childhood.

Isn't it just possible that this may have something to do with my being Daddy's favorite child growing up and having things come so easy my way? I wondered. But little do they know, I did not always live on the right side of Easy Street.

On my first trip back to Dehradun, Sanjay started to blatantly compare me in an unflattering manner with his wife, Pinki.

I resisted and privately resented my brother's statements. So it is probably understandable, why Mummy met with no resistance when she enticed me into joining in on grudge matches against her daughter-in-law.

Anjali, meanwhile, fooled us all. While there was unquestionable bona fide financial support from Antwerp that was critical to our survival, on occasion her assistance seemed to be somewhat self-serving, largely intended, I thought, to invite praise from Daddy. I was left with no choice but to gloss over a handful of sporadic condescending statements and patronizing actions randomly thrown my way, mostly because of my increasing reliance on her. I complained that she had left me high and dry at the time of my wedding. She protested that I raked her across the coals. We were both right.

It was all so confusing and would take some time, much thought, and, unfortunately for all of us, considerable pain to tease out.

I give myself a D-C grade for how I coped with this. Where D-C stands for Dunce-Cap. I would be remiss not to mention that there was enough foolishness and hurt on both sides. I was increasingly sensitive, easily wounded and would readily slide down the slippery path of feeling controlled, judged, used, abandoned, victimized --- cluster feelings that would become my pet-peeves. But not being believed would take the cake and trigger angst of blockbuster proportions. Nothing would anger me more than being subjected to unprovoked anger. Coupled with the professional hazard of reading between the lines and smelling judgment from halfway across the world, all this made for a deadly concoction.

I hate to admit, but I would've hated to be on my own wrong side.

Today, in the side-view mirror, I am loathe to confess that most of these conflicts sound rather petty and inconsequential, as most disagreements generally tend to appear over time. I think over the years, I now have a better understanding of my siblings' visceral reactions toward me. After all, it was encrypted in our dominant gene.

Perhaps if I'd been in their place, I would've done no better. I was never tested.

I need to be strong again, I promised myself. I need to be strong --- *now*.

The only way I knew how was through education and hard work. It had worked for me before. I was sure it would serve me well again.

So back to school I went. I studied hard, burning the midnight oil. And I worked arduously, white knuckling as I dodged fatigue.

And what better place to do this, than here in America?

IN THE EYE OF THE STORM

It was a difficult year when I started my four year residency training in psychiatry at the University of Chicago. Between our respective unpredictable call schedules, Arjun and I had started to become experts at innovating and juggling. We were desperate for nickels and dimes, so it became imperative that Mummy come from India to stay with us for a couple of months, to help out with the children. And, of course, Daddy came too.

Why does it always have to be a package deal? I asked myself.

Nothing had changed about my parents.

"Mani, fix me a bowl of yogurt. And don't forget to sprinkle some freshly-ground roasted cumin powder on it. By the way, on your way back, can you bring my garlic pills and vitamin E?" Daddy would command from his favorite post in front of the television, a copy of Playboy perched on his lap, complete with a bookmark from the Art Institute celebrating the French Renaissance to save the centerfold.

Stop that already! I dared not utter. You bug me to high heaven!

The family room is where Daddy would get his jollies, watching a nature show in his boxer shorts and wife-beater undershirt, pointing to the mating habits of other species in the garb of a focused and attentive study of procreation in the Animal Kingdom. That Daddy made no attempt to camouflage the rise he must have got from publically examining copulating beasts was both repulsive and revolting.

I wonder what the world looks like through his eyes, I would feel a fist twisting in my throat. But thankfully, the kids are totally oblivious to those grizzly bears humping each other in the open wild so free from care. I certainly don't want to be a prude, but, hopefully, they must think it's just a silly animal sport.

After the TV show was over, Daddy would start his own talk show, indulging in an uninterrupted discourse on the degradation of America amply evidenced by the content of white trailer-trash programming and the futility of daytime soaps. He would predict, with certainty, that the American civilization --- a contradiction in terms, he would instantly point out, would one day surely fall on its face like the great Roman Empire had done so many centuries ago.

I can never fully explain when I learned to loathe Dad's armchair dogma and pseudo-philosophy.

"Now, you are all intelligent people. You know that history repeats itself," he would remind us from the pedestal of his soapbox. "There's too much sex, drugs and violence in America. Mark my words, this country is going to the dogs and you can't do diddly-doo about it," he would pontificate from the armchair, twirling his mousse-styled moustache so that at least *it* would comply.

That wacky-a-doodle Dad-speak. All he really needs is just a good lockup! I thought.

"First of all Nargis, I must remind you not to address your parents as 'Mom' and 'Dad'," he would continue, as if he had just read my mind. "By the way, I do insist. These words sound extremely disrespectful. As if, they're names for dogs! What's wrong with calling us 'Mummy' and 'Daddy' like you did before you came to this country? In America people don't really care about their parents. As you must know, usually they show more love for their house pets! Marriage also has no meaning here. People divorce on a whim, expose their bodies without shame and sleep around with the next-door neighbor without a second thought. And not necessarily in that order. Now, there's nothing like our good old Indian culture and family values. Let me tell you, I *have* seen the world. Believe me, Nargis, it'll not be long before this nation is lost in its own ruins."

Why does he look at me when he's actually just talking to himself?

"Mani, when that happens, when this country falls on its face, Nargis and her family will fall on their knees and plead to return to the sanity, safety and prosperity of India. And India will forgive them, embrace them, and give them a second chance. They'll come back to their native country, like little ducklings who take to water the moment they're born. Back they'll go to the Indus Valley, to the crucible of civilization. That day is not too far off, when India will once again become a Golden Peacock like she used to be so many years ago before the looters and colonizers raped our country. Of course, you all know the sun did finally set on the British Empire. Nargis, now you know that I *can* see the future. One day, the sun will also go down for the West in the West. And when that happens, you and your family will not just crawl back to the homeland. Like dog-tired horses, who after a long and exhausting journey can finally smell home, you'll be galloping all the way back to the motherland!"

Jealousy or prophesy?

Daddy was back in town and back in the saddle: cunning, conniving, calculating and crass.

Sometimes, Daddy would talk about the bodies of women and comment on their cleavage or curves or a combination of all.

"It's rather pathetic when you think about how woman has been exploited by man through the beginning of time. Nothing has changed," he would explain. "Nothing will ever change. What's your opinion about this, Nargis?"

And I would get another spell of lockjaw, wishing I could immediately melt in my chair and disappear into the fabric instead of observing Daddy reflexively kick propriety to the curbside; watching him get sadistic pleasure in blindsiding me and assuring my continued subjugation through my silence.

Is Daddy being provocative? I'd wonder. Is he testing me? Or is it that I have now changed? That I can no longer suffer his slippery talk and mindless commentary? Is he trying to read my mind?

I remembered again, how when I was younger Daddy would prod me on those long walks, "A penny for your thoughts, Nargis," and I would have to quickly think of something to fill the pregnant pause that followed, to put an end to the volley of queries that would inevitably follow. All those years, when he would crawl into me to tell me what to say.

"Yes, Daddy," I would nod without thinking.

"Yes what?"

"You're right, Dad" I would answer aloud mechanically. When, what I really wanted to say but never could: "You can't buy my thoughts for just a penny. Take a long walk on a short pier, Dad."

Every evening during their visit, Mom would accompany Dad on his daily routine of "let's take a short walk to have a long talk about our children," with her trailing after him, always two steps behind. Sometimes, after these pow wows, he would return to our condo brooding and sulking. He could easily suck air out of the place! Daddy could spend an entire evening just moping around. There was no cheering him out of his dark moods. I did not know what set them off and dared not ask. Perhaps, he had started to sense my intent for Home Rule and baby steps toward Sovereignty. His own predictions about a possible insurgency were about to come true.

"Mind you, Nargis, that day's not far when our Indian rupee will be stronger than your U.S. dollar," he would persevere by the end of the day. "By the way, how much can your dollar buy anyway?" he would carry on. "My dear, as you're well aware, a single green bill can barely fetch three miserably green apples. You Americans pay an arm and at least half a leg for healthcare. No pun intended. And your plumber indulges in daylight robbery! Look, in this country of yours, people just dump their parents into nursing homes to die. Pray, what kind of culture is this? *I'll* tell you what kind. I call it *backward* culture. It's actually a total *lack* of culture."

Another brain-fart! Daddy has mastered the art of talking by pulling out all the stops. The only one thing you can't blame him for is being inconsistent.

The year was 1986. I wished Americans had been more responsible with STDs, so Daddy would not have fresh evidence for the closing arguments on his dissertation: The Inevitable Demise of America.

"Now, let's talk about HIV," Daddy ended the day at wrap-up. "It's a curse on this nation, a blight on its conscience. I do believe that it is, in fact, God's revenge on this promiscuous society. I've an inkling that one day, this nation will be so sick with an epidemic of HIV that you'll be creeping back to the Red Fort in Dehradun with your little tail between your legs. Like a frightened lost puppy pleading to be let back in after a storm," he would predict, arms crossed over his chest, taking turns to stroke each man-breast under his half-shirt.

Somebody, please change the channel!

A lot of Daddy's verbal diarrhea I had seen purged before. But hearing Daddy kill joy one more time and take the fuzz out of our effervescent feelings about immigrating to America, was downright cruel. When he was holding court, there was no point in arguing with Daddy. Or for that matter, at any other time. He would either prove me wrong and sulk. Or be proven wrong and sulk. On occasion, he would attempt to feign a heart attack somewhere along the way. Daddy would always win in the end --- or get angry and win anyway.

This went on all summer long, the entire two months Daddy and Mummy stayed with us. Secretly, I could not wait until it would all be over, but dared not let it be known. A poker face never came in more handy!

God is my witness, I can't wait for the day when I'll not need them anymore.

Privately, I told the children to stay away from 'that dirty old man.' Kids will be kids, after all. Mine were neither discreet nor submissive, as I was. Nor did they have the ability to filter their thoughts, the way I had mastered so well over the years.

One day, little Natasha was playing and twirling her stuffed Mickey Mouse in front of her grandfather, calling it Daddy *ji*, and boxing its ears as she did so.

"You're naughty," she laughed. "Mickey, you're naughty." And then, "You're bad," she giggled. "Daddy *ji*, you're bad."

And she boxed its ears again and again. And giggled and twirled around, again and again. Then she slapped it around a few times with innocent glee.

By God, was he livid!

"Why don't you tell her to stop!" he yelled at me. "Nargis, don't you teach your children how to respect adults? Can't you stop her from getting so mouthy! Is this what you're learning in this great country of yours? That's why there's no hope for this stupid Western civilization. Remember, one day, that sun *will* rise once again in the East. I also predict that this is when Europe will become a museum continent. Now let me tell you something. You ran to America like a little rat from what you thought was a sinking ship. You'll only realize this one day, when India will become a world power and your children treat you in the same manner in which you treat us."

Those were difficult days and awkward times. Two long months, when the mercury threatened to spill out straight past the tip of my thermometer. Sixty long days, when my Bullshit Meter worked overtime. The best way to survive, I had decided, was to try to dance between the raindrops. I would go about my business with blinders on and end the day with superficial and trite conversations. I consoled myself that I was listening, only via mental earplugs, to Daddy's conspiracy theories and pontifications on the downfall of the Great American Empire.

This is what life looks like on the other side of sanity. You didn't sign up for this. But don't get tripped, Nargis. Just bite the bullet. You reckon it's your turn to pay the piper, I would remind myself, over and over again. Be patient. It'll soon be over. Just play the tapes out to the end.

The human mind can do anything. It has the ability to travel to another place and leave the body behind.

It's so simple to clock-out, Nargis, I'd say to myself. Think of it as a nuclear zone and put your hard hat on. And also, after you've put that squarely in place, make damn sure you haven't forgotten the lead shield. Remember, hard hat and lead shield. Blinders and earplugs. Earplugs and blinders. Like a lobotomized patient with a locked-in syndrome.

When does dislike turn to hate? I pondered. I know that I don't do too well when I stay inside my own head. Never mind, Nargis. Don't feel boxed in. Just pretend you don't see anything. And make-believe that you can't hear anything. It's worked for you before.

And it did work. Actually, it worked for a while.

Until that last day.

"I FORGIVE YOU."

That last day started like any other last day. I remember it was a weekend. Arjun was on a flight home from a surgery convention in Japan and my parents were about to leave for India in a couple of days.

It was the end of another blistering August in Chicago. When the doggone days of summer are long and endless. The constant drone of air-conditioners mutes the carefree chirping of sparrows that cared to stop by for a brief visit on the small patio of our condo to peck at the tired black-eyed susans and the crumpled parched-brown grass.

There are times when it feels like what happened that day happened only yesterday. At other times, it feels more distant and hazy. Like bits and pieces from a dream. Or a nightmare. Or both. As if it happened to someone else I know really well, in some other place, at some other time, a very long time ago. It appears as if I am watching myself from outside my very being, from a place floating high up by the ceiling. Rather than head-on and up-close, with my feet squarely planted on the ground. An emotion as familiar as a blood relative. A memory as old as the carbon atom. It is a central hub of my very being. A feeling that has shadowed me through my life screaming for acknowledgement, when it suddenly appears from nowhere, to bob up and down like a troubled buoy in shadowy turbulent waters.

It is generally believed that little children feel what their mother feels, fear what their mother fears, and cry when their mother cries. Even if they do not understand what she might be crying about. Even if she becomes inconsolable and regresses into the craziness of hysteria, throws things about to openly declare her lunacy or alternately hits both herself and her children in her madness. They still feel and cry with her.

Mandy and Natasha did. They were eight and five that summer, and I was thirty three.

I cannot remember what started it. Was it because of something Daddy had said or not said, or was it because of the way he had looked or not looked? Or was it a buildup of my surging anger and naked rage at his provocative behavior and overt hypocrisy? Or was it because I did not need my parents anymore, simply because the mission of their visit had been accomplished?

Selfish me!

Or was it something that was just waiting to happen all my life?

My parents were packing and ready to go back to India. It just had to happen that day. It was a perfect storm.

Even if I had had a lifetime to prepare for it, I would have still come to the party mostly unprepared. *And* completely undressed.

Daddy was upset with Mummy about something and had retired early for the night to sulk in our bedroom. Most likely, he was waiting for her to come back to get him, apologize and cajole His Royal Highness, Daddy, as she had always pandered to him on similar occasions during their entire marriage. We had given my parents our bedroom, the children had theirs to share and Arjun and I used a mattress placed on the living room carpet --- for old time's sake!

Mummy had not gone to appease him yet. So, it was just she and I having freshly-brewed cardamom tea in the family room together. She was saying something about never needing to pluck her eyebrows, or having to use any makeup other than lipstick. Then she started to complain, about Daddy favoring both Pinki and her family.

"He's forgotten all of us because of Sanju's in-laws," she was confiding in me.

I told her that I felt the same way and we consoled each other quietly for a while.

In that moment, I felt we had a connection. Suddenly, feeling emboldened, I told Mummy everything.

"There's something about Daddy I have to tell you ---," I started.

Then I stopped. But I could not stop the tears. It was quite frightening that I could not stop my tears.

And I could not speak. It was scary that I could not speak.

My mouth was dry and my lips started to curl inward, but no words came out. Then I started to sob loudly.

The children were fast asleep and in spite of my attempts to muffle the sounds, my crying grew louder and louder. The more I tried to stifle it, the louder I got.

By now, Daddy had walked out of the bedroom. I knew he was there, but I could not look at him. Or Mummy. Or *anybody*. For what appeared to be forever, I could not see anything at all.

Between my choking tears and jerky gasps, I managed to say, "It's about Daddy ---" followed by more tears.

I could not stop myself from shaking. It appeared as if the room was spinning. Everything around me appeared crazy-blurry through my copious tears and droning moans. I was now gulping hiccups from crying so much.

Somewhere in the room, I heard Daddy tell my mother, "Give the girl some water."

She did so, like a robot. I gulped it down too, like a robot.

I still could not look at him. A weird non-feeling that I cannot describe had invaded my being and taken over my entire body. I cannot remember whether Mummy asked Daddy to leave, but now it was just the two of us alone again.

She was getting irritable, "Tell me quickly. Come on, Nargis, get it off your chest."

I looked at her. And then I looked away. Into nothing.

"It's about Daddy," I managed to say again, my voice getting low and husky. "And --- about something --- bad --- he did --- when --- I was --- a child --- with my chest --- and my ---"

The words were stuck in my throat. It felt as if I was dumb and mute at the same time.

"Nargis, now listen to me. If you tell me your secret," she encouraged me, "I'll tell you mine."

Then suddenly, it all came out. The floodgates had opened. Nothing could stop me now. The words were all jumbled up and not making any sense. I was not making any sense. There was no method, or sequence, or reason to it. It sounded like madness. And I sounded crazy. Out-of-a-movie crazy.

"Daddy used to *bother* me when I was a child," I told her very quickly, praying that he would not reemerge from our bedroom.

I told her that Daddy would touch me in girl places when I was young. It had happened many times. I told her that it started when I was nine years old. It happened because I was such a sucker for praise. It made me feel special. Daddy made me feel special. He took advantage of that. A father never should. I told her that as a child I could never tell anyone. I felt so much shame and guilt all my life. I could never trust anyone to help me.

"I was able to end it when I was thirteen. Daddy --- he would've never stopped," I ended.

Then there was nothing more to say.

For a long time there was silence.

I can never describe the expression on Mummy's face. She was both angry and matter of fact at the same time. She had that Mummy's "now-let's-get-to-the-bottom-of-this" face.

I thought, she must be anxious because she's blinking so rapidly.

"Tell me," she looked at me sternly now. "Was there any intercourse?"

I replied, rather too quickly. "No, Mummy, but he should've never done what he did."

I don't know whether she's relieved that there was no penetration. Am I responsible to make her feel better? I wondered. Or, does this exonerate him of the ultimate sin? Does she want him vindicated?

"How dare your Daddy do that!" I heard her say aloud. "He deserves to die. That *haramzada*! That bastard!"

I was shocked. It was extremely rare for her to hurl a curse word at Daddy. For some reason, this helped me get bolder.

In a few disjointed sentences and mixed up words that I cannot remember today, I told Mummy about what had happened to me over several years periodically and repeatedly. It is strange how a few words can describe everything that has occurred over such a long period of time. Throughout my narration, I remember referring to Daddy as 'he.'

I was now done talking about myself. It was strangely rather calm, barring the sound of a pack of coyotes in the distant Beach Park Woods howling with pain in the still of the night.

"What's your secret?" I reminded her. "Look, I told you mine."

What Mummy told me sounded too strange to be true. But I know that when it came to my father, truth was usually stranger than fiction.

"I think he did it with his youngest two sisters as well. I know he did something to them, but I'm not sure what it was. He used to say he was close to them and I always suspected that something was hanky-panky. Maybe that's why they went astray and had to be hurriedly married off. But, that's not all. I'm sure that Captain Mohandeep was his mistress. He told me that she was doing it with that new colonel she worked under after she had left your father's command. That's why she stayed around our house all those years, every opportunity she could get, to become a part of our family. I've been this innocent onlooker all along. I thought she was a great help with the simple chores at home, when actually ---"

I interrupted her, "How do you know all this?"

And Mummy answered simply, in her Simple-Mummy way, "I just know."

That should explain everything. Don't ask questions to which you don't want answers.

We were both quiet now. There were no further queries. From either side. And then, there was silence. But it was not a quiet silence.

Somehow I knew that Daddy was in the room. I could feel his presence looming in the background. Like a specter, or ghost. I could not turn around to look at him. But I just knew that he was there. Mummy, though, did turn around to look up at him.

"Shiv *ji*," she started. "Why did you bother Nargis when she was young?" she managed to ask.

For a moment, it felt as if he was frozen in time.

Then he started to advance toward me with a death-stare. He looked like an ant-lion ready to thrash me into smithereens. He was walking toward me with long purposeful strides. I was sure he would beat me black and blue or kill me cold or both.

"How dare you point a finger at me? You good-for-nothing girl! How dare you accuse me of such a cockamamie story? You *randi!* You whore! Who taught you to lie like this? You loose woman! You fucking *cunt!*" he shouted pointing at me, flinging his arms about, froth gathering on the sides of his mouth.

I shrank back like a wounded lamb. I was reeling from the sheer shock of hearing that word being used to describe me. I did not know that he knew this one syllable word.

I've been reduced to a four letter noun, I moaned to myself.

It was insulting at every level, down to the very roots of my shocked hair and the empty hollow in my miserable heart.

"You prostitute! You lousy little thing!" he went on. "What do you think of yourself? Because you've become a doctor you think that you're better than everyone else? Who made you such a topnotch professional anyway? It was me! It was *I* who sponsored your education. Time after time. Year after year. And what lies have you been telling your mother about me? You know that I never ever touched you, Nargis. I would never do that. Now look at me --- and tell your mother the truth. What decent father you know would ever dare touch a daughter like that?"

It was only Daddy doing the talking. It felt as if there were two of him. And two of me.

Things around me were starting to fog up, like they do when you flatten your nose and breathe against a cold windowpane. It was surreal.

"Mani, don't get worked up for nothing. Children forget and misinterpret things that happened a long time ago," he went on, licking his drying lips nervously. "Let me clear the air. All I did was hug you, Nargis. I loved you more than I did the other two children. You know that. You were the closest one to me. So this is what I get for giving you so much love. Now let's stop splitting hairs. Anyway, I forgive you. You were just a child. And children need to be forgiven."

By this time, I had started to wail. With both hands holding my head and my body rocking in place.

At some point during this heated exchange Mandy, hearing the commotion, came out of her bedroom. She was rubbing her sleepy eyes looking quite bewildered and scared.

Upon seeing her, Daddy smiled calmly and said, "Sometimes," he told her, "sometimes we all act a little crazy. Mandy, go back to bed now."

But he was not done yet. He then turned to Mummy.

"You were never a good mother to these girls. I had to be their mother, as well as their father. All in one. I had to hug them and give them the love you did not know how to show. And now look where it has gotten me! This country teaches people to think in strange ways. She imagines that I fondled her. Her mind is playing tricks on her. And you've the audacity to believe her? Haven't I always told you to think for yourself? I don't know when you'll ever learn how to do that. I give up."

After a pause, since nobody else was talking, he continued, "I think --- it's just possible --- um --- I think it might've happened that one time --- um --- after --- I must've had a lot to drink at a party. Mani, believe me, by God I thought it was you who was lying next to me. I swear, when I discovered it was Nargis, I moved away. The rest is a figment of her imagination. She always wanted special attention, this Nargis did. You know that. The baby of the family usually does. But she was just a child. I can't blame her for not remembering the past correctly. Mani, do you remember everything that happened to you when *you* were a child? You get the drift. So, now let's stop all this nonsense and go to bed. Let's move on. It's very late, and in a couple of days we have a long journey ahead of us."

I've a long journey ahead of me too, I thought. A long and rocky journey.

Now, for some reason, I *could* look at him. It seemed so bizarre, this whole thing. So weird that after all these years we were actually talking about this.

But no one was ready to go to bed just yet. Daddy went on talking, but I could not hear anything he was saying. I was looking alternately at his fingers and toes. And then at his face. His head seemed to grow smaller and smaller and started to become distant and hazy, as his eyes receded backward morphing along as they reversed all the way back into his skull. The same way it used to happen, when he would get crazy livid with me about something bad I had done when I was a child. That same apparition --- small head. Pinocchio nose. Big body.

He was telling Mummy how much he loved her, and how much he had sacrificed for the family. He had worked so hard all his life for us.

Daddy's in charge of station Damage Control.

"Look what I get in return for all my good deeds," he was telling Mummy. "I never knew that one day I would have to face such a strange accusation from one of my own children, and, that too, from the one I love the most. I should never have educated these girls. It's this education that has taught them to speak in this utterly disrespectful manner to their own father. It's this American culture that teaches them to fight with their own parents. I should've left Nargis back in the village to tend to a dozen kids with snot running down all their faces. Then it would never have come to this. Now, let's get out of this country as soon as possible. Let's go home tomorrow. Mani, you go help this girl wash her face. Nargis, you arrange for us to leave by the first flight out of Chicago in the morning."

Three Blind Mice. That would be the three of us, isn't it? The blind leading the blind.

Somewhere, also in the same room, Mummy was saying, "You must've done something, Shiv ji, or she would not be crying like this."

And I heard Daddy reply, also somewhere in the room where there were just the three of us, "She was always a crybaby, don't you remember? The youngest, the most spoiled, the most pampered. I should've treated her like I did the other two children. I should've spanked her around a bit as well, so she'd never lie again in her life."

Then just as predicted, he was hyperventilating, getting restless and sweaty. He slumped on the sofa and announced that he was going to die. He had folded his arms on his chest and closed his eyes.

"This is what you all want. You want me to die. I know it. You want to kill me. This'll definitely kill me. And both of you will be responsible for my death."

Then Daddy asked me to feel his pulse.

What if he actually keels over and dies at this very moment? On our couch? In our home? On *my* watch? Because of something that I just said?

Without thinking twice, I reached for his pulse. His arm was clammy and his pulse was skipping some beats. It had been known to miss a few beats on occasion, up to four to six per minute. He did take isoptin, even if only in homeopathic doses.

But, what if this time it's for real?

Then Mummy asked him to lie down and followed him into our bedroom. I cannot say how long they were in there together, or who said what, or if anything was said at all. It was very quiet behind the door. Finally, Mummy came out briefly for water.

What if he's really dying? I wondered for a moment, holding my own breath.

"Now let's get this over with. Nargis, you've said what you've wanted to say. It's over now," Mummy said quickly and firmly.

Then she asked me to go into the bedroom and give Daddy a

hug.

"Go and make up with your father. He's waiting for you."

I went into our bedroom. It felt as if I was walking all the way across the globe to where he lay limp, eyes half-closed, still breathing heavily.

"Come on. Give your father a hug. Quickly. Let's get it over with," Mummy was saying.

Is this what they call a day-mare? A nightmare when you're fully awake?

I leaned over and gave Daddy a hug. Like I used to when he would me mad with me and had to forgive me for some wrong I had done when I was a child.

And Daddy said, "That's okay. Sometimes, children do make up things."

His voice is coming back. *He* is coming back.

Then to Mummy, "I don't think we're welcome here, Mani. They only want you in their house to help out with the children. After I die, trust me, nobody will ask about you. Always remember that I was the first one to warn you about this. Nobody will want you like I do. Believe me, your children will never take care of you. One day, they'll accuse *you*, too."

Suddenly I do not know why, but I could not control my limbs to sit still anymore. That is when I stormed out of the room.

Who could I run to? Where could I go?

"I'm going to die!" I screamed. "I need to die *now*!"

I should kill myself right away. I'll hang by the door hinge using Daddy's belt, the one with the brass buckle and make him suffer. That'll teach him a lesson. When he sees me all cold and blue, he'll feel so guilty that he'll kill himself too. But wait, I'll not even be alive to see him take his own life. So what's the point, Nargis? You're too insignificant even to commit suicide.

I went and quickly bolted myself in the kids' bedroom.

It's safe here with Mandy and Natasha. They'll never harm me. Right now, this minute, this is the safest place in the world for me.

Then I started to cry hysterically, pulling my hair, slapping my face, beating my chest and punching the wall with my clenched fists. I must have scared the daylights out of my children. They were holding me. I was in Natasha's bed, crying hysterically, bawling my eyes out and rocking. I do not know what I was saying. My tears had found a new voice. But nobody could understand me. Not even me.

Mummy was outside in the hallway, pounding her fists on the locked door.

"For God's sake, Nargis, come out," she shouted, trying different keys to crank open the lock. "Come out now!"

"You *have* to believe me!" I screamed through the walls. "You *must* believe me! *Somebody* believe me! I *know* it happened. Somebody help me! Somebody please help me, or I'll die! Right *now!*"

I was shouting and screaming, hugging and crying with my daughters. Clinging to them and crying wildly. And the children were crying with me, for me.

"I beg of you. Please come out," Mummy implored. "Everything will be alright, Nargis," she promised. "Nobody will ever bother you again."

I do not know how long this went on, with my dry heaving and boohooing behind that locked door, running myself ragged. I tried to rein in the emotions. At some point, I am not sure why, I finally undid the latch.

Mummy came in and sat with me on the bed.

She was saying tersely, "What's happened has happened. Let's all forget the past. Nargis, you must forget the past. You've little children to take care of."

We talked some more. Rather, she talked and I listened. I was still in a daze. I cannot remember what we talked about. Whatever we talked about did not matter anymore. Whatever we talked about could never sound right anymore.

Nothing can make this right.

Then Mummy went again to check in on Daddy. He had gone to sleep, one hand on his chest where his heart should have been.

It was all quiet in the condo again, like nothing had happened. Everyone had gone to sleep. Except for me.

Surely, this reality show is not all over? It cannot all be over. It mustn't all be over. It's finally time to have my own well-deserved nervous breakdown!

I felt this urge to do something.

But what? Kill Daddy? Or kill myself?

I could picture myself hanging by the chandelier in the condo foyer, noose around my neck, head titled to one side like Jesus' on the cross, with the whites of my eyes bulging out like pale half-moons and toes pointing downward showing where my body should be laid. Flat line. Six feet under, like that doctor in the *Gunner's Song*. Cold and blue and very dead.

The neighbors would call 911, "A foul deed has happened in condo number 202," they would tell the police.

Crash and burn! That'll teach my parents a lesson. But wait. I can't do that to Arjun, Mandy and Natasha.

It's selfish to kill yourself, Nargis. Downright selfish and also quite stupid. You're brighter than that. It's just an escape thought, isn't it?

So, what *can* I do?

Confused and bedraggled from pulling my hair, teetering on the edge of insanity, in a moment of intense frenzy I stormed out of the condo. The chains were off.

I need some fresh air! Give me some air now!

In a raw fugue state, I made a dash to the end of a long tunnel. A tunnel that had no beginning and no oval sky at the end.

I ran one block in the dark to the nearby Kmart telephone booth to make a collect call to Anjali in Antwerp. Almost out of breath and between my sobs, I told her what had happened in condo number 202. Then I babbled on and on. I do not know whether I was making any sense, even to myself. I do not remember everything she said. Something about "keeping it under covers", since our parents were going to leave in the next two days anyway. Pun intended?

"The best thing is to let them go peacefully," she advised, rather calmly.

At some point during that conversation, she mentioned that Daddy had approached her once when she was in her teens. Most likely, he had been intoxicated and probably confused her for Mummy. She did not think too much of it and was able to let it go.

But why can't *I* let it go? Nargis, put a lid on it! Get a grip on yourself! You must return to your children. Your place is with Mandy and Natasha.

Somehow, I found my way back to the condo where my kids were fast asleep.

The rest of the night I tossed and turned, terrified of the morning light. I wished that I could creep back into the dark side of the moon. On all fours.

How much pain is too much pain? Is it like the sting you experience when you rip a Band-Aid off your entire body?

How can I stop the Brownian motion and get back to a Quiet Mind? God, help me! Help stop the buzzing in my head. I wish that my thoughts would spin in the opposite direction for once, so I can calm them down even for a minute.

I could not get my parents on the flight the next day as Daddy had instructed. So they left two days later.

Over the next couple of days nothing was said about the previous night. Actually, for many years, nothing would be mentioned again about that night.

Now when I think of it, those forty eight hours were the longest two days of my life. I am not entirely sure how I managed to go to work, treat hysteria and study Freud's analysis of dreams. But work and school had never stopped for anything before. It was business as usual.

I made sure that I was not alone in the room with Daddy even for a moment. I remember, I could not get myself to hug my parents goodbye at the airport without every muscle in my body flinching inside.

The following year, my parents made another trip to visit with us in Chicago. Another summer came and went and nothing was said about the night I had a freak-show meltdown in the condo. It was as if it had never happened.

Will there ever come a day when I can erase from living memory how I felt that night?

For it was on that night I realized, Daddy now knows, that I knew *he* also knew.

For some reason, this did not seem enough.

"PLEASE, DOCTOR ... CAN YOU HELP ME?"

She walked into my office, wearing a deep V-neck polka-dotted blouse, smelling of fresh daises. I will never forget how she looked. A drop dead gorgeous petite thirty three year old strawberry-blonde, with light freckles that stood out like pebbles on a sandy beach, and flaming hair that swept ever so often softly over smoky hazel eyes that twinkled like distant stars on a clear moonless night.

Then I noticed the deep gashes on Heather's arms.

Her voice was flat and her eyes were fixated. As if at the end of the universe.

"I remember it was a dark night. I could see the faint blue crescent of the new moon from my bedroom window. He had come silently into my bed. I couldn't tell who he was, but I remember the smell of Max Factor aftershave intermixed with stale wine. He lay next to me. With one hand he covered my mouth so I wouldn't scream. With the other, he started to fondle me. First my thighs. Then my breasts. And after that, my nipples. Next, he took off my panties and cupped my crotch with his hand. His unshaven chin dug into my bare shoulder as he carried me to the carpenter's workbench in the garage. There, he spread my legs on the table, and tied them to the metal hoops on either side. One by one. Like stirrups.

"Doctor, he penetrated me several times that night, convulsing to end each orgasm. All the while he had his tongue and his penis in my body. Both at the same time. That was one too many male parts in a child's body. There was no letting up. "Come baby, try this one on for size," he was saying, his voice husky and slurred. "I want to prepare you for your future husband." That's when I split into two bodies. Two people straggling between two worlds. One was real, and the other one did not exist in our universe. One had her head held down between his thighs to lick the come after he had first squirted it onto her face. The other one had floated away into outer space. When I finally looked up, he was peeing on my chest and spitting on me. And laughing.

Laughing himself silly. Long and hard. I recognized the laugh. But I could not see his face, because I couldn't stop my tears.

"I was about nine years old. Doctor, I've never shown this to anyone before," she said, as she rolled her pant legs up to her knees to show identical indentations on both her shins. "They are more than skin-deep, and stop only at the bone. Look, these are the scars on my soul from that night. I've been sexually anorexic ever since. And, I've never been able to walk straight either.

"Then last night, doctor, I shot him between the eyes. The same eyes that wanted my body. The ones that used to look at me covetously. I saw his brains leak out of his skull. The same brains that dared to think of me with lust. The ones that used to plan on how to rape me. I saw blood gush out of his body. The same one that used to rush to his penis, to prepare it before it entered me. The same blood that I also have, since we're related.

"Doctor, I killed my father in my dream. Now, I can't stop cutting on my arms. My thighs. My breasts. Over, and over, and over, again. Nor can I rid myself of the smell of Max Factor aftershave in my nostrils. I feel like a glass half-empty. I'm a basket case! Please, doctor. Please, can you help me?"

My vision got blurred through a film of tears as I tried to see past the pain in her smoky hazel eyes.

But of course, I must do my very best to help Heather, I told myself. She will never know this, but she's had it far worse than anything I've ever been though.

THE BEGINNING, OR THE END?
NINE YEARS LATER —

It was late spring of '96. When those yellow smiley faces in the white daffodils had dried up, waiting patiently on their stalks for an official change of season. When the tulip stalks were bare, sitting on a carpet of yellow and orange petals strewn on the ground around them, curled up in the sun. When the crocuses and hyacinths had finally reversed their upward thrust and returned back into the ground. Stymied by life.

I never truly believed that my father would die one day. He was as omnipotent and omnipresent as the God in whom he did not believe and just as invincible. He was God unto himself, who answered to no one. Unfortunately, not even to himself. With his practiced morning routine of snacking on amlas aged in vinegar alternating with downing Vitamin E laced with garlic, walking a daily ten-mile route, followed by sipping a couple of whiskey-sodas while reciting perfectly memorized tips from Eat Healthy Live Longer, he was not supposed to die.

For Daddy, life was a game of poker, where the opponent always started out with a stronger hand. In the middle of the game, Daddy would turn the chessboard around and show his rival how to win from a losing side.

Daddy had a final say in everything. He dictated how our family thought, felt, and breathed. Now it was *his* turn to breathe his last.

Did Daddy know he was dying when he took that first step off the cliff? What's it like to die, anyway? Is it like how they show in the movies, when a white glow beckons from the far end of a long dark tunnel and rapidly grows as it advances toward you swallowing everything in its path? Is it that final millionth of a second when your entire life flashes before your very eyes? When you get one last chance to own up to your sins before you become a part of that glow as it's being sucked into the depths of an eternal black hole and vanishes forever?

Did this happen to Daddy? Did all the rumors about him come true? Did *his* evil deeds flash before *his* eyes? Did he feel even the remotest desire to make peace with himself and or me and set the record straight once and for all? Did he give himself a final chance to whisper the truth with his last dying breath, even if he was the only one present to hear the words?

Did he acknowledge his wrongdoings, even if it was barely to the white-washed bare wall beside his hospital bed, since there was no other person close enough to see his lips move? Did his lips actually move when he spoke?

Did the words come out garbled, like hiccups of gibberish that blink and burp on a computer screen just before it suddenly dies down for good? Like, in an uncanny way, mine spluttered and conked off just now as I was writing this part of my story!

What *did* Daddy feel in that final moment of reckoning before he punched out? The moment when, for the last time in his life, the Sun went down on him. Like it is supposed to at the end of each day. Like he had taught me that it does, when I was just a child. The moment, when for the first time in his life, there was nothing between Daddy and death.

Daddy was a psychic. He could always foresee anything, couldn't he?

Like he had predicted that parental power would split his children by fueling jealously at the other's success. Mummy would believe more and more in everything that he himself believed in during their remaining years together and continue to do so for a long, long time even after he was gone. Like he had conjectured that I would have no communication with any member of my family, carte blanche, for six of the last nine years leading up to his death. Mostly, because I would never be able to shake off the expectation that my mother and my siblings must feel exactly the same way I did toward Daddy: hate him enough to shred any living memory of him. Like he had bet his last bottom rupee that Sanjay would have political ambitions to become Army Chief, and, as such, not want the family dishonor of his sister's past to muddy his image. Anjali would also choose to bury the shame, because she would now finally have a chance at becoming that favorite child she never could be growing up.

But, most of all, Daddy had prophesied a long time ago, that I would eventually succumb to my secret desire to be reunited with Sanjay because I missed his warmth, wit and the stories we shared together. I would feel desperately compelled to communicate with Anjali, past the lines that I myself had drawn in the sand, to fill that unfathomable void in my heart with my sister's motherly voice. And of course, I would reconnect with my parents, simply because I missed the accolades.

Sucker for praise!

One day, I would unlock the padlock on my heart and come back into that crowded space. Again. I would have an epiphany that once I had dead-bolted that door on my family for all those years, the firewall had shut everything out --- the good and bad, the happy and sad.

Like Daddy had predicted that I would never talk about the molestation! Or even write about it! Simply because I would want my story believed with no questions asked and no strings attached.

These were all *calculated* risks --- "it's all about time and distance". Similar to those Daddy had taken, when he would cautiously creep up upon Japanese soldiers to mercilessly ambush them in the thicket of Burma and shoot them cold. Or, when he would skillfully overtake a lorry on a narrow twisted mountain road. Risks that would not boomerang back to strike him dead!

I have often wondered about his final day. Did Daddy wake up that morning knowing it was going to be his last one?

For once, was he scared? Was he afraid to die?

I thought to myself, isn't it ironic that Daddy would die when I am now forty three years old. That's how old he was when he first started to abuse me. There must be a connection. I *have* to figure it out --- but later.

Did Daddy think of me in that last hour?

While gasping for life, did he get a chance to scribble a note. A line. A word. A syllable. Anything? Or perhaps even something like this:

Dear Nargis,

I should never have done what I did to you. I should never have destroyed your trust in a father. I've wronged you greatly and ask for your forgiveness --- And, I'll understand if you'll never be able to pardon me.

You must've gone through Hell carrying this yoke of betrayal all your life --- Mine is now ending, and it's now *my* turn to go to Hell.

Daddy

What else could he have scrawled to make it right for me? Can anything make it right for me?

Actually, there was no note from my father. He never did make it right for me. He left the world and my life forever. And he took everything away with him: The lies, the deceit and the paranoia.

But most of all, what he took away with him was the truth.

Now, I'm the only one left on Earth who knows what happened between us.

A bizarre accident had occurred. My parents had gone over to Terra Firma to correct a Labor Law violation, which insinuated that the quarry was mined too close to the retaining wall which endangered the lives of workers who were drilling blast holes on the upper benches. Nobody had died just yet. Mummy had stayed back in the manager's office, while Daddy went over to the excavation to inspect the site. Apparently, he was walking up to the edge of the retaining wall, when the limestone bench below him suddenly collapsed. This is when his whole life crumbled in front of him and he was engulfed into the mining debris.

'Let him be swallowed by the Earth,' just like I had written in my diary so many years ago.

I do not know how long Daddy lay prostrate in there, writhing in pain, crying for help from the bottom of a hole in the ground. When he was finally rescued, he had sustained a fractured spine and was immediately rushed to the military hospital.

This is what would now become the beginning of the end.

He was partially paralyzed from waist-down and would joke around with the female nurses, "I'm not good for anything now, since all my maleness is gone."

Sometimes in a fit of despair he would lament about the future of the world after he would be gone. Especially, the future of his family.

"Mani, after I die, I'm certain that you'll have a frolicking time visiting your daughters in abroad. I've seen many a merry widow in my time and I'm sure that you'll be no different. I know that it won't be long before you'll forget me entirely. All of you'll forget me in a jiffy. Just like that! In one millisecond! That's the way of the world. Your good deeds are buried with you. It'll be good riddance when I die, won't it? You might even find another man ---"

And he would curse her for being uncaring and unfaithful, even before she would have half a chance to consider it.

At other times, he would warn her ahead of time, not to be swayed by the opinion of her children.

"For sure, they will neglect you. Or use and abuse you. So never trust them."

There were other moments when he would tell her how she had always meant everything to him.

"Mani, you know, I could never do without you --- Please don't leave me," he would plead. "You're the best thing that's ever happened to me. You know that. I can't live without you. You're everything to me. You're the angel in my life. You're my Goddess. Please, I beg of you, please, please never leave me."

For the first few weeks after the fall, Daddy did not want his children to know that he had been injured. He could handle his family, especially those three children in the backseat, only when he had absolute control at the steering wheel.

It must have been sheer providence. A foreboding of ominous proportions. The day when I heard that my father was in the ICU, I had been invited to a *puja* at a friend's home in Chicago. We were throwing puffed rice and pine nuts into a fire, as a priest was chanting some mantras. I imagined my father's soul being scorched in the blaze. The flames were soaring high and for a little bit, even went dangerously out of control. Now when I think of that burning inferno, I believe it was an omen of galactic proportions of what was about to happen.

It was indeed a very strange day in my home in Chicago. And even a stranger night. The dark skies were ablaze with lightning like I had never seen before. With each clap of thunder, the whole house shook. The backyard lit up with streaks of dramatically convenient blue light caught between the old oaks, showing flashes of elongated miserable faces on their mature wrinkled trunks. The leaves flapped nervously in the rain. For some intermittent moments, however brief, it looked as clear as daylight! As if it was a cliffhanger to an Agatha Christie mystery thriller. You could easily have committed murder back there!

I had heard that it was quite possible that my father was dying that day. No one could tell for sure. The exact timings of birth and death are usually difficult to predict.

Is this a fact or could this be a rumor that he is spreading about himself to test my response? What if he actually comes out alive, healthy as an ox, only to catch me red-handed in my blatant lack of grief and mourning?

Arjun had gone to India to attend his brother's engagement, a significant part of which he missed because of the events spiraling around my father's terminal days. My husband's efforts went largely unacknowledged. Things have always been taken for granted by my family, where any imposition, however great, goes largely unrecognized. That arrogant presumption of entitlement.

Mummy, who is generally robotic in the best of times, is a class act in times of crisis. She was going through the motions, doing everything a dutiful wife should do. And, I am sure, blinking rapidly all along as she did so.

Arjun escorted his mother-in-law to where my father lay semiconscious, barely moving. They were informed that Daddy would need blood, so before returning back to New Delhi, Arjun, being a good Samaritan, donated his own and coaxed his driver to do the same.

"But, it'll make me weak, Sir *Ji*," the driver protested.

I believe none of that blood was actually needed for Daddy. I feel relieved that not a single drop of my husband's blood ever entered my father's body.

The doctor told the family that his patient had a good chance at recovery if he could get past this one last hump. The worst would then be behind him. The worst was indeed behind him, for my father died two days later.

No one will ever know what killed Daddy. Did the military hospital pump him with mega-doses of heparin, meant only for a mule? Is this what made him bleed to his death? Or did he in that split second of ultimate reckoning succumb to a web of lies of his own creation that strangled his heart? Or did God instruct his heart to stop?

I will never know.

The next day Sanjay flew in expeditiously from a military deputation abroad. He found Daddy lying in a hazy twilight zone.

Daddy could barely move but he spoke with amazing clarity, "Sanju, take care of your mother. She is special. She's simply the best."

He was stamping his legacy of control on her, for the rest of her life. He had said she was special. That is all it would take.

I should know, because this is the same specialness that did *me* in. And it would take me more than half a lifetime to break away free from it myself.

Daddy died that night. Lonely in a hospital bed.

"I want no ceremony after my death," he had strictly instructed Mummy, over and over again, during their long walks together. "Don't you dare call hokum priests and humbug pundits to contaminate my cremation. No hogwash. No nonsense. No nothing. I want it to be a pure and simple affair. I've done quite well without this stupidity during my lifetime and I certainly don't want even a semblance of it after I'm gone. Because when you're gone, you're *gone*. There's nothing beyond the beyond. There's nothing left except ash."

And nothing else, except a legacy of dysfunction peeking through the cinders and crying out loud.

So, there was no ceremony. There were only four people in his *baraat* on the day of his wedding. There were only four people in the funeral procession on the day of Daddy's cremation. This included his business partner and his man Friday. In her utterly distraught state, Mummy made a final gesture by taking off her shawl and placing it on his now still body. Then she stepped away from her husband for the very first time in her life. That was when my perpetrator --- my father --- became a part of the rest of the Universe.

In Chicago, I was up early that morning. Sanjay had called and I heard him as clearly as if it had happened only yesterday.

"It's the end of an era," he said. "Daddy is no more."

I felt oxygen being sucked out of the room.

This is what *The End* looks like. The End of Tyranny. The End of Everything. The End of Daddy. Now what?

Sanjay went on to tell me that in recent years, he had suffered recurrent and disturbing dreams of Daddy's death. The nightmares were different every time, except that they always ended in the ultimate demise of our father.

Of course, for Sanjay too, Daddy's death would signify the end of control and the beginning of freedom, I thought.

I put the phone down. I remember going to Mandy's bed and waking her up. Natasha walked in too, still rubbing sleep from her eyes. It was just the three of us. Arjun was on his way back home to us on a flight from India.

"Daddy *ji* is dead," I told my children, still in a daze.

That bastard has gone to hell! I muttered, but only to myself.

I remember feeling numb from the shock of it all. It was impossible! Daddy could not have died. He could *never* die. He was supposed to live forever.

For the next few days and weeks I am not sure what I felt. I am not sure what I was supposed to feel. I am not even sure that I remember everything that happened during that period. All I do remember, though, is that I did not cry. Not even once. I went to work the next day and the day after --- and the day after that, like nothing had happened.

Anjali could not stop crying when we spoke, "I can't believe Daddy's gone," she sobbed uncontrollably on the phone.

When I called Mummy, she sounded so far away. So distant. So angry.

Why angry?

"So *you* too heard about it?" she sounded harsh.

Why harsh? As if, I'm the *other woman*.

The compulsion to twist my arm through the telephone cord and shake her upside down into reality was irresistible.

I'll never get another chance to set the record straight with Mummy. She'll always be loyal to the man who made her feel like a Queen.

For a long time after Daddy's death, I was afraid to enter a room alone by myself in my house in Chicago. I was sure that I would find him there, sitting stiff on a couch, with both knees and elbows flexed, staring at me with those cold honey-brown eyes capped with those muddy-blue crescents.

If you turn around he'll see you and call out your name,

"Naaaaaargis!!!!!!" Don't look! Avoid all eye contact. Run, Nargis, just run!

I would imagine Daddy waiting for me each morning in the driver's seat of my car parked in the dark garage, holding the steering wheel with his rigid arms, staring blankly at me and beckoning me with his fixed gaze to ride with him.

During that week, the painters had covered the leftover cans of paint with tarpaulin in the basement of my house.

My God! It looks as if that's Daddy's body under the canvas! Run! Run fast! Run before he suddenly reaches out and grabs a limb or two as you pass by! God, help me! Don't leave me here alone with *him*. Run! Quick! Don't look back. Sprint up the basement stairs before he swivels his head to look straight at you like that skeleton-mother in *Psycho* and pulls you in with a single swing at your leg. This is scary. Good God! This is downright creepy! Is he *really* dead? Or will he suddenly rise like a Phoenix from the ashes?

While I was experiencing these bloodcurdling flashbacks, Mummy was going about her daily chores also imagining that Shiv *ji* was still there, watching her every move, testing her, even in her dreams. Sometimes, he would approve of her actions with a quick motion of his hand. At other times, he would guide her with his stony eyes as she would now begin to face the commencement of the rest of her life.

I had heard that my cousin, Priti, was having a tree planted in my father's honor in foreign lands. Anjali had accompanied Mummy to submerge his ashes in a canal by the ancestral village where he was born. Together, they gathered an assortment of the brightest rose petals from the Red Fort and later flung them gently where his ashes swiftly sank in a swirl of the fast current.

Death: That absolute perfect zero. When carbon atoms chased each other, to meet up with other carbon atoms. Atoms scattered to the wind and the water.

"We cheated on his instructions," Anjali later told me, knowing that Daddy would forgive her for her love. "You know, I've always had a different relationship with him."

Sanjay, in turn, was becoming more preoccupied with the money he was about to inherit. He would build a school or hospital or something. And have enough left over for charity.

But, what about me?

The pall of floating paranoia would be replaced by a cloud of secrecy. How large of an estate had Daddy actually left behind? Mummy would not talk about it and I felt that it would be too crass on my part to ask. The cracks in the family that Daddy had painstakingly created over so many years were now threatening to become gaping holes.

But really, our family had been broken a long time ago. It was Daddy who had meticulously applied crazy glue, which held it loosely together in a weird and crazy way.

Nargis, you'll hear the news of Daddy's death only this one time, I told myself. Here's your chance to free yourself. Completely. Remember, even though the monkey is off your back, the circus is still in town.

I will never know what Daddy was thinking about when he lay dying.

The evil that men do lives after them --- So let it be with Daddy.

You see, unlike him, I could never read *his* mind.

His actions, though, were larger than words. By taking the truth along with him, I knew that he cared only about himself. Even in death.

THAT FIRST WINTER FROST — "BRRRR ..."

The first winter frost portends a long bitter spell. When the dying grass, yellow in its paleness, is cloaked in a white coffin. When the bitter Arctic winds, a purveyor of the beginning of another long winter spell, blow a fine powder over a ground that appears stiff and cold and dead. When a stubborn layer of thin ice lays frozen on the puddles. If you peer into it, you can see your own face scowling back at you. But do not ever get tempted to skip over for you will surely fall short, skid and fall, to crack a tailbone or more.

That last farewell. One never knows at the time that it was indeed the last time.

The Shatabdi Express was ready to pull away from the platform at Dehradun station, smoke rising straight up from the exhaust of the diesel engine upfront. That too, without taking a pause. The guard blew a whistle, a green flag was waved and the bogies nudged each other with a light jolt. Forward. Then backward. Then forward again. Then the train picked up speed, ever so slowly, whizzing past until it became a square metal sheet seen receding into the distance straight down the tracks.

It was the end of our Indian vacation as we prepared for the journey back home to Chicago and both my parents had come to see my family off. Mummy had lingered on by the window. I do not remember what my mother was saying. Probably, some token send off wishes usually well meant.

Suddenly, Daddy interrupted her, "Mani, let's go home now. You know how much I hate goodbyes."

Then he instantly turned around and walked away. And Mummy followed. I remember waving to their departing backs until they were lost to the crowd.

That was the last time I saw my father. When he walked out on me. For the last time.

The first winter without Daddy was both odd and troubling

because of the other family members he had left behind.

I had lost Anjali a long time ago. The lowdown of what happened between Sanjay and me went something like this:

"If you think Aunty Tara was abused, as you implied she was, you're sadly mistaken, my dear Sister," Sanjay had said on a long distance line, somewhere between our Earth and outer space. "You should've seen her cry her eyes out after she heard about Daddy's death. You know, Nargis, some people break up their families by manufacturing lies about them. By the way, Anjali denied ever being approached by Dad like you alleged she had mentioned to you. And don't pedophiles repeat their crimes? You're a psychiatrist. You should know about this." And finally, the last nail in the coffin, "At least, there was no intercourse ---"

That did it for me.

I thought to myself, he's probably not gotten his rightful share of mother's milk.

Reflexively, I wrote a scathing note to him.

Dear Sanjay:

Maybe, it's just possible, you've forgotten the difference between right and wrong. Come on, roll the dice. Let's do this one last time. Heads or tails! Crap shoot! Either way I lose. My dear Brother, you've orbited around other people all your life. For once, go revolve around yourself! Farewell. For now and forever!

Your forgotten sister

And we stopped talking for a few years. It was worse than saying goodbye to him on that day, when he had looked so lonely and lost just before boarding a train to attend boarding school for the first time.

That first winter seemed even more long and cold because of Mummy. Some of this is blurred now, but there was a general pall of doom-gloom when we talked on the phone. While I felt internally relieved that she did not insist that I come for Daddy's funeral, I resented the fact that I could not break loose from a feeling of responsibility toward her. But, at the same time, I did not want to give either one of us a reason to sever all ties again. It had been painful enough the first time.

Those were strange conversations and awkward phone calls. I am not sure what was worse: The buildup of anxiety before we talked or the letdown after the final click. I would catch Mummy in different moods, all of which were disturbingly off-kilter --- sad, angry, sarcastic, hopeless and usually wallowing in self-pity. I am not sure which emotion bothered me more.

There she goes again, thinking only of herself. There's nothing that I can say at this time that can ever stick on her Teflon mind.

Mummy would talk about how lonely she felt, how much she missed Shiv *ji's* presence. It seemed as if dealing with her husband's death was like coping with both a divorce and a funeral at the same time. Of course, Shiv *ji* was watching and testing her every step of the way. Just in case she would slip up.

I could picture Daddy tending to his pet bees, brewing moonshine concentrate from homegrown grapes or weeding the okra patch in the backyard of the Red Fort in his boxer shorts. As he puttered around, he would picture life after he was dead, strangely amused and entertained by the prospect. If love means preparing someone for a life without him, he certainly did not love his wife.

Phone calls to Mummy continued to cause me great trepidation. Sometimes I would just hear her voice saying, "Hello ---, hello ---," before it faded out, when I would gently put the receiver back into its cradle. So she would assume, once again, that it was another wrong number.

Anger against Daddy was now turning into rage toward Mummy.

Does she not understand that he deserved to die? That he should burn in Purgatory forever?

How many times had I plotted to kill Daddy myself? With my own bare hands. How many times had I enacted the murder of my father in my own mind? Even if ever so fleetingly. So that he would finally pay for his deeds. Sometimes, I would even dream about doing him in all by myself. For all along, when he thought that he controlled my very being, Daddy could never actually control my thoughts.

I would take a hatchet and put it straight through his skull while he lay asleep and bludgeon him to death. I would watch his brains spill out, his blood splurge, and his body shrivel up. Then singlehandedly, I would cut him into pieces, and, with what was left of him after the vultures had torn him apart, bury the rest of him in the backyard. One day, a few police hounds would come by sniffing at his remains. I would surely be hauled to prison, his blood still fresh and stark red on my hands.

Nargis, don't listen to the devil sitting on your left shoulder. Turn to the angel on the other side.

How do I navigate through insanity and come back from the depths of grief and betrayal? How can I describe the anger that peels off several layers of skin? How can I describe the pain? Pain from a festering wound that has started to smell. Like shit.

The angst feels like it comes from somewhere deep inside me, from a place that I do not know actually exists. A place that I cannot reach myself. Somewhere deep inside my soul. Or what is left of it.

My soul begins to cry. Poor lonely lost soul. It is the child inside me who is lonely and lost. Lost and forgotten. Forgotten and abused.

She was an innocent child once, this Nargis. Not knowing good from bad, not knowing bad from evil, not knowing evil from sin. Not having a care in the world.

All she ever wanted was love. Look what she got instead. Even the memory of love has been erased.

I lost that little child who just wanted love.

THE U-CORD SNIPPED?

Difficult phone calls to Mummy continued. Her negative energy was unrelenting in her insinuations of my having a faulty personality. I reacted with a muffled convulsion to everything she had to say. She could never say anything right. When she was sad, I was angry. When she was anxious, I was angry. When she was in a lighter mood --- which was not often, I was still angry.

I had decided that my mother could never make it up to me.

One day when she phoned me up again, like so many times before, it was different this time. I did not know quite how to feel anymore.

"I've finally decided to tell you that the doctor found an ovarian cyst in my abdomen," Mummy sounded very upset. "It's the size of an orange. I'm informing you about this, only, because I don't want you to complain later that I didn't tell you."

I know I'm not ready for this.

I found myself peppering her with routine questions that I would ask of a patient. Routine, mechanical questions. The how, the when, and the what will happen next kind of questions.

And then, the question that I dreaded to ask, but must, "Is it benign?"

Mummy said she did not know yet.

She added, "My surgery will be done before the year is out. Sanju will come over to help me during that time and Anjali will arrive soon after. So you don't have to bother to make a trip."

Bother. How I hate that word!

The next time we spoke, Mummy was complaining, "My doctor said, 'Your daughter who lives in America should've been here to help you as well. Didn't you tell me that she's a physician?'"

Mummy, please shut up!

When she was grieving, I did not have the heart to confront her. And now, she is sick. How can you badger someone who's sick? What if she has cancer? What if she dies?

What'll happen to me if she dies? I know that I'm not ready for my mother to die. I know if that happens, I'll feel abandoned and cheated all over again.

When'll this torment ever end? Does it ever end? *Can* it ever end?

I wish that she *would* die. Then I'll be done with her once and for all. God, let me feel everything that I need to feel, all just once. But, only just once. Only this *one last time*. Then please, please let me go on with my life. Why's this pain dragging on for so long?

It feels as if I am walking barefoot on sharp pebbles floating on quicksand, where a giant whirlpool threatens to silently suck me into a quagmire of pain whenever I dare to stray nearby. Every time I fall into it, I forget the way out of there all over again.

Yes, she *should* die. Maybe, it'll be the right thing for both of us. It'll free us both. With her uterus out, that last link with her will be broken forever. The surgeon will expunge it from her insides and throw it out for trash, for stray dogs to chew on. Without that organ, she could never be called Mother again.

God help me! Lightning strike me dead!

Up and down --- Stop --- Down and up --- Stop --- When will this seesaw end? I want her dead. But dread it at the same time? Why do I still long for a bond with Mummy?

I cannot sleep anymore. I cannot think anymore. I cannot feel anymore.

I cease to exist.

A LONG AND TWISTED ROAD

It is hard to remember everything that happened during my first trip back to the Red Fort after Daddy's death. People must envy me, as I walk into the First Class cabin of a British Airways Boeing 747, like I used to. They must think that I am somebody special, someone who is so lucky, so happy ---

I feel as if I am walking into a forest of knives. The posh cabin appears overcrowded. The reclining flatbed feels like a pincushion. The plush leather seat is cold.

I cry most of the way back home. I am confused about my tears.

I hope they don't mean that I'm missing Daddy. It's true. I have not cried, yet, for losing him.

I cry into the tissue. I cry into the blanket. Then I cry into the pillow. I cannot stop sobbing. I shake with my tears. I shake with the anger of helplessness. I shake with the despair of betrayal.

I thought that I'll be finally happy and relieved after Daddy died. Why am I so miserable then?

I can barely talk without weeping.

It's a long story. It's a long, confusing, and complicated story ---

The salad tastes like blotting paper and the steak like tinfoil, but not because it is airline food. Over a lavish five-course dinner and a couple of glasses of Joseph Drouhin Rully chardonnay, Arjun talks about his mother. He tells me how, when he was a kid, every time his father would threaten to give him a good hiding for being lackadaisical with math homework, she would protect him.

"If you ever raise your hand one more time on my child, *Ji*," she would warn her husband, keeping little Arjun behind her, "I promise you, I'll kill myself, *Ji*."

Arjun would hide behind the folds of her sari, not daring to peek around her rounded silhouette. He said that deep inside he always knew that his mother would never actually kill herself. His father also knew that his wife would never commit suicide. But her standing up for her son made Arjun feel strong and protected.

"Don't you ever talk to him like that again, *Ji*," she would caution her husband repeatedly, briskly shaking her index finger at him.

Arjun's story makes me feel happy for him. But sad for myself.

I am sad, because in my heart I know that I never got to hear anything like that in my childhood. I am sad, because I know that my mother never did anything like that for me.

I wish Mummy had said that for me. I wish *somebody* had said something even remotely similar for me.

Finally, I muster up the courage to call Mummy from New Delhi.

"How long will you be staying this time," she asks. Her voice sounds harsh, distant. "Every year, you come home for only two days. And you hardly ever come without Arjun," she complains.

I respond gently, but firmly, "That'll depend on how our conversations go. There's a lot that I need to talk to you about. Actually, how long I'll be staying depends ultimately on you. On whether we can talk honestly. On whether you can speak from your heart. Also, Mummy, I hope that you're alone. I don't want anyone else there. If there're other people with you, I'll come some other time."

Mummy promises me that she is alone.

This is the first time in my life that I arrive at the Red Fort and my father is not there. Mummy was his shadow during all their life together.

I walk up the driveway by the manicured lawn and award-winning rosebush, The Pilgrim, which is in full bloom. Even without Daddy's keen supervision. For the first time, I walk into a Daddy-free zone. My feet feel heavy from the long journey and from the arthritis I have developed over the last several years. I feel like the walking wounded.

I ring the doorbell and wait. My heart is starting to pound. I can hear the thuds in my chest. They remind me that time is not still. That I am still alive. And that this is not a movie.

I hear slow shuffling steps from the other side of the large teak door, walking toward me. Mummy undoes the latch. She looks tired and frail. We hug cautiously.

Why am I so afraid of what I will surely see in Mummy's eyes? They still swell easily from crying. She has been rubbing them a lot. This has delayed her recovery from her recent cataract surgery. It bothers me that she still cries for him.

I sit Mummy down on the couch in the lounge, with the entire family staring at us from the photographs on the window sills. There is that one picture frame of Daddy in full military gear, flanked by other photos of the rest of his family. He is adorned with decorated ribbons for the wars that he fought and won, some of which have been documented in history books and others that did not quite make it there. Wars between the North and the South. Wars between the East and the West. Wars fought over God, Ego, and Oil. Daddy is looking straight at us. As if another war is about to break out. A war between Mother and Child. A war over Truth.

We start to talk. Rather, I talk and Mummy listens. I do not give her a choice.

"Mummy, every time I see a tear in your eye, it's a betrayal of me," is my opening salvo. "Sometimes, when I see you crying for the man who abused your daughter, I wonder whether you're really my mother. Something is not right with this picture. Don't you see? Remember, Daddy used to tell us those stories about adopting me, about finding me in a large black leather bag left in the gutter by the roadside and taking me home. Tell me, was that story really true? Or, did Daddy have an affair, conceive me out of wedlock and insist that you raise me?"

I don't think that Mummy is quite capable of having an affair.

"Do I have a different mother, after all? There has been such a web of lies hanging over our family that I don't know what's real anymore. So, now the time has come to tell me the truth. Mummy, do I have a different mother?"

I notice Mummy's gray hair peeking through the ebony dye. She is quiet. She is taking a long time to respond.

So I go on, "And, tell me, Mummy, when I was a baby did you actually nurse me?"

Mummy looks rather confused. She is blinking rapidly again. She appears anxious.

What might she be thinking about? How *does* Mummy think anyway?

"Are you saying that I picked you up from the gutter?" she says angrily and slaps me across the face instantly.

I am stunned by the assault!

"Your father left a will," she begins. "Is that what you've come to talk about?" she sideswipes me again.

I am livid.

"Mummy, that's what this family does. First you abuse me and then you insult me. You just go on abusing and insulting me. Is that the reason why you actually had me? So that you could practice target shooting on this pigeon? Is signing off on the property all that's now left of our relationship? Come on. Let's get it over with. Just tell me where you want me to scribble my initials."

Mummy is quiet again. I see pain on her face. Pain and anger. Her wrinkles appear even more pronounced when she is upset.

"Go on, Mummy, hit me again. Hit me between the eyes! You must know that slapping me is not the worst thing that's ever happened to me."

I notice sweat gathering on Mummy's upper lip and over the bridge of her nose. The wet circles on the underarms of her silk tunic *kameez* are ballooning as we speak, descending symmetrically further downward on either side, right in front of me.

"It's painful," I hear myself saying. "It's so freaking painful to be here in Daddy's house, knowing that you still keep his photograph by your bedside. When you fully know that for me, there is terror, dread and paranoia hanging around that frame. I get an internal convulsion every time I see his face. You know I've never felt free in this house, because it was always *his* house. I've never been able to speak my mind, because *he* would never allow that. So today, I want to say everything that's on my mind. Everything, Mother. *Everything*. And Mummy, you will have to listen until I'm done." I continue.

"So Mummy," I say, looking her squarely in the eye. "Look at me now. Look at your youngest child. Your last-born. Your baby daughter. Did you ever know what was going on between Daddy and me?"

Mummy responds, "Are you accusing me of knowing about it?"

She's referring to the sexual abuse as *it*.

"Remember," she continues, "I was always in the background when it came to you and your father."

"Whose fault *is* that?" I ask, incensed with anger. "Why were you not there? Where *were* you? What bothers me is that even after

I told you about the molestation, you never had the courage to leave him. Look at yourself now. You're crying for the man who abused your child. Your tears tell me that you don't really believe it happened. Your tears tell me everything. Tell me, would you have left him for me?"

"How could I have left him? Where could I have gone? I built this house brick by brick forty years ago. I would've never left it for another woman to occupy. You know how men are. He would've easily remarried had I left."

What *is* she talking about?

"You know Mummy, I don't think that I even know you. I'll never understand what you just said. We were never close, you and I. Pray can I ask, why? As a parent, do you take any ownership for that? For our lack of closeness?"

Mummy is irritated now. "Nargis, you know what? I've been bullied all my life! You harass me with your questions. Nobody can bully me now."

And I quickly retort, seething with anger. "Why didn't you ever tell Daddy what you just said to me? You were always so scared of him, weren't you? Only he could bully you, isn't it?"

"You live in America. Nobody talks about these things here in India. It's considered very shameful here, and ---"

"It's a shame that it happened, isn't it?" I interject, consumed with frustration.

"Do you know what it is like to live alone in this big house, like I do? Who could I turn to for help? Now, think about it. How long do I have? Five years? Ten years? Who will you argue with after I'm gone? And you never think of what the neighbors will say if they hear about your accusation. Dr. Negi, who lives down the street from us, always held your father in the highest regard. How could I face him? How could I face society?"

"What neighbors? What society? Mother, the ocean doesn't care about the fish. So, I see that once again, you're just thinking only of yourself. We hardly know anyone in this town anyway. Daddy kept us only for himself." And I go on, "But answer this if you can. You lived with Daddy for fifty long years, by *his* game and *his* rules. How nutty *was* he? And, how crazy was he as a sexual deviant?"

"I don't know what you mean," she sounds pensive.

"Actually, don't tell me. I don't think that I really want to know," I add quickly. "I don't even know why I asked."

Then after a pause, she continues, "All I know is that my brothers and sisters respect me," and she starts to cry. "They hold me up on a pedestal. I'm the most educated one and they've always looked up to me. They'll do anything for me."

"Then why didn't you leave Daddy for me, and go to them for help? You know, I don't believe anything you say anymore. And you know what makes it worse? I don't think that you believe it yourself."

Mummy sarcastically retorts, "Now, don't go on ranting and raving. Of course, there's no one in the family as bright as you. Only you understand everything. Your Daddy was right. This education has gone to your head."

I dismiss her last remark. That's how Daddy used to speak through her, for her. Just like he's doing right now, playing his Daddy Card.

I go on, "What family of yours are you talking about? You never spoke with your own father for the last few years before he died, just because Daddy was upset with him over a trivial matter. You even abandoned your own father. Now, he was a man well regarded by society. I should probably take solace in the fact that I'm not the only one who you betrayed."

"Your Nana understood my predicament. He knew that in our culture, I had to abide by my husband's wishes. In his heart, my father always knew that I loved and respected him."

I wish that I could feel the same way about mine.

"It's too bad that I don't believe you feel anything for me, Mummy. I've never felt your love. Tell me this, as you'd go puttering around the house --- spraying the *tardka* with cumin seeds, snipping roses for your vases, sowing the buttons on Daddy's shirt, or laying in bed with him --- did you ever think of me? Did you ever wonder what my life was like, being yanked around by sexual abuse? Did you ever take a moment to think of what it was like to go through that molestation, which I suffered as a child? Did you feel my pain? Now let me tell you something about pain. Sometimes, it's been so painful that I would go around driving in an ice storm in Chicago, with music blaring in my ears, wishing I'd get lost or die or something."

"Who ever told you to live in such a cold city? It's not for everyone. Especially with your arthritis. You should really stop working. Just try to enjoy life and be happy. Forget the past."

I've lost her completely. Is there even a point in trying anymore?

She goes on, "But, I want to ask you this. If what you allege about your father is true, then why did you leave your daughter Mandy with us when she was a toddler? Did you think this home would be a safe place for her?"

I try to explain, "It's hard to explain how well I had learned to block away the past. How I wanted so desperately to have a normal relationship with both of you. I wish that I had known better then. I wish that I had acted differently. I wish that I had made better choices. It's called *denial*, Mother. I was twenty five years old, and young and stupid. I wish that I had been stronger at the time. In my mind, I would justify that she was so little, so Daddy would never bother her. He had never touched me the wrong way when I was that little. And thank God for that. So I tried not to think about it. I was trying too hard to please you both. Remember, during that period in your lives, both of you had become empty-nesters after your kids had flown the coop. This house was big and empty. With Mandy reciting Humpty-Dumpty nursery rhymes in this lounge, your lives were once again filled with laughter and fun in caring for a grandchild. But it was all wrong. I should've never done that. I should've never taken such a risk."

Mummy sounds quite miffed, "You know what your problem is?" She does not wait for an answer. "Your problem is that you keep going back to the past."

Sock it to me!

"Mummy, how *do* you think? How *do* you understand why the Earth revolves around the Sun? You only knew how to revolve around Daddy. He *was* your sun. Or, why the moon shines? I wonder what made you as cold as the moon."

"I don't know what you're talking about. You keep talking like your father. You're just like him. You have to go on talking."

"How dare you tell me that I'm just like him? I've made mistakes, but I never sexually abused my children. And I've been able to admit to the blunders I've made. And, I feel remorse for having made them.

Do *you* feel any regrets? Children are so eager to forgive. All they ever want is to hear a parent admit to a mistake once, so that they can move on. As for you, Mother, you show no interest in me. Do you know how Arjun and I have lived and struggled, laughed and cried, together? How we ran ragged, fell on our faces, picked ourselves up and moved on? I've been afraid to tell you about the battles we lost along the way. Why am I afraid to be vulnerable with you? And you think my life is perfect, and resent that? Why, Mummy? Tell me *why*?"

Mummy, shaking her head and shutting her ears, "You're torturing me with your questions. Please, please don't ask me anything anymore. I beg of you. Stop! I can never win with you. You're just like your father. It's impossible to win with you."

"All excuses. In fact, it is *I* who can never win. It's a trap. This whole damn fucking family is a fucking trap. For God's sake, stop telling me that I'm like Daddy. At least, you can give me some credit for stopping the cycle of abuse."

I am shouting now. I must regain some control over myself.

"But tell me something, Mummy. Had I needed your help, could I have come back to live with you?"

"No, I could never live with you."

I catch her.

"Aha! You just said that I'm like my father! And you lived with him? And obeyed his every command? And abandoned your child for him?" I go on, "Would you've ever stood up for me if this had gone to court?"

"No," she says simply. "Nargis, it's impossible to talk to you. You're so temperamental."

I feel anger rising from somewhere inside my body.

Daddy will never buckle down. He's still here, in this room, right now, doing a voiceover.

My voice is shrill, "You call me temperamental! Headline News! Newsflash! Mother, *I'll* show you temperamental!"

When emotions get in the way, even bright people can act quite stupid.

I smash an empty glass on the floor! Mummy looks shocked. Then we both go down on our knees to pick up the pieces.

My patients should see me now! I'm a damn walking DSM-XXX!

I instruct angrily, "Stop Mother! Let me do this alone. Never mind if the sharp edges of the glass cut my fingers. Never mind the bruises, the blood or the pain. I've learned to pick up the pieces of my life all by myself. I'm accustomed to this. So let me do this alone, even if it hurts. I don't need your help anymore. No one can do anything for me in this house. No one ever has."

Suddenly, Mummy slaps herself. Then she starts to cry.

Now what do I do? It's all so confusing. Why's she crying? Does she feel sorry for herself, or sorry for me?

I feel like breaking something else. Then for some reason, the moment passes. But I still cannot get myself to comfort her.

Finally I say, "You know what I hate most about myself? I hate that I'm still emotionally dependent on you. I don't think Dr. Ezkiah did a complete job cutting that cord. Why should it matter whether you believe me or not? Whether you care about me or not? Or whether you're on my side or not? It's about taking sides, isn't it? This whole freaking thing has been a game. This relationship with you has never been easy. You're the last frontier left for me to overcome. You must know that the key to my sanity is still in that bunch you used to carry around."

Mummy has calmed down by now. I can still feel an artery throbbing in my temple.

I go on, "And when Daddy would hit us, you just stood there and said nothing. You would never leave his side. You'd never go anywhere alone without him. You used to explain that you couldn't leave Daddy by himself because of his heart condition. What heart condition? Do you really believe he had a sick heart? Now, we both know that he had a sick mind. You could never leave him, could you? And now, you dare ask me why I don't travel without Arjun? He's always taken care of me, that's why. Mummy, you believed everything Daddy said. Didn't you? You even gave up on God because of him."

"But Nargis," Mummy is able to interject, "in the last few years, you made it look like everything was okay."

"You know the truth, Mummy! Everything was *not* okay. Did you notice that in my letters home, I would put a tiny comma after the word Dear, and only after that add Daddy and Mummy? That was my silent protest. Did you ever notice that?"

Mummy says nothing.

"The day that Daddy died, I felt both of you had died. Do you remember how you responded to me? 'So, *you too* found out about it,' you said. How dare you use sarcasm with me! How dare you take your anger out on me! You have no right to be angry, Mummy. You've never been a mother to me, so I take that right away from you. Right now. This very minute. Here in this house. Now and forever. You're angry because you feel alone, now that Daddy is no more and you have to fend for yourself. That's what you're really angry about. Well, welcome to the club! I *too* was alone as a child and I *too* had to fend for myself. So, now you'll have to face life on life's terms. No Daddy to protect you. Remember how so many years ago you made a choice. Now you must live with it. As Daddy used to say, 'You made your own bed, now you must sleep in it.'

And, I go on, "I want to say this as clearly as I can. The myth of us being a special family has exploded --- It's over --- Control, Alt, Delete ---"

I'm certain that she doesn't understand this.

"Mummy," I go on, "New Rule! Let's not talk about other family members when we meet. Let there be no third person between us anymore. Let's try to rewind our relationship. Perhaps, we may have half a chance at having a connection."

My voice turns earnest, "You know, I'll never understand this. But now that Daddy is gone and you're finally financially, and hopefully, emotionally independent, why can you not think for yourself? Or have you forgotten how to? Or does his ghost still breathe inside this house? Does he still live inside you?"

Mummy answers, "It's so difficult to talk to you. You go in circles. I'm sure you've heard this before. So it must be true. You've always been so difficult to deal with. You're so sensitive."

I don't think I can singlehandedly turn the blades of the windmill to go anti-clockwise.

"So it's *sensitive, difficult, temperamental*. Good God, Mother! Go on. Make me a punching bag! Are you left with anymore stereotypes? How about --- prima donna --- or --- nutcase --- or --- straight out of a straitjacket? By the way, does pigeonholing me take you off the hook? It's all *my* fault, isn't it? That would make it quits, wouldn't it? Is that why you keep doing it? You must wonder how I got to be so sensitive. And, is it really such a bad thing? Thank God, I'm sensitive. Thank God, I'm aware of what can hurt others because I know what's capable of hurting me. Thank God I can recognize the power of judgment. Yes, sometimes it gets me into trouble. I can smell it from a mile away, even when my antennas are not up. Sometimes, I wish I didn't hear it as clearly as I do. It would simplify my life. Don't you see? That's what childhood abuse does. It completely messes with your mind."

After a brief moment I say, "But seriously, tell me Mummy. Was I a good child? Did I listen to you? Did I study well? Did I work hard? Did I make you proud?"

I do not wait for an answer. I know that Mummy does not have an answer.

Daddy would've certainly had one.

"I want to tell you, Mummy, that something has been lost over the years. There's a part of myself that's missing. The child in me is lost. I feel empty inside. Like an empty vessel," I end with one hand on my chest. "Right here, inside me."

We both look miserable. Misery loves company.

I'm not sure Mummy understands what I'm saying, or what I need from her. This needle will not move. I sound like a broken record, the kind when metal keeps drilling into plastic at the same spot, again and again. Mummy's face looks kind of plastic, too. I must've lost her several minutes ago. Actually, I probably lost her a long time ago.

Mummy looks lost and worn out. Suddenly, she looks really old.

I touch her lightly on the shoulder.

"It's late, Mummy," I say at last. "Let's both go to bed."

Mummy retires into her bedroom, while I spend the rest of the night painstakingly scrubbing off all my father's fingerprints in my mother's kitchen.

How can you kill somebody who has already died?

SHE TIES THE KNOT — "WHAT, AGAIN?"

I retire to the pink bedroom and slip under the quilt, the one with a maroon velvet cover embroidered over with green and purple peacocks fanning themselves to stay cool. It smells of home. Mummy has given me a rubber hot water bottle to warm my feet. I lie in bed and look up at the ceiling. In the haze of the night-light, I see a couple of lizards wrestling. They are the same two slithery reptiles with fat bellies and erect tails from that night, when Daddy came up to this very window and pointed a cold pistol at me.

I cannot sleep. The hot water bottle becomes cold. It feels rubbery against my feet.

That night I dream about Mummy.

There is a wedding in the family. I do not quite know who is getting married. A crowd is gathering at the Red Fort anticipating the arrival of the *baraat*. There is a sense of anticipation in the air to get just one glimpse of the bride and groom, customary at weddings the world over. Especially, to see them *together*.

I guess, since I'm also waiting in the crowd, I must be from the bride's side of the family.

It is just a little before the sun is about to set for the day, when the air becomes misty and heavy with the promise of romance and intrigue. The house is decorated with strings of triangular flags in a medley of every conceivable primary color, flapping jubilantly under the plaid tents. A mesh of naked bulbs twinkle like miniature stars high up in the mango trees. It is very festive.

Then, I see *her*. And I halt in my tracks.

It is not considered auspicious, if you cannot spot the bride at a wedding. Usually, she takes time to make her presence known, but when she arrives all eyes turn to her. Mummy looks just the way she did last night, all seventy two years of her. A light breeze is sweeping over her ebony-dyed hair, occasionally revealing stray patches of scattered salt-and-pepper gray roots like the first faded-out fall leaves playing peek-a-boo in a willow tree. Her back is hunched over, her steps are slow and halting, her eyes are red and swollen from crying.

But, no bridal dress?

There is noise everywhere. The continuous light chatter of a cluster of women huddled together in perpetual conspiracy, interspersed with the sporadic high-pitch laughter of other well-heeled guests flamboyant in their judgment. The rhythmic sound of a *dhol* drums out the continuous melody of a *shehnai*. In the background, there is a shrill band belting out *Tequila* to the compliments of an accordion and trumpets, blasting in different octaves, floating in and out of sync. But, no sounds of chanting by a priest.

Then, I see *him*. The groom, of course.

But wait. Something seems to be grotesquely wrong with him. And, why's he alone? Does he not have a family? Also, he does appear much younger than Mummy. Like forty something. And, why's he coming up the driveway ever so slowly?

At first, I think he must have a fractured leg, or a broken something. But as he comes up closer, I gasp! I notice that he is badly deformed. He has a clubfoot and the other leg is paralyzed. In fact, he can barely crawl as he advances toward the front Kota-stone steps leading up to the veranda, where Mummy is standing to greet her future soul mate and carrying a cheap garland laden with bright yellow double-string marigolds intermingled with crisp rupee notes. It is so heavy that she can hardly hold it upright. Her brow is furrowed with age. The blue veins on her hands are popping out, ready to burst, against her frail wrinkled skin. He looks like a wound-up injured animal, this groom. It takes him forever to get to his bride as he slithers up the stone pathway lined with orange-pink rosebushes and potted coral bougainvilleas.

I can hardly believe my eyes!

So, it's *Mummy* who is the bride and she wants to marry this creature? How did she ever agree to this? What *was* she thinking? No wonder she looks worried. Mummy always looks worried. Even when nothing bad is happening. She's always got that permanent crease on her forehead.

Then Mummy sees him, too. Suddenly, she becomes a changed person. She bows down to this all-brute half-animal, catering to his every need, cajoling, subdued and oh-so-sickeningly passive. She follows him everywhere without saying a word, carrying a weighty bunch of keys tucked away in her sari and making sure she is perfectly two steps behind him at any given time. Finally she goes away with him when he leaves through the gates, swishing his tail as he glides along, and they are both lost to the waiting crowd.

I do not know how this happens, but the Red Fort is now on an ocean. The entire foundation has been uprooted, revealing the jagged edges of cement that have erupted in the crisscross trenches where I used to play solitary hide-'n'-go-seek when I was a child. The whole structure is split apart and sitting on dodder, which looks a little bit like tangled angel-hair pasta. All nine bedrooms. The spiral staircase leading up to the library. The backyard vines. And the sitting room with empty velvet-cushioned sofas, which seem to be staring vacantly at Daddy's photograph as it is about ready to topple over off the edge of the mantelpiece. With each motion of the waves, the house seems to be getting closer and closer to falling on its side. The ocean is becoming rough and threatening, as the house bobs up and down like a buoy out of control.

For a while, it appears as if the house will surely go under. I try to hold the walls down to prevent it from being swallowed up by the tide. But it seems that it will be going down anyway.

Then I look at my hands. They look like little child hands. Like those of a ten year old girl.

This is when I wake up.

For a brief moment, I think that I am under water, free-falling to the bottom of the ocean. It is a vertical drop, as I plummet into the never-ending darkness.

It's cold down here. It must be way past the permafrost. I'm sure that I'm dying. Or already dead.

It is freezing in my bed. Then I hear someone at the other end of the house. I shake off the quilt and walk to up to the kitchen.

There I see Mummy, hunched over, silently stirring sugar in her teacup.

"TAKE TWO ... AAAAAAND CLAP!"

The next morning is another day. Like most next-mornings usually are.

I am writing furiously in the kitchen, hoping against hope that Mummy can see me scribbling my life journey. A story that I cannot wait to tell the world. A story the entire world *should* know. I catch her from the corner of my eye. I hope she realizes that the reason I am so feverishly scrawling our conversation from yesterday, is to make sure that it is never forgotten. So that it is not once again chalked up to another he-said-she-said.

It's just possible, that this'll scare her enough to finally get real. Maybe, the fear of the whole world knowing about how she abandoned me a second time over by not believing me will get her to be honest at last. Perhaps, it might even improve our relationship.

But in my heart, I know that the chances of this happening are pretty bleak.

I put down my pen and look my mother straight in the eye. She looks blankly back at me. I follow her to the lounge, where many an important tête-à-tête has happened before.

"Mummy, did you ever think of killing him?"

I will never forget what Mummy said.

"Now that's a stupid *fazool* question," she says sternly.

But I notice how she did not say no.

Last night must not have been good for her. She looks poorly rested with squishy dark bags under her eyes like dark concentric rings of half-Saturn. There she is, unyielding and unapproachable all over again.

"You won't think it's so silly, when this," I point to my writing, "when this goes into print. Will you still deny the truth after my manuscript makes it to the bookshelves at Barnes & Noble?"

It's too bad that I've to resort to being grandiose, I tell myself.

Mummy says, "I've only one last request for you. Publish your book only after I'm dead."

I'm already not liking where this is going.

"There's only one person who's really dead," I tell her firmly, "and that's your husband. And there's only one thing, Mummy, that I want you to do for *me*. I've never ever asked you to do anything just for me, have I? But, this is very important. Can you do this for me? Can you really do this for your youngest daughter? I want you to take your husband's picture and tear it into tiny pieces. Do it with your own bare hands. Please do this for me. I beg of you. Just for once. Kill him, that molester! Kill him slowly. Kill him again and again. Every time you shred his photo, think that you're killing him. Killing him for me. Only then will I know that you have even an iota of love left for me."

Mummy does not move. She is looking through me. Past me. To a place far away. A place I do not know.

I bring the picture from the mantelpiece in the sitting room and place it in her weary hands. The knotted veins on her palms are getting ready to explode straight out of the epidermis. I see a pulse throbbing on the side of her neck. The carotids are clicking twice as fast as the clock.

She holds the photograph. The same one that Daddy had saved for posterity. The one that I just finished removing from the large grand frame where it had been lying safe, flat and motionless and dead behind the thick glass, for the last few decades. That is how he had wanted his great-grand children to know who he was. That is how he had wanted to be remembered. The life-size headshot, with that heroic and accomplished look on his face that I knew so well. Children always get to know their parents' favorite look. He is in full army gear --- complete with the striped ribbons and medals hanging off his badge, in recognition of the wars he had fought and won.

He does not know this yet, but this is the first one that he'll lose.

Mummy tears the picture in half.

"There you go!" she says. "Are you satisfied now?"

I take the two pieces of Daddy's heroic and accomplished face from her and go on tearing the rest into little bits.

"You bad, bad, Daddy!" I shout, as I go on ripping it into pieces of nothing.

Then I spit on the pile of shreds and start to cry. The last part surprises me. In fact, I am shocked that I am weeping.

This was supposed to make me feel better, wasn't it?

"Nargis, why are you crying?" Mummy asks suddenly, "Do you miss him?"

I feel like a torpedo has hit me below the waterline. My face turns ashen and ghastly white, as if I am already long gone and dead twice over, but have simply forgotten to crawl back into my grave.

"Mummy, you probably don't know this about me. Like the many other things you don't know about me. I cry when I'm angry. I cry when I'm mad. I don't know how to express angst without crying."

"You cry too much. You were always a crybaby. The youngest and the most pampered."

There she goes again, sounding just like Daddy.

"Nargis, I'm pleading with you one last time. Stop this torture. What else do you want from me? *Maine kitni bar hath jodh ke mafi mang li.*"

She is clearly at a loss for words, now that she has switched to Hindi. She is telling me that she has apologized so many times already and wants to be pardoned.

I wonder why I haven't heard her admission of guilt yet. Nargis, here's your chance.

"Mummy, say this once to me. I'll help you out. I'll say it for you. All you have to do is to simply repeat after me, if you can. Word for word. Please say, 'I wish I had done something about it. I wish I had been there for you, Nargis. I wish I had protected you, my child. I wish --- that it had never happened --- to my baby.'"

She stares blankly at me, as if she is waiting her turn at a check-post to a foreign land. As if she has checked out already.

I feel hopeless, but I go on. "I'm almost certain that if Daddy were still here with us, you would've said, 'Let's end this nonsense, Nargis. Go give your father a hug. And everything will be okay.'"

No response.

"I don't think that I know enough about you, Mummy. What else don't I know? What are the other secrets in this family of ours? Tell me. Why did your sister have to die? Or was she killed?"

Mummy is still quiet.

"I remember like it happened last night. It was at Namgarh, the same place where I ended the abuse. By the way, I've never heard you give me credit for doing that. Daddy told us that your sister, Aunty Chandri, was given Old Monk rum laced with poison. It's a strange story. Truth is stranger than fiction, isn't it? Daddy said she shouldn't have fooled around with the other men in the family, since she was a widow. He said she was openly flirting with a few married male relatives and making an ass of herself. Is this true? Did Nana also know about it and condone her killing? Remember, it was all supposed to be hush-hush. We kids were not allowed to talk about it or ask any questions. Later, both you and Daddy changed the story on us and said that it had never happened. But, of course, you won't tell me what actually happened. Mummy, who killed your sister?"

"Nobody was killed. Who told you that?"

"Then, you'll have to tell me this. By the way, I hate to ask you this. Were you ever jealous and resentful of our relationship? Is that why you cannot feel for me?"

I don't know if I'll get an answer. So, I might as well go on asking questions.

I wonder if my father moved onto other partners, including little Nargis, because Mummy would say 'no' to him in bed. But I am too afraid to ask this one.

"I feel so stupid asking you all these questions, when you look like you don't hear them."

"That's because they're stupid questions to begin with," she says dismissively.

"Do you understand English?" I ask in utter exasperation. "Let me try this again. What's your opinion on the subject of sexual abuse?"

"It's a bad thing," she says simply. Then she quickly adds, "Why didn't you tell me about it when it happened?"

"I don't know if I can ever explain how it happened or why I didn't tell you. I couldn't tell you because I thought that it was all my fault to begin with. That's why. Who could I turn to? Our relatives? Daddy had always made them out to be uneducated, dimwitted and conniving. Our friends? We moved around all through my childhood like gypsies and were never allowed to have close friendships."

But I am not done yet.

"Sometimes I used to fear that Daddy would kill us all. Me along with, Arjun, Mandy and Natasha. All four of us. He would wipe any trace of my family from the face of this Earth. In fact, once I had this dream: Daddy was actually not dead, but just lying on the funeral pyre pretending to be asleep. His skin was all bloated and cracked and pink underneath. You were waiting for him to give you the final go-ahead to start his cremation. But he knew me too well. He knew how eager I was to see him gone. He could translate any expression on my face in a jiffy. He could read my mind. Before the fire had a chance to consume his body, he had picked up his old rifle kept hidden in his pants alongside his leg. It had six chambers, and only one bullet. He was playing Russian Roulette again. He liked playing games, didn't he? He fired all six shots at me. Then he proceeded to empty the entire cartridge into my body. Later from the ashes, I picked up a three-inch bullet that had grazed my leg. It had blood on it. Still warm and red. My blood.

"Believe me, I was terrified that he'd poison us all. You know, Mummy, he had no qualms, no conscience, no guilt. He had killed people in the war. He'd persuade you, 'Mani, my dear wife and soul mate, I'm sorry to tell you this. But our daughter, Nargis — she's really quite sick. She's lost her mind. She's gone completely bonkers!' He'd convince you that I had a disease, and, to cure the illness, he had to get rid of me. 'That's the only way out from under the shame of this false accusation, Mani,' he would've told you. And you would've been his willing and loyal accomplice. I would've died like your sister had died. And it would've all been hush-hush, like her death had been hush-hush. Both Daddy and you would've changed the story again: 'Nargis killed her entire family, and then she killed herself, too. She couldn't face up to the humiliation of her own lies.' By the way, was Daddy involved with your sister too? The one who was killed?"

If Mummy responded to my monologue, I do not remember her answers today. I do not remember whether I gave her a chance to counter or whether I was afraid of what she might say. Or, whether I am afraid to remember what she did say.

Or am I really more scared of her silence?

What I do remember, though, is that I just kept talking.

"Mummy," I go on. "Seriously, I really want to ask you this one last time. Have I ever, I mean ever, lied to you, Mother? Since you didn't believe me when I told you about the abuse, what did you think? Did you say: 'You know, this daughter of mine. She lies all the time. So, there she goes again. She just made it all up.' Is that what you said to yourself? I'm curious. When you think of me, what *do* you think? Daddy was right. If you don't bother animals, they leave you alone. It's people who bother each other. And one other thing. I'm forgetting when I heard this. But Daddy once said to you, 'You know, it's a well known fact. Animals do get intimate with their own young ones. It happens all the time in nature. It's very natural to do this --- this intimacy with one's progeny. It's a way to show love and closeness. Society curbs this normal behavior in us.' What utter baloney and bullshit! Do you believe all this bunkum too?"

"I've never heard anyone say that."

"Then, where's all this coming from? Don't credit me with such a vivid imagination that I've created such a story. You must think I'm super bright, don't you, to make it all up?"

My sarcasm is lost on Mummy.

"And my diary," I go on. "You must remember my diary? The one I wrote in the eighth grade. Where I'd written about Daddy. Where I had scribbled, 'He messed with me. I wish God would open up the Earth so he is swallowed instantly. One day he must pay for his sins. Jesus, help me!' Don't tell me you've forgotten about that, too? What *do* you remember?"

Mummy says quickly, "I don't know anything about a diary."

I feel, as if I am hanging upside down by my toenails.

"I guess it's your prerogative to forget. You must've been sleepwalking through most of my childhood. Why, you were there, when I had come back from Moscow that summer. We were sitting right here in the lounge. Daddy, you, and I. He told me that he had found my old diary hidden away in the dusty staircase attic. He asked me what I had meant in my writings. I couldn't answer. Or look at him. Then he said something about children going through different phases in their life when they hate their parents. He said it was normal for teenagers to feel that way. You were sitting right here, where you're sitting now. Don't you remember that?"

"I don't remember anything like that."

I am fuming aloud. I can hear my teeth gnashing.

"So since you don't remember, it didn't happen. And since it didn't happen, it wasn't said. And since it wasn't said, you wouldn't remember. Would you? I call it circular logic. Mummy, let me try this one last time. Now, look at me as I ask you this --- Do you really believe it happened?"

I notice that like her, I am also referring to the molestation as *it*.

"If you say it did, then it did."

"How do you change so suddenly? What makes you decide to believe me one minute, and not believe me the next? Do you flip a coin in your mind? What *do* you say to yourself? 'Today. Why, today is believe-day. And tomorrow? Tomorrow, let's play opposites again.'"

Mummy says, "You know, a daughter shouldn't constantly malign a parent. It isn't right."

"Who're you, Mummy, to teach me about right and wrong?" I counter.

Suddenly, it strikes me that at this very moment, I am just like my father. Tormenting her with a barrage of questions, just like he used to torment her. Questions she does not have answers for that he would then answer for her. And then, blame her for the answer. It dawns on me that I expect her to apologize for both of them.

Mummy starts to cry.

I lower my voice, but I am not done yet.

"Don't you wonder," I ask. "Don't you wonder how he got away scot-free? I can't tell you how obsessed I am with justice being done. If God were here to give you the authority, how would you make Daddy pay for his sins? But, I forgot. How can you find God again in your life? Daddy made you give up on Him as well."

"Sometimes, I don't know what to say to you anymore. What'll make it right? I guess I'm not as educated as you are. I haven't accomplished things in my life like you've done. So forgive me if it doesn't come out right."

"I want to leave you with this, Mummy. I've been so driven most of my life. First, I was driven to please Daddy. Then, I was driven to change my life and block away the past. Now, I'm determined to help others in need so they don't have to suffer as long as I did. I strive never to depend on a parent or anyone else in our family." I am surprised at how calm I sound, even to myself. "I made a vow to myself, a long time ago, that I'll never be vulnerable again."

In silence, I devour the meal Mummy had prepared for me. My mother shows her love through her cooking. At that very moment, my husband walks into the lounge.

"Arjun," I say in a pained voice, "you've seen me go through this rigmarole with my family for most of our life together. Don't you ever get tired of it? Don't you wonder when it'll ever end or if it'll ever end?"

Arjun responds gently, "Nargis, take as long as it takes."

THAT LAST DRY RUN

I visit my mother again. And then again a year after that. Like on previous trips home, I have mixed feelings. I feel raw pain. The kind you experience, when a scab that has been reluctantly healing suddenly curls back to expose the granulating pink sore pinching a million synapses on its way.

There's no failsafe way to prepare for this, I remind myself.

Once again, I do not know what to expect. And once again, there is only one thing that I *can* be certain about: it's not going to be easy.

Something that has become easier though, is bringing up the controversy right away. Strangely enough, Mummy starts it this time.

"Now, what happened between you and your father, only both of you know. And he's dead. So, it's your word against his."

Her opening lines bother me. They tell me that one whole year later, she still does not believe the story of my life.

It took us but one year to go right back to square one. So now, I'll be dragged uphill through mud and sludge one more time. With both feet dangling.

Aloud I say, "Tell me, what was Daddy's brilliant explanation? After both of you came back home after your visit to Chicago, how did he explain everything that transpired between the three of us on that night, when I finally had the courage to confront him?"

"He told me that you had the Oedipus --- what do you call it? --- The Oedipal complex. That you felt close to him because he was your father. Because he'd baby you, you know. He said little girls feel close to a father who pampers them, like he used to pamper you. It's very common to feel this, he explained. He said that you imagined the rest, about him touching you the wrong way. We all know how close you were to him. And how you always wanted it that way. Also, we all know that you're a bright girl with a vivid imagination."

"Did you really believe his explanation?"

"It could've happened like he said it did. Who knows?"

"NARGIS, JUST RUN!"

That night I have a nightmare. In my parents' bed.
I am alone in a shower.

It is like any other day. Nothing much is going on. It is quiet. Rather too quiet. I am in there, just by myself. Or so I think. By now, I have worked up the soap into a thick foam and slathered my body with lather. Soon, I have soapsuds all over: on my hands, over my chest, and even covering my eyes. I reach for the faucet, where I think it is supposed to be.

Why's it taking so long to find that godforsaken tap?

I turn it on full blast, but very quickly, it slows down to a mere trickle, to sounds of *"Haisha --- haisha."* Some of the soap is drying up now and then suddenly, the water stops.

Mummy had warned me about the water rationing in Dehradun. Stupid me! I should've paid more attention to that timing thing.

I am groping in the dark, desperately trying to get the water to run again.

But wait. Is there someone else in the shower with me?

This is when I get the heebie-jeebies!

Now, how in the world did *he* get in there? I'm sure it's a man. A portly man. Good God! How long has *he* been in there with me?

He is also nude. Just like me. And just like me, he also has soap all over *his* body. I do not know why, but I am sure that this other person in that enclosed space with me is my father. Something about him. I do not know what. I cannot see him with my eyelids shut so tight. But I just *know*. I try to squint through the soap blisters over my eyes, so I can at least get a glimpse of his apparition to confirm my worst fears. But it is all fuzzy around me. All I can see is a human form against the black tile with soap stains on it. My eyes are now starting to burn.

But, there is no time to wonder. Before I know it, his body grazes against mine. It is wet and slimy. I can feel his long tapering fingers reaching for my chest. It is very uncomfortable now. And very hot. Something is dripping down from under my armpits. It is not water. It is sweat. My sweat.

Then he quickly moves to block the door with his rotund frame. I'm scared! I must run!

But I cannot move. All of a sudden, I have lost control of my limbs. I am petrified! Petrified stupid. He is against me now. His body grazes against mine. This is when my nipples start to harden. And the skin on my face starts to peel.

I need to run *now*! God, get me out of here!

I scream and scream. I cannot stop screaming. When I wake up, I am still screaming. I realize that I cannot even make any sound when I scream.

It is four in the morning. Through the window, I see the winter sky starting to pale in the East.

It is deathly still inside the bedroom, lying next to Mummy. It is also deathly creepy. As if there is a spirit somewhere in the house. A ghost in flimsy white sheets floating around overhead in the dark. I wake up from a bad dream and go straight into another nightmare.

I'm in the wrong life.

It is impossible to go back to sleep. I try again, and again, to push those tired sleepless sheep over the fence. I count each one as it tumbles over to the other side onto crumpled grass, shaking its little behind, when it gets back on all fours and starts to run.

I will never sleep in Daddy's bed again.

HIS MASTER'S VOICE SOUNDS A BIT CRACKED

The next morning, we try again. This time Mummy and I are sitting on wicker chairs in the backyard lawn, sipping fresh lime sodas. Next to the vines loaded with humming bees that are busying themselves with the brightest flowers on the wall creeper and fussing over plump, deep-purple grapes that look like they are all set to crack and burst open with juice. Sweet-sour, gooey, sticky juice.

New place. New situation. Different outcome? I hope.

Mummy begins, "I'll never understand this. But why didn't you tell me before about the abuse?"

So yesterday was really just a sneak preview.

I go on to explain, "I probably realized this, even as a child, that you couldn't do anything about it. When the abuse happened, it happened slowly and systematically, over a long period of time. Daddy did it quite cleverly, you know. He was a clever and cunning man. It started as innocent hugging and back scratching. That's how I remember it. I was about nine years old then, a few days before we were going to leave Bombay. Then gradually, all this turned into a game. And before I knew it, it had evolved into something else. I cannot remember very clearly when it first started becoming uncomfortable. But by that time, I'd also started enjoying it. So it was too late to say anything. I felt that it was all *my* fault that it had happened in the first place. I felt it was *my* fault that it went on for as long as it did. Long before I finally had the courage to stop it, I knew it was all wrong. But, I also knew I would never be believed. And I was certain that I would be punished. By both of you. It was easier to forget all about it. So I thought. You would've never believed me, like you don't believe me now. If only my body hadn't responded, I wouldn't have felt so guilty."

"You could've told someone else."

"There was no one to confide in. Besides, Daddy had made me the Princess in the family. I don't think that I was ready to give that up yet."

"Had it happened to me, I would've never ever seen my father's face again."

"It's so easy for you to say that, isn't it, Mummy? Why, even after you'd heard about it from me, you continued not only to live with the perpetrator but also dedicate every waking moment to caring for him until his death."

And, most likely, also continued to sleep with him all along, I whisper to myself.

"I could've never left him. Where would I go? It's hard to live with anyone else. And, it's impossible to live with you."

Acid erupts in my stomach.

"So this is my fate. One parent abuses me. The other one abandons me." I start to wail. "Tell me. Why's this my fate? Why? Why? Why? Why can't you change how this story ends?"

I feel drained. My mouth is dry. Even saliva takes time to build back up again. After a few sips of fresh lime, I am able to go on.

"Tell me, did you miss me all those years? Even a single time?"

I continue moaning through my copious tears. They streak down the makeup on my face. Like empty railroad tracks. Tracks going to Misery-ville.

"Tell me that you missed me, Mummy. That you missed me even once."

I cry some more.

"And, Daddy would hold this property over our heads. As if lifeless bricks and motor would keep me silent forever. As you know, Daddy left his share in Terra Firma for me only because it would've been illegal not to transfer ancestral wealth. Sometimes I feel that this property was a payback for services rendered. It feels stained with his hands. The ones that used to touch my body. If I accept my inheritance, I'll feel cheap. If I reject it, I'll feel shortchanged because most of it was Grandfather's anyway. That's the dilemma in my life. That's what happens to an abuse victim. Your whole life becomes a fucking dilemma! Nothing that I do ever feels just right. Maybe, Daddy got the last laugh after all." Then I ask, "Mummy, do you think he included me in his will to make it up to me? Or, was his real intent to hang this yoke around my neck?"

Then out of the blue, Mummy makes a confession.

"Once," she says, "very early on in our marriage, I had packed up my bags to leave him and to go back to my father's house. We were fighting a lot. He was a difficult man to please. He wanted everything his way. He wanted to improve my English and my manners. He wanted to change everything about me. He wanted to control me. I should've left then and never had children with him. I could've lived alone and taught in a college to support myself. Then, I would've never had to deal with this pain today."

The should've, could've, would've. That makes two of us.

"Talking about all this makes me feel depressed," she keeps wiping her eyes. "Nargis, go back home to your own house. Never come back here again to see me."

"You're still thinking only about yourself. What about *me*?"

"Do you remember how I could never show any love to you children? I could never show any closeness to any one of you. He'd get very angry. He would feel insecure whenever he'd see me talking to anyone alone in a room. He would even eavesdrop, because he'd feel so terribly left out. And how he hated feeling left out! It would make him extremely upset for days. I'd even have to get his permission to see my parents." Then she adds, "You know, this time I did not even remember the anniversary of his death."

"I understand. But, what I don't understand, Mummy, is why it has taken you so long? Who is the real you? Good Lord! Will I ever know?"

Finally, Mummy turns to me and asks, "Nargis, do you want a relationship with me?"

"Mom, you'll be my mother until one of us dies. You're all I *have* left!"

We cry together. And then we hug. I hold onto her for a while.

Does she feel anything when she hugs me? I suppose she thinks, "This is the daughter who torments me. This is my difficult daughter."

Soon it is time to go. Time again to say goodbye.

When she comes up to give me an embrace, I see a wet transparent film starting to build in my mother's swollen eyes.

Who knows when we'll meet again, or whether she'll be alive when we do? I am embarrassed because when we part, I cannot bring myself to cry.

FREEZE FRAME

A year later, on the next visit home, nothing has changed. Except that Mummy looks a tad older every time we meet.

"I've had an unfortunate life. Do you know that?" she starts to say.

I hear the elastic band snap. The anger click. The one that was holding back my rage on the flight back home.

"Why did you use the word unfortunate for yourself? Remember, when all is said and done, when the dust finally settles, this time around it was you who started it. Shall we talk about who's really the more ill-fated amongst us? Do you want to compare your misery with mine? Why don't we draw up a chart, and put it all on a graph? Come on, Mummy, let's try this together. Let's put pain on the Y axis, and bars of red and blue that represent you and me on the X axis."

Nargis, don't get carried away with math illustrations and primary colors, I reprimand myself. And for heaven's sake, don't you ever get tempted to project complicated mathematical algorithms, draw a pie-chart or shade areas under a bell curve to make a point. Or as a last-ditch effort, collate P values to estimate the probability of rejecting the null hypothesis, or ---

She gets up and starts walking away from me. This is when I lose control completely.

"Mummy, do you know what you just did? You walked away from me. Don't leave me alone feeling like this. Please, I beg of you. Don't leave me again. *Never* leave me again. Please, never walk away from me again!"

Mummy comes back. She is quiet.

"Mummy, there're some things I've wanted to share with you to get your support and understanding. After Daddy's death, I used to see him everywhere in our Chicago home: In the basement, under the tarpaulin; in my car, with his hands frozen on the wheel; in the backyard, hiding behind the big oak; or floating on the pool, playing dead. I still feel haunted by his spirit. I've had to deal with all this. And I've had to deal with you and my siblings, too."

"It's strange. But I used to also feel that. I still think he's watching me, just to see if I make a mistake."

It is oddly comforting to learn that Mummy has felt the same paranoia I have also experienced.

"Mummy, do you remember after your last trip to our condo we didn't talk for six years?"

"I never said that your Aunty Tara was abused. I only said I had a doubt in my mind."

I'm at my wits end. I must sound like I've just unzipped myself out of a straitjacket and escaped straight out of a loony-bin.

I can imagine the pixels on all the overhead signpost warnings on every major national highways blinking, "--- LOOK OUT FOR CRAZY PERSON --- FUGITIVE --- RESPONDS TO NAME 'NARGIS' --- CAN BE VERY DANGEROUS ---"

"Do you say this again and again, to psyche me out? So that one day I'll finally give up? Or go batty or something?"

Again silence.

I pause, just to inhale.

"Do you have the faintest idea how hard all this has been for me? I hated it when I returned on vacation from Moscow, and discovered that Daddy had started to favor Sanju over me simply because he was a son. I always thought that I was supposed to be the son. Daddy insisted all along that girls and, boys are equal. That's how he had raised us. So it was a shock when all this changed so suddenly."

Pause.

I sound like a stupid broken record. One that is stuck in skip. But I go on.

"Well, let's move on. I want you to remember everything that I'm about to say. Remember, Mother. Remember this time what I'm about to tell you. So Mummy, let me try this one last time. For a moment, imagine that all this is actually happened to you, and not to me. That you were abused by *your* father. How would you feel?"

"That never happened to me. So I can't answer your question."

I feel as if my insides are trailing behind me. All the way past Exit. And I'm running out of runway. Woe is me!

"Let me try this one last time. It's happening in a film. Do you watch movies, Mummy?" I ask, my voice wavering with exasperation.

"I don't anymore. The glare bothers my eyes."

"I promise you, this'll be a short one, Mummy. Let's peel the onion together, layer by layer, peel by peel. So, this is how the story goes. The movie is about a little girl who's molested by her father. It's quite clear that he's the leader of the pack. He has some great visionary ideas, but cannot tolerate any difference of opinion. He feels largely unaccomplished and has this crazy dark side, which he's usually able to cleverly rotate away from the public eye. Now, let me tell you about the mother. She starts out being strong, but loses her clout through twists of fate. She can't hold a candle to her husband. When she says, "Eh?" he replies, "Grrr." When he tells her to jump, she asks, "How high?" Nevertheless, she does put every effort in assuring that all her children, including her daughters, are educated and learn to be independent. Unfortunately, along the way, she forgets how to think for herself. Later, she even forgets how to remember. It makes life so much easier when she cannot think. And when she cannot remember."

I take a break to breathe

"Now let me cut to the chase. Both the older daughter and the only son feel edged out, because the father showers special attention just on the little girl, who thrives on it. She can't get enough. Don't you see how this is a perfect setup for exploitation? A Petri-dish for breeding muck? A fertile ground for abuse? Brilliant that he is, the father does not count on the fact that one day this little girl will grow up to be self-reliant. That one day, she'll become old enough bold enough to confront him. To regain her strength, she has to shut herself out of the family. Completely. For many long years. She needs to shut out the noise that rattles her very insides. She realizes that she has to give up that special place in her family forever, in order to get her sanity back. It's a huge price to pay, but she knows that there *is* no other way. She had gotten used to that special place. She used to blossom in that special place. It was *only* for her. But now, she chooses to go down to the bottom of the totem pole and stay there. It's safer there. That's when the mobile begins to swing. Actually, it swings wildly in the *other* direction. That's what mobiles are known for. That's how a child learns to see what's on the other side of its cradle. The mother still cannot think for herself and leans more and more on her oldest daughter, who, in turn, has now finally become the favorite child. And she holds onto that position for dear life, since she never experienced that in all her years growing up. The son, who was never made to feel male enough to help his little sister, can't make up his mind or take a stand. So he vacillates back and forth between the two ends of that mobile and ends up getting caught in the crossfire. This is how all three of them abandon this poor little abused girl — How do you feel about this story? How do you feel about the actors in this movie?"

Mummy is silent again. Maybe to her it plays like a cheap novel.

I feel like a scarecrow that needs to be sewn back together again into myself.

"I don't know how I feel. They're just actors," she says finally.

"How do you feel about the little girl, the one who was abused and abandoned?"

"I don't know how to feel anymore," Mummy says simply. Then, "Nargis, why do you keep on *bothering* me? Why don't you just kill me! Just let me die! You kill me with each and every question you ask. You torment me whenever we meet. Promise me this. Promise me that you'll never talk about all this nonsense ever again. I know that it'll shorten my life if you do. Will that make you happy? To see me dead?"

Mummy is old.

Mummy will never change.

Mummy is too old to change.

I feel, as if I am dangling from the end of a rope. One that is now low enough from the ground.

Nargis, try to free yourself. Walk away, I tell myself. You're capable of swimming back to the shore from the deep end. All by yourself. You've been able to swim up to the surface from muck. Singlehandedly. You've done it before. Time to reel yourself back in from the edge. Yes, you *can* turn the page of the calendar. Nargis, you *can* start a new day.

I promise my mother that I will never talk about sexual abuse again. Actually, I promise her that I will never talk about this again. *With her.*

I have kept that promise.

FOOTSTEPS IN THE SAND

I dream again that night.
Those freaking dreams? They never end!

I know that after everything that was said earlier that day, it will once again be a difficult night.

I am sitting on a beach with throngs of other people. We have all assembled as extras in a background scene for a movie shooting. I am sitting on the bleachers with my daughters to my left, watching intently, as I hold my face in my palms. I am waiting for the director to call the next shot.

For some reason, it looks like Colaba beach in Bombay. The sea is choppy and the waves keep coming at us, building themselves into a frenzy as they crash against the rocks. I can feel the spray of water sting my face as it splashes around. I can taste the salt in my half-open mouth, as I gaze at nature's wonder-filled ride.

The movie is being projected into the night, where the water meets the sky. All the actors in the motion picture look larger than life, even though their profiles are not very clear because they zigzag along the horizon.

We are all watching this movie together.

It is about a little girl who is trying to say something to her family over dinner, reading from flashcards. The plates and silverware have been laid out meticulously, but the first course has not yet been served. It is hard to say how many people are sitting at that table. The girl has short straight hair, pulled tightly back with a red headband. She could be about nine or ten years old.

It is kind of odd, but the girl keeps forgetting her lines. Then she repeatedly apologizes for forgetting them. Occasionally, the reel starts to blurb and burp with exclamation marks, questions and stars!!! ???
***

"Never mind," I explain to little Natasha on my left. "At the end, they'll be able to snip off the sketchy parts from the spool and put the story back together again."

I turn to my right. This is when I see my father. He is sitting barely two or three seats away from us. If he is aware of us, he does not show it. He is also watching the same movie. There is no expression on his face. I do not know why, but his honey-brown eyes are strangely glassy as are their waning muddy-blue crescents. The kind you see on dead corpses. I know that my mother is sitting on the other side by him, but I cannot see her. Daddy's frame is blocking her from my view. I can picture her blinking with rushed and rapid movements, as she continues to chew on her nails.

I am aware that sometimes she does this when she's confused, or anxious. Or when she thinks of the most inane things. Or when she cannot think for herself.

It is quite strange that Daddy and I are about the same age. We are both in our early forties.

I think, I've finally figured it out. That's how old I was when he died. That's also how old he was, when he first started to molest me.

Then the shooting abruptly stops, and the actors relax to take a break. The crowd is now quickly thinning out. Suddenly, it is just my daughters and I who are left. Mummy has gone, too.

This is when Daddy looks at me for the first time. He beckons me with his eyes to follow him.

So, he's not really dead, is he? But, why do I feel compelled to go with him?

We all stand up to leave. His back is now turned to us. He starts to walk on the sandy beach, expecting me to follow.

I do not know why, but I find myself walking away from Daddy. He does not look back even a single time. The three of us walk in single file, with my daughters just behind me. First Mandy. Then Natasha. They look like little ducklings. They appear much younger.

It is now deathly still on the beach, except for the sound of our feet crushing the sand with each step.

I turn around to look at Daddy. He is walking alone. His body is now bent double, as if he is carrying an invisible load. Silently. All by himself. I observe that he is starting to age as he walks on, morphing into an aberration beyond human recognition as his head and his toes merge into each other. He seems to be barely gliding over the sand, like a ghost. This is when I notice that he is not leaving any footprints behind him. Soon, he becomes a mere speck on the horizon.

I turn around to look at the ocean. The waves have stopped. It is very calm now.

I wake up thinking, Nargis, don't get carried away --- it was just a dream. You've been watching too many movies lately.

"DEAR NARGIS"

"YOUR PATH IS A DIFFICULT ONE ---
BUT YOU'LL BE AMPLY REWARDED"

Cheap wisdom retrieved from a fortune cookie.

I am sitting alone in the backyard of our home in Chicago, with an open letter in my hand and my completed closed manuscript on my lap. The sun kissed double-zinnias and single petal daisies are vibrant with color this summer. A tapestry of every shade known to mankind: salmon-pink, flaming-red, boldly-mauve and simply-white. The storm from earlier today has brought out the beauty and radiance in the flowers around me. Some of the maple leaves, palm-size and still fresh, are lying unabashedly on the ground. In the distance, I see a hesitant fawn gingerly following a doe out by the fence.

The flowers remind me of our garden in Indore. Where the joy of the outdoors would come alive with Sanjay. I think back to the times when we would hunt and fish together. When we would retrieve the warm flattened old *khota* paisa off the tracks. There are no more granny-pennies or old *khota* paisa around anymore.

There is some sadness, too. It is so confusing when both these emotions come together to clutter my mind and muddle my thoughts.

When I play mind games with my own mind.

I am surrounded by a colorful medley of summer flowers when I open the letter. I read it aloud. There is no one around to hear it except myself, and the house sparrows pecking for seeds that only they can spot in the grass.

My dear Nargis,

I've been thinking about writing to you for a long time now. This is the first time I'm writing a complete letter to you. This is the longest letter I've ever written in my life. To anyone. It is not just another PS: I love you letter. I'm not content, anymore, with squiggling just two lines in the tiny space left by your father at the end of our letters to you over the years.

I salute you for your energy, spark and zest for life. At the same time, I tremble to think of what you must've gone through all those years. All alone. All those years when you were just a child. By yourself. So dependent. So innocent. So trusting.

I want to understand everything that has happened to you. I want you to know that what happened to you saddens me, because it saddens you too.

I'm aware that you hang up the phone every time I say, 'I love you,' because you cannot say it back. I wish that it had been different between us. I wish that I'd been stronger and more responsive to your needs.

I want to learn how to help you, by learning how to think for myself. I want to hold you, if that'll take away the pain. I want to be a part of your life, because you'll always be a part of mine. Before I'm finally gone, I yearn for even a single moment of honesty and love between us. As you can see, I'm using I-statements, because you told me that this is one way of taking responsibility.

I wait for the day when the demons will be gone forever. And I pray for the day when there'll be no more ghosts between us.

To my baby daughter, who is the love of my life ---

I sign 'Mummy' at the end.

Then I put my pen down.

I read this letter to myself, again, quietly in my mind this time. I want to remember every word in it. I want to make every word in it a part of my being, because every word in there feeds my soul. The one that hungers for love. I know that these very lines will surely soothe me the next time confusing emotions whack-out my mind. The next time when I decide to crackup.

Then I close my completed life journey and walk back into the house.

I guess, I've not been handed anything that I cannot deal with. Adversity is a resume builder. And pain is known to bring grace.

Outside, the sky is clearing up after a storm. I look through the rain-splattered window. I see twisted little branches scattered all over the trampled summer grass.

The leaves on the trees are brighter and fresher than ever. The songbird emerges from the bushes serenading the advent of summer, its mouth larger than its body, as it bursts into song.

It is time to go. I hear Arjun calling for me.

My husband of thirty years puts his arm around me. "Remember, Nargis. Einstein once said, 'Time moves only in one direction: forward,'" he tells me gently. "Only humans have the capacity to take it backward. Is there any point in defying that great scientist's logic?"

EPILOGUE

HOW THE YEARS HAVE PEELED AWAY ---

It is generally believed that there is a penalty for trespassing into the future. I am not sure that this is entirely true. There comes a time in one's life, about the time when one is getting ready to be a bit carbon-dated, when the past ebbs away and becomes one with the horizon.

I went back in a rented Mercedes to my ancestral village, Raipur, in UP. Today, you have to drive over a mishmash of newly built flyovers to get there. In the New World Order, India is now slated to become a superpower just like Daddy had predicted so many years ago.

Time is the best marker. The old family home is decrepit and infested with rats and snakes. The thick weather warped walls made of slender eighteenth century bricks stand silently, while the desiccated twisted weeds peeking through between the cracks scream to be noticed. The caked courtyard, fractured in a thousand places, is lined with rows of stubborn anthills. The once sturdy hand pump has long since dried up.

At the entrance, the tired swing door stays open all the time, mostly because the hinge is rusted and cannot budge anymore. Nobody dares pass through the front doorway today, but for reasons starkly different from the era when my great-grandmother, Ma ji, ruled the roost. Gone are the days when she would keep the untouchables, who timidly begged for an odd paisa or random scraps from the table, standing mute and drenched in a thundering downpour of the monsoon outside that door.

Nobody lives here anymore. Even the beggars have declined squatter status in Grandfather's house.

Across the street, where that poor old mud house stood, is a spanking new villa built by Uncle Deshraj's oldest son, the one who was not a staggering drunk and swigged his life away into oblivion. His daughter has a Master's in Education. The house boasts of a neatly tiled red roof, wall to wall marble flooring, granite-top kitchen counters, over five hundred channel satellite TV, a nervous dishwasher, a couple of shiny Maruti cars in the dusty driveway.

The family still opens up its hearth and home when a guest comes through the doorway, even if unannounced --- guests still come unannounced. Especially if a family connection can be established, however remote.

More than half of my thirty three first cousins have immigrated overseas, spread out like spokes from a hub. Some of them live in Australia, grow wheat, and have worked industriously to become wealthy farmers. I have never told them my story. Recently, at a family wedding, I ran into my light-eyed cousin, Priti, Uncle Shankar's daughter, the one who Daddy wanted to adopt. She told me that she misses my father because he had always been so kind to her. It is heartbreaking to see that she also has an arthritic condition similar to mine.

Anjali had an unfortunate divorce and soon thereafter moved in with Mummy. Regrettably, she married somebody like her father who could not be faithful to his wife. At least she took a stand on the matter. While being immersed in her meaningful work in social causes pertaining to girl-child trafficking in Nepal, she has also raised three charming daughters. They may never know this, but I am proud of all four of them. Somehow, Anjali and I are still careful about what we say to each other, although I am now able to stave off any judgment in my general direction. I cringe every time I hear her mention how she misses Daddy so much. I am not certain she believes my story. She does not want to talk about it. For that matter, neither do I. For reasons not very clear to me, it does not seem that important anymore.

Moreover, I have a fear of losing a relationship with her a second time over. Not experiencing a deeper connection with my nieces has been an enormous price I paid that first time.

Sanju is now General Sanjay Yadav. He is blissfully married and dotes on his children. My brother tells me that one of his daughters reminds him of me. "She's brilliant and beautiful just like you," he says. I miss his warmth and wit when we are not together and have been mostly unable to replicate that banter with anybody else. Interestingly, we both blow-dry between our toes after a shower! I look forward to spending time with him reminiscing about the great adventures we have shared. On most good days, he is still my favorite Yadav --- especially in the right doses. I suppose now he does believe most of my story. This means a lot. But, for reasons not very clear to me, we also do not talk about it when we are together.

Mummy still lives in the Red Fort. It is now a white and red house. A few years ago, termites invaded the library and ingested a better half of the books Daddy had so painstakingly stacked up on the shelves. Including *Lolita*.

I am not sure what Mummy really believes. I promised her several years ago that I will never bring up the past with her again. So, I try to keep Daddy out of the equation in our conversations. It has not always been all easy. Since she can never be the mother I have pined for all my life, often times, I have had to become my own parent.

Mummy chooses to live on the opposite side of the globe. I am thankful that she is still there at the other end of the line when I dial her number. I am a poster child of codependency, who was eventually able to move out of Pain City, I continue to struggle with negotiating and navigating healthy boundaries with her. It is so tricky to land the plane on the Hudson River each and every time! Sometimes, I sway dangerously on that tightrope: too close causes angst, too far leads to guilt. But I cannot risk being unhinged again. Or getting unplugged.

Fortunately for both of us, it has generally become easier to visit with Mummy, especially when I hearken back to my childhood and narrate the fun stories to amuse her. I enjoy amusing Mummy.

It warms my heart when I hear my mother laugh. She sounds so much younger when she laughs. Like she did during those three memorable years when just she and I lived together in Lilliputian house. When she would cook my favorite bitter-gourd peppered with crushed pomegranate seeds. When she would wake me up way before the newspaper boy would toss a copy of *The Indian Express* on our front lawn, shake me out of bed and firmly lead me to my study desk with sleep still stuck between my eyelids. When she would relate how she got goose bumps every time she would remember how I was almost lost to the bad, greasy underworld at Howrah station on my way back home from boarding school. When she would give me a spoonful of sugar before every exam. When she would insist that I put my arm around her whenever we slept in the same bed, simply to confirm my presence.

All memories from my childhood. Control Save. Some bitter-sweet, like marmite. Some sweet-sour, like tamarind. Others tangy-sour, like mustard.

Having one parent alive allows me to be still called a child. Every time we meet I wonder if this will be my last meal with Mummy, even though this feeling has been going on for several years. I often think of the losses she has had in her lifetime. I am still working on forgiveness. I hope that I will be able to pardon her during her lifetime. For some reason, letting go of the past is getting easier. And then, some memories are a gift. Especially, every time I give her a hug and smell Mummy. When I find myself searching for a whiff of Pond's Cream.

"SAVE that page," Nargis, I tell myself. "Learn to STAY in the moment." "Remember, HEALTHY boundaries." I leave these Post-it notes for myself everywhere. On my steering wheel. Beside my appointment book. And inside my vanity case.

We are, after all, a family of survivors. Even if not all of us are aware of it. We each have had our own chinks in the armor and our own cross to bear. Mummy, Anjali and Sanjay keep Daddy's photos displayed in picture frames in their homes, while I keep him securely buried away in an album. Not quite six feet under yet. Sometimes, when I look at his photograph --- the one with his face emerging stern and remorseless above his bowtie, I think of him not as my father but as a person who just chanced his way into my life. A person whose cells changed so many times during his lifetime that, even though he started out as my father, he ended up as a completely different person: a stranger who molested me. I have discovered that this is one way to relegate him to my rearview mirror. I confuse his birthday and have forgotten the date when he actually died. His brother has toes identical to the ones Daddy did and matching hands with long tapering fingers. The ones I was born in. The ones that groped my body. I still find it hard to look at them, whenever uncle and I meet.

Myth buster: Daddy does not need to believe my story. Because Daddy *knows* my story. But Daddy is still dead. From down there he can do no more harm. Is it even possible in the human repertoire to love and loathe, admire and abhor the same person? At the same time? They say that success is the sweetest revenge, but I am now way past retribution. There is no ill-will greater than humanity. I feel sad about my father's life, but sadly not about his death. I hope that I can forgive Daddy during my lifetime. For now, I will let him sit on the bench a little longer. When his turn comes, I may have to redefine the word.

I have long since ended self-flagellation and forgiven myself. I am done asking the same questions over, and over and over again, and expecting different results every time. I am done crying alone, stirring up the silt at the bottom of the ocean with my tears, or turning rocks upside down looking for love. I am done banging my head on a windowpane like a dumb trapped fly, when the window just behind me is actually wide open.

It never ceases to amaze me what one person can experience during a single lifetime. A long time ago, I vowed to myself never to miss the ecstasy of another tequila-colored sunrise. The one that burns out yesterday's angst. Or the quietude of another unhurried coral sunset, when the dust settles the hubbub of fireflies for the night. Screen savers. After all, there are only so many sunrises and sunsets in a lifetime.

Ample time has been spent to explore the myths and explode the other half-truths about my family. I am grounded in my resolve to temper my expectations and have learned to accept that what was my kind of, sort of, family is no more. I am slowly learning to work my way into the gray zone, make a graceful exit out of triangulated relationships, drop that tug o' war rope to let the other side win and walk into my fears. I have stopped being a pall bearer of misery. But most of all, I try to get out of my own way. And that allure of specialness? There is such bliss in feeling special with the special people in my life and reciprocating this privilege. And that holding onto resentments? They just rot the container and hang around to haunt and hurt. *Only me*. I am passionate about the work I do, helping my patients and learning from them. Most of the world would agree that work is the best therapy, especially when you are helping others..

This emotional clearing house called life. How do you stay sane, in insane places? How do you prepare to cope with the next all-consuming 'oholic' experience, looking through the kaleidoscope of time? When do you stop sorting through the tangled mess your family has become, a bit like what you just pulled out from last year's Christmas lights to put up on the tree? Inside-out, and topsy-turvy. When every family member remembers the same episode differently?

When will life teach us how to fall without getting hurt? Why are we sent on Earth without an instruction book, on how to expunge scars and snap back broken wings? No shortcuts. No cheating. No blueprint. Not even cliff notes? Why do we have to muddle through happenstance and be tested and tried, toasted and roasted, battered and weather-beaten in order to be battle-ready? Why do we have to endure snafus over life's squabbles? When will we realize that the spoken word can kill? And that our deeds can make another person invisible?

There are many things I am so very grateful for. I feel blessed that I belong to two out of the three most powerful nations, which happen to also be the largest democracies on our planet. Both countries boast of having the largest populations of English language lovers. Both triumph over a sound secular standing and abominate racism and communalism. India has done much more for me than I will ever be able to do for her, even though I am still ashamed of her poverty and appalled by the corruption within her borders. But, whatever else I become, you cannot take the Indian out of me. America is now my home, even though I have yet to develop a taste for peanut butter and apple pie! I am proud to be an Indian and eternally indebted for having been accepted as an American. This has probably something to do with needing both roots and wings. I have chosen to be socially liberal and fiscally responsible. I have learned to trust the free-market system. I still do not believe in God. And this is not because of the trials I have stumbled on or the tribulations that have stumped me.

If belief in God means not hurting others, then, I suppose I do try to believe in Him.

The mind can never understand everything. It's impossible to see past a closed door.

I remain busy with philanthropy that has given a new meaning to my existence. Between those bookends of life, the joy you experience from giving back is the best kept secret. While I enjoy deep and lasting relationships with humor as a steady friend on my pillion seat, sometimes I still struggle with detachment. Buddha *was* right. There is a reason why there is only one word, *kal*, for both yesterday and tomorrow in Hindi. It *is* all about expectations: The glass is indeed half-full.

Loaded words: (In ascending-descending order)
Mindfulness
Radical Acceptance
Work At It
Will Take Some Time
Don't Give Up Too Easily
Two Steps Forward, One Step Back
It's The Only Way To Move Forward
Worth Every Drop Of Blood In Your Body
No One Benefits From This More Than You Yourself

Arjun and I look for each other every morning in our sunshine filled home. Every now and then, we are pleasantly surprised when both of us have the same thought as we wake up together with the sun just coming in from the East. It is a three-way setting: trust, love, and friendship. We are privileged to greet people who come through our front door, to enrich our lives. We are blessed by the company of close caring friends and savor our time with them, reminiscing in the backyard, sharing stories from our travels over the drone of crickets playing hopscotch in the underbrush. When I want to hang on the pendulum to stop time.

I can smell the different shades in the fall. I can feel the singular pitch in a song. I have tasted the sweetness of love. It is amazing how you can find love in so many places.

Mandy and Natasha have grown up to be beautiful independent young women who include us in their lives and look forward to coming home for Christmas. They say that when children do so, one has, at a minimum, made an honest attempt at being a good parent.

Most people try not to repeat the same blunders their parents made. Sometimes, it does take work. I try to acknowledge and learn from the past, and have gotten help when I have been unable to do so on my own. It is so much easier to be nice. Isn't it?

I have vowed that I will never again lose a relationship that is important to me. I have vowed, to myself, that I will never shut that door on someone I love ever again in my life.

My name is Nargis --- and I work at being vigilant about fending off the ghosts that come between us.

POSTSCRIPT

L istening to the heart-wrenching stories of scores of families in my professional work impelled me to create a fictional protagonist, Nargis. She is a composite character made from many people I have had the privilege of knowing during my life who have demonstrated the courage to cope with the struggles of childhood abuse, and the abandonment and loss of loved ones.

My goal in writing this novel is to enhance the awareness of abuse issues. Nargis's first-person narration of a complicated relationship with her father helps the victims of family dysfunction obtain solace in the thought that they are not alone, and acquire coping tools to move on in their lives.

Even though the characters in *The Ghosts That Come Between Us* are fictional, Nargis' story that celebrates the triumph of hope over despair is a universal one.

--- Bulbul Bahuguna, M.D.

GLOSSARY

Unless otherwise stated, the words listed below
are of Indian (Hindi) origin.

aaloo	potato
amla	gooseberry
azuu	meat stew (Russian)
baithak	living room
bakshish	alms
Bania	person from trader/broker class
baraat	groom's party
barfi	Indian sweetmeat made from caramelized milk and sugar
beta	son (girls are also affectionately addressed as 'beta')
Bhai Saab	older brother, addressed respectfully
bhajan	religious hymn
bindi	decorative dot on forehead
borshch	beet and cabbage soup (Russian)
chaat	sweet sour appetizer
chakki	mechanical grain grinder
chappals	slippers
chunni	stole
churidar	women's tight pants
chusne-wale	cheap variety of mango, meant to be sucked
dakshana	homage fee offered to a Hindu priest
dal	lentil
desi	of Indian subcontinent origin
dhaba	country diner
dhobi	washer man
dhol	drums

didi	older sister
dzurnaya	female on duty (Russian)
fazool	foolish
gazal	soulful Urdu music
gurdwara	Sikh temple
Gutka	pocket version of the Sikh religious scriptures
halwa	blessed sweetened wheat flour distributed in temples
haramzada	bastard
Jaat	person belonging to the farmland owner class
jhola	satchel
ji	used as suffix to address a person with respect
jutha	food or drink soiled by taste
kalai	nickel polish
kameez	long tunic
kartoshko	potato (Russian)
kathak	North Indian classical dance that tells a story
khadi	handspun fabric
khleb	bread (Russian)
khota	bad penny
kolkhoz	Soviet cooperative farm (Russian)
kurta	tunic shirt
laddoo	sweet dessert balls made from flour or powdered lentils
lassi	drink made from churned yogurt and spices
Madrassa	Islamic school
masala	spice
maulvi	Moslem priest
memsaab	female employer
morozhenoe	ice cream (Russian)
nada	drawstring used to tie pants
namaste	spoken salutation

otlichno	excellent (Russian)
paan	betel nuts, tobacco and other spices wrapped in betel leaves
pakoras	fried fritters
palto	long overcoat (Russian)
paratha	sautéed wheat flour flat bread
Pathan	person from the North Frontier region of the Indian Subcontinent
pechene	cookie (Russian)
phukni	tubular metallic stoker
Pioneersky Laager	activity camp for young Communists (Russian)
pithu	game played with seven stones and a soft ball
pucca	authentic
puja	Hindu prayer
purdah	veil
puri	puffed fried bread
randi	prostitute
roti	flatbread
Saab	Sir
saag	cooked spinach and mustard leaves
salwar	loose drawstring pants
samosa	fried or baked pastry with a savory filling
sannyas	renunciation
sepoy	soldier (Indian army)
shapka	winter hat (Russian)
shee	cabbage and bean soup (Russian)
shehnai	flute, often played at Indian weddings
tamasha	scene
tardka	sauté in oil